The REAL STORY

RJ Layer

Bella
BOOKS
2014

Bella Books, Inc.
P.O. Box 10543
Tallahassee, FL 32302

Printed in the United States of America on acid-free paper.

First Bella Books Edition 2014

Editor: Medora MacDougall
Cover Designed by: Linda Callaghan

ISBN: 978-1-59493-344-8

About the Author

Born and raised in the "Heart" of the Midwest, RJ still resides there with her partner of twenty-four years, their feathered chatterbox and two new furry feline rescues. When not working the day job, she loves to work at writing lesbian romance. In addition to traveling to new places, RJ can be found relaxing in the rolling hills on the water. Their hideaway is the perfect place for dreaming up engaging characters and moving stories. She also loves taking photos and enjoys reading every free minute she can find.

Dedication

For Lori—forever and always—till my last breath.

Acknowledgment

Thank you to Karin Kallmaker and Linda Hill for giving me the opportunity to share my passion for writing. Bella's dedication to bring lesbian literature to readers is coveted, and I feel especially proud to be a part of the Bella family. A special thank you to editor extraordinaire, Medora MacDougall, for your guidance, motivation and expertise. "Onward and upward!"

Chere, your mention so many years ago that I was the "creative one," and I could do anything, sparked the dream that began this journey. I give my deepest heart-felt thank you, to you and all of our family, for a lifetime of love. My dear friends Linda and Dori, your encouragement and support have inspired me to arrive. Thank you!

And, Lori—my one—the reason—my all.

CHAPTER ONE

Kate Bellam deposited her mask, cap and gown in the bin before dropping with a thud into the hard plastic chair at the end of the locker room with its fading gray walls and blue metal lockers.

"God, I feel like I just ran a marathon." She rubbed at her tired eyes before closing them against the harsh overhead fluorescent lights and leaning her head back against the wall.

"For every long, tired hour you just spent in there, there's more than one grateful friend or family member out there," said Eric Morgan, Denton Memorial Hospital's general surgeon, nodding in the direction of the surgical waiting room. He pulled off his own cap and tossed it in the bin. For as commanding as Eric Morgan's presence always appeared in the OR, it never ceased to amaze Kate the quiet, low tone with which he spoke. "Your ability to remain so cool under pressure—and not bailing on doctors when it takes hours longer than scheduled—is why you're the most sought-after surgical nurse on staff."

Kate glanced at the clock over the door. "Crap!" She jumped to her feet, patting frantically at her pants' pockets.

He cocked his head. "You didn't lose something in that guy's abdomen, did you?" He flashed a playful smile.

Kate rushed to her locker and fumbled at the combination lock. "Damn it!" She spun the dial again. "I was supposed to pick Megan up and take her shopping hours ago." She jerked on the locker handle, and when it didn't open, she let out an exhausted sigh. "She's going to be furious with me." She took a calming breath and tried the lock again.

Eric straddled the scarred wooden bench in front of the lockers. "Tell that pretty little niece of yours it's my fault you missed your shopping date, but I am eternally grateful for your skills. I assume you also know that you were invaluable in saving that guy's life."

Kate pulled her phone out of her locker and started dialing. "She's hardly little anymore, you know. She's a seventeen-year-old now and I seriously doubt she cares what my excuse is this time."

He rubbed at the stiffness in his neck as he watched her. "Wow! Seems like she was just becoming a teenager last year." While Kate paced, he continued, "So—seventeen, you've about got her raised. Time to start thinking about a life for yourself."

He was well aware of Kate's dedication, not only to her job, but also to her niece. Kate liked and respected Eric. Of all the surgeons she'd worked with, he was the most compassionate and least egotistical. If things were different, a *lot* different, she would, without a doubt, pursue him.

Megan finally answered and Kate launched into her apology. "Megs, I'm so sorry I missed our shopping date, but there was a trauma surgery, they needed me." Eric poked her, then pointed to himself when she glanced at him. "Dr. Morgan said I should tell you it was his fault."

"Is he that hunky doctor with the soft, sexy voice?"

Her niece's description of the surgeon made Kate's cheeks grow warm. "Megan!"

"Well, is it him?"

Kate wandered to the corner and nearly whispered, "Yes, it's him."

Her niece laughed lightly before saying, "Okay, since you were busy with him, I'll excuse you blowing me off."

Kate shook her head in response to Megan's single-mindedness.

"Just tell me he's at least going to buy you dinner."

Kate watched as the subject of their conversation stripped off his scrub shirt. "Afraid not, sweetie. That's not on the schedule for this evening."

Megan sighed loudly. "That suc..." She coughed. "Sorry, I mean that really stinks. You two would make the cutest couple."

Kate glanced quickly at the handsome form across the locker room and let out a tired breath. "If you say so. Listen, I'll be home in about thirty minutes. Why don't you order us a pizza for dinner, and if you want, we can hit the mall tomorrow evening."

"Did you already forget? I have to be at the paper first thing tomorrow. I'll probably be wiped out by evening."

Kate slumped against her locker, the reminder making her feel worse than she already did at missing the time she had committed to Megan. Bracing for a typical teenage response, she asked, "I'm a pretty horrible excuse for a mom, aren't I?"

Megan snorted. "Nah—I got friends with moms a lot worse." She hesitated. "You do the best you can. Hey, you're buying me pizza, right?"

Slinging her purse over her shoulder, Kate pushed through the door and into the hall. "I'm heading toward the exit now. You call in the pizza and I'll pick up something yummy to go along with it and see you shortly. There's money on my dresser if it gets there before I do."

"Sure, drive carefully. I'll see you in a few."

Kate pulled out of the parking lot, lowering the car window. Although the humidity had started to climb in recent weeks and they were predicting record highs for the summer, the fresh air was welcome as it ruffled her blond hair. Feeling the weariness of her day, she thought about Megan. She hated that she'd forgotten tomorrow was her first day as a summer intern at the *Denton Daily News*. She'd been so focused on Megan beginning her senior year of high school next fall and how she would pay for college after that. Megan was a smart girl—no, she was a brilliant one, much as her mother had been at the same age. And Kate wanted to make sure she had every opportunity to achieve everything she hoped for her life. She deserved no less.

* * *

Kate hurried up the walk from the driveway of the cozy two-bedroom ranch they called home. She smiled, admiring the results of her and Megan's hard work weeks earlier. In the beds that fronted the house, the flowers burst with vibrant color and set their house apart from the others on the quiet residential street, like a cardinal outside the window on a gray winter day. She rushed through the door, handing Megan a white paper sack. "Please put our sundaes in the freezer."

Megan peered into the bag as she headed for the kitchen. "Mmm…what flavor?"

"What else but decadent chocolate?"

"So where's the beer?" Megan asked playfully as she slipped the bag in the freezer.

Kate's stomach roiled at the thought of Megan getting caught up in things like alcohol. She kept her voice light. "Much as I hate to sound like a mother, as long as you're living under my roof, there'll be no drinking until you're of age, young lady."

Megan laughed. "Relax, Auntie, I meant for you. You look beat." She guided Kate toward the kitchen table and the waiting pizza. "You're forgetting that I live outside the stereotypical box that most kids my age live in, like Mom did."

The day's long surgery had left her anxious and exhausted in the same breath. "I'm sorry, honey, I forget sometimes how grown up you are."

Megan snorted. "Not grown up, Aunt Kate, that makes me sound old. I'm just trying to be smart about my life."

"That you are, Megan, and I'm so proud of you for it." Kate dropped heavily into the chair.

"Guess you'll be having a soda like me." Megan returned to the fridge.

Kate rolled her shoulders and stretched her arms, stifling a yawn. As Megan set the soda in front of her, she asked, "Is there a reason you think I should ply myself with alcohol this evening?"

Megan flopped into her chair, flipping open the pizza box, plucking off a mushroom and popping it in her mouth. Placing a slice on a plate, she handed it to her aunt. "You work so hard all the time, I just thought you might like to kick back and relax for once."

Kate took the offered plate. "Honey, I'm sure after a few pieces of pizza, a chocolate sundae and a soak in the tub, I'll be as relaxed as I can get. I'll have no trouble falling into bed and sleeping like a baby." She took a bite, savoring the taste and realizing she'd not eaten anything since about eleven thirty and it was now going on eight. "Besides, Megs, when have you ever seen me drink beer?"

Megan swallowed her mouthful. "Okay, okay, I get it." They ate in silence for a few minutes before Megan broached a new subject. "You know, Aunt Kate, I still think you should let me ride the bus and you keep your car."

Kate swallowed her bite, washing it down with a drink of soda before responding. "Sweetie, we've already been through this. I don't want you riding a bus downtown every day. It's not a problem for me to take one to the hospital, and it will be a much shorter ride for me than it would be for you."

They had discussed it at length, and even though Megan had only been driving for a year, Kate felt the experience and responsibility of getting herself to and from the newspaper would be invaluable for her. Besides, her six-year-old Honda Accord was paid for. Surely it would survive a few door dings from being in a cramped parking garage.

Megan snatched up another piece of pizza. "I just feel bad taking your car away from you is all."

"I appreciate that you care so much, but it's only for a few months. I've suffered worse hardships in my life, believe me."

Megan rolled her eyes. "Yeah, yeah, I know, you had to walk like five miles to school in the snow or something. Right?"

Kate narrowed her eyes. "Very funny." She wadded up her napkin and tossed it at her niece, and they both laughed. Kate turned serious again. "We're clear on the rules? Only driving to and from the paper and no hauling any other kids around?"

Megan cocked her head. "By 'we,' you mean me?"

Kate felt bad for feeling any need to remind Megan. She had proven in recent years to be responsible and mature beyond her years. "It's not you, sweetie, so much as your friends. I know how persuasive peers can be. I trust you, I hope you know that."

Megan rose from the table with her empty plate, then returned a minute later with the sack from the freezer and spoons. She dropped with a thud and a sigh back into her chair. "Yes, I know," she said, handing Kate a sundae and a spoon. "Can we not have one of those deep conversations now, though?"

"Shutting up now," Kate said, digging into her dessert.

* * *

Tommie rushed into her closet-sized office in the newsroom. She had the info she needed to quickly knock out a bio on the newly signed pitcher for Indiana's only pro ball team, the Carson Cougars. With his addition to the team, this just could be their year to go all the way. She was pleased. Her laptop came to life, beeping to let her know she had new emails. Of course she did. She'd been out most of the day and hadn't turned the computer on once. She preferred to do most of her writing the old-fashioned way, with pen and paper. For her the computer was nothing more than a glorified typewriter, a voiceless phone and compact library. She knew, of course, there was more to the thing than that, but she limited her use to only what she absolutely needed it for. She'd met hundreds of people in the under-thirty crowd who lived by their computers. She was an aberration. She'd just as soon type out her stories and toss them in her boss's in-box on her way out the door.

She clicked on the mail icon, watched as her email in-box added one message after another, and then began weeding at the top, clicking delete as each "General Delivery" message was highlighted. After a dozen or so she stopped on one from her boss. It had a time stamp of nine fifteen that morning and was copied to her, the woman who wrote the local entertainment news and some guy listed as "typeset supervisor." Her genial mood dissolved as she read, "Starting three summer interns tomorrow morning from the local high schools." She groaned. "You each will be expected to teach these eager, aspiring young minds the ins and outs of the newspaper reporting business, which shall include all aspects of your individual jobs. Please keep in mind these young people are working for mere peanuts, their main focus being to learn, so do not use them for fetching coffee, lunch, picking up dry cleaning, etc. You get my drift." She read on, but all that registered was "blah, blah, blah…"

She mumbled to herself, "Great, you give us a day's notice that we're going to be babysitting for the summer." She punched hard on the delete button. "Well, we'll just see about that. I've got better things to do than drag around some know-it-all teenager looking for something to fill their summer and their class credits." She'd storm into her editor's office in the morning and have a loud, closed-door meeting with him. As a sixth grader, it had been a pain in the ass being more than a head taller than the rest of the kids her age. Now being tall had definite advantages, especially when it came to dealing with male athletes, coaches and managers—and her runt of a boss.

* * *

Two young gals clinging to each other stumbled into Tommie in the doorway as she entered Lili's Pad an hour later. Reminded of the email that had soured her mood earlier, she slid onto a stool and muttered, "Kids! Parents should lock them in the house until they're thirty." Even as she said it, she realized how ridiculous it sounded. After all, she herself was only twenty-eight.

Jamie slapped down a napkin in front of her. "Unusual seeing you in here during the week. What'll you have?"

"Just a beer. I'm waiting on a carry-out order from next door."

Jamie moved to the cooler. She was well suited for her job, Tommie thought, easy to talk to and definitely easy on the eyes. She always seemed to be wearing something sleeveless to show off her perfectly toned arms, even in the dead of winter when it was only twelve degrees outside.

"So you think the new pitcher is going to take the team all the way this year?"

Tommie took a long pull on the beer, the icy brew cooling her mood as well as her throat. "I think this is the best shot they've had in years. If his arm holds up, his win record speaks for itself. We just might be scrambling for Series tickets this season."

Tommie raised the bottle to her lips, pausing as a hand gripped her shoulder and a warm body pressed against hers.

"Hey, stranger. Did you miss me?"

A tingle flowed through Tommie at the sound of the low sultry voice. She turned to meet eyes dark as night, darker even than her own, and received a quick kiss on the lips.

"'Cause I sure missed you, Tommie Boy."

Tommie had last seen Carly Torres ten months earlier, two days before she left for a temporary assignment with her job in Colorado, and had last been with her a month prior to that. She was, hands down, the best-looking woman Tommie had ever had the pleasure of having. She was built exactly the way a woman should be, in Tommie's opinion—curvy in all the right places. She was *sexy hot*, doing things to Tommie's body she didn't know could be done.

Jumping off her stool to fully embrace her, Tommie felt pressure against her lower abdomen. Holding Carly at arm's length, she saw she was sporting a bit of a baby bump. "You're not thinking I'm responsible for that, I hope." She cocked her head.

"If you were, would you make an honest woman of me?" Carly batted her long lashes.

Tommie swallowed a big lump in her throat before she could answer. "Ah, you know me—love 'em and leave 'em," she shrugged. "Don't think I'm the settling-down kind, you know." She grabbed her beer, taking a big gulp. "Besides, I'd never sign on for kids," she said, shaking her head. "Just don't care for them much."

Carly squeezed her hand, winking. "Well, I had to give it a shot. Can I join you?"

Tommie glanced at the clock on the wall behind the bar. "Sure, but I've only got a few minutes. My dinner should be ready next door anytime." She offered Carly a hand as she pushed up on the barstool before seating herself again. "I'd offer to buy you a drink, but I'm guessing that's out of the question. Unless Jamie has some milk back there."

Carly patted Tommie's hand. "I'm fine. You're such a sweetheart. I just stopped in to see if there were any familiar faces in here...and here you are."

Carly wouldn't have thought she was so sweet if she'd run into her when she was raging about her idiot boss earlier, thought Tommie. Not that she needed Carly to be thinking kindly about her just now. When she charmed women it was purely for the possibility of sex and that was the last thing Carly's condition made her think of at the moment.

Tommie swigged the last of her beer. "I gotta go, good lookin'."

Carly caught her hand. "Maybe we can get together for dinner and..." She allowed her words to trail off as she gazed seductively at Tommie.

"Uh, sure, call me. I'm still at the paper." She pushed off her stool, but Carly kept hold of her hand.

"You know, just because I'm pregnant doesn't mean I can't still... you know..." She bit her bottom lip while trailing a lacquered nail up Tommie's arm. Tommie felt a warm surge between her thighs, fully aware what "you know" meant.

Knowing she was probably flushing because Jamie was listening intently to their exchange, Tommie leaned over and whispered, "Then call me, and we'll...you know..."

She kissed Carly's cheek lightly, then strolled toward the door, feeling in her underwear the sticky wetness that women like Carly so easily aroused in her. Out on the sidewalk, she cursed herself. "You're like a horny damn dog. I hate dykes with no self-control." She smiled, though, at the thought of the woman who had caused her that loss of control.

* * *

Kate took her cup of chamomile tea to the bathtub and, slipping out of her robe, slid into the steamy, scented water there, her tired muscles giving a silent "ah" as she submerged her body up to her chin. She got her mind to stop whirring for only a few minutes before thoughts of Megan and her impending adventures in the summer intern program crept back in. She was thrilled and proud beyond words that Megan was one of only a few seniors to be accepted in the program. But having grown up in suburbia she worried about her going downtown daily by herself. She told herself to stop worrying. Megan was a smart girl and if she didn't know how to handle herself now, she would quickly learn.

Kate inhaled the soothing scent of bath oils and smoothed her hands over her arms and down her thighs. "Relax," she muttered. "Just relax."

She moved her hands slowly up her stomach and lightly over her breasts, feeling the day's stresses leaving her body. When her fingers reached her pubic hair, she hesitated, but her body was screaming for release. It had been far too long...And far too long since a hand other than her own had pleasured her. She pushed two fingers into the wetness building there, her body twitching in response, even as she struggled with the guilt and embarrassment that giving herself this kind of release gave her.

Bodies shouldn't demand this unless you were with someone that could accommodate their need, she thought. But they did. So every now and then you just had to take matters into your own hands. She reached over the side of the tub, pulled a little submersible vibrator from the folds of the towel on the floor and within minutes achieved an orgasm. She closed her eyes, recalling the last time she had shared this with anyone. Remembering a rare evening out two years ago and a stranger.

* * *

She'd gone out for the evening with three of her fellow nurses after seeing Megan safely off to a sleepover at a girlfriend's house. After dinner at a nice restaurant, the others insisted on going to a strip club—where they promptly went overboard drinking and groping the club's handsome, hard-muscled male dancers. While the whole atmosphere was very arousing for Kate, a male body wasn't what she wanted to touch. When they'd had enough, she poured them into a cab, explaining that she wanted to hang around for another drink. The second their taxi was out of sight, she hailed one for herself and headed to The Underground, the gay bar on the perimeter of downtown. Located there at least since she'd been in college, it was known as the best dance spot for women in a hundred miles. Seating herself at the bar, Kate quickly downed a first drink and was getting started on a second when a woman sidled up and leaned close to be heard over the noise.

"I was going to buy you a drink, but I see you just got one."

Kate turned, appraising her. She was gorgeous and the closeness of her body to Kate's set every nerve in her on fire.

Kate moved until their shoulders touched and said, "You can buy the next one."

The woman's lips curved up in satisfaction. Setting her glass on the bar, she extended her hand to Kate. "It'd be my pleasure. I'm Carly. And you are?"

Feeling the pulse beating between her legs, Kate took the woman's hand. "Kate, and it's a pleasure to meet you."

The woman didn't release Kate's hand but slid her arm across the back of the bar stool Kate was sitting on, pressing herself closer still. In a sultry voice she said, "No, Kate, I'm sure the pleasure is all mine."

Something about the woman was so electrifying and hot, Kate wanted to take the hand that held hers and put it between her legs to relieve the ache. She couldn't believe she was in a bar entertaining the thought of sleeping with a stranger, and yet she was. They made the usual small talk, jobs, music, the current movies. Then they finally danced. One dance led to another, then another drink and more dancing. By the time they made last call, Kate's head was abuzz with alcohol, her body demanding sexual release. This Carly seemed normal enough…safe enough. Or was the alcohol clouding her judgment?

Outside on the sidewalk Carly asked, "So, do you live around here?"

Here comes the awkward part, Kate thought. "South of town, I was just going to get a cab." Somehow they'd never got around to discussing where either of them lived. "How about you?"

She hooked her thumb over her shoulder. "Just a few blocks from here actually. I have a loft on Washington." Kate didn't miss the sexy, inviting look illuminated by the faint glow of the nearby streetlight. "You want to join me for another drink, or do you have someone to rush home to?"

Kate's pulse quickened. "No one, and I'd enjoy another drink."

Carly hooked her arm through Kate's. "Wonderful, let's walk."

They walked mostly in silence, then entered a secure building, riding up six floors. After Carly dropped her keys and jacket on the table inside the door, she helped Kate off with hers in a way that made Kate want to wrestle her to the floor where they stood. She motioned Kate toward the kitchen.

"I'm sure I have beer and wine, but beyond that, I don't know for sure."

Nervously, Kate said, "Wine will be fine."

She yanked open the fridge and pulled out a bottle. "It's white."

Kate gave a nod and Carly poured two glasses. She looked around the open, airy space. The colorful wall art and throw pillows stood out starkly against the muted off-white carpet, furniture and walls. "Your loft is wonderful."

Before Kate knew it, Carly was standing close enough she could feel the heat from her body. "I really like it."

She put the glass in Kate's hand, which she quickly sipped. Then she placed the glass on the counter turning toward Carly.

Carly reached up, touching her painted nails to Kate's cheek. "You have the prettiest blue eyes I think I've ever seen."

Kate tried to suppress her nervousness. "I've…uh…never, uh…"

"You're a virgin?" Carly flashed Kate the same seductive look she'd given her at the bar.

Kate shook her head, feeling the flush creeping up her neck. "No, I've uh…been with women before."

Carly gave a knowing look. "But you've never picked up a woman before just to fuck." Kate's face felt hot, and she reached an all-time high on the nervousness scale. Then Carly said, "It's okay, honey."

Kate slowly brought her eyes up to meet Carly's. "I'm sorry, maybe this is a mistake."

Carly cocked her head. "Why? Because you don't want to?"

"No, I'm not looking for any kind of entanglement. I can't…" Kate lowered her head.

Carly laughed lightly before touching Kate's cheek again. "Oh, honey, don't worry. The word 'relationship' isn't even in my vocabulary." Kate shuddered when Carly stroked her fingers down her arm. "So tense, like you're ready to pop. Why don't you let me make you scream with pleasure?"

Kate felt like a gangly teenager again trying to have her first sexual encounter. She *was* ready to scream.

Carly took her hand. "Come on now, I promise I'll be gentle."

Kate allowed herself to be pulled to the bedroom, where Carly slowly undressed her before seductively undressing herself. In the back of her mind, Kate knew how reckless it was, but her body wouldn't let her say "no." It was something extraordinary. When the orgasm hit, she'd never experienced one like it.

* * *

Kate had the vibrator deep inside as her fingers stroked her swollen flesh. She bit her lower lip to stay quiet as she shuddered through an orgasm bigger than the last, then slumped weakly in the cooling water. Tears brimmed in her eyes as she considered what her personal life had become—lonely nights and self-gratification. She wondered if she'd ever be happy and in love again. Feeling more drained than she had when she left the hospital earlier, she pushed herself out of the tub and dried off. Washing her "friend"—

no one else took care of her the way it did—she placed it in its case, ready to be secreted in the box in the bottom of her bedroom closet.

When she pulled the door open, she found Megan standing there, fist poised to knock. Kate quickly put the case behind her back, hoping her niece hadn't seen it.

"Megan!"

Megan eyed her sheepishly. "Sorry, you were in there so long I was worried you might have fallen asleep and drowned."

Kate reached with her free hand to push errant strands of hair off Megan's face. "I'm fine. I just got caught up in a daydream." She leaned in the doorway so her hidden hand wouldn't be so obvious.

Megan stepped away, then stopped. "You know, you should hook one of those eligible doctors at the hospital so you don't have to work so hard all the time to support us."

Her niece's concern for her own well-being was more than touching. "Sweetie, I promise you that I don't work any harder than anyone else to support us. But I'll put that on my list of things to do."

"Good." Megan turned. "I'm going to bed now, have a big day tomorrow."

"Goodnight, Meggie, sweet dreams." She winced internally at the slip of the childhood nickname she'd used to comfort Megan after her mother died. She should probably quit calling her that, but then again, if she didn't…maybe she'd never grow up.

With a yawn, Megan said, "'Night."

CHAPTER TWO

When Tommie saw George Dixon moseying toward his office, she jumped up and followed him in, closing the door behind her.

"We've got to talk about this ridiculous intern thing." She allowed him to sit behind his desk before stepping up to it and placing her hands on her hips. He looked at her with disinterest. "I don't have time to babysit some kid. I'm not even in here most of the time. Am I going to have to get a permission slip signed by his parents every time I need to go somewhere because I have to drag a teenage boy around with me?"

George wasn't successful at hiding the tiny smile. Tommie knew he was enjoying making her life miserable. He tried to look serious when he said, "It's a young lady you'll be mentoring, not a teenage boy."

Tommie slapped her hands down loudly on the desk, making him jump in his chair. "No freaking way I'm going to drag around some...some..."—Tommie was at a loss for words, one of the few times that had ever happened—"some...Barbie looking for a cool way to spend her summer vacation." Her cheeks were on fire and she had an intense urge to leap across his desk and wrap her hands around his stubby neck.

Defensively, he crossed his arms over his chest before saying, "I thought you'd be thrilled to have some girl following you around like a puppy."

Tommie took the comment for what it was, a personal dig. It was no secret she was gay. Except for a few snooty old biddies who worked in administration and this jerk, most everyone at the paper treated her like a person. He was taking this opportunity to slam her because he could.

"That's a low blow, George, even coming from you." Tommie pushed off the desk and straightened to her full, menacing height of five foot ten. "I won't do it, George. You can take your little pet project and shove it up someone else's ass." She headed for the door. "I'm going to Mr. Foster with this." Mr. Foster was the executive editor, and Tommie was sure he would put George in his place.

George called after her, "This was his pet project, in fact." She turned to face him. "I told him you wouldn't do it. He said you're a consummate professional and would gladly accept the challenge of shaping a young mind." He gave her a smug look.

Tommie immediately knew the score. He could have included that little fact in his email and saved her the humiliation of losing it for no good reason. But no—he'd probably made a bet with someone that she would storm his office this morning. The smirk on his pudgy face made the muscles in her fingers twitch into fists.

Foster was one of the good guys in the otherwise cutthroat business of news reporting. He respected Tommie and she respected him for respecting her. If he wanted her personally to be involved with this little "do-gooder" project of his, she would quash her distaste and attempt to make him proud. George stood, placed his hands on his hips and puffed out his chest in a show of victory. She strode back and leaned over his desk, towering over the foul, little man by more than six inches.

"I'm doing this because I like Mr. Foster so much. You know how I feel about you." She turned toward the door again, muttering under her breath, "You putz."

"We're meeting in the conference room at nine sharp."

Tommie waved a hand as she left the office. "Yeah, yeah, can't wait."

She hoped Foster wouldn't be in the meeting, but he probably would be since she'd chosen to dress down today. Five minutes shy of nine o'clock she popped into the ladies' room, tucked in her baseball shirt, pulled on her jacket and smoothed a hand over her short dark hair. She checked her appearance in the mirror and pressed down a few more standing hairs.

"Yep, you look like a big ole dyke," she said, "but it's gonna have to do." She smiled at her reflection. "I am what I am, and there ain't no changing that."

When she entered the conference room a few minutes later, she saw three kids huddled at one end of the table and "Ms. Entertainment," as Tommie liked to call her, sitting at the opposite end obliviously typing away on her laptop. Putting on her best poker face, she stepped toward the kids' end of the table and extended her hand.

"Hi, I'm Tommie and I write the sports column, among other things."

The interns stood one at a time, introducing themselves.

"I'm Megan Bellam." She gave Tommie a firm, but ladylike handshake. "I'm not much of a sports person, but you write a very interesting column." She flashed a pearly white smile. Definitely not a sports person, Tommie thought, assessing her dimples, mid-length blond hair and girly blouse and skirt. In fit-looking shape, though. She turned to the next student.

"Bradley, uh...Brad Schaffer. Nice to meet you." He offered Tommie a damp hand. He was no taller than Kid Number One. Megan, was it? About five foot four. And definitely nervous.

The last girl stood. "Tiffany Cooper." She promptly plopped right back down into the cushy conference chair. She took the prize. A "Ms. High Society" Tommie thought, and probably thought herself above everyone else in the room, including Ms. Entertainment. If Tommie got stuck with that one, she'd quit or kill herself. Either way, she wouldn't be returning tomorrow.

Tommie sat a few chairs away from Kid Number One, whose name she'd forgotten again. A guy from production who had just entered sat across the table from her beside Ms. High Society. A few minutes later Mr. Foster blew in, in a rush, George following in his wake.

After introductions were made all around, Mr. Foster launched into his "rah, rah" speech about his program. Ten minutes later Tommie was wishing she grabbed a cup of coffee on her way. She stifled a yawn. A lot of what was said went in one ear and out the other as Tommie considered where to go for lunch. But finally, after half an hour Mr. Foster announced who would be mentoring which student, and thank the Lord the kids were paired up as Tommie suspected. Her summer adolescent would be Kid Number One, Megan…Something.

When Foster dismissed the meeting, Megan immediately placed herself at Tommie's side, saying, "I'm really excited about this opportunity. Writing's all I ever think about."

She was a little bubblier than Tommie liked in the female gender—hell, in anyone. But at least it sounded like the kid was going to take it seriously. Tommie reminded herself of the declaration she made to make Foster proud of her.

She forced a smile. "Let's get to work then."

As Tommie led them toward her office, Megan asked about the current state of affairs in newspaper printing.

"There's been a shift of seismic proportions in journalism," Tommie began. "I personally hate most of the technologies these days. The 'do more with less' and the whole downsizing of the newspaper reporting business. But…what are you going to do? Move ahead or get left behind is what. It's a new world—be courageous and try to shine any and every way you can. Learn all you can about the use of social media and the Internet in journalism. Be hungry…be flexible. Because I'll tell you what, when Grandma's generation is gone, God rest their souls, so too will be print media probably."

When she pushed open the door and stepped inside the cramped space, Megan stopped, mouth agape. Tommie started to clear stacks of files and paper from the spare chair set at the side of her desk to catch the overflow from the desk. Now she'd have to come up with a new plan.

"They don't give you much room to work," Megan said, stepping around a pile of precariously stacked magazines.

Tommie didn't look up from her task. "Tell me about it. They expanded some areas," Tommie made quotations with her fingers, "and consolidated others, basically cutting my old office in half. But hey, they're still printing papers every day so I still have a job. If you repeat this I'll deny it to my grave, but if I were you I'd maybe think along the lines of becoming a best-selling author and being a journalist on the side." Tommie didn't have any notion why she was sharing so much with this adolescent stranger, except she had a very honest, trusting look about her. Successfully clearing the chair she finally made eye contact with the girl. "You can set this wherever you want to."

"How about I move some of these piles around so I can sit across the desk from you?" Tommie looked at her with a stricken expression. "Or I can just sit right here." She hung her purse on the back of the chair before taking a seat.

Tommie dropped into her own chair and, taking a breath, said, "Look, you can move my stuff around if you promise to only do it when I'm standing here so you can show me what's moving where. That way when I need to find something it doesn't have to turn into a scavenger hunt. Believe it or not, there is a method to my madness." She waved her hand around the tiny room.

"That sounds reasonable."

Tommie started to lean back, then stopped. "Shoot!" Megan looked on questioningly. "I meant to get coffee on the way back." Tommie got up and stepped around the desk. "You want some?"

Megan crinkled her nose. "I don't drink coffee, but something else would be great."

Tommie motioned. "Come on, I'll show you where the 'Roach Coach' is."

"'Roach Coach'?"

Tommie shortened her stride so the girl could keep up with her. "Yeah, you know, a truck with vending machines on wheels. They have the best coffee." Tommie cupped a hand over her mouth and said quietly, "The coffee in here stinks worse than instant, but they won't do anything about it."

The elevator deposited them in the basement, where Megan followed Tommie through a huge garage area, up a ramp and out into an alley. Half a block down they stepped onto the sidewalk beside the courthouse building and about ten feet away from the vending truck. Midmorning pedestrians hustled up and down the courthouse steps, rushing in to plead their cases or away in celebration of freedom. Tommie was grateful not to have to worry over the quagmire that was the criminal justice system. Her job was stressful enough...made more so now with her new charge for the summer. *Please just let me survive this.*

"Voila!"

While Tommie filled a cup with coffee, Megan selected a can of juice, then said, "Darn, I left my purse upstairs."

"Don't sweat it. This one's on me." She dug wadded bills from her pocket and paid. "Next time's on you, though."

"Fair enough."

As they headed back down the alley, Tommie said, "Do me a favor and don't ever walk through this alley by yourself."

"Why?" Megan asked, sipping her juice and recapping the bottle, giving the area only a cursory glance.

Tommie halted abruptly, glowering at Megan. "Look, you seem like a nice kid. I wouldn't want some street person to happen upon you alone out here or some slimeball who just got set loose on some legal technicality." *Man*, she thought, *I sound like somebody's mother.*

"You walk down this alley by yourself, don't you?"

Tommie snorted. "That's different. I'm bigger than most of the bums that hang around here. You're not."

"I'm not a weakling, in case you're thinking I am."

Tommie stopped at the dock door they'd left through. "If you don't promise me you won't come out here alone, I'm not going to give you my code to use on the door."

Megan cocked her hip and planted a hand on it. "And just who would I venture out here with?"

God, Tommie thought, *you knew what you were doing when you made me a lesbian. If I had a kid I would surely kill it.* Megan was beginning to wear down her resolve to be on her best behavior.

"I don't know, maybe Barbie up there."

"Barbie who?" Megan asked indignantly.

Tommie answered, "The red-nailed, porcelain-faced blondie that came here with you and what's-his-name today."

"For your information, I don't know those two. We each come from different high schools and I never met them before this morning." She cocked her head to match the angle of her hip. "And furthermore, I'm pretty sure I wouldn't ever become friends with either of them. He's too dweebie and..."—she shuddered—"she's got her nose so high in the air if she went out in a rainstorm without an umbrella, she would drown." She took a breath. "No disrespect intended."

Tommie had to stifle a laugh at hearing Megan's colorful, and probably accurate, descriptions of her peers. With a straight face she crossed her arms over her chest, taking care not to slop the hot coffee on herself. "Still, if you don't promise me you'll stay out of this alley, you don't get my code. Shortcuts are great, but only when they don't get you in trouble."

"I do know a little something about life's tough challenges." Megan removed her hand from her hip. "But fine, whatever."

One side of Tommie's mouth curled up. Spoken like a true teenager. She admired the girl's spunk and determination. If she chose to be a reporter, both qualities would come in handy.

"It's my birth date."

"Your code is your birth date?"

"Right." Tommie punched in the three digits. "Two-fourteen."

She opened the door for Megan who mumbled, "That's creative" as she entered. Tommie was certain she meant it to be heard, but she let it pass. They weren't getting off to a very good start. The three-floor elevator ride was silent as was the walk back to Tommie's office. Tommie closed the door and settled into her chair.

Megan's expression reflected her defiant mood so in an attempt to diffuse it, Tommie leaned back casually and said, "So, Megan, tell me about yourself."

Megan's tight expression relaxed. "I go to South View High School, and English, of course, and history are my favorite subjects. I live with my aunt, and for fun I like to read and research things on the Internet. If I have a tough day for any reason, I like to write in my journal. It helps clear my head. And to get into this program I had to submit a paper."

"What was your paper on?"

Megan boasted, "The educational and social struggles of inner-city kids in cities like ours."

Tommie nodded, duly impressed. "Wow! That's an impressive topic. I'd like to read it."

"I'm sure your boss has a copy of it," Megan said coolly, nonchalantly crossing her legs.

Tommie winced at the mention of George. "I'm sure he does, but maybe you can bring me a copy of my own tomorrow?"

"Sure, I think I can find a copy at home." Megan thought for a moment. "Or I could email it to you. It's on my computer."

Computers, Tommie thought, *does anyone exist anymore without one?*

"A hard copy would be better if you can find one. I prefer something tangible to read from."

Megan pulled a small notebook from her purse, flipped it open and wrote herself a reminder. After checking her email, Tommie took Megan on a grand tour of the building, including the production area where they printed the papers.

They strolled through layout where one of the photographers whose photos frequently accompanied her articles called out. "Hey, T."

"Hey, Eddie. This is my intern for the summer, Megan Bellam."

Eddie simply nodded and Megan said only, "Hi."

"So, Eddie, you ever shoot pics at a Series game?" She knew the answer without asking. Eddie was a hometown boy. He'd only been on staff a few years, coming there straight out of college. The Cougars hadn't been to so much as a play-off game since Tommie was in junior high.

He laughed. "Yeah, right."

Tommie clamped her hand on his shoulder. "Well, buddy, you just might get a chance this season."

He crossed his fingers on both hands. "That would be a career boost, for sure."

"For you and me both."

Walking past an enclosed area that nearly covered the north end of the building, Megan asked, "So what's in here?" Cupping her hands to her face she leaned in against the window, attempting to see through the closed blinds.

The cold draft of air blowing under the door wasn't what made Tommie shiver. "Uh, they store stuff in there. Come on." Tommie moved hurriedly to the elevators. *They store servers and computers and geeks in there, and those IT guys detest me.* Tommie always jokingly referred to them as the paper's "It" guys. Of course calling them that to their faces had garnered her more than one verbal complaint from the top "It" guy. *What a bunch of namby-pambys.*

They went again to the basement, heading this time in the opposite direction from the garage. The noise of the running presses increased exponentially as they neared a set of steel doors down a long hallway.

"Here," Tommie plucked two small packages of ear plugs from the dispenser next to the door, "put these in."

"Seriously?"

"Only if you want to go inside." Tommie cocked her head.

Megan stuffed the pieces of foam in her ears. Inside, the floor vibrating under their feet, she caught Tommie's arm. "So this is what fresh ink smells like?" She yelled over the reverberating noise, wrinkling her nose.

Tommie inhaled deeply, her own memories of her first time down here flooding back. "That's right, kiddo." Megan frowned at her.

* * *

When lunchtime rolled around, Tommie deposited Megan in the cafeteria and left to run an errand. Megan had tried to protest, acting precisely like a teenager, and Tommie had explained that her lunch break, on the rare occasions she got one, was *her* time and not the paper's. Of course, there was no errand. She had just needed a break from the girl. Standing on the sidewalk a block away, she wondered anew how parents managed to raise kids. Thinking of her own unruly self as a teenager. "Could be worse," she muttered, "she could be more like I was." *God, the things I put my parents through as a teen!*

They spent the remainder of the day researching. Tommie was sifting through one of the many piles of "stuff" in her office. "The most important thing in newspaper reporting is to get your facts straight. Careers die in a heartbeat when you don't get that one right."

"Why can't we just look this stuff up on the Internet?"

Tommie kept her aversion to pretty much all-things computer to herself. "I tend to do a lot of my research the old-fashioned way." Megan sighed. "But here," Tommie scribbled two things on a piece of paper. "Search away." She indicated her laptop. "I'll help you sort out credible sources."

"I do know how to surf the net," Megan said in a snarky tone.

Tommie's patience was dwindling. She grabbed up the piece of paper, scribbling more notes. "These are reliable sites." She handed the paper back. "If you need to print anything—"

"Why would I need to print? Can't I just save the links to use next time?"

Tommie was at her wit's end. "Fine. Just please don't blow up my laptop. Me and the IT guys don't exactly get along."

Megan lowered her head. "Guess that's why you didn't take me around to meet them then."

Tommie called it a day at four thirty, sending Megan off toward the parking garage before heading around the corner in the opposite direction to Sam's Pub for a beer and a little decompression. Fifteen minutes later, after chugging a cold one and chasing away the remnants of the day, she headed back to her office to do some real work. It smelled different, she noticed. Like Megan. It was a fresh and pleasant fragrance, but it reminded her what the next nine weeks would entail. She groaned, parked herself in front of her laptop and started drafting a guest article for a blogger on the newest right fielder for their own minor league team, the Denton Dragons. When the lingering fragrance proved too much of a distraction, she gathered her notes and the laptop and headed home.

Sitting at home in her favorite lounger, sipping a beer, she continued working on the article, wistfully yearning for the days of scribbling notes in her notebook then sitting down at her electric typewriter and the tap, tap of the mechanical keys. She loved that old thing, which her father had purchased for her, not without a lot of haranguing on Tommie's part of course, at the neighbors' garage sale. It had been a difficult adjustment for her when she started at the paper and was forced to submit her work via computer. "Times they are a'changing," she murmured aloud, reminded of her advice to her young shadow for the summer. She blew out a long, tired breath. It just might be the longest summer in history.

* * *

Hoping to get home a little early for a change, Kate rushed from the hospital around twenty after four—and discovered that her bus wouldn't be around for another ten to fifteen minutes. Grumbling to herself, she sat on the bench in the little glass enclosure. She needed to remember to tuck one of her many paperback romances in her bag for times like this.

A heavyset woman sat beside her with a grunt and a thud. After a moment she pulled a magazine from her bag and fanned her face.

"They're saying this summer's gonna be a hot one."

Kate had been on her feet all day, getting only a short bathroom break between surgeries and little else. She was tired and hungry. Still, she couldn't just ignore the woman, could she?

"Is that so?"

Apparently those three words were all it took to open the floodgates. The woman began talking like a talk radio host about everything from the weather to her job and then a history of her family and kids.

An iPod, thought Kate, *that's what I need. And a big stick.* If the woman had touched Kate's arm and said, "Oh, honey" once, she'd done it a dozen times. If she did again, Kate was going to clock her. Before that could happen, fortunately, the bus arrived. As they waited their turn to board, her bus buddy decided it was time to introduce herself.

"My name's Margie, maybe we'll be riding the same bus again tomorrow."

"That's possible." Kate silently sighed.

She allowed the woman to board ahead of her and made her way past her to the back and an empty seat. She hated how she felt at the moment. She was always kind and considerate with strangers. Her job demanded it, but it had also always been who she was. She chalked her mood up to her growling stomach. Closing her eyes, taking a few calming breaths, she decided some soft music right now would be so soothing. She'd definitely make Megan take her shopping this weekend for something she could use for listening to music. She was feeling more like herself when the bus reached her stop. As she stood to exit the bus, she noticed the woman still sitting in her seat.

"Have a good evening," Kate said when she passed by.

"You too, honey."

Two blocks later Kate was letting herself in the house, and although all she wanted to do was drop into a chair in the living room, she went to the kitchen. It was Megan's first day and Kate wanted to have a special dinner. She pulled out the steaks she'd thawed last night and got started. Megan came in five minutes later, excitedly calling Kate's name.

"In the kitchen." Megan bounced in. Kate wished she had half the energy of her niece. "How was your first day, sweetie?"

Megan poured herself a glass of juice, gulped half of it and took a seat at the table. "Well, they teamed me up with the sports columnist—"

"Sports?"

"Yeah, thankfully. I might have had to back out of this if they'd stuck me with the uppity lady that writes the entertainment stuff. I don't think I would have liked that at all." Kate turned to look at her. "I know, I know, I shouldn't give up on something until I've tried it. That's why I didn't get upset about the sports thing. You know me, Aunt Kate, I'm about as sports-minded as that knife in your hand. But this writer is really interesting and I think I can learn a lot."

"How long has he been at the paper?" Kate asked, picturing Megan working with some retired athlete or some hunk who couldn't make the pros that Megan would develop a crush on.

She got up and placed her empty glass in the sink. "Oh, it's not a he, it's a she."

"Really?"

Megan backed against the counter a few feet from where Kate worked. "Yeah, she's kind of cool and she knows everything about sports. She knows all these statistics about all the professional baseball, football and basketball players. Like, did you know there's only ever been one baseball team to have a perfect season? I mean in the whole history of baseball." When Kate gave her a blank look, she said, "In eighteen sixty-nine the Cincinnati Red Stockings posted a record of sixty-five and zero. Better known now as the Cincinnati Reds—you know, our rivals across the state line. Oh, and they were the first fully professional baseball team. She knows all these little tidbits of information about, like, every sport imaginable. It's pretty amazing, I'm really impressed."

Kate wiped her hands. "She must be a library of knowledge if she's impressed you."

"I'll tell you, though, the little office she works in is a disaster area. If my room ever looked like that you'd ground me from *everything* for *eternity*. Oh, yeah, and I'm pretty sure she's gay."

Kate hoped she successfully concealed her alarm. "Megan, why would you say such a thing?"

"Well, she doesn't wear make-up and wears her hair super short. She dresses more like a guy than not, and probably wouldn't be caught dead in heels unless they were on a pair of motorcycle boots or something." Megan shrugged. "She just looks the part."

Kate's chest tightened. She couldn't tell if Megan was bothered by the fact that her mentor might be a lesbian or not.

"So how was your first day on the bus?" Megan popped a cherry tomato into her mouth.

"Why don't you get changed, then help me with the salads? I'll fill you in then." Kate was still trying to process Megan's assumptions about her new mentor. And she wasn't entirely certain she was ready to approach the gay/lesbian topic, unless Megan pressed it.

"Sure." Megan started from the room, but stopped. "Aunt Kate?"

"Hmm…" She didn't look up from the sharp knife she was trimming with.

"Thanks for letting me have this opportunity. I think it can be a life changer."

"You're welcome, Megan. Now go get changed. You're not done working for the day."

Kate started the grill, Megan returned minutes later to begin chopping and within the half hour they were enjoying dinner on the deck.

"So, really, how was the bus experience?"

Kate paused briefly, then said, "It was okay. It kind of reminds me of high school, only the people all look older." Megan laughed. "We need to go to the mall so you can pick me out something to listen to music with."

Megan asked, "Like an iPod?" When Kate nodded, Megan offered, "You can use mine."

Kate smiled. "Meg, honey, I hardly think you and I enjoy listening to the same kind of music. The first thing you did in my car was change the radio station. Right?"

"Guilty as charged. Could we look for some kind of book bag for me while we're there?"

"Sure, sweetie. We'll make a girls' day of it this weekend. Okay?"

"Sounds good."

Megan told her more about her day at the paper over dinner. Kate was thrilled that she was happy about her summer internship. Her greatest worry was that Megan would spend too much "alone" time in her room and take steps backward to the angry, confused teen she'd been a few years ago. Life had not been fair to Megan. Her father abandoned her before she could say "Daddy" and had never been heard from since. Then her mother, Kate's vivacious, nonconformist, artist sister, Nikki, had died. Kate did her best to make a happy life for her niece, but she wasn't sure she herself could have held up under those circumstances.

"Hello?" Megan's voice pulled her from her reverie.

"I'm sorry, Megs, what?"

"I was asking if you wanted me to clean up tonight."

While pleased at her thoughtfulness for asking, Kate knew Megan was probably busting at the seams to get on the computer. "That's okay, I'll do it if you'll just carry in your own dishes. I'm sure you need to report on your day to all your friends."

Megan rolled her eyes. "Yeah, right, all my friends. I have one that even cares."

They entered the kitchen. "Megan, honey, one good, trusting, lifelong friend is better than a handful of any other kind. Go fill Ashley in."

Megan placed her dishes on the counter, then quickly kissed her aunt's cheek. "Thanks again for everything." She gave a little wriggle. "I can't wait to go shopping this weekend."

Kate didn't miss the sparkle in Megan's eyes. She looked truly happy and Kate prayed to be able to help her stay that way. "Me too, sweetie. Say good night before you go to bed."

Megan nodded, then disappeared, and Kate began her cleanup. In her twenties she hadn't been sure if she had that maternal instinct that most women do, but then Megan was dropped in her lap. An eight-year-old third grader, suddenly alone in the world, her mother lost to the ravages of a brain tumor. Megan had struggled as any child would to understand why the one person she most loved and trusted was being taken away. If anything could be thought of as fortunate in such a devastating situation, it was that by the time Nikki went into hospice care, Kate and Megan were becoming somewhat comfortable with each other.

Kate had had adjustments of her own to make, of course. Having Megan in her life had helped her to move on from her sister's death. Being responsible for a child required a lot of focus. Sacrifices too. Like being single. Hayden, her partner, had fled the minute Kate confirmed she would become Megan's guardian. Sex was a small thing to forgo for now in exchange for having Megan in her life and being a good role model for her. She peeked in on her, said her good nights, before retiring to a bath with her tea—tonight minus any tub toys.

CHAPTER THREE

The days mirrored each other for the remainder of the week. Kate continued to get off work in time to beat Megan home or follow quickly on her heels. Kate kept her nose in her book at the bus stop, but mouthy Margie talked anyway.

She was thrilled to get behind the wheel of her own car on Saturday and drive them to the mall. They had a good day shopping. She even splurged on a new pair of shorts and summer top for herself, one that was "hot" enough, Megan said, to enable her to land the eligible doctor of her choice. They picked up a romantic comedy on the way home and Megan invited Ashley over to watch it. The intimate scenes made the girls giggle—and made Kate long to be held and touched in such a tender way.

* * *

Tommie didn't arrive until nearly twenty after nine on Monday and found Megan standing outside her office, wearing a scowl.

Oh crap! She dug her keys out of her pocket.

Megan muttered, "Nice of you to show up. It's not like I had anything better to do than stand around here with my thumb somewhere I'd rather it not be."

Tommie unlocked the office. "Sorry to keep you waiting, kiddo. Two days away from this place and I kind of forgot you'd be here this morning. I had to stop and pick up some reference materials." She slapped a stack of paper down on her desk. Red-faced, Megan remained in the doorway. Tommie turned up her palms. "Look, I said I'm sorry." She motioned between herself and Megan. "This is something I'm going to have to adjust to."

Tommie watched Megan cross her arms over her chest and braced herself. She'd seen many a woman take that stance with her right before they started to rip on her for doing something offensive or just plain stupid.

"Might help if I could call you, huh? You may not like computers much, but I notice you're practically married to that phone of yours, checking it for whatever is constantly beeping at you."

"I wouldn't even have it if I didn't have to, but some technology is essential. I get scouting reports on Twitter. Nothing like good old-fashioned reporting," Tommie said sarcastically. Megan frowned at her and Tommie whipped her phone from her pocket. "Point taken. What's your number?"

She keyed the buttons as Megan recited the number. Megan let her cell ring twice, terminated the call, fished Tommie's number out of Recent Calls and saved it to her Contacts list. When she finished she said, "You know this is about more than a phone call."

Oh God, Tommie thought. She sounded like some weekend fling she'd scorned.

"You think I'm just an annoyance, hanging out here for the summer and that I could care less if I have anything to do."

Tommie groaned mentally at the teenager's tirade. She was sure the Barbie kid wouldn't have cared if she'd had nothing to do for an hour or so. She'd probably have just sat in the break room and done her nails or something mindless. Still... She opened her desk drawer and rummaged around. Finally producing a key, she offered it to Megan.

"Here, now if for any reason I'm late, which you should know about in advance"—she waved the cell phone still in her hand—"unless for some reason I'm dying on the side of the road, you can let yourself in. But…" Tommie paused, "don't move anything." She narrowed her eyes at Megan. "You promised, remember?"

Megan dropped the key into her purse. "You don't have any respect for me at all, do you? To you I'm just a kid."

Tommie dropped helplessly into her chair. "How long you gonna beat this dead horse?"

Megan's tone was angry. "What's that supposed to mean?"

Tommie decided it was time to use her well-honed ability to schmooze women. "Never mind, I'm just talking out my ass… oops, sorry. And I'm sorry I didn't tell you to take an extra hour off this morning. I promise to get better. I'm just not used to having someone shadow me…or, I mean, working with me."

Shut up, Tommie, she cautioned herself.

"Look, let's start over." She pasted on what she hoped was a charming smile. "Good morning, Megan, I'm sorry to be running late." She began sifting through the stack she had just piled on her desk. "So, how was your weekend?" She quickly glanced sideways at Megan.

Megan eyed Tommie suspiciously before she answered. "It was nice. Aunt Kate and I went shopping Saturday." Tommie was intent on the newest stack she'd introduced to her already cluttered office. "Do you really care?"

Tommie stopped, giving her full attention to Megan. "I wouldn't have asked if I didn't, and just a tiny bit of info about me, I can multitask with the best of them. Just because I'm doing something else doesn't mean I'm not listening." She added impatiently, "Go on, tell me all about your weekend."

"She let me invite my best girlfriend, Ashley, over to spend the night. We watched a movie and had popcorn." She leaned toward Tommie as if she were going to share a national secret. "After Aunt Kate was in bed we were online chatting with this guy that just graduated. He's oh-so cute. If my aunt knew, I'd probably lose my computer privileges for a week."

Shoot me now, thought Tommie. It looked like she was fast becoming Megan's second best girlfriend. Which meant, no doubt, that she would be subjected to hearing every detail of "teenage girl living" in the latest generation.

Megan sat back. "So, what did *you* do this weekend?"

Tommie's mind flashed not only to what she'd done, but whom—the blond fitness trainer, a friend of a friend, she met at

The Underground who convinced Tommie to drive her home. The young woman had an insatiable appetite. Tommie had worried at one point, in fact, that she might be having a coronary or a stroke or something equally debilitating. She felt sorry for the woman's clients. What was her name? Candy? Sandy? Something "Andy" sounding. She had written it down somewhere, along with her phone number. The next time she needed to lose a few pounds, she decided, she would hook up with the woman and drop them overnight.

"Hello?" Megan was waving her hand in front of Tommie.

Tommie looked up. "Oh, uh…I just went out for a few beers Saturday night. Nothing special for me." Megan was studying her, and her overly warm cheeks probably indicated there was more to her weekend than she was saying, but Megan seemed satisfied to let it go.

"Here." She handed an envelope to Tommie.

"What's this?"

"It's my paper. You asked me to make a copy for you."

"So I did." She laid it on the corner of her desk.

"Aren't you going to read it?"

"Now?"

Megan sighed loudly. "Yes, now. It's only four pages long and I didn't bring it so you could just lose it in all of this." Her eyes moved over the chaos that surrounded them.

Desperate to avoid another go-around, Tommie pulled out the contents of the envelope, read them quickly, as was her nature, and returned them to the envelope. Reaching it out to Megan, she said positively, "Good work."

"You can keep it. Maybe some day I'll be a famous writer and you can sell this on the Internet."

"Thank you." Tommie slid the envelope into her desk drawer. "Shall we get to work?"

They managed to make it through the rest of the day without any further misunderstandings, miscommunications or head butting. And through the rest of the week, though at some point each day Tommie lost her patience about Megan's lack of sports knowledge and having to explain things that were a natural part, it seemed, of her own DNA. Conversely, Megan acted like a typical teenager regarding Tommie's seeming lack of knowledge about any recent technology except her smartphone—never hesitating to point out all the features Tommie was failing to use. Still, by week's end, they were settling into a better working relationship. For all the teenage behavior Tommie had to endure, she couldn't deny the girl was smart, focused and maintained a good work ethic.

* * *

Kate enjoyed hearing about Megan's experiences at the paper—except for the parts about when she and her mentor had clashed.

"I hope you're not being disrespectful with this woman, Megan."

"No way, Aunt Kate." Megan's head shook adamantly. "She just makes me so mad sometimes. One minute she treats me like an adult coworker, and the next she's acting like I'm a kid. The next time she calls me 'kiddo,' I'm going to scream."

Kate laughed to herself. "Well, don't get yourself fired. It wouldn't look good on your résumé to be fired from an internship. It might suggest you're not trainable."

"Don't worry, I'm pretty sure Tommie likes me, but I'm sure she'd never admit it."

"Does she have kids of her own?"

Megan snorted loudly. "Kids, no way. I told you: I think she's gay."

Kate kept her tone even. "Families come in all shapes and sizes, Megan."

"I know." Megan looked a little uncomfortable. "She doesn't wear any rings. I just get a feeling she's still single."

Kate let it go, still unsure that she was ready for a discussion of life choices with Megan.

Thursday evening as they cleared their dinner dishes, Megan asked, "Ashley wants me to go up to their place at Sweetwater Lake for the weekend. Can I?"

"You mean, 'may I?'" Kate began running dishwater. "Exactly whom are you going with?"

Megan grabbed a towel, ready to dry. "Well, we'd be going up with her mom Friday evening. Her dad is driving up Saturday and I'll ride home with him on Sunday. He has to go back to work. Ash and her mom are staying part of the week." She didn't give her aunt time to ask more questions. "Please, Aunt Kate. I've been responsible, going to the paper, practically since school was out. And just think, you can have a peaceful weekend without me in your hair. Hey, maybe you can go out with some of your friends, meet a guy and get lucky."

Kate turned abruptly. "Megan!"

She shrugged. "Well, you can if you want 'cause you'll have the house all to yourself." Megan waggled her brows.

Kate shook her head at her brazen comments. "Get Ashley's mother to call me this evening. It's not even up for consideration until I talk with her."

Megan tossed the dishtowel on the counter and started from the room.

"Hey, where are you going? We're not finished here."

Megan called as she disappeared down the hallway, "I'll be back to finish, I'm just going to text Ash to have her mom call you."

After Kate finished washing, she filled a cup with the last of the coffee and settled back at the table to sort through the day's mail. Half an hour later her phone rang and vibrated on the counter. Before Kate could get to it, Megan came bounding back in, scooped up the phone and handed it to her. She waited anxiously while her aunt conducted a three-minute conversation, ending with, "Thanks for the call. I hope you enjoy your vacation."

Kate had no sooner pulled the phone from her ear when Megan was clamoring, "Well, what'd she say, can I go?" Kate stood, carrying her phone back to the counter and prolonging the suspense. "Ah, come on, Aunt Kate, you're killing me here. Can I go or not?"

Kate leaned a hip against the counter. Megan stood paralyzed, watching her for signs. She finally said, "If you promise me you'll call the minute you get there and let me know when you're headed home. I don't want to spend the weekend worrying about you."

Megan danced barefooted over to Kate, chanting, "Thank you...thank you...thank you." She threw her arms around her aunt and squeezed. "I promise to call you, and...I promise you won't regret letting me go."

Kate welcomed the affectionate gesture. They had been few and far between since Megan entered high school. Kate didn't understand. Affection had been a natural part of their relationship.

She had been very close with her mom at that age—until she came out in college, which had not just strained the relationship, but fractured it beyond repair.

Megan released her hug. "You're the greatest, Aunt Kate." She popped a quick kiss on Kate's cheek.

Before Megan could get away, Kate cupped her face in her hands. "You're a pretty terrific girl yourself, you know."

Megan's cheeks flushed pink as she wriggled away from Kate. There wasn't a conceited gene in the girl, Kate thought. She did harbor some insecurities, however, although she covered them well around people who didn't know her as Kate did. Megan backed out of reach.

"I've gotta go let Ashley know I get to go and start packing. Thanks again."

Kate smiled. "You're welcome, sweetie. I'm sure you'll have a wonderful weekend."

* * *

Kate caught the earlier bus the following morning, hoping to begin and finish earlier than usual so she could see Megan off for her weekend away. She liked being requested specifically for some surgeries, but she disliked being scheduled into one at the last minute just because the scheduled nurse found some reason not to come to work. As a precaution, she called the house before entering the surgery wing just after two and left a message for Megan, saying that she might miss her before she left, to have a wonderful time and please, please call.

She was beat when she entered the house at six fifteen. Megan was long gone, but she had left a note on the kitchen counter: "Aunt Kate, sorry to miss you, but Tommie let me leave an hour early when I told her what I was doing for the weekend. Hope you're not mad. Enjoy the peace and quiet, and I *will* call like I promised. Love, Megan P.S. Thanks a million, again, you're the best!"

Kate smiled, returning the note to the counter, and pulled open the fridge and removed the wine bottle there. Only after pouring a glass and enjoying a few sips did she go change clothes and fix some dinner. After Megan called as promised, she relaxed on the couch with another glass of wine and began surfing the TV channels. She decided eventually to watch a romance she'd seen at least twice before, then sighed heavily. Even knowing how it ended, she knew she would probably still cry at the end.

Most of the time she could handle the loneliness. The hospital kept her extremely busy and the rest of the time Megan was usually around. Megan was the reason she had chosen to remain alone, but she had never for a moment begrudged making her such a big and demanding part of her life nine years ago. She chalked it up to destiny. Besides, she wasn't sacrificing her personal life, just putting it on hold. Megan would go off to college in another year and she would have all the time she wanted to go out and play the field again. No matter how you viewed the situation, it was Megan who'd been shortchanged, not her.

Kate cried less during the love story than she'd expected to, but she went off to bed with a heavy heart. She wanted to meet and fall in love with someone who'd want to share her life. To feel the touch of another woman, a touch, she knew, that would reach places inside her she never could. She drifted off, dreaming of a woman holding her in strong, comforting arms.

On Saturday she cleaned house, finished the laundry and grocery shopped, all before dinner. Bored out of her mind, she considered going out for a bit. She stared at her closet, hoping an article of clothing would make a decision for her. Her better sense kept telling her to stay home and out of potential trouble. Cruising a bar could be a dangerous venture. She'd worried for weeks after her indiscretion with that woman a few years back. A tiny dark little corner of her brain kept replaying the scene from that night, though, and the ecstasy she had experienced. Finally, it drove her to the closet for a top to complement her best-fitting jeans and favorite sandals.

Half an hour later, she pulled into the parking lot of Gurlz Club, an obscure little bar on the north side of town. The neighborhood was more industrial than anything else, so on a Saturday night there weren't people other than bar patrons around. She'd never been to the place before, having only overheard a clique of nurses and aides gossiping about it over lunch. She sat outside for more than fifteen minutes, watching couples and singles enter the bar, loud music shattering the dark quiet every time the door opened. Finally mustering the courage to go in, she told herself as she crossed the parking lot that she'd just have one drink. If no one approached her during that time, she'd drive herself home and dig her friend out of the box in the bottom of her closet.

She took an empty seat close to the door and ordered a strawberry margarita from the woman behind the bar, a skinny, tattooed girl with peach-colored hair and a cocky but pleasant butch attitude. She sized Kate up, winked and said, "Coming right up, babe."

Kate scanned the crowd while she waited for her to return. The average age looked to be under thirty, five or so years her junior.

Setting her drink in front of Kate, the bartender said, "Don't think I've seen you here before. I pretty much know everybody. You new in town?"

Kate sipped slowly on the drink, buying some time before she answered. "Not exactly."

The gal tipped her head knowingly. "Ah, just new to this kind of bar." Kate held the drink straw between her lips and just shrugged, prompting the peach-haired girl to lean close over the bar. "Understood. Listen, my name's Tammy and if you need anything," she leaned closer still, "anything at all, don't hesitate to ask me." She gave Kate a "got your number" kind of look.

Kate's cheeks warmed. She hadn't dressed ultra feminine, but the bartender had automatically assumed she was straight. She knew if she caught someone's attention here, it would probably be because some lesbian thought she played for the other team. Unfortunately after more than an hour, Tammy, though overly attentive, was the only one to have paid any attention to Kate. She was second-guessing her decision to check out this bar instead of the one downtown. There she would likely have at least met someone to have an interesting conversation with by now.

She was getting ready to leave when a voice rose above the loud music. Turning her eyes to a table next to the dance floor ten feet away, she saw a woman towering over six seated women. All were laughing, their laughter escalating every time the tall woman leaned over the table. As Kate watched, the woman straightened and started toward the bar. She shifted her eyes to her drink, pretending to sip it as the woman moved into the space between Kate and the empty barstool beside her.

The woman slapped her hand on the bar. "Women...you gotta love 'em."

Tammy approached, giving the woman a nod. "Hey, babe, how's it going?"

"It'll be perfect if I can get one of those pretty ladies to escort me home tonight," the large woman responded. She turned to look at the table of women she'd been entertaining moments before, brushing against Kate's shoulder as she did so. "Sorry, hon."

Without looking in her direction, Kate said, "No problem."

Tammy asked, "Whatcha having?"

The woman brushed Kate's shoulder again as she turned back, offering no apology this time. "The ladies think we should shoot Slippery Nipples, so a round of those and another pitcher of beer."

Tammy scrutinized the larger-than-life woman closely. "You gettin' drunk there, my friend?"

"I just might be." The woman dug in her pocket, pulled out a set of keys and dropped them on the bar. "Here, if I can't get one of the ladies to take me home, I'll walk."

"You get a driver and you can have them back," Tammy said, picking the keys up from the bar.

The woman bumped her arm against Kate's shoulder and said, "Or maybe I'll get this pretty young thing to drive me home."

Pretending she didn't hear what the brusque woman had said, Kate stared into her near-empty glass. Her heart racing at the thought that this woman might engage her in conversation when Tammy left, she pushed the glass away and slid off the barstool. "Good luck," she said, heading for the door without a backward glance.

* * *

Tommie leaned an arm on the bar and watched the blond with the nice tight ass walk rigidly to the exit and disappear into the night.

"Who was that?" she asked Tammy.

"The woman of my dreams. Looks like you scared her off."

Tommie feigned insult. "Not me, sweet pea." She glanced at the exit door and back. "I think she was in the wrong bar."

"We'll probably never know." Tammy headed off to fill Tommie's order, returning with the tray full of shot glasses and a pitcher of beer.

Tommie partied the night away, finally charming the dark-haired Colleen, she of the round bottom and nicely matched breasts, into taking her home with her after guaranteeing Colleen she wouldn't be disappointed.

The next morning, with a hangover to beat all hangovers, Tommie called a cab to take her back to her car, cursing herself with every throb in her head. One of these days, she'd learn not to drink that sweet liquor stuff so many of the young girls drank. "Slippery Nipples," she mumbled as she climbed behind the wheel of her car. "How can something that sounds so erotic make you feel so crappy?" She popped open a cold beer the minute she entered her apartment and felt better by the time it was finished.

* * *

Megan arrived home two hours and fifteen minutes after she called Kate to say they were leaving. After depositing her bag in her room, she joined her aunt on the deck.

Kate asked, "How was your getaway weekend?"

Megan dropped into a cushioned chair. "It was okay."

Kate laid her book aside, viewing Megan with a critical eye. "If you were any more enthused about it, you'd be considered contagious."

Megan frowned. "Ashley's parents don't get along real good. They bicker a lot. It was kind of a bummer. And then on the drive home, her dad complained some about Ash's mom, and I really like her, Aunt Kate. I think she's nice and really cool like you."

"Thanks, sweetie. Ashley's mom seems very nice from the conversations I've had with her." Kate shot a serious look at her niece. "You know, Megan, sometimes adults don't get along well even after they've been together for a long time."

"You mean like my parents, who figured out pretty quick they didn't belong together?" She paused, then added, "Or like your boyfriend, who dumped you when I came along?"

Kate scooted her chair to face Megan and took her hand. "Sweetie, don't think for a minute you are the reason my relationship ended." That was true or half-true, at least. It wasn't Megan's fault that Kate's girlfriend of several years took off when Kate was faced with taking custody of her. The situation just made it very apparent to Kate that she and Hayden had very different plans for their lives. While Kate had not ruled out the possibility of having children if the circumstances seemed right, Hayden had said she intended never to be responsible for any bratty kids. That knowledge, along with Kate's declaration that they would not spend nights together until such a time that Megan could be told the truth about them or she'd grown up and moved out, started a battle Kate decided she didn't intend to fight. They parted ways and Kate never looked back, resolving instead to approach each new day with a positive attitude and good intentions. Kate let Megan assume what she would about the relationship, though the half-truths had filled her with guilt on more than one occasion. If Megan ever asked anything more specific, she vowed she would be honest with her and hope for the best.

"You are the best thing in my life, Megs. You are wonderful, and caring, and I'm so proud of you every day." Kate pushed hair off Megan's face and behind her ears. "As far as your parents... unfortunately you're right. They weren't meant to be together, but for the short time that they were, they created something truly amazing." Kate hooked her finger under Megan's chin, smiling warmly. "You."

Megan was clearly embarrassed by her aunt's praise. "Yeah, yeah, I know." She squirmed uncomfortably. "So, how was *your* weekend? Peaceful, quiet? Or did you go out? Did you meet anyone *special?*" Megan waggled her brows.

Kate chose her words carefully. "I did go out to a bar Saturday night for a little while, thinking I might run into some of the nurses from the hospital, but I didn't. And before you ask again, no, I didn't meet anyone special either. You know I'm not much for the bar scene."

"So you enjoyed the peace and quiet without me here?"

Kate shook her head. "Megan, you are not a burden or a hindrance in my life. You don't get under my skin or in my hair, and you've never made me feel like I want to run screaming from the house." Kate's lips curved in amusement. "Promise you're not going to start either."

"As if," Megan cocked her head. "Did you drive Grandma crazy when you were seventeen? Ashley's mom says she drives her crazy."

Kate chuckled. "Oh, I'm sure I probably did, sweetie, more often than not." *And then I drove them halfway across the country,*

Kate mused. It had seemed like a relief in her sophomore year of college that her dad's job had taken them to Texas. Their family gatherings had become uncomfortable, to say the least. Now they were non-existent and Kate would keep it that way. She had shared with Megan only that her grandparents and mother had had a major falling out after Megan's parents divorced, and alluded to a number of further confrontations that surrounded Nikki's decision to leave Megan in Kate's care. She didn't want Megan to ever find out that they'd used the words "devil's spawn" in one such heated conversation while describing Megan. Of course Kate was simply labeled a deviant. Kate had vowed to Nikki to keep Megan away from their parents' poisionous ideas—anyway, anyhow—that she had to. Kids should be able to make their own judgments regarding other human beings without the tainted notions of narrow-minded individuals like the senior Bellams. Megan had been curious when she was little, but now seemed to accept it as a fact of life that she and Kate were on their own.

CHAPTER FOUR

When Tommie strolled into the office around ten thirty on Monday, she found Megan hard at work at her desk, drinking a cup of tea and, as Tommie had directed in the note she'd left atop the folders, sifting through the material there on the minors' up-and-coming catcher, Joe Hawthorne She began gathering up her stacks of paper to move, but Tommie stopped her.

"Stay put. I don't want to interrupt your progress." She sat instead in the chair at the end of the desk.

Megan finished writing a note and asked, "You didn't mention a deadline on this. When do you need it by?"

Tommie appreciated Megan's use of the word "deadline." Just maybe the kid was cut out to be a writer. "None yet." Megan looked at her curiously. "There's talk they're going to be moving him up to the majors in the next few weeks to replace a guy on the disabled list who will probably be out all season. I could hit better than his backup." Tommie shook her head. "If that happens, we need to be ready with a story."

Megan asked, "If?"

Tommie clarified, "More often than not the rumors I hear in the minors' locker room come to pass. I like to be ready with my stories so they can hit the paper the day the announcement comes down from the guys in the head office."

"So, do they have press conferences to make the announcements, or do they come out as tweets or blogs?"

"All of the above." *Smart kid.*

"So sometimes it doesn't happen?"

"Rarely. I usually get good info. That's half the job. Knowing what the news is going to be." She eyed Megan seriously. "I was thinking if you draft a good story on the guy and he gets called up, I'd run what you write under my byline. How does that sound?"

Megan's face lit up. "With my name too?"

Tommie tapped a finger on her notepad. "Sure, if it's worthy." She paused. "Of course, you have to agree to let me be your editor."

"Deal."

Tommie stood. "And speaking of the minors, I need to run. I've got an interview scheduled for eleven thirty. You okay to work here on your own?"

"I think I can manage." Tommie thought there was a bit of an edge to her voice, but if she was pissed about something she managed to bite her tongue.

"Terrific. I probably won't be back until after lunch so you're on your own. If you go out, be careful." She hesitated, then added, "Please," unsure why she felt this need to worry about the girl.

Megan asked, "Can't I just get something from the cafeteria and eat in here?"

"That's fine, just don't..." Tommie stopped herself from lecturing the girl, "Sure, I'll see you after while."

* * *

Kate actually managed to beat Megan home by five minutes. She was standing in front of the fridge trying to decide what to make for dinner when she burst in yelling, "Aunt Kate, where are you? You're never going to believe what happened today."

Kate braced herself as Megan dropped her backpack in the middle of the kitchen floor. Breathlessly she started, "You can't believe how great this day has been."

"Slow down, honey, and take a breath."

Megan paused only a moment. "Well, Tommie was late to start with, but she left me something to work on. Something worth working on, not just grunt work like pulling research stuff together." She rolled her eyes. "Anyway, she asked me to put together a story that might make it in the paper."

"That's wonderful!" Kate pulled her niece into a hug and kissed her forehead. "I'm so proud of you."

"Aunt Kate, will you read it?"

"Your story? Of course I will, sweetie, along with everyone else in Denton."

Megan shook her head. "No, I mean before I turn it in to Tommie."

"Oh, honey, you know I know nothing about sports. I'm not sure I'd make a good critic."

Megan explained. "It's not so much about sports as it is about this guy that plays sports."

"Well…"

"Think of it like a book report on some guy in history."

Kate mentally rolled her eyes and thought, *Great, I hated history*, but said, "Sure, sweetie, I'll read it." She made a shooing motion. "Go get ready for dinner."

* * *

Tommie paced the tiny space of the office, reading Megan's draft. When she finished, she met Megan's eager gaze.

"There are a couple of things I think we need to tweak." She rolled the pages and shook them in her hand. "But this is really good work, Megan. If Big Joe Hawthorne gets called up to the majors as I expect, your story will run with your name under my byline." A moment later, Megan was wrapped around her and squeezing Tommie's lunch out of her.

"This is incredible!" Her voice had a note of high-pitched giddiness. She bounced as she continued hugging Tommie. "Thank you, thank you, Tommie."

Even after Tommie grabbed the girl's arms and extricated herself, Megan continued to carry on in the same gleeful voice. "Whatever we need to do to punch it up, just tell me, I'm here to learn."

Tommie relished Megan's eagerness, but the hug had left her red-faced and more than mildly uncomfortable. She backed around her desk and, taking a seat, said, "I want to read it over again, then we'll discuss it."

Megan agreed enthusiastically.

* * *

Tommie arrived Monday morning just shy of lunchtime. "I had an interview scheduled with one of the Cougars' injured reserves down in Carson. I forgot about it until this morning."

Megan shrugged. "No problem. As long as I have things to keep me busy I don't mind." She handed Tommie her rewrite. "I made the changes, if you want to take a look." Tommie quickly scanned it, nodding her head as she read. "You were dead-on with every note you made. You're a good teacher. I'm really learning a lot."

Tommie's heart swelled like a proud parent. She hadn't wanted any part of this little program and had never viewed herself as the mentoring kind. But when Megan wasn't making her nuts, it was kind of fun. The relationship between the two of them was unquestionably reaching a whole new level.

When Megan arrived Wednesday morning to a smiling Tommie, relaxing with her feet up on the desk, she asked suspiciously, "What?"

Tommie flipped over the proof page of the sports section. Under Tommie's byline was the caption, "Will the 'Thorne' Help Secure That Elusive Championship?"

Megan's eyes sparkled with excitement. "Does this mean...?"

Tommie stood, extending her hand across the desk and announcing, "Congratulations, kiddo, on your first news story."

Megan gave Tommie's hand an excited shake, then picked up the paper and began reading it.

Tommie waited an adequate amount of time, then asked, "What? You're not going to read me the riot act for calling you 'kiddo'?"

Megan just continued skimming her article.

Tommie decided their working relationship had indeed reached a new level. "This definitely calls for the mentor to take the person being mentored to lunch. There's a great sports café just up the street. Let's plan on going at noon."

"Sounds great." She dug in her purse and pulled out her phone. "I have to tell Aunt Kate the news. That okay?"

"Sure, sure, call whomever you like." She handed Megan a slip of paper. "Here's your next assignment, some things to research when you're done. I need them before the end of the day if you can manage it."

Megan gestured an okay with her thumb and index finger as she stepped just outside the door. Tommie chided herself for being so considerate. She was normally crabby and demanding at work, especially in the morning. But the girl was growing on her.

"Aunt Kate! I'm so glad I caught you before you went into surgery. I've got some news for us to celebrate tonight." She paused, then, "Oh—no—I understand." Through the doorway Tommie saw Megan's shoulders drop. "Okay, I'll see you when you get home."

As Megan snapped the phone shut, Tommie busied herself with the papers in front of her. She didn't want Megan to think she'd been eavesdropping. She was hurting enough already, judging from the pasted-on smile she was wearing when she returned to the office. "My Aunt Kate is the greatest," she said, setting her purse down in the corner again. "She can't wait to celebrate my good news."

Right, Tommie thought. It sounded like the woman was some "mightier-than-thou" surgeon who was much too busy for her niece. Tommie pasted on a fake smile of her own in response.

* * *

They were seated in a booth at one of Tommie's favorite sports bar and grills. As much as she craved a cold beer with her burger and fries at "Frankie's," she wanted to be a good role model for Megan so she too ordered iced tea.

She wondered where this newfound conscience came from. She'd never been one to give a hoot about what people thought of her. She'd grown like a weed when she reached puberty. She was bigger than any of her classmates as they entered high school and stronger than many. That had gained her some respect, if nothing else, especially from the boys. It didn't take them long to learn that if they got smart and called her "Tomboy," Tommie had ways to make them sorry.

Before long, she had more friends than she needed, male and female—every kid who was afraid of another in the school. If you were friends with her, they saw, you didn't get picked on by the bullies. These included a number of girls as well as boys. One was Diana Cain, the captain of the cheerleading squad. The first time she confronted Diana, telling her to leave shy little Mindy from choir class alone, Tommie got all sweaty and tongue-tied. But she finally managed to get her point across. She also realized during the confrontation that she wanted to kiss the uppity girl more than she wanted to yell at her.

That was the moment she had recognized her libido was only stirred by the female gender. A number of her classmates soon recognized that too. In high school her boyish looks netted her a half a dozen girls on whom to try out her kissing skills. Most were merely curious, but during senior year little shy Mindy developed a pretty serious attachment, only to be brokenhearted when Tommie went off to college. She had heard a number of years later that Mindy had become an accomplished violinist and was performing with the Chicago Philharmonic.

"So, any more stories I can write or help write?" Megan brought Tommie back from her trip down memory lane with her question. She munched on a bite of lettuce, waiting for Tommie's answer.

"I'll see about setting up an interview you can tag along on." Tommie took a gulp of tea, then asked, "Do you always eat so healthy?"

"Healthy?"

"Yeah." Tommie pointed at the salad. "Salads, yogurt, fruits. Don't you ever eat chips or cookies"—she picked up a fry and wiggled it—"or greasy fries and burgers?"

"I eat burgers occasionally." She shrugged. "I just eat the way I always have since I can remember. It's how Aunt Kate eats. I never really thought of it as healthy or not."

Aunt Kate, Aunt Kate, Tommie thought, adding "health food nut" to the list of unappealing qualities the woman possessed. Tommie was getting a picture of a woman she didn't much care for. How was it, she wondered, that Megan was so "normal" and not uppity like the Barbie who had entered the intern program with her? There was an interesting story there, Tommie decided, and, like any good reporter, she intended to get at it before Megan departed at summer's end. Including why Megan lived with an aunt and not parents.

* * *

Megan was studying in her room with headphones on when Kate knocked and entered. She took a seat on the bed as Megan removed the headphones.

"I'm sorry I'm so late. The on-call cardiac surgeon had a particularly delicate procedure late this afternoon and he requested me. Did you eat something?"

"One of those frozen microwave dinners."

"So…good news?"

Megan nodded. "Yes, but you look pooped. Have *you* had anything to eat?"

Kate sighed deeply. "No."

Megan popped up, grabbing her hand. "Come on, I'll prepare you a fabulous dinner and tell you my news while you're eating."

Megan made Kate sit at the table while she microwaved a dinner, then set a plate and a glass of lemonade in front of her and took the seat opposite.

"Remember that story I had you read and comment on last week?" With her mouth full, Kate nodded. "Well, it's going to appear in tomorrow's sports section—and with my name on it!"

Kate quickly swallowed and reached a hand across to Megan's. "Oh, sweetie, that's wonderful. I never doubted you had the talent for writing."

Megan's excitement bubbled over. "I'm going to be in print!"

"The Fourth of July holiday is next weekend. How about we turn our annual cookout into a celebration of your first published work?"

"Can I invite Ashley? If she doesn't have to do something with her folks, that is?"

Kate pushed her half-eaten meal aside. "Sure you can, sweetie. Invite other friends too if you'd like. Just let me know how many are coming before I go grocery shopping."

"Will do." She jumped up. "I'm going to go email Ash and ask her right now!"

* * *

Kate stopped on her way into the hospital the following day, picked up two copies of the newspaper and placed them in her locker. She'd clip the article out of one for Megan and the other she'd tuck into the treasure box under the bed where she kept special mementos. She took one of the papers to the cafeteria to read when she finally got a lunch break, beaming with pride while she ate her apple and yogurt.

She had finished reading and was preparing to fold the paper away when she heard a female voice a few tables away mention Gurlz Club, the bar she'd been to on Saturday night. She lowered the paper slightly to take a peek in the direction of the voice, then quickly hid herself again. She didn't recognize the face as one she'd seen Saturday night, but that didn't mean the gal with the close-cropped hair hadn't seen her. Common sense told her to make a hasty exit from the cafeteria, but curiosity kept her in the seat. The women seated at the table were making no attempt to keep their voices down.

"Can you believe she left with that dark-haired woman?"

"Lucky girl," another said, lowering her voice the tiniest bit before adding, "I've had the pleasure of her company before."

"Do tell."

"Well…" Kate could tell by the sound of the woman's voice that she was smiling as she talked. "You know that song 'All Night Long'? Whenever I hear it, I think of her."

"Oops! Time to go." After a series of moans and grumbles, the women headed back to work and the table emptied. As the group dispersed, Kate chanced another quick look—and wished that she'd picked up on their conversation earlier. Her curiosity was certainly piqued as to whom this infamous woman was who could go all night.

CHAPTER FIVE

Megan was so giddy and eager to please on Thursday that Tommie didn't know if she could take much more. Then, remembering how jazzed she'd been the day her first story ran and frankly proud of her role in grooming the young writer, she decided to grin and bear it. When Megan was still bubbling on Friday, though, she'd had all she could stand. She gave the girl a list of research materials she needed and sent her to use a computer in the paper's library for the rest of the day.

By the following week, Megan was considerably more subdued about the whole publishing thing, much to Tommie's relief. On Wednesday as they stood at the hot dog stand in front of their building Megan asked, "Do you have big plans for the holiday this Saturday?"

Tommie gave the second hot dog she was devouring a rest and wiped her mouth. "I hadn't given much thought to it. Maybe I'll drive down to the Cougars' stadium and see if I can get a scalped ticket for the game."

"So you don't have any plans?" Megan persisted.

Tommie cocked her head. "Why are you asking?"

"I thought—" She gave a little shrug. "I thought I'd invite you to the Fourth of July cookout Aunt Kate and I have every year."

"That's a nice thought, Megan, but I'm sure I'll find something to do."

"But if you don't have plans you should come over and hang out with us. I'd really like Aunt Kate to meet you."

Judging from Megan's frown she was frustrated with Tommie. *What else is new?* Tommie did a mental eye roll. Aunt Kate? The last person Tommie wanted to meet was that uppity, self-centered surgeon. She'd rather sit at a bar and get turned down by every woman she tried to pick up.

"It'll be fun and Aunt Kate is really cool. You'll like her. She even drinks sometimes. Please, say you will," Megan pleaded.

Tommie wanted desperately to have an excuse not to accept Megan's invite, but she didn't, not without lying. "I'll think about it" was all she would commit to.

"Okay," Megan said, looking dejected, "but I kinda gotta let Aunt Kate know before she goes to the grocery store Saturday morning."

Tommie felt pressured. Part of her couldn't care less about this woman, but a tiny part of her was curious. Curious about how Megan could speak of her aunt like she was the greatest, when Tommie suspected she was anything but. She told Megan again that she'd give it some thought.

* * *

At dinner that evening Kate asked, "Is Ashley going to come over and cook out with us Saturday?"

"Yeah, she said she would."

"Did you invite any of your other friends?"

"Nope, but I invited Tommie. You know, the woman that I work for at the paper."

Kate was rather surprised but said only, "Really."

"She said she'd think about it."

Kate understood that was probably just the woman's way of putting Megan off. "Don't be too disappointed, sweetie, if she can't come. She probably already has plans."

Megan stood with her empty dishes. "She said she didn't have any, that's why I invited her. I'd really like you to meet her. She's kinda cool."

Oh joy, Kate thought. She might actually have to meet this woman that Megan had been butting heads with. "You'll have to keep her entertained then if she does come, because you know I know nothing about sports. I can't imagine what we could possibly find to talk about."

Kate wasn't going to worry. She suspected this woman had better things to do on a holiday weekend than hang out with a teenager and a stranger. She hoped so anyway.

* * *

Tommie was already hard at work Friday morning when Megan practically floated into the office. "Well?"

Frustrated by the interruption and Megan's energetic enthusiasm, she responded, "Well *what*?" Her Friday was starting out sour. The Carson Cougars had lost their starting second baseman, a homerun hitter, to an injury the evening before. With him gone she foresaw the championship pennant sailing off in a hard wind. The team would have a serious struggle now to even make it to the playoffs.

Megan eyed her curiously. "What's got you in such a bad mood on a Friday? It's almost the weekend."

"Yeah, well, tell that to the Cougars. Ramos is out for the rest of the season. Without his bat they can probably kiss the championship goodbye."

"Sorry to hear that." Megan took a seat. "So, did you think about coming to our cookout tomorrow?"

Tommie exhaled deeply. She'd forgotten all about it. Well, her team was circling the drain. She might as well suffer right along with them. "Sure, why not? Just write down the address and time."

Megan wore a full-face grin as she scribbled on a sticky note and handed it to Tommie. "This is great, I can't wait for you to meet my aunt. She said you wouldn't come, but I knew you would."

That comment alone was enough to make Tommie go even if she weren't curious about Megan's aunt. Predictable was something

Tommie worked hard not to be. So if Megan's aunt was so sure she wouldn't join them, wild horses weren't going to keep her away.

"What should I bring?"

"Nothing, Aunt Kate always fixes everything."

She glanced at the note. "Okay, then I guess I'll be meeting the amazing Aunt Kate tomorrow at five." Megan looked pleased. Tommie just wanted to growl.

* * *

Tommie cut Megan loose early and drove to the Dragons' stadium for an interview with one of the coaches before the evening game. Afterward she picked up a few things at the paper, ordered carryout from her favorite burger joint, Pop's Diner, and headed next door to Lili's Pad to wait for it to be prepared.

Jamie placed a napkin in front of her. "You're kind of early. The hot babes never get here before eight o'clock."

"Yeah, well, the hot babes will have to get along without me tonight." She hooked her thumb. "I'm waiting on dinner and I've got work to do, but I may come by tomorrow night and see what kind of fireworks I can set off."

"Girl, are you ever gonna pick just one and settle down?"

Tommie thought about it only a moment. "Nah, been there, done that. Everything else has changed so much, gotta keep one thing consistent. Besides, relationships are a lot of work. I already have one job, I don't need another."

Jamie chuckled. "Whatever you say. You want a beer?"

"Just one, I need to be clearheaded to work this evening."

Jamie placed the beer in front of Tommie. "So any other plans for the big holiday tomorrow?"

She took a long drink. "Not tomorrow night yet, but I do have a dinner cookout thing."

"Anyone I know?"

Tommie shook her head laughing. "I seriously doubt it." She took another drink of her beer. "The intern working with me and her aunt. Both straight as an arrow."

"Wow! They must be real babes."

Tommie nearly choked on a swallow of beer. After a few coughs, she cleared her throat enough to speak. "The intern is only seventeen and I've never seen the aunt. Good-looking or not, she doesn't sound like someone I'd be remotely attracted to."

Jamie wiped absently at the bar. "Sounds like loads of fun. I don't envy you."

Tommie gulped the last of the beer. "Yeah, well, I'm just doing it as a favor to the kid. I guess she doesn't have any parents or something. She just got her first piece printed in the paper so I agreed to stop in for their little celebration." She pushed off the stool. "I'll probably be by as soon as I can excuse myself without being rude." She gave a wave. "See you tomorrow."

Jamie tucked the towel in her waistband. "I'll be here."

* * *

Kate barely managed to open the front door that evening when Megan bounded down the hall from her room to greet her.

"Add another steak to the grocery list. Tommie said she'd come by to cook out with us."

Kate was stunned. "Really?"

Megan followed her down the hall to her room, stopping in the doorway. "I told you she'd come."

Kate dropped her purse and bag next to the dresser. She turned to face Megan, her fingers going to the buttons on her blouse. "Just remember it's going to be your job to keep her entertained."

Megan turned from the doorway as Kate's blouse fell open. Kate wasn't sure why it embarrassed Megan to see her in various stages of undress, but it did. "I know, I know, you don't know anything about sports." She disappeared into her room across the hall.

As soon as dinner was over, Megan started the cleanup and Kate rushed out to the grocery. It would be the first company they'd entertained in quite a number of years, except for occasional visits by some of Megan's friends.

* * *

By four o'clock Saturday the house was cleaned, all the food preparation was done and Kate had a pitcher of margaritas chilling in the fridge. Dressed in the shorts and top she'd bought while shopping a month earlier with Megan, she settled into the lounge chair on the deck with a sample of the margarita. Kate didn't realize she had closed her eyes until she heard the doorbell ring.

Megan had already reached the door and was pulling it open when Kate entered the living room. Her mouth fell open as she recognized the woman filling her doorway. Her heart raced so rapidly that she felt light headed.

"Come on in," Megan said.

The woman's eyes met Kate's, and she braced herself for what would come next. When the woman's face showed no signs that she recognized Kate as well, she released the breath she was holding.

Megan began the introductions. "Tommie, this is my aunt—"

Tommie cut Megan off. "Aunt...no way...more like sister." Kate thought her dark eyes actually sparkled. "Kate, right?"

"Kate, Kay, Katie, Katlyn, I answer to all," Kate responded nervously.

Tommie asked, "And what do you prefer?"

"Just Kate is fine."

Tommie extended her hand. "Okay, Just Kate, I'm Just Tommie."

Kate's lips twitched in response to this big powerful-looking woman's easy good-natured humor. She watched her small hand disappear into the massive but gentle hand extended to her.

"It's nice to meet you, Tommie. Megan talks about you often."

Tommie's face blushed a light pink. "Lord, I hope not as much as she talks about you." Tommie leaned closer and talked quietly out the side of her mouth. "Even so, I have to tell you, Megan was a little conservative in describing you."

The woman is flirting with me. Kate's heart fluttered. She was suddenly aware she was still holding the sportswriter's hand and slowly extracted it. She alternated her gaze between the woman and Megan before saying, "Perhaps if I had some idea what my niece has said about me, I would know if I should thank you for a compliment or..." she looked again to Megan, "ground you."

Megan moved to take Kate by the arm. "Aunt Kate, you know I couldn't possibly say anything bad about you."

Kate rolled her eyes. "Not unless I were about to ground you from using the computer or take away your phone."

Megan playfully stuck out her tongue. Kate quickly returned the gesture. *Well, aren't we acting silly in front of our guest?* She felt her cheeks warming and chanced a glance at Tommie. Rather than looking put off by it all, she appeared to be fascinated by their interaction.

Tommie raised the six-pack of imported Mexican beer she was carrying, along with a lime tucked between the bottlenecks. "I wasn't sure what you liked to drink, so I brought these."

As Kate accepted the carton their fingers brushed, the innocent contact making her heart skip a beat. "I made margaritas if you'd like one. Or would you rather have one of these?"

Tommie's voice interrupted her distracted thoughts. "I could drink a margarita before dinner." She trailed Kate into the kitchen. "I'm pretty much just a beer drinker, though."

Beer chased by Slippery Nipples, Kate thought. That was what the women had been shooting at the bar two weekends ago. "I'll just put these in the fridge. Megan, why don't you show our guest out to the deck while I get our drinks."

"Sure, and you can make mine a margarita too."

Kate laughed lightly. "Very funny, young lady. Would you and Ashley like iced tea or a soft drink?"

Megan held the door for Tommie. "I'll be right back." Passing Kate on her way back to the living room, she said, "Ash and I will have soft drinks."

"Where are you going? You have a guest on the deck."

"Ash is chatting with someone online. I'm just going to get her."

"You promised me when you invited her that you'd entertain this Tommie woman..."

Megan sighed. "I know, I know. We'll be right back."

Kate hurriedly poured the drinks and rushed outside with one for Tommie and a fresh one for herself. Tommie was comfortably seated in the lounger Kate had nearly dozed off in moments earlier. She placed the glasses on the adjoining table and took a seat in a chair on the other side of it.

"Sorry to leave you sitting out here alone. Megan said she'd be right out."

Tommie said, "No problem. It's nice out here, peaceful. I like peaceful. I live in an apartment surrounded by a lot of noisy people."

Kate nervously sipped her drink as the silence grew between them. After several long awkward minutes, she said, "So...Tommie, that's an interesting name."

She wondered what on earth was keeping Megan and Ashley from joining them. She would have to have a conversation later with Megan about social etiquette. How it was improper to invite a guest to your home and then leave her in the company of a total stranger.

* * *

Tommie took a drink of the tart concoction. "My last name is Tommelson, so it's a nickname." Reading Kate's curious expression, Tommie went on to explain, "A bunch of kids I played with in grade school said I looked more like a 'Tommie,' so the name just stuck." Tommie was not shy or embarrassed by her butch appearance. She was more than comfortable with who she was and with her sexuality, although she couldn't tell for sure how Megan's aunt felt about it.

"And your first name is?"

Tommie, who was hardly ever shaken by anyone, was suddenly embarrassed to admit her real name to the woman seated beside her. In a voice that was barely audible, she mumbled, "Grace." She watched as Kate's eyes brightened and her lips curved in amusement.

"Grace is a very pretty name."

Tommie snorted, "Pretty, right." She indicated herself with a gesture of her hand. "This is pretty? I'm thinking not." She took a gulp of the drink. "Til the day I die, I don't think I will ever be a 'Grace.' I mean, really, at the age of twelve I was already five foot eight and probably a size twelve with all the baby fat still hanging on."

Tommie's pulse quickened as Kate gave her a quick once-over.

"I managed to grow another couple of inches in high school. Hell...sorry, I mean heck, I was taller than most of the guys in my classes."

"No middle name?" Kate asked.

"Ann."

"You could have gone with Ann. Or Annie. Like Annie, get your gun, Oakley."

Damn, Tommie thought. *She's beautiful wearing that expression of amusement, even when it's at my expense.* She shifted uncomfortably and shook her head. "My parents obviously suspected I would be a handful and this was their retribution. If it's all the same to you, I'll stick with Tommie. I think it suits me." She awaited Kate's next jab.

"I suppose you're right." Kate tipped her head to the side. "You do look like a 'Tommie.'"

"How do you mean?"

Kate hesitated a moment, then said, "You have a commanding personality, a powerful stature. You hardly look like a 'Grace' or 'Ann.' So I would have to agree— 'Tommie' suits you."

The way Kate was looking at her threatened to melt her into a puddle right there on the deck. *Wow*, Tommie thought. *Intelligent, thoughtful and the woman's got looks to die for.* She bowed her head.

"So you do the whole sports section of the paper, edit it or something?"

"Or something," Tommie answered, thrilled that Kate cared to ask. "I have a byline. Sometimes I attend games, you know, football, basketball, baseball…" Her nose wrinkled. "Occasionally hockey. The one sport I don't much care for—too bloody violent." She chuckled at her own pun. "Anyway, I write what they assign me, whatever the hot topic is or whoever the big-ticket athlete is at the time. I get to pitch my own story ideas and every once in a while they let me help lay out the sports page."

Kate seemed genuinely interested as she listened. "Lay out?"

"Oh, you know, pick out the photos that go with a story and help decide which is the best scoop for the front page of the sports section and what belongs on the last—golf." Tommie poked her finger in her mouth. When Kate laughed it was like sunshine washing over Tommie's skin and flowing through her veins at the same time.

"I'm sorry, I must sound ignorant. I have to admit I've never looked at the sports section in the paper, and Megan's done nothing but talk about it since she started working for you—"

Tommie cut her off, "She doesn't work for me. She works with me." She laughed. "Actually…sometimes it feels like I work for her." She hoped her comment wasn't perceived as a slam about Megan.

"I feel your pain." Kate rolled her eyes. "Megan's tried telling me about what you two do all day long, but honestly, most of it goes right over my head."

"Most women aren't into sports, so you're in the majority."

"So that puts Megan in the minority?"

"Hardly." Tommie waved a hand dismissively. "Megan's not interested in sports. She's interested in writing. She must have drawn the short straw to end up with me instead of the woman who writes the entertainment section."

"No, no. I recall her saying that she preferred that position over any other."

Flattered, Tommie took a shot at flattering Kate in turn. "I imagine you're more interested in current world events or the financials." She glanced around the spacious, private backyard they were sitting in.

Kate laughed lightly. "Actually, I'm more interested in the coupons and sale flyers."

Tommie swallowed the last of her margarita. "Ah, spoken like the typical mom." Tommie winked at her. "But your secret is safe with me."

* * *

If men were as charming as the woman next to her, Kate thought, she might be persuaded to switch teams. But she'd never met a man who'd had the effect on her that Megan's mentor was having.

"I'm such a bad hostess. Would you like another drink or one of those beers you brought?"

Tommie reached for her arm as she started to get up. "Relax there. I don't need to be waited on." She stood. "I'm a big girl, no pun, I can get my own beer. Can I freshen up your drink?"

"Thank you." Kate handed Tommie her glass, feeling the flush rise up her neck. "The pitcher is next to your beer in the fridge."

She fanned her face after Tommie disappeared into the house. The woman in her home today was a far cry from the one she'd encountered at the bar. That one had seemed to be a crude womanizer; Kate certainly would never have entertained the idea of inviting her to her home. So why had Megan? Obviously, she had been right about Tommie's sexuality. Did Megan know or suspect something about *her* that she wasn't sharing?

Tommie returned a few minutes later, followed finally by Megan and Ashley, who Megan quickly introduced as her best friend.

Megan asked, "How soon are we going to eat?"

"Whenever all of you are ready. I just have to turn on the grill and throw on the steaks."

"We're ready." Megan looked at Tommie. "Are you?"

"I can eat anytime." When Kate stood Tommie asked, "What can I help with?"

Kate lit the gas grill. "Nothing, it's all done, but grilling the steaks."

Tommie got a cocky grin on her face. "I can't really cook a lick, but I'm pretty darn good at grilling." She touched Kate's elbow as she stepped by her to the door. "Why don't you let me take care of that part of dinner?"

Kate shivered inside. Was it Tommie's touch or the sound of her voice? That charming smile, or…*oh, God, stop it, stop it,* Kate commanded her out-of-control body. "I'm not in the habit of having company help me with the meal, thank you. I can manage."

Taking a long drink of beer, Tommie perched a hand on top of the fridge as Kate opened its door. "I imagine you can manage all kinds of things expertly. You've done all the hard work. Let me do this part of dinner. What do you say?"

Kate wondered if perhaps Tommie liked her women helpless and submissive. *And why on earth would I even care?* She picked up the apron from the counter, holding it out to Tommie. "As you wish."

Tommie hung the apron around her neck, giving a look of satisfaction as Kate placed the platter of steaks in her hand. "You can make the girls' medium well and I'll have mine medium rare."

Tommie tipped her head. "Coming right up."

* * *

When the grill was hot, Tommie dropped the steaks on, whistling as they sizzled. She couldn't believe how far off she'd been in her assumptions about Megan's aunt. She was very genuine and down to earth. And, straight or not, she looked juicier than the aged prime beef she'd just flopped on the grill. Lost in a little fantasy about the petite blond, she didn't sense her returning. She jumped when Kate spoke.

"How's it going?"

Tommie wasn't sure why she felt embarrassed. It wasn't like Kate could read her mind. She said nervously, "I'm glad I wasn't turning your steak when you snuck up on me. I might have dropped it on the deck."

"I'm sorry, I didn't mean to startle you." She gazed up at Tommie. "Did you want another beer?"

Tommie was nervous as hell. She swallowed a tight knot in her throat. "Uh, no, I'm good. I want to eat something before I drink any more." Much to Tommie's relief Kate returned into the house.

Seated around the table, Megan got the conversation started. "Oh, yeah, Aunt Kate, I forgot to tell you that Tommie's going to take me on an interview with one of the Dragons' players."

"That sounds exciting."

"Will you have to go into the locker room?" Ashley asked.

Megan looked over at Tommie. She swallowed a mouthful. "Maybe. Depends on where they want to do it."

"Ew." Ashley scrunched up her face. "I hear guys' locker rooms smell gross." She too looked at Tommie. "Do they?"

"Depends on your definition of gross. I have brothers."

Both girls shuddered simultaneously. *Well*, Tommie mused, *girly teens haven't changed much in the last decade.*

"Those guys won't be naked, will they?" Megan's eyes went wide and Kate frowned at Ashley's question.

"They only pulled that on me once. After I made a disparaging comment about my pen being bigger than certain bits of certain players' anatomies, they started making it a point to keep their clothes on until I leave." Tommie chuckled and her cheeks heated up at the memory of the confrontation. She had been unbelievably embarrased by the blatant display but decided the only way to earn a crumb of respect was to make "the boys" feel her embarrassment ten times over. It had worked like a charm.

She listened as the girls chattered on about classmates and who was dating who and who was on the outs in which cliques. It reminded her of all the evenings she'd spent around the family dining table. The memory warmed her inside. Almost as much as the glances she kept catching Kate casting her way.

When they'd finished eating, the girls asked to be excused to Megan's room. After clearing the dishes away, Kate joined Tommie back out on the deck, where she was nursing her second beer.

"This is a really nice place you've got."

"Thanks, we're pretty comfortable here." Kate settled back into the chair.

"I imagine cutting on people pays pretty good, huh?"

"'Cutting on people'?"

Tommie clarified her statement. "Yeah, I figure docs get paid a lot to do surgeries, right?"

"You think I'm a surgeon?"

Tommie felt the flush of embarrassment creeping up her neck. "Uh, yeah," she said. "You're not?"

Kate shook her head. "No, I'm not. Mind me asking why you thought so?"

"I overheard Megan on the phone say she was glad she caught you before you went into surgery. And, then, you live in this nice house in this neighborhood. I assumed you must be a doc to afford it on your own…" Tommie pursed her lips, then laughed. "Maybe I should try using my reporting skills and ask some questions instead?"

"Let me just give you a brief bio." Tommie accepted the offer with a tip of her head. "I'm a surgical nurse and have been for about seven years. I worked mostly in the ER prior to that." Kate hesitated a long moment before continuing. "Your assumption about my marital status is correct. I am single."

Tommie took a swallow of her beer. *Hmm*, she thought. A politician's answer—concise and to the point. No more, no less. "Sorry, I didn't mean to pry into your personal life."

Kate gave a little laugh and Tommie felt the same warm rush envelop her again.

"Oh, I'm sure you didn't get more information than you could acquire through the right Internet search. Or so Megan is always telling me."

Tommie swung her legs off the lounger and faced Kate. "Sometimes I think it's a shame what you can find on the Internet these days. Technology…it keeps moving forward whether you like it or not. I'm sure by summer's end Megan will teach me everything

I don't know." She looked at the bottle in her hand. She really wanted to finish it, get another beer and sit talking to the lovely Kate Bellam as long as she'd allow her to do so. She knew, however, that the more she drank the more amorous she'd feel, and Megan's aunt deserved better than Tommie's alcohol-induced flirting. Kate Bellam had class all over the women Tommie was used to spending time with, and Tommie felt she deserved to be treated accordingly. She placed the bottle down on the table and stood.

"I need to get going." Kate started to get up, but Tommie stopped her with a hand on her arm as she had earlier. "Don't get up, you look too relaxed sitting there. I can let myself out." She nervously shoved a hand in her pocket. "Dinner was terrific and I'm glad I got to meet Megan's Aunt Kate."

* * *

It was probably just as well that Tommie was leaving, thought Kate. She was enjoying the feel of that hand on her arm more than she should. "Well, perhaps we'll have the chance to meet again." She realized the moment she made the statement, though, that she was going to have to stay away from the bars now for fear of running into her.

Tommie nodded. "I look forward to it. Tell Megan I'll see her Monday at work."

"Enjoy the rest of your holiday weekend."

Tommie fumbled with the door handle, her eyes never leaving Kate's. "Uh, yeah, thanks, you too."

Kate finished her drink and leaned her head back in the chair. She envied Tommie. She suspected she might very well be on her way to a party or one of the lesbian bars to finish celebrating the holiday. She wished so badly sometimes that she had the freedom she had a decade earlier but knew she'd never trade it for taking care of Megan. This was her life. She accepted that.

* * *

Tommie walked into the bar and dropped her keys in Jamie's hand. "Here, I know I'm going to be too loaded to drive tonight."

"Do tell."

"Nothing to tell, just in a mood to. Can I get a beer?" She started to turn toward the crowd, then stopped. "A bottle, no draft tonight."

Tommie leaned back against the bar to survey the bigger-than-usual Saturday night crowd. It wasn't long before Colleen spied her, sauntered over, placed her foot between Tommie's and leaned in against her thigh. "Hey, handsome. Buy a girl a drink?"

Warmth flooded to Tommie's center as she remembered the previous summer and what Colleen had looked like padding naked to the bed where earlier Tommie had tortured her into begging for release. "Hi, Colleen." She passed her eyes quickly over the five-foot-two, well-proportioned woman, pausing briefly at the spot that pressed into her thigh. "What are you having?"

"Before or after you?"

Tommie shook her head. "Let's not get ahead of ourselves." She could feel the perspiration starting at her hairline.

Colleen played her fingers over Tommie's stomach, around her back and down across her backside before sliding her hand around to rest on the thigh that her own wasn't pressed to. She leaned closer to press her breasts into Tommie's middle.

"I haven't been able to think of anything but those strong hands of yours and…" She reached up and traced a manicured nail over Tommie's mouth. "Those masterful lips."

Colleen licked her own lips and Tommie thought she might have an orgasm on the spot, fully clothed. The loud music slowed, prompting Tommie to grab Colleen's wandering hand. "Let's dance." She didn't wait for an answer but dragged her out to the dance floor. Colleen quickly adjusted, locking her hands behind Tommie's neck, resting her head between Tommie's small, firm breasts and swaying slowly to the music.

Tommie closed her eyes. Her mind drifted away with the music and the warm body in her arms. She imagined she was holding the beautiful blond with the amazing blue eyes she'd met earlier that evening and the feeling made her tingle where she was being touched. She wanted Kate Bellam more than she'd ever desired a woman, in spite of the fact it could never be. A whiff of Colleen's signature perfume snapped Tommie out of her fantasy. She looked down. Colleen's light brown eyes were burning golden with want.

The way she was riding Tommie's thigh as they moved to the music was making her agonizingly horny.

She leaned down, her lips to Colleen's ear, and asked, "You want to get out of here?"

Colleen responded by taking Tommie's hand and dragging her toward the door. An hour later Tommie was lying in Colleen's bed, sweating, panting, frustrated. Colleen was nestled in the crook of Tommie's arm, drawing her fingers lightly from Tommie's breastbone to her pubic bone and back. As hard as she tried, though, Colleen wasn't able to push Tommie over that edge.

Tommie had thought all she wanted was a mind-blowing release, but she couldn't get the image of Kate out of her head and that was putting the brakes on any chance of an orgasm. Colleen liked hard, rough sex, and Tommie knew in her heart of hearts that Kate Bellam would only make love nice and slow, reveling in every touch, every kiss and each sensation. No, Kate Bellam would never be a quick screw. She'd be an "all night long" kind of woman, in the softest, most sensual way. Of that, Tommie was certain. Much like the woman who had broken Tommie's heart years ago when she was too young to know how deeply invested her heart had been in the relationship.

Colleen interrupted her musing. "Hey, baby." She slid her leg between Tommie's thighs, applying a little pressure. "What's it going to take to get you off tonight?" She positioned her body on top of Tommie's and began pumping her center.

"I'm more interested in making you scream. I'm good."

Colleen began kissing her way down Tommie's stomach. "I can't dispute that."

Tommie caught Colleen's arms and pulled her up her body. "I want to taste your luscious lips while…" Tommie slid two fingers into Colleen's wetness. Colleen began riding them hard, moaning with pleasure. "While I take you there again."

Minutes later Colleen screamed out, "Oh, God, yes," and collapsed on Tommie.

Tommie liked the feel of a woman's spent, hot and wet body pressing down on hers. She wondered what Kate would feel like, then quickly reminded herself that Kate would undoubtedly prefer to have her head resting against a male chest.

When Colleen's breath slowed, she gasped, "God, you're amazing."

Tommie allowed Colleen to lie on her until she suspected she was about to doze off, then she gently rolled her to the side, eliciting a faint moan from her. When she was sure from her breathing that she was asleep, Tommie quietly slipped from the bed, picking up her clothes, which had been shed between the front door to the bedroom. Quickly dressing in the living room, she made her escape, the door clicking closed behind her. In the lobby she called a cab. Hoping the evening breeze would cleanse the smell of sex from her, she sat on the stoop waiting for her ride.

* * *

Kate tossed and turned, unable to sleep. It must have been the last margarita she drank after everyone left and Megan went to bed. The clock registered a little after one thirty in the morning. She threw back the covers in frustration. Pulling a silk robe over her nightie, she quietly made her way to the kitchen. Filling a glass with water, she went out to the deck. After standing several long minutes taking in the peaceful quiet of their neighborhood, she stretched out on the lounger, relaxing back into its cushions.

Her mind came alive with the image of Tommie sitting in the very same chair. Based on the tales Megan had told when she first started her internship, Kate had concluded that Megan's mentor was bitchy and arrogant. And then she discovered Tommie was the very same butch whom she'd labeled as a womanizer after their encounter two weekends earlier. She couldn't imagine why Megan would invite someone like that into their home.

Remembering now how she had gazed across the table at Tommie when she spoke—*Oh, God*—she was suddenly worried. Had Megan witnessed the schoolgirl way that she had been hanging on Tommie's every word? Megan was far from naïve. Then again, Kate reflected with great pride, she was never one to judge a book by its cover. She'd obviously seen or found something more to the woman that endeared her. Kate realized in the few short hours they'd spent together earlier, Tommie had managed to endear herself to Kate too. She was witty and charming, if not a bit on the flirtatious side, which Kate didn't seem to mind. She was also smart and articulate about her craft. Kate didn't doubt that Megan could learn a lot from her.

Drawing her arms across her chest against a chill from the breeze, she couldn't help but smile, certain that Tommie had assumed she was straight. She had observed years ago that gay women flirted differently with straight women than they did their own. She wasn't sure why, but she liked the idea of Tommie having enough of an attraction to her to flirt. Even though Tommie was not the kind of woman Kate had ever pictured herself with, she closed her eyes and remembered how gentle Tommie's touch had been, especially when she'd taken Kate's hand to shake it. Feeling the stirrings between her legs, she quickly popped open her eyes and tried to think of something else. Charming or not, there was no way Kate could be aroused by this "what you see is what you get" Amazon of a lesbian.

CHAPTER SIX

Megan's presence in the newspaper office reminded Tommie of the attractions of her pretty, but straight aunt for a few days, but before long, the blond was pretty much off her mind. Or so she thought until several weeks later when she was returning from a Cougars game down in Carson. Kate didn't even enter her mind as she drove past the hospital. But then a block down the street she happened to glance at the crowd at a bus stop, did a double take and found herself whipping a U-turn in traffic, to the blaring protest of car horns. Circling back, she pulled to the curb at the bus stop. The cheery, rotund woman seated beside Kate eyed Tommie curiously, but the nurse, who was wearing headphones and had her nose stuck in a book, was oblivious to her presence.

Tommie called over the traffic noise, "Could you get her attention?" She pointed to Kate.

The woman tapped Kate's shoulder, then pointed toward the Jeep.

Kate removed the headphones, eyeing her suspiciously. Realizing she was having trouble recognizing her in her ball cap and sunglasses, Tommie removed them. "You're not waiting on a bus, are you?"

"I am."

Tommie motioned. "Come on. I'll give you a ride."

Kate tucked the book into her bag and walked to the Jeep. "You're not heading my direction, are you?"

Tommie shrugged. "I could be." When Kate gave her a questioning look, Tommie said, "Ah, come on, you couldn't possibly prefer public transportation over my company." Tommie grinned.

"Are you sure it's not an imposition?"

Tommie leaned halfway across the passenger seat and spoke in a low tone. "Are you kidding? Being seen cruising around town with a knockout like you will do wonders for my reputation." When Tommie winked, Kate blushed.

"Well, I certainly wouldn't want to jeopardize that." Kate tossed her purse and bag on the floorboard as Tommie extended a hand to help her hop up onto the seat. "Just promise you won't roll us over in this thing."

Tommie raised her hand. "Scout's honor."

They made the ride mostly in silence until Tommie pulled in the drive behind Kate's car.

As she reached for her things, Kate asked, "Would you like to come in for a beer? You left some behind a few weeks ago."

Tommie hesitated a moment. "I don't want to mess up your schedule."

"We don't have schedules. My job makes it nearly impossible, so we fly by the seat of our pants a lot."

"As far as I'm concerned, seat of the pants is the only way to fly." Kate laughed. "A cold beer sounds really good right now if you're sure I won't be intruding on anything."

Kate hopped out. "Not at all, come on."

Tommie enjoyed watching Kate's behind as it moved gracefully up the driveway. She had this odd sense of déjà vu as she did so, but couldn't quite put her finger on what she might be recalling.

Their voices brought Megan from her room. "Hey, Tommie." She looked confused. "Did I forget something at work?"

Tommie shook her head. "No, your aunt here was hitchhiking, so I gave her a lift."

Even more confused now, Megan looked at her aunt.

Kate looked at Tommie. "Very funny." Tommie gave her a sheepish look. To Megan, Kate said, "She saw me sitting at the bus stop and offered me a ride home."

Megan scrutinized her aunt.

"What?"

"Your hair looks like you've been in a tornado."

Kate smoothed a hand over the loose strands of hair escaping the tie at the back of her neck. "I can assure you that if you took a ride in a vehicle without any doors, windows or a roof, yours would look worse."

Tommie waited for Megan's retort, enjoying the banter between the two.

Megan merely shrugged. "So what's for dinner?"

Kate offered a shrug of her own in response.

Megan asked Tommie, "You hanging around for dinner?"

Kate eyed Tommie, awaiting her answer. Tommie was suddenly nervous at the prospect of an impromptu dinner with Kate and Megan. The cookout had been different. It was planned, for starters, it was out on the deck and there was another outsider there beside herself. For some reason, the thought of sharing an intimate dinner with the two, probably at the dining table, made Tommie apprehensive.

"Uh…" Tommie shrugged. "I just stopped in for a beer." Nearly choking on the growing knot in her throat, she hooked a thumb toward the door. "I've got some work I need to get to."

Kate dropped her things next to the chair where she stood and kicked off her shoes. "Oh, c'mon. Stay and have dinner with us. I can put a meal together in under thirty minutes." Kate moved beside Tommie, taking hold of her arm. "Your work can wait a little while longer." She tugged her arm lightly.

Kate's touch fired nerves that made Tommie's heart race and her stomach flutter and stopped her protest on her lips. She allowed Kate to pull her to the kitchen, where she motioned Tommie to a small table with only two chairs.

"Sit, make yourself comfortable."

Kate pulled a bottle of beer and a lime from the fridge along with an opened bottle of wine. Tommie watched as she sliced a piece of lime to stick in the beer after she opened it, then poured herself a small glass of wine.

Tommie tried to pull her eyes away as Kate turned and approached the table, but she only succeeded for a few seconds. Hard as she tried, Tommie couldn't make herself not admire that inviting body, curved in just the right places. Kate's amused expression told her she'd been caught looking.

"Thanks," Tommie said, taking the bottle, knowing she was probably blushing.

Kate raised her glass. "Cheers."

Tommie shoved the lime in, took a quick sip and nervously licked the tart lime from her lips. "Absolutely."

She watched—inconspicuously, she hoped—as Kate delicately sipped her wine, noting that she waited one, two, three, four full seconds before she swallowed it. She'd never seen a woman savor anything quite like Kate was savoring her wine. Oh man, Tommie thought. *If I kissed her now, how sweet would those lips taste?* She blinked, trying to banish the thought. Her cheeks were on fire.

Why was it the women she'd found herself the most attracted to were the ones who were unavailable? They were either straight or already in a relationship. The kind of relationship that seemed likely to Tommie to stand the test of time.

She would never find herself in that kind of relationship, Tommie thought. Spending every night with the same woman. Looking at the same face, hearing the same voice, day after day. It would take a long time, though, to grow tired of looking at Kate Bellam. She could almost feel how incredible it would be to lie in bed on a lazy morning with Kate curled in her arms.

"Tommie?" Tommie blinked repeatedly. "You looked like you were a million miles away."

Tommie took a quick swig of her beer. "Sorry," she lied, "I was just thinking about this story I'm working on."

"Megan mentioned you were out of the office all day today on assignment."

"Yeah, I was."

"What kind of assignment requires you to dress like that?" Kate asked, motioning toward Tommie's T-shirt, which was tucked neatly into a pair of cargo shorts, and the sneakers on her feet.

Tommie laughed lightly. "Doesn't exactly look like working clothes, does it?" Kate shrugged. "I was in the stands at the Cougars game." She took another pull on her beer. "My press pass will get me into any game anytime, but it's not the same as sitting with the fans and listening to what they have to say."

When Tommie said no more, Kate asked, "Did your team win? Did you get your story?"

Tommie beamed. "They did actually pull it out in the bottom of the eighth." She let out a long deep breath. "They've got a tough road ahead of them if they hope to have any shot at a playoff spot, but…" she turned her palms up, "you never know. Stranger things happen all the time."

* * *

"Stranger things happen all the time." Yes, they do, Kate thought. Here she was, after all, having a drink in her kitchen with a lesbian. An obviously "out" and butch lesbian she didn't think she'd ever see again if she stayed away from the bars, not unless the woman somehow ended up in her OR.

And no one, not Megan or this not-so-unattractive woman, suspected how much they had in common. She savored this secret kinship with Tommie. It's not like she would ever be with Tommie. And she certainly wasn't Tommie's type, based on what she had witnessed at the bar weeks before. Her type, she guessed, was the young, wild, partying kind. Not the reserved, settling-down kind of homebody that she was.

Tommie interrupted Kate's thoughts. "Something wrong?"

"No…I was just contemplating what's available for dinner. Is there anything you won't eat?"

"No, but I don't want to interfere with your time with Megan. I really do have some work I need to get to."

Tommie started to stand, but Kate placed her hand on her forearm to stop her. "Sit…please. Megan and I have dinner together nearly every night. I'm sure she'll welcome a different face across the table as much I as will."

Tommie didn't resist. "You make a convincing case."

Kate stood. "Would you like another?" she asked, indicating the beer bottle.

"I'll pass."

* * *

As promised, Kate threw dinner together in about thirty minutes.

Megan finally broke the silence at dinner, which judging from the slight awkwardness in the air was normally conversation-filled, Tommie guessed. "Must have been some assignment you were on today. You didn't even check in on me." She stabbed a vegetable and popped it in her mouth.

Tommie met Megan's eyes. "You know I don't feel like I have to babysit you. I trust you to do what you're supposed to and stay busy."

"Mind if I ask what the assignment was that you can dress like that?"

Wow, Tommie thought. She phrased her question very much as Kate had earlier. She laid her fork down, took a drink of water and said, "I was at the game today. I'm working up a story on their pitcher, Pedro."

"That's so cool you get to go to games as part of the job."

"You think it's cool to go to baseball games?"

"Yeah, sure," Megan responded. "Why wouldn't I?"

"Have you ever been to a game?"

Megan shook her head. "No, but I bet it's fun."

"Megan, I had no idea you enjoyed baseball."

"It just sounds like fun."

Tommie asked, "Do you think you'd like to go to a game sometime?"

Megan's expression brightened. "Really? Yeah…that would be too cool."

Tommie swallowed another bite of food, then said, "I'll see about some tickets. Maybe your aunt would like to join us?" Tommie shifted her gaze to Kate.

"Oh, I know nothing about sports. I don't think baseball games are my kind of thing."

Tommie nodded her understanding, but Megan pleaded, "Ah, come on, Aunt Kate. I've never been to a baseball game before, but I'm willing to check it out. It sounds like fun."

Tommie interrupted, "It's okay, Megan. I'm sure your aunt has better things to do than watch a bunch of guys trying to hit a silly ball so they can run around in circles."

"Come on, Aunt Kate, be adventurous, try something new. Isn't that what you're always telling me?"

Kate looked at Megan with skepticism. "You really want me to tag along with you to a baseball game?"

Before Megan could answer, Tommie butted in, saying, "Yeah, come on, Aunt Kate."

Kate threw her hands up in the air. "Fine, fine, I'll go. I hope they play on a Saturday or Sunday, because I can't take off any unscheduled weekdays for the next few months."

"Great! I'll round up tickets for a weekend game then. Do either of you care who they're playing?"

Kate shrugged and looked to Megan, who shrugged in turn, then asked, "Should we?"

Tommie laughed. "I guess not. But you do have to care about who wins."

Kate agreed, "Of course."

Tommie was developing a serious liking for this pair. It was a given that she would be attracted to Kate's physical beauty, but she was also feeling a pull to something else, a part of the woman that seemed deeper somehow.

Tommie couldn't wait to get to work the following day and start lobbying for some weekend game tickets. She managed to scour up three for a Saturday game a week and a half away. She immediately let Megan know, telling her to tell Kate, and if for any reason Kate changed her mind about going, to let her know so she could find a substitute or give the ticket to someone. Megan told Tommie the next morning that her aunt still planned to attend the game and wanted to know what to wear. Tommie laughed and just said, "Something comfortable."

* * *

Tommie didn't think the days could pass any slower. She was dying to see Kate again, but she couldn't think of one good reason to knock on her door. She'd even driven past the bus stop by the hospital a couple of times in hopes of seeing her and was disappointed when she didn't. By the Friday night before the day she would spend at the game with the Bellam women, she was like a caged tiger. She had so much pent-up energy she thought she would combust. She pulled on a fresh shirt and headed to The Underground. She'd have a few beers, find a little "hottie" and let off some of the pressure building in her.

She stood at the bar nearly an hour nursing her first beer before the cutie she'd been eyeing finally sauntered over and stopped directly in front of her.

Tommie took a quick drink of beer and said, "Hi!"

"Hi, yourself." She flipped her blond hair off her shoulders. "You were looking at me like you wanted to buy me a drink." Tommie stepped aside and motioned her to the barstool beside her. She hopped up. "I'm Melinda." She extended a hand to Tommie.

She took it gently. "Tommie," she offered and leaned closer. "I don't suppose I have to tell you that you're the best looking woman in this place."

Melinda kept hold of Tommie's hand, squeezing it as she leaned back. "Aren't you the sweetest thing?"

Game on, Tommie thought. Her charm never failed her with the younger ones. Women, once they hit the thirty mark, were much more skeptical and suspicious, but she figured little Melinda here to be just of the legal drinking age and easily delighted by the attention.

"What are you having…Melinda?"

She offered a coy smile. "Now or later?"

Well now, she'd be too easy to get into the sack, Tommie thought. "To drink?"

"Strawberry daiquiri."

Tommie ordered the "fou-fou" drink and another beer. They toasted with a clink of the glass to the bottle and began the ritual of small talk. Ten or fifteen minutes later, Melinda hooked her finger in a belt loop on Tommie's pants and pulled her closer.

"Do you like to dance, Tommie? 'Cause I love this song."

Tommie answered by placing her beer on the bar and leading her to the dance floor. As Tommie slipped her hands to the girl's waist, she locked her hands behind Tommie's neck and pulled their bodies close. As the slow sensual music filled Tommie's head, Melinda steadily rocked her body against Tommie's groin. Each thrust pushed Tommie toward a need that could only be satisfied by flesh against flesh. Tommie pressed her lips close to Melinda's ear.

"You're making me too hot for this place."

Melinda's lips twitched when she looked up at Tommie. She slowly slid a hand over her chest and a rock-hard nipple and continued down, around and over Tommie's backside. Melinda pressed more firmly against Tommie as she held her gaze.

"I really need a drink," Tommie said. She slipped from Melinda's grasp and led her back to the bar, where she quickly downed the rest of her beer. Melinda ran her hand over the plane of Tommie's chest again, between her breasts and over her flat stomach, stopping only when her finger's curled into the top of Tommie's pants. Tommie shook as a shiver raced up her spine and fire ignited between her legs.

Melinda bit her lower lip, then said, "I have a big backseat in my car…" She watched Tommie's eyes. "Just right outside." Tommie's head began a slow up and down movement.

Outside, Melinda led her across the parking lot to, surprisingly, a Cadillac. *Great*, Tommie thought. *I'm going to have sex with a barely legal girl in her parents' car.* She slid into the spacious backseat anyway.

"Nice car."

Melinda closed and locked the door before crawling over to straddle Tommie's lap. "Thanks, I just got it last month."

Surprised, Tommie said, "It's a pretty ostentatious car for someone young."

Melinda feigned hurt. "It's the best car to drive in my profession."

Afraid of the answer, Tommie asked the question anyway. "And what is that?" At that moment, she realized Melinda had been slowly grinding herself in her lap.

"I sell real estate. My clients trust in my success because of the car."

Tommie didn't doubt the truth in her statement. As relief washed over her that the young woman wasn't a paid escort or something, she pulled Melinda's top out of her pants, placing her hands on her bare waist.

Tommie cupped Melinda's breasts, allowing her thumbs to play across the fabric that separated hardened nipples from her touch. Melinda moaned softly and rocked her hips hard against Tommie's, as Tommie released the front-open clasp of her bra to touch the satiny soft skin of Melinda's breasts.

"Oh, God," Melinda murmured as Tommie teased her nipples simultaneously between thumb and forefinger. When Tommie pushed her top up and replaced the pressure from the fingers of her right hand with her tongue, Melinda grabbed hard onto her shoulders. "Oh…yes…" Melinda hissed.

Tommie's hand slipped down to Melinda's building heat. Even in the car's darkened interior, Tommie could see the girl's pale blue eyes change to a steely gray.

"I need…I need…you to touch me…there." She reached a hand down to unbutton her pants, giving Tommie easy access to her waiting flesh. Tommie's fingers deftly entered her satin panties, sliding effortlessly into her slick wetness. She stroked slow and deliberately as Melinda once again grabbed her shoulders and rode her movements.

Tommie groaned, "God, you feel good." Her own arousal grew, building from the feel of Melinda's heated center.

Tommie slid two fingers inside Melinda, forcing all the air from her lungs. She gasped, "Oh, baby," as Tommie pushed her toward the pinnacle. Within minutes Melinda had her face buried against Tommie's neck, muffling a scream as she came hard and shuddered. She slumped against Tommie trying to catch her breath. "God, that was amazing."

Making a woman scream in pleasure did so much for her ego.

After several long moments Melinda whispered, "I want to get you off like that." She scooted down Tommie's thighs, working her pants open.

Tommie stretched her arms across the seat back and closed her eyes in anticipation of release. She had gone commando for the evening, which made it easy for Melinda to quickly make contact with her throbbing, wet flesh.

Melinda leaned in to kiss below Tommie's jawline. "How's that baby?" Tommie groaned in response. Melinda continued working her fingers back and forth through Tommie's wetness. She rocked against the movements of Tommie's hips, pressing into her hard, and whispered, "I'm going to make you scream…come on…scream for me, baby."

Tommie's breathing was ragged with the increasing intensity each stroke of Melinda's fingers drew from her. As she neared orgasm, she gasped, "God, Kate, you're incredible."

Melinda leaned close to Tommie's ear. "I don't know who Kate is, but I'm happy to help you get over her."

Tommie's breath caught in her chest and her eyes popped open.

Melinda checked her eyes, then quickly kissed her. "It's okay baby, I don't mind being a rebound after what you just did to me."

She continued to slowly stroke Tommie, but the moment was lost. Tommie took Melinda's face tenderly in her hands and shamefully whispered, "I can't, I'm sorry."

Melinda stilled her hand but left it buried in Tommie's wetness. She pushed the fingers of her other hand through Tommie's dark locks. "Baby, you have nothing to be sorry for. I'm just sorry I wasn't able to help you over your heartbreak from…Kate, was it?"

Tommie shook her head as if to say, "Oh well, you tried." They put themselves back together in silence. When they exited the car, Tommie leaned back against its door, studying Melinda in the glow of the nearby streetlight.

The blond stood close, resting her hand against Tommie's chest. "You come back and find me, lover, when you're ready." Tommie gave a slight nod of her head before Melinda pulled her head down to place a parting kiss on her lips.

Tommie remained leaning against the car, watching as she crossed the parking lot to the bar. She let out a deep, exhausted breath. Kate…why had she called out Kate's name as she was about to come? Tommie had never confused women in her life. Some would say that she went through women like rock stars did groupies. She might not always remember their names, but she never mixed them up. And Kate, of all women! She could never be with her, as badly as she might like to be. She scrubbed a hand over her face. She needed a drink desperately, but she went home instead, putting herself to bed, alone and frustrated.

* * *

Tommie knocked on the storm door and heard a voice call from somewhere within to "come in." As she stepped into the living room, Kate entered from the hallway, fussing with the tie she was placing in her hair. Tommie was pretty sure she'd managed not to let her mouth fall open—at least she hoped so—but to be safe she kept her dark sunglasses in place.

"Make yourself at home. We'll be ready in a few minutes."

Tommie knew she was a little early. She couldn't move from where she stood, though, her feet somehow anchored to the floor as she watched Kate with her arms raised above her head and her hands at the back of her neck. The white cotton of her blouse was stretched taut across her chest, revealing the unmistakable outline of nipples through the fabric. She averted her eyes when her fingers twitched.

God, get a grip before you turn into a blundering fool, ordered the voice in Tommie's head. She blew out a slow breath when Kate turned and disappeared back down the hallway.

As they climbed in the Jeep, Kate mused, "So we're going topless today."

Tommie's face got hot, but that could easily be blamed on the August heat. "Yes, is it a problem?"

Kate smoothed a hand over her head. "No—it will just play havoc with my hair."

"Not a problem." Tommie reached in the glove box and pulled out two Cougars ball caps, handing one to each Kate and Megan. "Here, these should help." Kate placed the cap on her head, which only served to make her more attractive than she already was to Tommie. "If you pull your hair tie higher on the back of your head you can tuck your hair through this hole." Tommie pulled her own cap off the gearshift, pointing out what she was talking about.

Megan leaned forward from the backseat. "Here, let me help."

After they successfully threaded Kate's hair into the cap, they headed down the road. Once they were on the highway the noise all but obliterated any possibility of conversation. Kate closed her eyes and leaned her head back. The sun kissing her skin made her more stunning than Tommie could have imagined possible, and she stole as many sideways glances at her as thought she could get away with. She didn't have a clue that Megan caught nearly every one of them.

They entered the stadium with its crush of people thirty minutes before the start of the game.

"If we get separated for any reason," said Tommie, "just ask someone where your seat is." She indicated the number on the ticket.

Kate said, "Wow! This place is huge."

"This is awesome!" Megan exclaimed, standing on her toes to see over the crowd to the field.

Tommie's senses were on overload as she inhaled the smell of popcorn, pretzels and hot dogs and anticipated that familiar crack of the ball against the bat and the cheers of the crowd. These were the things that made baseball Tommie's favorite sport, going all the way back to childhood. This was a place of comfort and bliss for her. A place where she wasn't a big butch lesbian, but just another devoted baseball fan. It didn't get any better than this.

"Okay, bathroom, drinks or food before we go down to our seats?"

Kate and Megan looked at each other, then said in unison, "I'm fine."

Tommie thought how true a statement that was about Kate. The Bellam women decided on sandwiching Tommie between them when they reached their seats, which was also fine by her. Soon after the game started, so did the questions. Tommie welcomed the feel of Kate's fingers on her arm each time she leaned close to ask something. And each time Kate crossed and uncrossed her legs, Tommie had to sit on her hands to keep herself from reaching over and touching skin that she was certain was as soft as silk. Megan soon struck up a conversation with a young fellow sitting beside her, so Tommie was left to devote all her attention to Kate.

By the seventh-inning stretch the Bellams were into the game, and standing, cheering and yelling along with the thousands of strangers that surrounded them. When the game ended with a disappointing loss, they waited in their seats for the crowd to thin.

Kate commented, "If that guy who was stealing the base and got caught hadn't been they might have won?"

Tommie nodded and thought, *Probably not*, but she agreed with Kate that it was a bonehead call. The first baseman was not a base stealer. While it probably didn't make any difference, you just never knew what could change the course of a game. She pulled a small notebook from her pocket and jotted a couple of notes, then stood and stretched her cramped legs, certain this was the first time she'd ever sat through an entire game without getting out of her seat and walking around. But no beer meant no need to go to the bathroom. They'd each had a watered-down soft drink and a pretzel and that hardly warranted a long climb up the steps for a break. It was nearing six o'clock as they ascended the steps.

"You two hungry for some real food? 'Cause there's a great place on the way back to the interstate where we can grab some dinner."

Kate took a peek at her watch, then looked at Megan, who said, "Sure."

Kate said, "That sounds good, but only if you let me treat, since you treated us to the ball game."

Tommie chuckled. "The game tickets were free, and there's no way I'm gonna let a pretty lady—" she abruptly stopped herself, saying instead, "Listen, you've had me over for dinner twice now. It's my turn."

"Having dinner at the house with Megan and me is hardly the same."

"I disagree."

"I suppose we're just going to have to fight over the check then."

At the top of the stadium steps, Tommie stopped and planted her fists on her hips. With a devilish grin, she said, "I don't think you want to pick a fight with me."

Kate took her own imposing stance, with one hand on her hip and her head cocked. "Are you going to bully me?" Her lips curled up.

She looked so damn cute in her ball cap and shorts that showed a mile of leg. Tommie really wanted to see where those legs ended.

Kate continued, barely able to hold back a laugh, "You have to watch out for the little ones you know." She straightened her shoulders. "I can be very scrappy in a fight." She couldn't hold back any longer and began to laugh, joined quickly by Tommie.

When they finally regained their composure, Tommie said, "Tell you what, we'll flip for it."

"Fair enough."

Tommie fingered the coin in her pocket that her dad had given to her when she attended her first-ever ballgame, which seemed like forever ago. She liked to think of it as her lucky charm. The dollar-sized coin carried the faces of two baseball legends, one on each side. It was, in other words, a two-headed coin. All she had to do was get Kate to call tails when it came time to flip over the check.

The conversation at dinner centered mostly on the game since both Megan and Kate were full of more baseball questions. When the waitress came to take their drink order, Tommie nudged Kate.

"Order a margarita, and I'll have a beer. Megan can drive us home." She looked at Megan. "You can drive a stick shift, can't you?"

Megan's face lit with surprise. "Uh, sure. I can drive if it's okay with Aunt Kate."

Tommie looked at Kate and waggled her brows. "Ah, come on, Kate, live dangerously." Kate gave in.

Tommie took care of the check under the pretense of a trip to the bathroom, asking when she returned, "Are you two ready?"

"We need to settle the check. Are we fighting or flipping for it?" Kate asked brazenly.

"I think it's been taken care of already."

The waitress appeared, slipping the credit slip to Tommie unseen before asking, "Is there anything else I can get for you?"

"The check," Kate said.

"Already been taken care of," the waitress replied.

Kate cast a scornful gaze at Tommie. "You said…" When Tommie shrugged, she said, "Don't be so sure this is settled. I *will* figure out a way to even things up."

Tommie could think of a number of ways Kate Bellam could even things with her. None of which would cost a dime. "I'll entertain discussion in the future on the matter."

She sat behind Megan as she drove them home so she could sneak peeks at Kate.

In the driveway, Megan hopped out and headed toward the house, calling out, "Thanks, I had a blast," as she went.

Kate asked, "Are you okay to drive yourself home?"

Tommie nodded, then wondered briefly if Kate would have invited her for a sleepover if she'd said no.

"I think I'd feel better if you came in for a cup of coffee or tea before you drove yourself home." Kate kept her gaze firmly fixed on Tommie as she stood with her hand resting on the roll bar on the driver's side of the Jeep.

"It's late. I really should go."

"I can stay up until at least midnight on Saturday nights. Are you telling me you can't? It's not even ten yet."

Tommie tipped her head and remained still, mesmerized by Kate's eyes as they flickered in the moonlight. She could spend every minute of the rest of her life in Kate's company, but doing so lately was sometimes torturous. Like after she'd had a drink.

In a child-like voice Tommie said, "I stay up past midnight too…" She paused and in her normal tone said, "But I was out kind of late last night, so I'm actually pretty worn out this evening."

* * *

Had Tommie been at the bar last night, buying women drinks in the hopes of getting one to take her home, as she had been doing the first time Kate had laid eyes on her? The thought caused a feeling in Kate's stomach she wasn't sure she understood.

"Well, then, I would imagine you should probably put yourself to bed. Thanks for everything, I had a wonderful time." Tommie started the engine but sat in the driveway until Kate reached the door. There, she turned, gave a quick wave and disappeared inside.

Kate went directly to the fridge. She needed a drink, but there was no wine chilled, no margaritas made, and it was too late to make them now. All she could find was a bottle of Tommie's Mexican beer. She had never been a beer drinker, barely tolerating the smell and caring less for the taste. Searching the crisper, she found a lemon, not the lime that Tommie had placed in her beers, but she decided to give it a try. Megan was already seated in front of her computer so she took the concoction out to the deck. Stretching out in her lounger, she took a sip, wrinkling her nose at the strong carbonated taste that assaulted her palette. Setting the bottle aside, she gazed up at the bright sky, lit by a nearly full moon.

Breathing deeply, she tried to relax her body, which felt strung tighter than a rubber band nearing its breaking point. She knew what the problem was, and it was named "Tommie." Tommie was fun and full of charm. Charm, it seemed to Kate, that had this irresistible effect on her—and she liked it. She knew Tommie assumed she was straight, and yet she was still attentive to her. Kate didn't understand it, but she enjoyed the special way it made her feel. She had never spent time around anyone as openly gay, and…well…just so plainly comfortable in her own sexuality. And Tommie was big and butch and didn't try to hide that fact. Oh, she was careful in her speech and behavior around Kate and Megan, but her very presence was a constant and frustrating reminder to Kate of who she herself was under all her secret layers. And beneath all those layers was a woman who yearned for the soft feel of another woman's lips on hers, and tender touches that could fire a burning desire in her.

She closed her eyes and in her mind's eye saw dark eyes full of desire looking back at her. Tommie could probably arouse desire in any woman who asked to be taken, straight or otherwise, she thought. She had caught the occasional glances from her, had seen the desire burning just below the surface in Tommie's eyes. Tommie was a woman who loved women. She probably viewed every woman the same, a trait Kate didn't particularly like. Still, there was something about her.

* * *

Tommie was grateful for the cool evening air. She was hotter than a nomad in the desert. If she didn't know better, she'd swear she was having one of those hot flashes her mom was always complaining about.

She tossed her cap on the couch, grabbed a beer from the fridge and started pacing. What was she doing stewing in her cramped little place on a Saturday night, when she knew full well there were women out there just waiting to have sex with someone like her, someone who could read a woman's sexual needs like a trashy romance novel?

Actually, she knew why she was here pacing around like a horny dog and not out prowling—it was Kate. How could one straight woman come into her life and turn everything she knew about herself into something so foreign? She'd lusted after unattainable ones like Kate before, but never had they wreaked havoc on her life the way Kate was doing. She easily recalled last night with Melissa, or Michelle or whatever her name was, and her inability to get off. Just like it recently happened with Colleen. "Oh, God," Tommie groaned. It was humiliating to even think about.

She stripped off her clothes and stepped under a cool shower, trying to wash away the ache between her thighs. After fifteen minutes, frustrated, she toweled off and fell into bed. When she closed her eyes, though, she saw Kate looking so cute in that baseball cap and so sexy in her short shorts with those legs. Reluctantly she began stroking the need between her own legs, something she hadn't resorted to in more years than she could remember. She knew, though, that the frustration wasn't going to go away without a little help. When she finally managed to achieve a small orgasm—and it wasn't without a lot of effort—she collapsed into her pillow. She needed to put some time and distance between herself and this woman, who'd undoubtedly put some kind of spell on her.

CHAPTER SEVEN

Kate saw the posting about the fundraiser on the board in the locker room. The hospital was a co-sponsor of a program that provided summer sporting activities for underprivileged inner-city kids. *Wow*, she thought. *Fifty dollars a person. Way too rich for my blood.*

Then something else jumped off the page at her. A guest speaker at the dinner and recipient of a community humanitarian award was going to be *Denton Daily News* staff writer G. Tommelson. This had to be Tommie. She jotted down the web address for information on the event, which was scheduled for the following Friday evening.

Kate stopped at the library on her way home to use a computer, not completely sure why she didn't want Megan knowing she was checking out something involving Tommie. Megan's internship had ended weeks earlier, and since she had returned to school, neither of them had mentioned Tommie's name.

Going to the site listed on the posting, Kate read the article there about the summer program and co-organizer, G. Tommelson, sportswriter for the *Daily News*. The article included the tiny, smiling photo of Tommie that headed her column, something which Kate had found herself reading more often than not of late, despite her general disinterest in sports. She wrote down the phone number to call for tickets to the semiformal affair and called it as soon as she left the library, hoping that there would still be some left. Assured that her ticket would be waiting the following Friday, she drove home.

She was looking through her closet and humming when Megan plopped on her bed and cleared her throat. Startled, she turned. "You should give warning before sneaking up. You nearly gave me a heart attack."

"Sorry." Megan eyed her curiously. "You seem extra happy this evening…big date or something this weekend?"

Kate returned to her searching. "A date…no. This weekend… no again. I'm attending a fundraiser the hospital is co-sponsoring next Friday." She turned briefly back toward Megan. "Would you like to go with me?"

Megan wrinkled her nose. "Fundraiser, as in a lot of older people you probably don't know standing around talking all evening?"

"Something like that. I think there might be a few speeches thrown in there." She turned back to the closet. "Oh, and dinner just to entice people to come."

Megan stretched on her side, pulling a pillow under her head. "Gosh, Aunt Kate, as much as I like all that do-gooder stuff, I think I'll pass on it, if you don't mind."

She'd known Megan would prefer not to go, though if she had known her mentor was going to be there she might have. Just as well. Kate would have a hard time justifying spending a hundred dollars so Megan could see Tommie speak at a public event, even for such a good cause. Kate, on the other hand, was dying to see how the burly, "in your face" woman handled herself at such an affair.

Aha! She had found what she was looking for. Granted it was a few years old, but she was sure she could still squeeze into the dress she'd worn to be a bridesmaid for one of the few women at work that she'd developed a kind of friendship with.

"So, I'm going to be home alone next Friday?"

Kate hooked the dress on the top of the door and pulled away the plastic that was covering it. "For a while. Why, did you have something planned?"

"No," Megan answered innocently. "But if I'm going to be here alone, can I ask Ash to spend the night?"

"That's fine, sweetie." Kate pulled her top over her head, prompting Megan to jump off the bed and head for the door. "As long as you two promise not to get into anything you shouldn't." Kate's words of warning were lost on Megan since she'd already disappeared down the hall.

* * *

Kate arrived a little late, looking to skip the social drinking part of the evening. She hoped to be seated at the far back in the ballroom since she purchased her ticket so late. She wanted to get in and out without being detected if that were possible. Only a few people were still milling about as she entered and quickly found her table. She didn't know anyone there, but that was not a problem. She dealt with strangers on a daily basis and typically under far less pleasant circumstances. As she chatted with the others at the table, she kept her head down. She figured she'd get a good look at Tommie when she received her award.

Exactly twenty minutes after the dessert was served a gentleman in a suit, minus a tie, cleared his throat at the microphone.

"If I can have everyone's attention, please?" He paused as the chatter died down. "We have a number of people to recognize and thank this evening, starting with all of you for making your generous donations toward this very worthy cause." He began the applause, which lasted at least half a minute. As it died off, he continued, "And now it is my honor to introduce our hometown captain of industry and philanthropist, Richard Baxter."

The room erupted again in applause as everyone rose to their feet. When people returned to their seats, Kate caught sight of dark hair above a white shirt toward the front of the room and knew it must be Tommie. Baxter's commanding voice droned on and on, thanking every organization that had a hand in the charitable cause and finally introducing Anthony Foster, "the man behind the *Denton Daily News* and behind this successful project."

Foster was direct and to the point. "Thank you one and all, but I must say right off, I am merely one of the pairs of arms that help row the boat this project represents. From heads of business to community leaders and local ministries and clergy, we have all worked hand in hand to provide something of great value to future leaders in sports, our businesses, community and churches. And to each of you who have had a hand in our successes, I extend my deep thanks." He raised his hands before the applause could spread too far. "As it is with any great achievement, this one began with the simple idea that every child in a community should have the opportunity to be a part of something exciting and challenging, regardless of his or her economic circumstances. I am honored to say that I work with the individual whose dream became 'Project Summer Fun.'"

Kate thought that the man's taut, tanned face might crack from the wide, proud paternal grin he was wearing.

"Ladies and gentlemen, please join me in saluting, G. Tommelson, better known as Tommie, one of the head sportswriters at the *Daily News* and the recipient of this year's Outstanding Community Achievement Award."

Chills raced over Kate's skin as the crowd once again rose to its feet and applause thundered throughout the ballroom. Kate sat as soon as the occupants at her table did, wanting to remain anonymous. Tommie appeared completely at ease as she leaned on the podium in a casual stance. Her voice seemed soft and demure compared to the men who had spoken before her, but it was far more exciting to Kate's ears.

* * *

"Thank you. Please let me start by saying that I'm not a public speaker...at all, so don't expect me to come across like Mr. Baxter," Tommie nodded toward his table at the front, "or my boss, Mr. Foster." She met his eyes and Foster tipped his head. She flipped between the two note cards on which she'd written some names. She knew exactly what she wanted to say. More than one successful athlete had overcome insurmountable odds growing up and had managed to achieve stardom or in some cases simply a career to be proud of and a way to make a living. Every aspiring athlete should have an opportunity to do that. She would challenge individuals in other fields and careers to take action to help a child.

"It's no secret that I like sports. I grew up in the shadow of three brothers, whom I'm sure my parents blame for me becoming such a crazed sports nut." Her comment garnered a few chuckles. "But more importantly, I grew up in the right neighborhood and went to the right schools. I was able to participate in the sports of my choosing because the school had money to support the programs and my parents could afford the costs the school didn't cover." She glanced at her notes, then scanned the crowd, trying to connect with them. "A lot of kids don't have—"

Her eyes spotted on pair of familiar blue ones in the back of the room and in a split second she lost both her voice and her train of thought. Kate held her gaze, then smiled encouragingly.

"Uh—" Tommie stuttered and looked at her now-shaking hands before risking a glance back at Kate. Kate nodded as if to say, "Please continue."

Tommie cleared her throat and looked to her boss for a confidence boost. "Sorry...As I was saying, too many kids, especially in the inner city, don't have the opportunities kids from the suburbs have. I wanted to try and rally our community to take action to remedy that sad reality."

Hitting her stride again, Tommie spoke for another ten minutes about famous athletes who had achieved monumental success because of one simple act by one person who could make a difference. She took care not to allow her eyes to meet Kate's again, though, until she was through.

She raised the plaque her boss had presented her and said, "I challenge every one of you to do one thing that will make the difference in the life of a child who needs a little bit of help. Thank you." She held the award aloft a long moment, watching as Kate applauded with the rest of the room like she was someone to be proud of. As people started to move about, she began to make her way from the podium to the back of the ballroom.

* * *

When Megan had first spoken about Tommie, Kate had gotten the impression that she was a real hard-ass who didn't particularly care for young people. The chance meeting at the bar hadn't bolstered her opinion either. Tonight she was seeing for the first time another side to this woman, one she'd certainly never expected. Under Tommie's tough, powerful exterior was something much different. Kate was only now realizing how different, how soft and gentle a person Tommie truly was. Kate hadn't been able to pull her eyes away from her as she spoke, not eloquently but from the heart. A heart Kate now suspected was as big as the woman herself.

As for her own heart—at the moment it was thumping with excitement that she knew this big-hearted, larger-than-life woman. She was proud to be a part of same "sisterhood" with Tommie, even though her part was a secret. It wasn't any wonder she felt so drawn to Tommie. Why she was attracted to her. Kate didn't think it was possible for anyone who knew the woman not to like or care about her. And she was just so...so handsome this evening all dressed up in that white oxford shirt, those creased black slacks and polished shoes. Kate had never seen her looking so formal and so...commanding.

Knowing she could hardly skip out now that she'd been spotted, Kate waited anxiously as Tommie made her way through the crowd, stopping regularly to shake hands and receive pats on the back. Ten or so feet away, someone else congratulating her stopped Tommie again. The sensation that enveloped Kate as Tommie's eyes moved over her caused her breath to catch.

* * *

Tommie's view of Kate was unimpeded. She was gorgeous—and the last person Tommie had expected to see this evening. The tasteful, but revealing royal blue dress she was wearing highlighted deeper hues in her already mesmerizing eyes. She looked like she'd been kidnapped from a fashion runway. Tommie's eyes traveled over every inch of Kate's magnificently displayed body as she listened without hearing the person who had stopped her.

Finally Tommie managed to break free. Stepping within a few feet of Kate, she offered a cheerful "Hi!"

Kate responded with a lighthearted "Hi" of her own. Before Tommie could say more, she extended her hand. "Congratulations." Tommie welcomed her touch, which was accompanied by a heart-stopping squeeze.

Tommie was as speechless as she'd been earlier when she'd glimpsed Kate in the crowd. She felt a pulse beating in the hand that still held Kate's, but she couldn't tell if it was hers or Kate's. After what seemed an eternity, she finally found her voice.

"Uh…thanks."

Tommie released Kate's hand. Not because she wanted to—she relished the feel of Kate's hand in hers—but because she realized they'd been standing there, unmoving, for too long. And while Tommie couldn't care less, she worried that someone would conclude she and Kate shared some kind of deeper or more "special" bond. She didn't want that, for Kate's sake.

"This is an amazing thing you've started, Tommie. I have no doubt you'll find deep pockets in this city that will help keep it going."

Tommie shrugged nonchalantly. "Hey, it's all about the kids."

Kate nodded in agreement. "Yes, the kids are what matters." She glanced at her watch. "And speaking of kids. I've got two at home alone. I should get going."

Tommie's stomach clenched. She wanted to grab Kate's hand and ask her to stay, have a drink, sit and catch up. Not to mention look at her until every fine line and faint freckle on her face and partially exposed chest were etched in her mind to conjure up at a later time. But she didn't, even though she hadn't seen her for a month. Instead she touched her fingers to Kate's elbow, turning her toward the exit.

"Come on, I'll walk you to your car."

Kate hesitated. "That's okay, I'm sure there are people that would like to talk with you."

Tommie rolled her eyes. "I'm sure there are, but they can wait a few more minutes."

* * *

"I was really surprised to see you here this evening," Tommie said as she walked Kate to the main exit.

"The hospital co-sponsored the fundraiser," Kate said, offering a truthful, if somewhat evasive statement. She couldn't possibly tell Tommie the real reason she'd come. Tommie might misinterpret her motivation. "I must say I was quite surprised too. This whole charitable project you created—you never even hinted at it to Megan or me." Kate suspected that was because Tommie wanted to maintain her "tough guy" façade.

Tommie shrugged off Kate's comment, but as they pushed through the door outside, she said, "I've missed seeing you...you and Megan, I mean."

Kate wanted to say the same. She missed being around Tommie for very selfish reasons and enjoyed immensely the time she could spend with her. She made Kate feel like setting free the hidden part of herself that she desperately wanted to embrace—if only that were possible.

"I know Megan misses working with you. We should find something we can do together." They stopped beside Kate's car.

Pulling a thin wallet from her pocket, Tommie retrieved a card. "Here are my numbers. Call me if you think of something."

"Okay."

Tommie opened Kate's door. "Thanks for coming tonight."

"It's all about the kids, right?" Kate noted how devilishly attractive Tommie was as she smiled back at her.

Tommie nodded. "Right."

CHAPTER EIGHT

Ah...the wonders of the world of sports. The Cougars had rallied as the season began to draw to an end and now had a chance—slim though it might be—of making it to the Series. And to make life even better, Tommie had secured tickets to an "at home" playoff game, a game that would likely help cinch the league championship. She could barely contain her excitement as she dialed the number from her office.

Disappointed when the machine picked up, Tommie said, "Hi, it's Tommie. Can you give me a call back? I have some exciting news."

It was only two fifteen. Realizing that she wouldn't hear back for a bit, she called it a day and headed up the street. She took her time with the bottle of Dos Equis she ordered, occupying herself with listening to the TV as a commentator on the sports channel marveled at the impossible turn of events that had made possible the Cougars' current playoff hopes. Her phone vibrated just after four.

Megan's voice sounded unusually sweet. "Hi, Tommie! What's up?"

"Have you been following any baseball at all?" She knew it was a stretch.

"Kind of, some. I know the Cougars are doing pretty good."

"Better than good. They're in the playoffs for the league championship."

"That's cool..."

"Very. So listen, I've got tickets to Game Number Two, which is here at home next Wednesday, and I thought I'd see if you and your aunt would like to go with me."

"Seriously?"

Tommie chuckled. "Seriously."

"Wow! Um...okay, I mean, I want to say okay, but I have to wait until Aunt Kate gets home and ask. What time is the game?"

"It starts at ten after seven, so I'd like to leave by a quarter to five at the absolute latest and get ahead of some of the traffic."

"I'll ask her as soon as she gets home and call you back."

"Sure, I'll talk to you later then."

* * *

Kate wasn't home from work when she arrived at the Bellam house on game night. According to Megan, she probably wouldn't be back before seven. Tommie was more than disappointed. Since seeing her at the fundraiser weeks before, Tommie hadn't been able to get the vision of her in that amazing dress out of her mind.

Still, she was enjoying being with Megan, who was almost as caught up in the excitement of the fans as Tommie was. This was the first playoff run for the ball club since she had been in junior high and the Cougars had been battling her home state team. She clearly remembered watching the game back then with her dad and brothers. When the Cougars took the field at the bottom of the eighth inning, they were holding their own and keeping the score close.

Megan leaned over. "I'm going to the bathroom."

Never taking her eyes off the field, Tommie asked, "You want me to go with you?"

"I'm almost eighteen," Megan huffed. "I hardly need my hand held for the bathroom."

Tommie waved a hand. "Sorry."

"Do you want anything?"

"Yeah, don't get lost. Okay?"

Megan shook her head and headed for the restrooms. Ten minutes later, two outs down, the batter cracked a foul ball that headed toward their section and everyone rose to their feet, watching the sky. In the hubbub, Tommie didn't notice Megan descending the steps and Megan didn't realize a ball was headed her way. Not, that is, until a mass of bodies surrounded her.

Tommie caught a glimpse of Megan's frightened face as a dozen guys competed for the ball that was dropping almost into her hands. After that, she disappeared in the crush of bodies. Panicked, Tommie pushed frantically at the people between her and the group that had converged on the foul ball and apparently swallowed up Megan. Then the guys began stepping back from the spot where the ball had fallen—revealing Megan lying on the steps at an odd angle.

She shoved at the last guy who stood between her and Kate's precious niece. "Move, you Neanderthal." Daring him to protest, she knelt next to where Megan's head rested. The skin on the girl's forearm was stretched to near breaking point over what Tommie could only assume was a major broken bone.

She touched the back of her hand softly to Megan's cheek. "Megan…Megan, can you open your eyes?"

The girl's eyelids fluttered, then slowly opened, and her right hand reached toward the broken left arm, but Tommie caught it before it could connect. "Don't move, kiddo."

Tears crowded the corner of Megan's eyes as she croaked, "It hurts."

Tommie gave her hand a gentle squeeze. "I know, but just stay really still, okay. Squeeze my hand if you have to." She looked at the crowd around them and yelled, "Someone get some help. Call nine-one-one. Something!"

It seemed like hours to Tommie, but within minutes a medic was asking her to move aside. She did so reluctantly. She stayed where Megan could see her, although her eyes were again closed. The medic made quick work of checking her pulse, heart and breathing, then gingerly slipped a blood pressure cuff on her uninjured arm.

He gently placed his hand on her shoulder. "Miss…Miss, can you open your eyes for me?" Megan's eyes opened slowly and he looked into both with a tiny flashlight. While he was making his assessment another guy was securing her neck in a brace. Then together they splinted her obviously broken arm. When she moaned and cried out in pain, Tommie's heart squeezed hard in her chest.

"Who are the parents?" the medic asked the crowd standing around watching the action.

Tommie stood from her squat. "She's here with me."

The guy looked her up and down, then handed Megan's purse to her. He and his partner quickly strapped her to a backboard and started up the steps, Tommie close on their heels. Once they secured her to the waiting stretcher, he asked, "She a minor?" Tommie nodded. "You riding with us?"

Tommie was anxious. "Yeah, let's go."

* * *

The ambulance pulled away from the stadium and Tommie listened as the medic spoke into his radio. "BP normal at one twenty over seventy-two, pupils were equal and reactive, pulse rate normal, but reps have slowed. I think she's going into shock." He rubbed lightly with his knuckles on Megan's sternum. "Hey, cutie, can you open your eyes for me again?" Receiving nothing but a twitch, he asked Tommie, "What's her name?"

Tommie felt nausea wash over her. "Meg…" She cleared her throat. "Megan."

He tried with his knuckles again. "Megan, hey girl, can you open your eyes? Megan?" Into his radio he said, "No response."

Suddenly Tommie became deaf, as if she were in a dream in living color without the sound. She saw the medic place a needle in Megan's undamaged arm, hang a bag of clear liquid and insert a tube into the needle. She heard "IV set and flowing at…" and then tuned out again, this time saying a silent prayer, "Oh, God, Megan, open your eyes and talk to this guy. Open your eyes and look at me."

Just as suddenly she was back again. *Kate*, she thought, *I have to get hold of Kate.* She opened Megan's purse, which she'd been clutching so tightly that there were dents in the leather from her nails. Pulling out her shiny pink phone and flipping it open,

Tommie located the menu and began scrolling until she found "Kate, Aunt." She took a deep breath and held it as she punched the dial button.

Kate answered on the fourth ring, her voice recognizable and cheery. "Hey, sweetie, is the game over already?"

Tommie exhaled slowly and swallowed hard. "Kate, it's Tommie."

Kate said, "Oh, hi, Tommie…" and then was abruptly silent.

Tommie went into her professional mode. "Listen, Kate, there was a little accident at the ballpark involving Megan. We're on our way—" The driver blasted the siren and laid on the horn as they approached a major intersection.

"Oh, God, Meggie."

The anguish and despair in Kate's voice shook Tommie to her core. *Take charge*, she told herself. "Listen to me, Kate. We're on our way to…" She touched the tech's arm, "Where we goin'?"

"Children's, since she's a minor. It's right off the interstate on the north side of the city." Tommie repeated his words to Kate. He asked, "Is that her parents?" When Tommie nodded yes, he said compassionately, "Her vitals are all stable. I think she's just in shock from the pain of the bone break."

Tommie nodded her head in understanding. "She's going to be just fine, Kate, I promise." When she heard nothing in return, Tommie asked, "Are you okay to drive?"

Kate's voice sounded frantic. "Yes."

Tommie asked calmly, "And you know where you're going?"

"Yes."

Tommie heard the slam of her car door. "Kate?"

She sounded distracted. "Yes."

As soothingly as she could manage, Tommie said, "Please drive carefully. I'm right here with Megan and I promise you nothing else is going to happen to her. Call Megan's phone when you're heading in to the ER so I can meet you and take you to her."

"Okay." Kate sounded distant as the call ended and Tommie flipped the phone closed.

No more than ten minutes later they were pulling into the ambulance bay and in only a few more they were rolling Megan into a trauma room where a nurse stopped Tommie at the door.

"Are you related to this girl?"

"No, her aunt's on her way now."

"I'm sorry, but I'm going to have to ask you to wait out here, please."

Tommie realized then she should have lied. Said she was her sister or her aunt. Aunt—Kate—that thought sent waves of guilt and anxiety through her. She stood in silence as the nurse disappeared through the doors, then watched as gowned nurses, doctors, and whatever all the other people were in the room hovered around Megan. Tommie checked her watch. It couldn't have been more than fifteen, twenty minutes tops since she'd spoken to Kate. That meant a minimum of an hour before she would arrive. Tommie paced the hall. Finally, after nearly thirty minutes, the nurse came back out looking for Tommie.

"How is she?"

The nurse offered a comforting smile. "She's going to be fine, I'm sure. She's kind of out of it, though. They gave her something for the pain before they tried setting the bone." Just the words made Tommie cringe. "They'll need more X-rays before they can do any casting and I'm pretty sure they're going to do a CT scan as a precaution since she got a pretty good bump on the head." Tommie listened intently. "She keeps asking for someone named Kate. Is that you?"

Tommie shook her head. "No, but she should be here soon. Any chance I can see her for just a minute?"

The nurse patted Tommie's arm. "Wait right here, hon."

Ten minutes later she poked her head through the door. "You can come in for just a minute or two. They'll be here shortly to take her down to radiology." The nurse steered Tommie to the right side of the bed. Megan's eyes were open but glassy.

Tommie touched her hand. "Hey, kiddo, how ya doin'?" Megan rolled her eyes toward Tommie and licked her lips. Tommie patted her hand. "That's okay. Don't try to talk. They say you're going to be just fine and your aunt's on her way. I'll bring her to see you as soon as I can."

Megan's fingers reached around and squeezed Tommie's hand.

"They're going to roll you down the hall in a few minutes to take a look at that hard head of yours." Tommie gave Megan a wink. "Tell you what, though, I'm so proud of you. You managed what a dozen guys couldn't, and most of them were bigger than me." Tommie produced the ball she'd been palming since they'd put Megan on the backboard. She held it before Megan's eyes. "You had this hidden under you on the steps." Tommie gave it a little toss and caught it. "Yep, we'll get it signed by whoever you want to sign it."

Two guys in white coats entered the room and one said, "Bellam, Megan?"

Tommie said, "Yes."

"She's going to radiology. Probably be back within thirty minutes if they're not too behind."

Tommie stroked a few locks of hair off Megan's forehead. "I'll hold on to this for you while you take your little ride, and I promise to have Kate here when you get back."

When Megan squeezed Tommie's hand again, Tommie felt it all the way to her heart. She looked so helpless and small. All Tommie wanted to do was wrap Megan in her arms and keep her safe. Tommie followed a short way as they whisked her off, then paced the waiting room until Megan's phone vibrated in her pocket.

"Kate."

"I'm pulling in the parking lot now."

Her voice sounded even and controlled. "I'll meet you right inside the emergency doors."

She moved quickly down the hall, meeting her a few feet inside the door.

Kate wore a stricken expression. "Where is she?"

Tommie was about to answer when she noticed the color draining from Kate's face. As she started to slump toward the floor, Tommie caught her under one arm, holding on firmly until she could scoop her other arm under Kate's legs and pick her up.

Before she got her to an empty seat, a woman in scrubs was at their side. "Is she all right?"

Tommie gingerly placed Kate in the chair and squatted in front of her. "I think she may have just fainted. Kate?" She tipped her head up by her chin. "Kate?"

The nurse was checking her pulse when Kate slowly opened her eyes and looked into Tommie's.

"Maybe we should take her back and check her out."

Kate protested. "No, I'm okay, I just got a little light-headed. I'm a nurse. It was just anxiety, I'm sure." She looked intent but said meekly to Tommie. "Please take me to Megan."

The woman vacated the seat beside Kate. "Her color's coming back. She's probably fine, but if she feels faint again, let us know."

"Thanks." Tommie returned her eyes to Kate. "She's in radiology getting a CT scan. She got a bump on the head and they're being abundantly cautious." Kate's eyes shone with tears. "Her left arm's broken, but they say it looked like a clean break and it should heal just fine."

Her heart breaking, Tommie watched the first of many tears slide down Kate's cheeks. She seemed at first to be taking it all in with controlled emotion, then she pressed her hand to her mouth and sobbed.

"Oh, my God, Meggie." She sucked in a breath and let out another cry.

Tommie moved to the chair beside her and placed her arm around Kate, who dropped her head onto Tommie's shoulder and continued to cry softly. As Tommie gently rocked Kate, she had the same feeling she'd had with Megan earlier. She only wanted to make her feel safe and secure.

Tommie's voice was barely above a whisper when she spoke. "I'm so sorry I let her get hurt, Kate. I promise you she's going to be just fine, and I won't ever let anything happen to her again."

Kate's crying had subsided, and she reached for Tommie's hand. "I don't blame you. It's just...she's all I've got."

Tommie looked at the delicate hand resting upon her own. "I swear I'll help you keep her safe."

When Kate squeezed Tommie's hand that powerful surge she'd felt with Megan returned. It all felt foreign and so confusing. A few minutes later Kate leaned away from Tommie's shoulder and withdrew her hand.

Tommie slipped her arm from around her shoulder and stood. "Let's go see if Megan's back from radiology."

The room was still empty so Tommie found a chair and pulled it close enough to see the doors to the room and made Kate sit.

"You want something? A soda, coffee or a water?"

Kate sat fidgeting with the zipper pull on her purse and only shook her head no. Tommie checked the time.

"They should be coming back any minute."

It was another ten before Tommie recognized the guys in the white coats rolling a bed their way.

"Here she comes now."

Kate stood and waited anxiously as they swept right on past her and Tommie into the room.

The nurse caught them before they could enter and asked, "You're the relative?"

Kate took a step closer to the door, trying to see through the window. "Yes, her aunt and her legal guardian."

"She's going to be fine, honey. Let them get everything hooked back up and you can go in. I'll find the doctor and have him come in to talk to you."

She moved down the hall and a moment later the two guys left the room. Tommie held open the door in front of them, but Kate stood unmoving, her eyes fearful and pleading. Tommie tipped her head toward the room.

"I'm right behind you."

Kate moved to the side of the bed where Megan's left arm, encased in an inflatable cast, lay propped on pillows. The only thing showing below her upper arm were her fingers. Kate touched them briefly, leaning over to kiss Megan's forehead.

"I'm here now, sweetie, and you're going to be just fine." Kate drew back, blinking away the threatening tears. She stroked Megan's hair at her temple. "Megan...sweetie..." Megan's lids twitched, her eyes opening slightly. Kissing her forehead again, Kate repeated, "You're going to be fine, honey. Are you in pain?"

"Tired," croaked Megan before her eyelids drifted closed.

Kate stroked her hair. "Of course you are."

Kate stepped back, turned from the bed and pinched her eyes shut. Without thinking Tommie moved to her, slipping her arms around her shoulders and drawing her close.

"Oh, God." Kate's head fell against Tommie's chest and she began to cry again. Tommie held Kate until the doctor came in, when Kate quickly pulled from her warm embrace.

"Mrs. Bellam?"

Kate dabbed at her eyes. "Ms."

He extended his hand. "I'm Dr. Cooper. I treated Megan when she came in." He picked up the chart on the foot of the bed and looked it over carefully before continuing. "Megan has suffered a break in her left forearm..." He indicated where on his own arm.

"The radius bone."

"Yes, that's correct."

"I'm a nurse."

He nodded. "From the pictures it looks like they got it properly set. The orthopedic specialist will be placing the hard cast within the hour, I would imagine. We did a CT scan since she suffered a pretty good contusion to the side of her head and lost consciousness for more than a minute or two. The neurologist and I both confirmed there's nothing to be worried about, but we would like to keep her overnight just to monitor her and make sure no swelling develops. Other than that she's in fine shape. Once the cast comes off in eight to twelve weeks, she'll be good as new."

Tommie saw the slightest bit of relief wash over Kate's face.

"Any questions?"

"I can take her home tomorrow?"

"I don't see any reason you can't. Kids are very resilient, unlike us old folks." He winked, which garnered a half-smile from Kate. "They're generally very hard to break, but they bounce back quickly when they do."

When he left, Tommie pulled a stool to the bedside and directed Kate into it. "She'll want to see you when she wakes up."

As promised, someone came in shortly and cast Megan's arm, explaining the break, how they set it and what to expect. Tommie stood protectively at Kate's side.

An hour later as they settled Megan into a room Tommie said, "I'm going to catch a cab over to the ballpark and pick up my Jeep. I'll bring you back something to eat."

Kate moved to where Tommie stood in the doorway. She crossed her arms over herself, not in annoyance or fury, but as if she were cold. All Tommie really wanted was to wrap her arms around her, hold her and make her feel warm and safe.

Kate said softly, "You should go on home. You've done enough already."

Tommie dropped her head, shoving her hands in her pockets and mumbling, "Yeah, no kidding."

Kate curled her fingers around Tommie's arm. "I'm sorry, that came out wrong. This is not your fault." She tilted her head, trying to capture Tommie's eyes. "Accidents, they just happen."

Tommie shook her head in disgust. "But I failed to protect her."

Kate's eyes glowed with compassion. "It's not your job to keep her safe. That's mine."

Tommie knew in that moment that was the job she wanted. Not only to keep Megan safe, but Kate as well. She wanted to be their protector, a guardian, a spouse and a parent. All the things she'd never dreamed she would desire or need in her life. She suddenly realized she wanted that thing her parents had and that each of her brothers had sought in recent years. Being in bed with a hot woman and having hotter sex was fun and stimulating for her libido, but she knew now she wanted that thing that made her feel warm all over—especially in her heart.

"Tommie?" Her eyes traveled from Kate's hand on her arm to meet her eyes. "You should go on home."

"There's a lot of things I should do—" Tommie let the words die. *Like tell you how much I care about you.* But she held back the words and onto her emotions.

Kate steered her into the hallway. "I've got this, really. I'm fine and Megan's going to be just fine." For the first time since she'd arrived, Tommie thought, Kate did look like she was okay. "Thank you for all you've done."

Tommie's face was growing warm from the gentle hand that still held onto her arm. The spot on her arm that Kate was touching felt like it was on fire. "Sure…no problem. I kinda like the kid, you know."

"Yes, I know."

*   *   *

The cabbie raced diagonally across the marked spaces of the stadium parking lot toward Tommie's Jeep, which under the glow of the lights looked abandoned. He stayed only long enough to make sure it started. Several blocks from the stadium she stopped at a twenty-four-hour burger joint and got a quick sandwich and an extra-large caffeinated soda to go. Driving up the highway she took the turnoff for the Children's Hospital. When she got there, she walked boldly past the security desk to the elevators. When she exited on Megan's floor, the eyes behind the nurse's station desk were immediately trained upon her.

As she approached, the fortyish woman there stood. "Can I help you?"

"I know where I'm going."

The nurse started around the desk. "Visiting hours aren't until—"

Tommie cut her off with a wave of her hand. "I'm not a visitor." She continued down the hall without looking back. She stopped in the doorway, seeing Kate's head resting on the back of the semi-reclined chair. Except for the arms she had crossed tightly over her breasts, she looked perfectly relaxed. *Or,* Tommie thought to herself, *just plain perfect.* She got a blanket from the closet and gently laid it over Kate, who emitted a barely audible moan and shifted her head to one side. Tommie took up sentry near the foot of the bed, sitting crossed-legged on the floor and leaning back against the wall.

* * *

The voices drifted into her head on a whisper, at first, then grew louder. Tommie blinked her eyes open, instantly noting the tingling in her legs and the blanket draped over her shoulders. She struggled to unfold her legs and get the circulation going again.

"You hear what the nurse just said, sweetie? We should be out of here before lunchtime."

When the nurse had gone, Tommie got her still-tingling legs under her and pushed up off the floor, groaning involuntarily. She stretched her aching body, stifling a moan as Kate stepped closer.

"You can't possibly have slept well like that, so I won't even ask."

Tommie twisted one way, then the other until her back popped. "I'm sure I slept in worse places in college."

Kate arched a brow. "They say Megan can go home as soon as the doctor stops in and signs her release."

Tommie roughly combed her fingers through her hair, frightened as to how disheveled and unruly she must look. "That's just great."

"Yes…it is."

It was seven thirty. Tommie rushed down the hall to a lounge area and left a message for her boss that she'd be working out of the office all day and he should call if he needed her. She slipped into the restroom, splashing cold water on her face and finger brushing her teeth before returning to Megan's room.

"You don't have to hang around here," Kate said, to which Tommie responded, "I know," before sitting down to wait on the doctor.

When he finally arrived, he checked Megan's chart, then his handiwork and at last the hand and fingers that protruded from her lavender-colored cast. He patted her leg. "Everything should heal just fine, and as a nurse," he directed his remarks to Kate, "I'm sure you know what to keep an eye out for." Kate nodded and he handed her a prescription for pain medication. "She will need this, believe me, for at least a few days."

As Kate prepared to help Megan dress, Tommie said, "Let me get that filled for you down at the pharmacy and I'll meet you in the lobby."

Kate rummaged in her purse, then handed Tommie her insurance card and a credit card. "Thank you, we'll see you downstairs."

Kate and an orderly helped Megan into the passengers seat of Kate's car, Tommie holding the door wide open to facilitate things.

When Kate placed the cast gently in Megan's lap she winced and said with tears in her eyes, "It hurts."

Kate smoothed back her hair as Tommie handed her the prescription bag. "Maybe you should take one of these now." She opened the package and reached across Megan to the console for a water bottle. "Here, sweetie." Kate placed the pill in Megan's hand. "It's not cold, but it'll wash the pill down."

Megan's face contorted as she swallowed both, then leaned her head back. Kate carefully buckled her in, closed the door and turned to Tommie.

"Thank you...for being here...and helping."

"Hey," Tommie shrugged, "it's the least I can do, considering..." She looked closely at Kate's eyes. "You seem kind of tired. Are you sure you're okay to drive?"

"I'm going to hit the first drive-through for a coffee. I'll be fine."

"Right there with you, sister. I seriously need a caffeine jolt."

Kate smiled at her "sister" remark. Tommie followed them to the drive-through and then all the way to their house. Kate opened the passenger door. "You really didn't need to follow us home, but I'm glad you did. I might need you to help me get her in the house." Kate knelt inside the car door, gently squeezing Megan's thigh. "Meg, honey, we're home. Let's go inside."

Megan's head lolled to the side. "Hmm…"

Kate shook her leg. "Come on, Megan, wake up so we can go in the house." Another "hmm…" was all Kate got from her. Kate pulled Megan's legs out of the car, being careful of her injured arm. "Can you help me with her?"

Tommie placed a hand on Kate's shoulder. "Let me. You get the door." She scooped Megan up in her arms. Kate rushed to unlock the door, quickly dropped her things inside and led the way to Megan's room, where she pulled back the covers on the bed. Kate marveled at how easily Tommie carried Megan and how carefully she placed her on the bed. Lacking a father, Megan had missed out on so much. Like a daddy who would cradle her broken body in his arms. Kate was amazed at how natural Tommie looked with Megan in her arms. *A gentle giant*, Kate thought, recalling the previous night when those same strong arms had held and comforted her.

"I can hang around a while if you want to get some sleep. You look exhausted. I can sit in here with her in case she needs anything."

Kate led Tommie out of the room and toward the kitchen. "We'll be able to manage fine, but let me get you something to drink. A cup of coffee or something to keep you awake."

"Only if you're having something yourself."

Kate let out a huge sigh. "I'm thinking a cup of tea would hit the spot about now, but I can make you some coffee."

Tommie crossed her feet at the ankles and leaned back against the counter. "Whatever you're having is fine with me."

Kate motioned to the kitchen table. "Please, sit down and relax."

Even completely exhausted, in rumpled clothes, Kate looked incredibly beautiful. Tommie couldn't keep her eyes off her as she moved about the kitchen.

With the teakettle on the stove she said, "I'll be right back."

Minutes later Kate returned wearing a robe tightly wrapped around her and her hair pulled back. Her face looked freshly scrubbed. "I hope you don't mind," she said, indicating the robe. "I needed to get out of those clothes."

Tommie couldn't find her voice to reply. She was about to have tea with Kate Bellam and all that separated her from Kate's bare, naked skin was a thin layer of chenille. Tommie tried to concentrate on the cup in front of her, but her eyes kept wandering to Kate's tired expression and the exposed skin of her chest that led to the valley between her breasts before disappearing beneath the robe. God, she wanted to hold Kate, maybe kiss her, but definitely soothe the weariness from her body with feather-light touches in just the right places. Deciding to stop torturing herself, Tommie stood up from the table.

"I should get going and you should get some rest."

Kate followed her to the door, catching one of Tommie's hands in hers and turning Tommie back to her. Kate said quietly, "Thank you."

Tommie looked at the small, soft hand holding her much larger one, trying desperately to stop the nervousness and desire that was welling up within her. She only managed to mutter "sure."

Kate didn't release her hand and Tommie feared it was about to tremble the way her insides were. She couldn't recall a time she'd ever felt like this around a woman.

It was a struggle, but she found her voice. "You suppose I could stop back in the next day or so and see how Megan's doing?"

Kate continued to hold onto Tommie's hand. "I think Megan would appreciate that." Then Kate did something totally unexpected. She pushed up, lightly touched her lips to Tommie's cheek and squeezed Tommie's hand. "Thanks." She stepped back, gazing up into Tommie's eyes with her baby blues, looking as sweetly innocent as the day is long.

God, you're beautiful, Tommie thought, but she certainly couldn't say that. She barely managed to say "I'll see you in a few days" before pulling the door open.

"Stop by anytime."

* * *

Kate leaned in the doorway and watched as Tommie walked down the drive to the Jeep. She couldn't begin to imagine why Tommie wasn't in a relationship with someone. She'd make a perfect partner for some young gal looking to start a family. As tough as she looked on the outside, there was clearly a gentle, caring soul within her.

* * *

Tommie followed through and stopped in to see Megan Friday after work. She was much more alert than the last time Tommie had seen her and anxious to return to school. Tommie had a surprise for her. As tired as she had been after seeing Megan and Kate home safely from the hospital, she had driven back to the stadium the day after the accident and, using her press credentials, managed to speak with the player who had hit the foul ball that had landed Megan in the hospital. And coming off a win the previous night, he was happy to sign the ball for the girl.

Tommie presented the ball to Megan, who read the autograph aloud. "To Megan, a great catch, Nat Warner." Her lips curled in delight. "Wow! This is too cool." She turned the ball over in her hand. "Is this scuff where he hit it?" She held the ball out for Tommie's inspection.

"That or it's where it hit your hard head." She poked Megan's arm playfully.

"Really?" Megan asked, "I thought I got clobbered when I fell."

Tommie shrugged. Might as well let the kid think she went down for a good reason. Kate tried unsuccessfully to get Tommie to stay for dinner with them, but after holding Kate in her arms and having Kate place that kiss on her cheek, she just didn't trust herself not to flirt uncontrollably, and Kate deserved better than the behavior Tommie reserved for the women she picked up in bars.

CHAPTER NINE

Time passed, but a day didn't go by that Tommie wasn't thinking about Kate. She'd close her eyes and feel the soft warm skin of her hand and the tender lips that had touched her cheek. Something Tommie couldn't begin to understand made her want Kate more than she'd ever wanted a woman in her life. And Kate was not a woman she could have. And the women she could have were becoming less and less inviting, which only increased her frustration.

After another two weeks Tommie decided she should at least call Megan to see how her arm was doing. She waited until she suspected their dinner hour had passed and settled in her comfy old recliner with a beer and the phone.

"Hey, Tommie!" Megan answered in a bubbly tone. "I was starting to think you just wrote us off"—she giggled at her own play on words—"or fell off the face of the earth."

Tommie took a swig, then lied. "I've been pretty busy, you know, what with the playoffs, then the Series, and football being in full swing now."

"Sorry about the team. It kinda looked like they were going to go all the way...for about five minutes."

Tommie chuckled. Megan must have read or heard that, because those words had been spoken and printed just about everywhere about Tommie's beloved team.

"Yeah, well, there's always next year." She took another sip of beer. "So I called to see how the arm was doing."

"I had to go in two days ago to have it X-rayed. They said it was healing like they hoped and I could probably get this cast off in a month."

"That's good news."

"Yes, I guess I'm just a tough and fast healer."

Tommie laughed again. "I have no doubt about it...the first part anyway."

"Did you want to speak to Aunt Kate?"

Did she ever, Tommie thought. But why? So she could ask her out? So they could date for a while, get married and have kids? There was no good reason for her to need to speak to Kate, other than wanting to hear her voice, but that would only serve to torture her more.

"Tommie?"

"Uh...sorry there, kiddo, I got distracted for a minute. What were you saying?"

"I asked if you wanted to talk to Aunt Kate."

"Oh...no...I don't think there's anything I need to talk to her about. I just wanted to check on you and...uh, good news on the arm. So, I'll let you go and check back again in a few weeks."

"Okay, thanks, Tommie."

Tommie clicked off the phone and dropped it on the table. *Hell yes*, she wanted to talk to Kate—more than she wanted the beer in her hand. She closed her eyes and remembered the warm hand and soft lips one more agonizing time.

* * *

Kate had been folding laundry off the kitchen when she'd heard Megan's voice through the wall, then decided it could have just been something on her computer. When Megan entered the laundry room she startled Kate, causing her to put her hand to her chest to slow her racing heart.

"Sorry," Megan said in all sincerity. "You'll never guess who just called me."

"Hum…" Kate thought for a moment. "The president's personal assistant."

Megan laughed. "No, silly, it was Tommie."

Kate's heart picked up the rapid rate again. She tried to sound casual when she responded. "Oh, really. And what was she calling about? Did her team win their thing…" —she waved a hand around—"that thing they were trying to win?" She already knew the answer, but she didn't want Megan to question why she was suddenly following baseball.

Megan laughed again. "No, her team"—she mocked Kate's hand gesture—"didn't win their thing. She just called to see how my arm is." Kate raised her eyes to look at Megan. "I think it's sweet she called to check on me."

"That was a very thoughtful gesture."

"Yeah, thoughtful. You know…I should have asked her to go with us to the festival Saturday. She likes beer and they have plenty of it there. Better still"—she laid her phone on the dryer—"*you* should call and invite her. Then she won't have to wonder if I have permission to be asking."

Megan quickly left the laundry room, leaving Kate to either invite Tommie or provide Megan a good excuse for not doing so. Tommie had crept into Kate's thoughts more than she'd thought the woman should since Megan's accident, but Kate had decided to chalk it up to Tommie's likeable, friendly personality. When she couldn't come up with a good reason for Tommie not to join them at the festival, she let the phone redial the last number received and chewed her lip while she listened to the phone ring once, twice…

* * *

Tommie was surprised to see Megan's name reappear on her phone. "Hey, did you forget to ask me if I could get tickets to a pro football game?" She wasn't expecting the response she received.

"I detest football, it's so…so brutal," she heard Kate say in a low tone.

Tommie immediately sat up straighter in her recliner. "Kate—uh, hi! I thought it was Megan calling back."

"Yes, well, she wanted me to call and invite you to go to the fall festival with us downtown on Saturday."

Before Tommie could stop them, the words tumbled out. "And did you want me to go with you too?" She realized how lame she just sounded. *How very schoolgirl—like, I like you, do you like me?* But she couldn't take it back now.

"Actually, I thought it would be nice if you could either join us or meet us there."

Tommie paused to make sure she sounded completely indifferent when she said, "Uh, yeah, sure, I can probably meet you there at some point. Maybe I can just call Megan's phone and catch up with you two that way?"

"Sure, that would be fine. Megan never strays far from her phone. So call us and we can meet for some of that wonderful festival food. And I'll treat, because if I recall correctly, I still owe you a meal."

Tommie chuckled. "You don't owe me anything, but if you feel so obliged, I guess I better show up so you can unburden yourself of that debt." *Did Kate sound a little flustered?* Tommie wondered. Or was that just wishful thinking on her part? She hoped she sounded more composed herself, but somehow she doubted it.

* * *

"Then it's a date, sometime between noon and one." Kate felt like a teenager. She groaned silently. *I hope I didn't sound like one.*

"Okay, so I'll just call Megan when I get there and we'll figure out where to meet up." Tommie's response sounded…sedate. Unlike the excited anticipation Kate felt bubbling up at the prospect of seeing Tommie again.

"Wonderful, we'll see you Saturday. I'm sure Megan's anxious to see you." Kate added quietly, "I think she misses seeing you every day." *And even if Megan doesn't miss you,* Kate thought, *I do.*

She carried a stack of Megan's laundry to her room, the cell phone perched on top of it like a royal scepter on a velvet pillow. "Tommie is going to call your phone and meet us downtown on Saturday."

Megan grabbed her phone. "That's cool, but you should have given her your number."

"And why is that, young lady? I do believe this was your idea."

"Because now I have to hang around waiting for her to call. All my friends will be there and I'll be standing around…" She exhaled loudly.

"Megan, I seriously doubt you will be ostracized by your friends if you are seen with me or with Tommie, for that matter. Again, I remind you, it was your idea for me to invite her."

Megan's shoulders slumped. "I know. I just thought if Tommie came, you guys could hang out, you know, and I could hang with my friends." She held both hands before her, palms up. "You know." She raised one hand. "Teenagers." Then she lifted the other. "Older adults." A frown creased Kate's face as she eyed Megan, but she said nothing. Megan shifted nervously in her desk chair before trying again. "I just meant"—she made the same hand gestures—"big people, little people. Ah, don't be mad, Aunt Kate. I wasn't saying you were old or anything."

Kate finally laughed. "Believe me, Megan, I understand. I was a teenager once too. And contrary to what you might think, it wasn't all that long ago."

* * *

Tommie stopped in at Gurlz Club Friday evening for a couple of beers on her way home.

When she got up to leave just before eight, Tammy asked, confused, "You buggin' out of here before the babes arrive?"

"Yep." Tommie slapped a few extra bills on the bar.

Tammy cocked her head. "You got a woman at home keeping tabs on you or something? You barely come in anymore, and when you do you seem all kinds of distracted and always seem to leave alone." When Tommie just shrugged, Tammy leaned closer. "You either got a woman stashed at home or you're not really Tommie, you're a clone."

Tommie laughed. "You're right there, Sherlock." She spun quickly on her heel and left Tammy standing there with a questioning expression.

Despite the two additional beers she had at home before she turned in at midnight, Tommie woke just after six. After tossing and turning for more than a half an hour she gave up on sleeping. Once the coffee had brewed, she paced the confines of her small apartment, her anxiousness increasing with every sip of caffeine.

She had a "date with Kate." Kate had actually called it that. Even though she tried to convince herself that she had only used the word as part of a standard line, Tommie's heart was palpitating at the thought of spending time with her.

She forced herself into the shower around nine, then drove to the paper. Making herself do some work would be a good distraction for a few hours. And it almost worked too. She got a couple things cleared off her desk, but she also watched the clock persistently. At eleven forty-five she headed to her car for the ten-minute drive to the location of the festival. She was walking the several blocks to the park when her phone rang.

It was Megan. "Hey, Tommie, are you still coming down?"

"Sure. I'm about half a block from the park. What's up?"

"My friends are standing around, waiting on me, and I don't want to leave Aunt Kate waiting alone. Besides, she might get mad."

"Where are you?"

"She's looking at stuff in a tent next to the statue of the guy with the gun."

Tommie chuckled at Megan's description of the military soldier statue and her obvious eagerness to be off with her friends. "I'll be there in less than five minutes. You think you can hold on that long, kiddo?"

Megan sighed. "Do I have a choice?"

Tommie laughed again. "That's between you and your aunt, but I'm almost to the park entrance. I'll see you in a few." As Tommie approached the statue she saw Megan standing with a group of girls. When she stepped behind Megan, tapping her on the shoulder, the girl jumped and spun around.

"Hi, Tommie! Am I glad you're here! Tell Aunt Kate to call me if she's ready to go before I find her later."

"Sure thing—" she stopped before calling her "kiddo" and embarrassing Megan in front of her friends. "See you later."

They were gone in a flash. Tommie stood on the spot where the girls had been so Kate could find her. A few minutes later she emerged from the tent. Tommie saw her before Kate noticed her and, remaining hidden behind her sunglasses, turned and pretended to read the plaque at the base of the statue. When Kate stepped behind her and spoke, she could have melted from the sound of her voice.

"Hello."

"Hi!"

Kate responded with a dazzling smile that made Tommie's heart pitter-patter. "I see the girls abandoned you."

"I sent them on their way. They had better things to do than stand around with me. You know how teenagers are."

Kate rolled her eyes. "Yes, better than I ever thought that I would." She checked her watch. "What shall we do, eat, shop or have a beer?"

"I didn't think you liked beer. Do you?"

"Well, no, but you can certainly have one. Isn't that one of the big draws for this festival, all the different beers?"

"It is, but just because I'm a big beer drinker doesn't mean—"

Kate cut her off. "I'm sorry, I didn't mean to insinuate anything." When Kate's fingers brushed lightly down her arm, Tommie's heart jumped to her throat. "I just meant if you truly enjoy drinking beer you should…" She stopped. *She's nervous*, Tommie thought, and when she chuckled Kate joined her.

"I do enjoy beer and there is one I wanted to try today, but I thought I might do that when we eat, whenever that may be, and now or later is okay with me. Are you finished shopping?"

Kate looked sheepishly at the single bag in her hand, then up at Tommie. "Well…"

"I don't want to plan your day for you, but why don't we do the shopping thing, then take a break and eat something? I can have my beer then."

"You don't strike me as the shopping type."

Tommie locked her gaze on the sunglasses that were hiding Kate's magnificently blue eyes. "Are you assuming I have a what… personal shopper to pick up my groceries and pick out my clothes? Or do you think my mom still does that for me?" She shoved her hands in her pockets and fought to maintain a serious expression as she played with Kate.

"I guess if I want to know something I should ask instead of assume."

Tommie shrugged. "That's what I do." *Well, most times*, she thought. "What with being a reporter and all." She hesitated before answering Kate's unasked question. "I don't shop for sport." She gave a wide grin at her pun. "But I do my own grocery shopping and I don't mind too much when I have to go clothes shopping."

She so wanted a look at Kate's incredible eyes. "It's a beautiful day, so let's shop. I'm sure there are all kinds of unique and interesting things in all these tents." She turned in a slow circle.

"There are only a couple of things I'm looking for. Then we'll get some food and sit down to enjoy this beautiful day."

Tommie nodded and signaled Kate to lead the way. Tommie couldn't care less if she ate or ever had a beer. She was enjoying being with Kate and very glad to be hidden behind her sunglasses so she could allow her eyes to investigate every inch of the beautiful woman in her company.

Sometime later—Tommie hadn't kept track of the time, but she was carrying six shopping bags for Kate—Kate said, "I'm starved. Let's get some food."

Balancing the plate like a waitress while carrying the bags, Tommie located a table in the shade of a big old oak tree.

Once Kate was seated, she said, "I'm going for a beer. What can I get you to drink?"

"Just water, thanks." Pushing up her sunglasses Kate dug in her purse for some money. "Here, wait."

Tommie rushed off toward the big semitruck with the long lines.

While they ate they talked a little, Tommie asking about Megan and her going off to college the following year and Kate asking Tommie about the baseball team. Eventually they were done eating and sitting across from one another in an awkward silence. They began to speak simultaneously, and after volleying back and forth Kate convinced Tommie to go ahead.

"If this is being too nosy, just tell me okay?" When Kate bowed her head slightly, Tommie asked, "Where are Megan's parents?"

Kate seemed momentarily surprised by the question, then met Tommie's eyes. "They're both gone. Megan's father took off when she was a toddler. My sister handled it very well, which I was glad for because he was an ass and I'm certain would have made a terrible father." Kate hesitated, taking a drink of water before dropping the big one on Tommie. "Megan's mom died from a brain tumor when she was eight." Kate's eyes glistened with unshed tears.

Tommie felt all the air rush from her lungs, immediately regretting having asked the question. "God, Kate, I'm so sorry...I shouldn't have—"

Kate reached across and placed her hand on Tommie's hand and said in a quivering voice, "It's okay. It's going on ten years now, and we've managed to move past it."

Tommie felt like a heel. "Unfortunately," Tommie said, "I have this habit of—"

Kate stopped her again with a squeeze of the hand still resting on Tommie's. "It's really okay." She tipped her head. "I actually wondered why you hadn't asked about it before now."

"I figured Megan would tell me and when she didn't I thought…" She held Kate's gaze. "I thought maybe it was something you didn't talk about and…I didn't want to pry." She shrugged. "So essentially you've been Megan's mother? You've raised her?"

Kate nodded. "Yes and no." She took another drink of water before continuing. "I never expected Megan to think of me as her mother and I told her so. She was young, only eight, as I said, but she understood what happened to her mom and I made sure she knew it was okay to keep a big part of her heart for only her mom. She asked about calling me 'mom' when she was about ten, I think, but I told her I like the sound of Aunt Kate. I couldn't possibly replace her mom. Nikki was one of a kind."

Tommie didn't want to pry for more details, Kate's pained expression was tearing at her heart, but she figured since she had Kate talking she might as well say it. "And you never married." She decided it could be a statement or question, however Kate wanted to take it.

Kate picked at the napkin under her water bottle. "I was in what I had thought was a serious relationship. It's amazing how fast some people run at the mention of kids." She shrugged. "Megan's been my focus. She'd already had more to deal with than any child should."

Tommie raised her beer to Kate as a salute. "You've done a good job as far as I can see. She's a great kid."

"Thanks, we manage pretty well together. So what about you?" asked Kate, feeling awkward and a bit shy as she did so. She couldn't seem to stop her mouth. "Are you in a relationship, have a significant other or partner?" There, she'd finally put it out there. Tommie had never said she was gay, but what Kate witnessed at the bar made it impossible to conclude anything else.

Tommie's eyes went wide at first, then she said, "Gosh, Kate, I thought you'd never ask." Kate could feel her face blushing with color. "I'm sorry, that was uncalled for," Tommie quickly added.

Kate didn't take her eyes off Tommie as she spoke. " I kind of figured, but I wouldn't necessarily throw it in someone's face, you know. I mean I don't want to make you feel uncomfortable around me." Kate shook her head. "Who you do, or don't, sleep with is of no concern to me. As long as it's not my niece." Kate narrowed her eyes at Tommie before she laughed lightly and patted Tommie's hand. "I'm kidding."

Tommie laughed too. "Of course you are." She leaned in close. "As cute as Megan is, she's a little young for my taste." *God*, she thought, *did I really just say that? Shut your mouth now, Tommie. That was an inappropriate and inexcusably crude thing to say to Kate of all people.* "I prefer my women a little more mature." She paused. "Not that Megan's immature, she's..." Tommie put her finger to her lips, then said, "I probably should just shut up." *Yeah, before the hole you're digging is big enough to swallow your big ass!*

Kate sensed Tommie's naturally in-control nature shifting toward flustered and was enjoying the tiniest bit her ability to cause it.

When Kate didn't say a word, Tommie finally said, "No...no one, no commitments. Truth is, I've never really seen myself as the settling-down type." Tommie chuckled and leaned in close. "Maybe if I grow up someday, I will." She lifted a shoulder. "When I'm done sowing all my wild oats, that is."

Kate was too busy listening to Tommie to pay much attention to the woman approaching their table—not, that is, until she stepped behind Tommie and placed her hands on her shoulders.

"Hey, Tommie Boy...fancy seeing you here."

The woman's tone sounded flirtatious and somehow familiar to Kate. Tommie swiveled sideways in her chair as the woman ruffled her already unruly hair. The woman pushed her own dark sunglasses atop her head.

"Hey, Carly...wow!" Tommie looked at her protruding belly. "Are you ready to pop or what?"

When Carly smiled at Tommie's remark, Kate had a flash of memory. "I've got about ten weeks to go still."

Tommie immediately stood, directing her to the chair. "Sit down here." She touched Carly's lower back. "That just looks painful to carry around."

Carly poked a finger into Tommie's ribs, making her jump back, then settled into the chair.

Kate held her breath. If she'd passed the dark-haired woman on the street she wasn't sure if she would have recognized her, not in her current condition. But did the woman remember her? *Good Lord, please do not remember me.*

Carly looked up at Tommie and cleared her throat. "Aren't you going to introduce me to your friend?"

Tommie jerked her head, her eyes meeting Carly's. "Oh, sorry. Carly, this is Kate Bellam. Kate, this is an old friend, Carly Torres." Kate thought Tommie seemed even more flustered than before.

Carly reached a magnificently manicured hand across the table, offering Kate a comfortable handshake. "Very nice to meet you, Kate."

"You too," Kate barely managed to say.

While still holding onto Kate's hand, Carly glanced at Tommie. "I always knew Tommie would get snagged by a pretty young thing like you...Kate." She locked her eyes back on Kate's.

Kate could feel the flush creeping up her neck as Tommie stuttered, "Uh, no...Kate's not..." Tommie shook her head, "We're not...you know." Tommie swallowed noticeably. "Kate and I are..." She gave Kate a questioning look. "Friends, right? Just friends. Her niece worked with me during the summer in an internship program."

Kate gave a slight nod in Tommie's direction while Carly gave her a knowing gaze. "Of course, how silly of me to assume you two were—well, never mind." When she pushed on the table to stand, Tommie slipped a hand under her arm to assist her. "I'll let you two get back to your lunch." She placed a light kiss on Tommie's cheek. "Always good to see you, sweetheart." Tommie blushed and Carly turned to Kate. "And nice to meet you, Kate." She poked Tommie in the side and said, "Watch out for this one, she's a charmer."

Kate nodded, feeling her cheeks flame. She kept her eyes on Tommie as she watched Carly waddle away. When she turned back to Kate, Tommie's blush was still evident and curiosity was getting the better of Kate.

When Tommie dropped back into her chair, Kate asked with the lift of a brow, "So, an old friend, huh?"

"Yeah." Tommie looked over her shoulder in time to see Carly disappear into a crowd. "She's a great gal." Tommie shrugged.

A "great" gal, Kate thought, remembering her night with Carly. *How about incredibly arousing, amazingly sensual or maybe wickedly awesome, as the teens would say? Just great? Tommie, Tommie, what is it you do for a living—write?* Kate continued to keep her eyes intently on Tommie.

"She's not married or anything." When Kate tipped her head, Tommie leaned in over the table. "She's like me, you know, even though no one would ever suspect it. We used to go out a while back."

Kate wagged a finger. "Did you, you know, help her get pregnant?"

"No way." Tommie laughed. "Not me. I don't do kids."

Remembering the fundraiser months earlier and the tender way Tommie had held Megan in her arms after her injury, Kate simply said, "Right."

At the designated time they met Megan with Ashley and her dad back where they had split up earlier. Megan begged Kate to allow her to hang with Ashley and after assurances that her dad would deliver Megan safely home, Tommie and Kate left the festival. Tommie, being the gentlewoman, insisted on helping carry Kate's purchases to her car.

After the packages were secured in the trunk Tommie held Kate's door. "Thanks for the invite. It was very thoughtful."

"You're welcome, but I can't take the credit. It was Megan's idea for me to invite you." Kate slid behind the wheel. "I'm sure the plan was to get you here so she could ditch me for her friends."

"In that case, tell Megan I said thanks. It was fun," Tommie closed the door.

Kate started the car and powered down the window. "Yes, I enjoyed myself. We'll have to do something fun again."

"Yes, we will."

Kate watched Tommie, staring after her in the rearview mirror. She had thought she would choke when Carly had joined them briefly. She wasn't sure if the woman was just being polite when she excused her assumption about Kate and Tommie or if, in fact, she hadn't recognized or remembered Kate. She hoped the latter because if she did know who Kate was she might share that with Tommie privately at some point.

It didn't surprise Kate that Tommie and Carly were friends or more than that. She suspected there was no shortage of attractive women in Denton and elsewhere who would want to be with the big butch softie. Even though Carly was older than herself, Kate figured the woman wouldn't be any more immune to Tommie's charms.

* * *

Tommie stood in the street watching as Kate drove off. Carly's appearance at the festival and her assumptions had thrown Tommie, but Kate had seemed to take it all in stride. Had Carly somehow been able to discern her feelings for the beautiful blond? And if she had, was Kate able to pick up on it too? Tommie could have hugged Megan for the selfishness that had allowed her to see Kate today. Being around Kate was better than—well, almost anything she could think of. She shook her head and started off in search of her own vehicle.

She could hardly miss the raven-haired woman leaning against the front of her Jeep as she strode up the street. Stopping a few feet away, she engaged Carly's dark eyes. "Hey."

"Where's your pretty blond?" Carly asked.

"She went home, and I told you she's not mine." Tommie paused a moment, taking in Carly standing there so casually. She decided it was true what they said about pregnant women being beautiful. She had never seen Carly look so enticing. "So what are you doing hanging around? Shouldn't you be home with your feet propped up or something?"

Carly looked up at Tommie through long dark lashes. "I was on my way when I saw your Jeep." She reached out and hooked her finger in the waist of Tommie's pants. "I thought I'd try and bum a ride."

"You walked here?"

"I did. It's only five or six blocks." She tugged on Tommie's waistband as Tommie looked around nervously. "Give a girl a ride home?"

Tommie returned her eyes to Carly's, giving a slow nod. How could she refuse a pregnant woman? "Sure, come on."

Tommie helped her up in the Jeep and drove them slowly toward the downtown loft she had probably spent more time in than at any other woman's place. She'd thought briefly when they were seeing each other on a pretty regular basis that Carly might be the kind of woman she could live with. Then one night after a rather raucous romp in the sack, Carly had snuggled up to her and started asking questions about Tommie's future plans. When she mentioned that she wanted kids, Tommie knew it was time to cut and run. She couldn't see herself as a parent. She thought perhaps she'd been passed over by the nurturing gene. They had only been together once since then. It was the night after they left the downtown bar too intoxicated for Tommie to drive. The plan was that she'd sleep it off on Carly's couch. She slept it off, all right. In Carly's bed, after mind-blowing sex. She promised herself it wouldn't happen again, and it hadn't.

Tommie parked half a block from the loft and raced around to help Carly out.

She held onto Tommie's arm. "Thanks, you're such a sweetheart."

Tommie felt a tiny tingle, but she ignored it. "You're welcome."

Carly squeezed and gave her arm a tug. "Come up and have a beer. You can help me pick out the baby's name." Carly's eyes gazed up hypnotically at her.

Tommie got a nervous twitter in her stomach. "I can't. I should get going."

Carly persisted. "Come on, Tommie. I promise to be on my best behavior."

Tommie regarded her for a moment before giving in. "Okay." She held up one finger. "One beer, and you promise."

"Scout's honor." She looped her arm through Tommie's as they strolled down the sidewalk.

Carly disappeared into the kitchen while Tommie took a seat on the couch, picking up one of the several baby name books from the coffee table. She returned barefoot minutes later, handing Tommie a cold beer and perching on the coffee table in front of her.

Taking a long drink of the beer first, Tommie asked, "Do you know if it's a girl or a boy?"

"No. I want to be surprised." She absently rubbed her extended belly. "That sounds kind of old-fashioned, doesn't it?"

Tommie shrugged. "To each his own."

Suddenly looking surprised, Carly sat up very straight, pressing her palm against her belly.

"What's wrong?" Tommie asked, alarmed by Carly's movement and expression. "Are you all right?"

"I'm fine. The baby's kicking." She reached out to Tommie. "Give me your hand. You have to feel this."

Tommie knew her face probably showed her fear.

"Don't be silly, it's not like it can bite you...yet."

Tommie reached out her hand tentatively, allowing Carly to place it against her abdomen. Her hand jerked involuntarily at the first movement. Then she was awestruck.

"Wow! That's pretty amazing to think you got this little person inside you."

When she sipped the last of her beer, Carly asked, "You want another?"

The pure sensuality that Carly exuded gave Tommie pause—for a long moment. "Nah, I should get going."

When Tommie shifted to get up, Carly stood, placing a hand on her shoulder. "You don't have to run off, do you?"

Tommie gazed up into eyes dark as a moonless night. *God*, she thought, *she's such an incredibly alluring woman.* She eased back on the couch under the insistent hand on her shoulder, and without warning Carly straddled her, lowering herself into her lap. Tommie squirmed with the familiar feel of arousal. She looked away from Carly's mesmerizing gaze, then finally choked out, "You promised to behave."

Carly stroked a painted nail down Tommie's cheek and under her chin, tipping her head up to look in her eyes.

"If I recall correctly, I promised my best behavior. And when have I ever given you anything less?" Tommie's thigh muscles clenched as she closed her eyes.

"Tommie...are you telling me you don't want what you know I can give you?" Tommie looked into her eyes but said nothing. Carly pleaded, "I need you to touch me so badly." She worked herself deeper into Tommie's lap. "Please, I promise you won't go away disappointed." She slid her hand between them, curling her fingers around Tommie's heat. She purred, "Oh, baby, I want you." Leaning in she nibbled on Tommie's neck.

Tommie dropped her head back against the couch in defeat. "I've never—"

Carly silenced her. "It's easy, hon." She pulled up her sweater and pulled out the stretch panel on her pants. "Maternity clothes are made for easy access...see."

Tommie knew as she slipped her hand in and past the damp curls that Carly would be slick with invitation. Carly emitted a low moan as Tommie's fingers slid back and forth through her folds.

Carly's hands clamped onto Tommie's shoulders. "Oh, God, yes...that feels so...good."

Tommie's fingers teased at her opening as she watched Carly's desire smolder in her dark eyes. Tommie reminded herself she was doing this as a favor only and for no other reason.

In a throaty voice she asked, "You want me...right here?" She slipped a finger through the contracting muscles, and Carly responded by pushing herself against it. She leaned forward, pressing her cheek to Tommie's.

Barely above a whisper, she begged, "Please, Tommie, make me come."

Pulling her finger out slowly, Tommie said in a hushed tone, "I don't want to hurt you."

Carly gasped, "No baby, you won't." She pressed her lips closer to Tommie's ear. "Please fill me."

When Tommie's two fingers hesitated to enter Carly completely, she pushed down hard on Tommie's hand. Tommie heard the air rush from Carly's lungs as she pleaded, "Oh...yes, baby, don't stop."

Tommie moved in and out with the rhythm of Carly's hips until she felt her muscles tighten fiercely in an effort to hold Tommie inside her. With one last thrust, Carly shuddered, releasing a "God...yes" and slumping against Tommie's shoulder, her breath hot against Tommie's neck.

As Carly's breath evened out, she whispered, "I want to make you come, Tommie Boy. I want to taste how much you want me." She once again pushed her hand between them to cup Tommie. "Mmm..." she murmured against Tommie's neck. "I can feel how much you want to come." When Carly fumbled to unbutton her pants, Tommie caught her hand. "Let me have you, baby."

Tommie didn't release her firm grip on her hand. "I can't," she sighed heavily. "I'm sorry...I can't."

Carly leaned back and stroked Tommie's cheek. "I'm probably the one who should be sorry for seducing you." She eased off Tommie's lap and sat beside her. "You want to talk about it?"

Tommie felt her guard go up. "There's nothing to talk about."

Carly shifted to face her. "Tommie, I have you hotter than a wildfire and you don't want my mouth on you. Something is definitely wrong." She took Tommie's hand in hers. "Come on, talk to me."

Tommie just shrugged and avoided Carly's eyes. Those eyes had the power to extract most anything she wanted from Tommie.

"It's the pretty blond, isn't it?"

Tommie huffed too quickly in response, "No..." She leaned forward, picking up her beer bottle. Discovering it empty, she set it back on the table. She wanted a beer, not to talk about Kate. Irritated, she said, "I told you we're just friends. Besides, she's straight."

"Since when has that ever stopped you?"

Tommie pushed up from the couch, angry, and crossed the room. Jamming her hands in her pockets she fumed. She was hot and wet, and she wanted to come. But not with Carly. She wanted the soft touch of Kate Bellam to bring her to orgasm and that seemed so wrong to Tommie for so many reasons. Carly interrupted the beating Tommie was giving herself when her belly brushed against Tommie's backside.

"It's okay to care about someone, you know." She hugged Tommie from behind. "I do."

Tommie stiffened as the panic rose in her chest. She extracted herself from Carly's embrace and said, "I gotta go," moving swiftly to the door.

Carly called out. "If you think you love her Tommie, go tell her."

And Tommie was gone with a slam of the door.

She drove past The Underground but didn't stop, instead heading for her favorite place on her side of town. She was more than a little upset with herself for her apparent inability now to have sex with women for the sheer pleasure of it. She couldn't fathom how a crush on a straight woman could dampen her formerly overactive libido.

"Damn it, Kate Bellam," she cursed as she passed by the other bar and headed for home. "How on earth did you get to me?"

* * *

Megan called an hour after Kate arrived home to ask if she could spend the night at Ashley's. She had the house to herself or—she thought for a brief moment—she could go out. Frustration settled with the realization that she couldn't go out, probably ever again. Running into Carly today was a reminder she could end up bumping into someone she absolutely didn't want to in a women's bar. Someone like Tommie. That had already happened, though Tommie didn't know it. Kate couldn't stop wondering how it would feel. To be in a place where she could be herself and have Tommie's charms and all of her attention focused on only her. She closed her eyes, imagining Tommie holding her in a slow dance and those big strong arms of hers holding her solidly against Tommie's body.

Good Lord, Kate thought, *that's the last thing that can ever happen.* She couldn't come out. What would Megan think of her? Even though Megan seemed to accept Tommie and was, Kate was certain, aware of her preference for women, Megan had never thought of Kate in that way and she wasn't sure if her niece could accept or handle it. Kate had vowed almost ten years earlier not to be a source of hurt or disappointment in Megan's life if it was within her means to prevent it. She poured a glass of wine, started the bath and dug out her little bathtub friend to help scratch that itch burning deep inside.

CHAPTER TEN

Nearly a month passed before Tommie and Kate spoke again. Kate finally mustered the nerve on the Sunday before Thanksgiving to give her a call.

Tommie didn't recognize the number, but the prefix seemed familiar.

"Hello."

"Tommie, hi, it's Kate."

Tommie immediately straightened her posture as if Kate could somehow tell she was slouching in her recliner. "Hi!" Tommie responded cheerily.

"We haven't spoken in a while. How have you been?"

Tommie wondered why Kate's normally confident voice sounded so off. "Doin' okay. Is everything okay with Megan?" She wondered if that was the reason for Kate's call out of the blue.

"Megan is Megan. She's just fine, the cast is off and her arm is good as new."

Tommie's voice took on a deeper, richer quality. "And you?"

"I'm just fine too."

Tommie's first thought was to agree wholeheartedly, but that would be inappropriate.

When the silence became deafening, Kate finally said, "The reason I'm calling is"—Tommie's heart raced in anticipation—"I was wondering if you had plans for Thanksgiving."

Tommie's heart dropped to the pit of her stomach as she slouched back in the chair. "Yeah, I'm driving to see my parents. They live just outside Chicago."

"That sounds like a great way to spend Thanksgiving, with your family. Are your—brothers, right?—going to be there as well?"

Tommie couldn't muster the enthusiasm Kate's voice held. "Just my oldest brother Mark and his wife and three boys."

"That sounds like a wonderful time. Guess I...we don't have to rescue you from a microwave turkey dinner, then. Maybe some other time. Have a safe trip."

"Thanks," was all Tommie could think to say.

"Well, then, maybe I'll talk to you again...sometime."

Kate sounded disappointed, or was she imagining it? "Sure" was all Tommie managed in response.

"Have a good evening."

"You too." When Tommie heard the click of Kate hanging up she dropped the phone in her lap and leaned her head back. "Damn it!"

She wondered how she could get out of her family commitment and if she did what Kate would think of her for blowing off a family gathering for a meal with a casual acquaintance. After all, that's what they were—just acquaintances. Kate had made such a deal about Tommie being with family for the holiday. She raised the phone and pulled up her parents' number and stared at it for a long while before she cursed again, "Damn," and tossed it aside.

* * *

Megan bounded into the kitchen. "Aunt Kate, are you okay?"

"Hmm..." Kate slowly turned her gaze to Megan.

"You seemed so far away. Is everything okay?"

Standing, she shook off her disappointment. "Sure, sweetie. I was just thinking about some work stuff." She brushed her hand lightly down Megan's previously injured arm on her way to the sink. "What are you up to this evening?" As Kate dumped the remnants of her tea, Megan pushed herself up on the counter.

When Kate turned around she asked, "Do you suppose I could invite Ashley over for Thanksgiving dinner?"

"Doesn't she have plans with her family?"

Megan sighed. "Her parents are getting a divorce and things are pretty crappy for her now. I thought she might like to get away from it for a day." She hopped off the counter. "Please."

Kate took Megan's face in her hands. "You're such a sweetie"—she kissed her forehead lightly—"and a good friend."

Megan squirmed in her grasp. "Is that a yes?"

"Yes, Ashley can have Thanksgiving dinner with us."

Megan started to bolt from the room, then suddenly halted. "Hey, you ought to invite Tommie too."

Kate leaned a hip against the counter. "Perhaps I will."

Megan disappeared.

* * *

Neither woman could come up with a good reason for phoning the other on a whim so another month passed. Kate considered inviting Tommie to join them for Christmas dinner, but she assumed she would be spending the holiday with her family in Chicago. Tommie kept hoping for an invite from Kate. She was fully prepared to make a quick drive to her parents, stay a few hours and return home in a hurry if Kate invited her to do anything at all, but, disappointingly, she didn't.

While out shopping for her nephews two days before Christmas Tommie had a brainstorm about how to give Megan a memorable gift to commemorate her internship. Knowing her own wrapping wasn't going to cut it, she rushed home to pick it up and back to the mall to have it specially wrapped, then tucked the package in her glove box. She had a plan that she hoped would provide the opportunity to see Kate. She spent Christmas Eve at her parents', sleeping in her old room, now converted to an office, on a less-than-comfortable pullout bed. When the presents had all been revealed and dinner was done on Christmas Day, Tommie passed out kisses and hugs, then anxiously headed toward home.

Half an hour outside of town she pulled out her cell phone and dialed the number she'd saved just before Thanksgiving.

Four rings later Tommie was anticipating voice mail and about to hang up when she heard the click and "Merry Christmas!" Kate's voice sounded so warm and dreamy, Tommie thought she felt it physically enter her.

She closed her eyes for a second, then responded. "Kate, hi! Merry Christmas."

The background noise abated. "Are you having a merry visit with your family?"

"I was. I'm almost back to town."

"Back in town?" Kate couldn't stop the words as they tumbled out. "Big date?"

Tommie chuckled. "Nothing like that. I have a little something for Megan. I thought I'd drop it by if she's there and you're not in the middle of some big holiday party."

"No, no parties, so you're welcome to stop by if you want."

"Great, I should be able to get there within the hour."

"No need to rush, we're not going anywhere. Just drive carefully. There's probably more than one idiot on the road today."

"Sure, I'll see you in a little bit."

"Okay."

Kate returned to the sofa and the old holiday movie she and Megan were watching. When the doorbell rang, she actually managed to get to her feet before Megan.

"I'll get it." She pulled the door open to see a smiling Tommie on her doorstep. "Come in."

Megan glanced toward the door briefly. "Hey, Tommie," she looked back again. "What are you doing here?"

Kate tugged on her sleeve. "Let me have your coat."

Tommie shrugged out of her knee-length leather coat, pulling a small shiny box from its pocket before allowing Kate to take it from her. "I had a little Christmas gift for you, Megan." As she handed over the package, she noticed the bowl of popcorn and the movie playing on the TV. "I've interrupted."

Kate said quickly, "No, no, we've seen this movie more than once. You're not interrupting anything." She moved to sit on the arm of the couch next to Megan.

Megan turned the slender, rectangular package over in her hands, studying it, until Tommie finally asked impatiently, "Well… are you going open it or make me take it back?"

Megan carefully tore away the red bow and ribbon before ripping into the silver foil paper. The black case didn't give any clues to its contents. Megan undid the snap in the middle and flipped open the two pieces of the top. Her eyes widened at the sight of the shiny black pen. "Oh—wow!" Megan gasped, carefully lifting the pen from the plushly lined interior of the case. "Aunt Kate, look, it's a real Mont Blanc pen. Wow, Tommie, thanks!"

Kate noticed the look of gentle satisfaction on Tommie's face as Megan turned the pen over in her hands and marveled as if it contained some unseen power.

"What's this?" Megan asked, pointing to the script on the cap. "It's the same as what's on the case." She closed half of the case's top. "And this?" She indicated the deep blue sapphire on the cap's clip.

"It's a special edition and that is the signature of someone famous." Megan looked at her expectantly. "I doubt you've heard of her, but I bet your Aunt Kate has." Tommie winked at Kate. "Marlene Dietrich."

"Well?" Megan looked at her aunt.

"Tommie is correct. She was an actress from many years ago, known for her glamour and exotic looks. She was still making movies into her fifties." Megan appeared astonished by Kate's knowledge and Tommie looked on curiously. "I enjoy old movies, right, Megan?"

Megan rolled her eyes. "Oh yeah. Like the first ones ever made…before there was color." She snickered, turning the pen over in her fingers again.

"I first learned of this iconic actress while researching a paper in college. I discovered her last piece of work was a documentary film about her life in nineteen eighty-four—my birth year." Tommie had been fasinated by her body of work, and after watching nearly every film she'd made, she had developed a serious "admiration" for the German-born actress with the melodic, sultry voice. Tommie's cheeks warmed as the memory of how she came to own the pen filled her mind.

"So, my big-mouth brother, Mark, told Mom I had this 'obsession,'" she gestured quotations, "for Marlene Dietrich and thus this became my graduation gift. Anyway, enough history." Tommie noted the look of concern Kate was suddenly wearing and raised a hand. "You deserve it for all your hard work. I probably learned as much as you did from the experience." *Some pretty serious, adult things I sure wasn't expecting.* "I really want you to have it. It's a keepsake so take good care of it—it's made to last a lifetime. I have no doubt you'll pen many a great work with it."

Megan leaned in and placed a kiss on Tommie's cheek so quickly that Tommie didn't see it coming, then jumped up. "I've got to go try this out. Thanks, Tommie, you're the best."

Tommie watched as Megan disappeared down the hall, then stood and turned her dark eyes to Kate. "I should get going."

Kate hopped up. "Stay and at least have something to drink."

For the first time since she'd come in, Tommie looked Kate over—from the lightweight red sweater that hugged her full breasts down to her snug-fitting jeans and socked feet. Man, did she ever look good. Like the perfect Christmas package.

Kate took a step toward her, drawing Tommie's eyes back up to meet hers. "I have eggnog." Tommie crinkled her nose. "Okay." Kate thought for a moment before turning to the kitchen. "I don't have any beer, but I have wine." Tommie followed like an eager puppy until Kate stopped in the kitchen, freezing Tommie in the doorway. "Or I can make some coffee or tea."

"Uh…coffee would be great it it's not too much trouble."

Kate motioned Tommie to the table. "Not at all. Have a seat. It only takes a few minutes to brew."

Tommie watched, envious that Megan had this woman to take care of her. The thought surprised her. She hadn't felt a need to have someone take care of her since she was probably fifteen, except for sexual needs. Kate's every move made Tommie want to run her fingers through the blond hair that fell like silk over her shoulders and kiss along her jawline and down to the hollow of her neck.

Suddenly Kate was sliding a steaming cup of coffee in front of her and asking with concern, "Are you okay, Tommie?"

Tommie nodded. "Yeah." Wrapping her hands around the warm mug, she watched Kate slide into the chair across the table. "My nephews had the whole house up before the rooster ever crowed this morning. I'm just a little worn out." She raised the cup. "But I'm sure this will help." She blew the steam away and took a sip.

"It must be fun…and exhausting to have little ones around at Christmas."

Tommie returned the cup to the table. "It is, but I don't know how my brother and his wife manage that every day. They have three." She shook her head. "They're two, four and six. Any one of them alone is enough to wear me out."

Kate watched Tommie's expression over the rim of her cup as she sipped. "So, you don't ever see yourself with kids?"

Tommie snorted. "Me?" Kate nodded. Tommie couldn't meet her eyes so she stared into her cup. "I guess I just figured with me being the way I am...you know, it wasn't an option. Honestly, I've never given much thought to it." She met Kate's eyes briefly. "I'm not so sure I'm good parent material."

Kate absorbed every word but noticed something deeper in Tommie's eyes in the brief moment she glanced up.

"So you ever going to have some kids of your own?"

It was Kate's turn to get lost in the darkness filling the cup in her hands. "I've thought about it, once Megan's gone. I don't think I can be without someone to take care of." She met Tommie's intent gaze. "I just never wanted anything to take my attention and focus from Megan. She deserved..." Kate hesitated. "No, she needed, all of me."

Tommie lifted her cup. "Megan will be out of here when she starts college next fall from what she's told me." Kate nodded. "That's less than nine months away, you better get busy." Tommie gave a playful smile. "Them babies don't make themselves."

Kate's face got warm.

Tommie chuckled lightly. "Sorry, sometimes I have no control over what comes out of my mouth."

Kate just shrugged, then leaned in over the table as if about to share some top-secret information with Tommie. "That's okay, but I am only thirty-three. I don't think my clock has run out yet."

Now Tommie's face flushed. She turned her palms up. "See, it just shows how much I know about the whole parenting and baby thing."

Kate sat back. She suspected Tommie knew a lot about a lot more things than she let on.

"So, you have some big plans for New Year's?"

Kate dreaded thinking about the plans she'd been talked into by Christy, a friend at work. She had tried to get out of it, but Christy and the other girls had been relentless, so Kate had finally given in.

"I'm supposed to attend a party with a group of gals from the hospital. You?"

Tommie nodded. "Same—some party everyone's claiming is the party to beat all parties."

"Sounds fun."

Fun? Only if you were going to be there, Tommie thought. She stood. "I need to get going."

Kate jumped to her feet. "So soon?"

Tommie picked up her empty cup, but Kate reached to take it from her, lightly brushing her fingers against Tommie's in the process. Tommie felt warmth surge inside her from the innocent touch.

"Yeah, uh…I have to do some work tomorrow. Sports don't take much of a holiday. I'm lucky to get the few days off I do."

Kate handed Tommie her coat from the closet. "Let me get Megan to—"

"Ah, don't bother her. She might be back there writing the next great American novel. I'd hate to be the one to disrupt the creative flow and all that. Tell her I said to enjoy."

Kate lightly grasped Tommie's wrist. "That was a wonderful gesture, thank you." Her voice was soothing and quiet.

Tommie's shoulders rose in an embarrassed shrug. "I think Megan's got potential."

Kate's hand remained on her wrist, and Tommie glanced quickly at it, enjoying the warmth that was spreading through her like wildfire.

Kate gave a light squeeze before letting go. "And you inspire young people with potential."

Tommie felt the flush creeping up her neck. "Ah, heck Kate… now you're just embarrassing me."

"Well, have a Happy New Year."

"You too." Tommie hated having to go.

* * *

Kate dressed with reluctance for the party. Megan had left an hour earlier with Ashley for a slumber party at another friend's house, so she really didn't have a good excuse not to go out with the girls from the hospital even though she would have rather been spending the evening home alone with a good book and a few glasses of wine. The last New Year's Eve she could recall enjoying had occurred a decade ago. She'd had soft lips to kiss at the stroke of midnight and a reason to be celebrating. She had been in love, for whatever good that had been. Or at least she'd thought that was where she was in her life.

She got to Christy's just before eight thirty, and they arrived at the party fashionably late not long after nine o'clock. They were sought out immediately by the rest of their hospital clique and did what every group of two or more single women did—gossip and survey the crowd for a potential somebody to lock lips with at midnight. Kate wasn't the least bit interested in anyone the girls pointed out, although, there was more than one woman in the crowd she'd be pleased to kiss. She suspected Megan was having a much better time than she was with her friends at the slumber party.

* * *

Tommie didn't want to show her face at this affair she'd been goaded into attending by Carly. Carly, a mere two weeks out from delivery, had said she needed just one night out to dance, flirt and do whatever other unholy, but not unhealthy, things she could squeeze into one night before her child claimed the next eighteen years of her life. Still, Tommie had never failed to have fun with Carly, so she even rented a tux in order to serve as her unofficial escort for the evening.

The party was being held at The Underground so Tommie parked at Carly's loft. They walked the few blocks in the crisp night air, arriving around ten. Vowing to limit herself to no more than two beers so she could drive and not have to crash at Carly's or call a cab, Tommie sipped her first drink slowly and casually surveyed all the women packed into the place.

An hour later, she was taking the first sips of her second beer and trying to have a conversation with the gyrating brunette a few feet away when her cell phone vibrated in her pocket. Megan's name appeared on the screen and her heart stopped.

Loudly she said to the brunette, "I've got to take this," waving her phone and heading toward the alcove by the restrooms.

By the time she reached a spot where she could hear and flipped the phone open, the call was gone. She debated, waiting a few minutes to see if a voice mail would come through. Pacing down the hall past the restrooms she kept looking at the phone in her hand, anxiously waiting for something, a beep or another call. Finally it beeped notification of a voice mail and she dialed, listening with a finger in her other ear. The sound was horrible at best, but she managed to make out Megan's teary voice asking Tommie to please call her if she got her message. She quickly located Carly and pulled her away from a pierced and tattooed twenty-something-year-old.

"I have to go. Something's come up that I have to deal with right now." When Carly gave a pout, Tommie said, "Have a good time, be careful." She looked past Carly at the punked-out woman. "She looks kind of dangerous." She planted a light kiss on Carly's lips. "Have a Happy New Year."

"Call me if you need to." She hooked her fingers in the waistband of Tommie's pants. "Tommie to the rescue."

Tommie gently took Carly's hand. Leaning down, she pulled it to her lips, then said, "Something like that." She cocked her head and said to the young woman growing impatient behind Carly. "You take real good care of my woman here, understand?" The girl's eyes grew wide as she nodded a "yes" very cautiously.

Tommie stepped out into the night before she dialed Megan's number. When the phone was answered all she heard was sniffling.

"Megan?" Tommie's heart raced as she ran toward where her car was parked.

Between sniffles, Megan managed a tearful, "Tommie."

Tommie was in a panic. "God, Megan, what's wrong?"

Megan finally pieced together some words. "I'm in trouble…I… don't know…what to do."

Tommie stopped dead in her tracks. "Where are you, Megan?"

Again, Megan's sentence was broken, but Tommie was able to hear, "At some…guy's house…a party."

Tommie took a calming breath, exhaling slowly. "What's the address, Megan? I'm coming after you." After several attempts Megan was able to say the address and Tommie confirmed it. "Are you safe where you are right now?" Receiving a shaky "yes," she said, "Then don't move, I'll be there in fifteen minutes."

Thankful she'd only had one beer, Tommie drove only slightly over the speed limit, avoiding the intersections that she knew would have sobriety checkpoints. She was sober as a judge, adrenaline quickly quashing any effect the one beer might have had, but she couldn't even think about taking the time for a sobriety test—Megan needed her.

As Tommie turned the corner, she saw Megan's form flash in her headlights. She was crouched on the step out by the sidewalk, her arms wrapped around her knees and her head resting there. Tommie stopped in the middle of the street. Getting out, she looked around as she crossed to where Megan remained unmoving.

Stooping in front of the small figure, she said softly so not to startle her, "Megan."

Megan's head came up and she launched herself at Tommie, throwing her arms around her neck and crying uncontrollably. Tommie's heart broke in an instant. She wrapped Megan in her arms and held her tightly.

"Shh…" She rocked them ever so gently. "I'm here…you're okay…everything's going to be all right now."

Megan sobbed loudly and shuddered violently against Tommie's shoulder. Realizing Megan wore no coat, she loosened her hold so she could slip her jacket off and put it around Megan's shoulders.

She again held her and quietly reassured her as her sobs began to abate. "Hey, hey, whatever's wrong we'll handle it, I promise. I need you to talk to me, though." Megan pulled back, wiping her sleeve across her eyes. "Where's your coat?"

Head hanging, Megan sniffed. "Inside…I guess."

Tommie stood, pulling her up and feeling the sway as Megan stood. She picked up the distinctive smell of alcohol.

Gently she asked, "Megan, have you been drinking?" The question prompted another round of sobs. She pulled Megan against her chest. "Shh…it's all right, kiddo, we'll figure this out." When Megan stopped the tears again, Tommie said, "Let's get your coat and get out of here."

Megan pushed away from Tommie, nearly toppling over. "No." Tommie caught her arms and held her upright. "I can't go back inside…no, please…no, Tommie."

"Come on then." Tommie placed an arm around Megan's shoulder. "Let's go."

The old Nissan Sentra her older brother had handed down to Tommie to drive in the winter didn't look like much, but everything still worked perfectly. She cranked up the heat as they pulled away.

Megan settled her head on the seat, holding Tommie's jacket tightly around her. After several minutes of silence she began to cry again. Tommie found a spot on the residential street to pull over and killed her headlights. Unbuckling her seatbelt, she shifted so she could see Megan a little more clearly in the car's dim interior.

"Tell me what happened. Did someone do something to you?" Tommie prayed the answer to the last question was no or she'd have to turn them around and go hunt down the SOB and hurt him.

Megan rolled her head away and looked out the side window. In a whispered voice she answered, "No, I did this to myself." She began to tell Tommie what had happened.

Afterward, Tommie patted her leg. "It's okay, people make mistakes and at least you realize that."

Tommie's words of comfort triggered another bout of crying. Between sobs she choked out, "I'm...so sorry."

Tommie took her hand and clamped it between hers. "Listen, it's going to be okay."

A few more minutes passed before Megan managed to stop crying again. Tommie was sure she must have run out of tears by then.

In a shaky voice, Megan finally said, "Aunt Kate—" She shook her head. "She's going to hate me." She sucked in a deep breath, trying to hold back more tears.

"I'm sure if you talk to her, Megan, she'll understand."

"No," Megan shook her head again. "She'll be so disappointed... it'll kill me."

Tommie could see fresh tears streaking Megan's face in the faint glow from the streetlights. She reassured her, "Nobody's going to die over this. You and your aunt, I'm sure, are going to work through this. Let's get you home." Tommie slowly pulled the car from the curb.

Megan murmured, "I'm sorry."

Tommie gave her a quick glance. "Believe me, kiddo, I know firsthand that we all make mistakes. What's important is how we deal with them."

"But...but, I ruined your night."

Tommie shook her head. "Trust me on this one, you didn't ruin anything. You see how I'm dressed. Do you think I enjoy these kind of things?" She tugged at the too-tight collar of her shirt while Megan simply shrugged. "Well, I don't, so thank you for getting me out of there. We'll just call it even for the night."

Megan closed her eyes and the remaining twenty minutes of the drive was silent. Seeing Kate's car in the drive, Tommie wondered why she was home so early. She parked on the street, then gently shook Megan's shoulder.

"Come on, Megan, you're home."

Opening her eyes slowly and confused, she asked hoarsely, "Did you call Aunt Kate?"

"No, I swear, I didn't call her." The girl's eyes teared again. "Come on, might as well get it over with." Making their way up the drive Tommie asked, "You got your key?" Megan dug it from her jeans pocket, handing it over.

Kate was obviously startled by the sound of the door lock. Her eyes going wide with alarm, she jumped to her feet as they came in the door, dropping the book she'd been reading.

"What's wrong?" The panic in Kate's voice was as clear as the frigid night's sky.

Megan's eyes were brimming with tears as Tommie stood behind her vehemently shaking her head "no" and waving her hands. Kate stopped short of taking Megan in her arms.

"I'm so sorry, Aunt Kate—" Megan's voice quivered with the words.

Heeding Tommie's warning, Kate merely wrapped Megan in a hug, prompting her to cry again.

"Shh…" Kate cooed, "it'll be okay, we'll talk about it in the morning. Go to bed, honey. I'll check on you in a minute."

Kate stood numbly, watching as Megan disappeared down the hall. Tommie remained silent and still, not sure what she should do, if anything. Kate returned to the couch, sitting with her hands pressed together between her knees. Tommie moved to perch on the edge of the chair across from the coffee table, her arms resting on her knees.

With tears glistening in her eyes, Kate said, "Please tell me what's going on."

Tommie blew out a breath and after a moment began to report what she'd found out. "Megan and Ashley went with some other girls to a party. They all lied to their parents about staying

overnight with each other. There was drinking at the party"—
Tommie mocked surprise—"and apparently someone convinced
Megan to try it. She said she didn't want to, but you know how peer
pressure can be. And with all the upheavel in her life, the divorce
and all, Megan said Ashley was bent on finding out if alcohol really
does dull the pain." Kate nodded slowly. "She knew it was wrong,
Kate. I'm pretty sure she's regretting it. The other girls were all
drinking so much too she didn't trust any of them to drive her
home when they left."

Tears wet Kate's cheeks and her voice was so soft, Tommie
hardly heard her. "But she didn't call me."

"She's afraid, Kate—afraid she'll disappoint you. Hell, there's
nothing in the world she loves or respects more than you."

"Oh, God," she sniffed, "I could never be disappointed in her."

Tommie couldn't stand watching the tears streak down Kate's
face any longer and moved to sit beside her on the couch. "Look,
she probably called me 'cause I'm like…I don't know, a big sister
maybe." She laughed lightly. "Although, most of the time she acts
more grown up than me."

Sniffling, Kate said, "But she's afraid to talk to me."

Tommie gently took Kate's hand in hers. "I don't think so, but
you two need to talk this out in the morning. Heck, I've never liked
kids much, but she's become the little sister I never had. You've got
a really smart girl, Kate. Drinking is stupid at her age, but at least
she acted responsibly about not getting in a car with an impaired
driver. And I really think she's going to regret this for a long time."

"I don't know what I'd do if anything happened to her." That
admission broke the dam and a sob wracked Kate.

Tommie automatically wrapped her arms around her, just as
she had with Megan. "Ah, Kate, please don't cry. Man, it kills me
when women cry."

Kate's body shook in Tommie's arms. God, Tommie thought, it
was selfish to revel in how good it felt to have Kate in her arms. As
good as it had felt when she'd held her months ago.

Kate finally drew slowly away. "You're missing your party."

"Nah, I didn't really want to go in the first place. Don't worry
about it."

Kate still sat close enough their thighs brushed. *This is right
where I want to be,* Tommie thought again, *taking care of you and*

Megan. It briefly occurred to her how foreign that sounded—wanting so much to care for and about someone else.

Standing, Kate picked up her wineglass and swallowed the last of the drink. "Would you like something to drink, Tommie?"

"What are you having?"

"Some tea, I think."

Tommie said, "Okay," and started to get up. Kate held out a hand to stop her.

"Stay put, I'll be back in a minute."

When she returned with the tea, they talked for hours, Tommie telling Kate stories of stupid behavior from her college days that involved drinking and reinforcing how smart Megan had been that night. Just after two she stood and stretched.

"I should go and you should get some sleep, so you'll be clear-headed to talk with Megan in the morning."

"It's so late, Tommie. Why don't you just stay the night? You're welcome to bunk here on the couch." Kate patted the cushion. "I've fallen asleep here many times and it's pretty comfortable."

The prospect of sleeping under Kate's roof had Tommie shaking inside. She moved to stand in front of the door, feeling the need to make a quick escape.

"Your jacket!" Kate said. "Let me get it for you. It's freezing out."

When Kate reached out and took Tommie's hand in hers and squeezed, Tommie swallowed hard, feeling her heart in her throat. Kate's voice was as soft as her skin touching Tommie's.

"Thank you for taking care of Megan again."

"I told you I'd help you keep her safe…and I intend to keep my word."

Involuntarily, Tommie reached her free hand up to brush her fingertips ever so briefly over Kate's cheek. Kate leaned toward the offered tenderness, but Tommie stepped back.

"Tell Megan I said to behave herself." With great effort she pulled her hand from Kate's and opened the door. "Good night, Kate."

To Tommie's ears, Kate's voice was like a whisper on the wind. "Good night."

Tommie lowered the window as she started the car. The nighttime temperature was in the low thirties, but it felt like the

Fourth of July under the weight of her clothes. Her body was on fire, head to toe. But it wasn't the kind of fire that sparked the familiar throb between her legs. It was different, completely different from anything she'd ever experienced. She glanced through the tinted passenger window as she put the car in gear and saw Kate in the doorway. Yeah, it was definitely different.

She wanted to go back, sweep Kate into her arms and carry her off to the bedroom. She wanted to take Kate to bed, but only in order to hold her and reassure her life would go on as planned and that for her and Megan it would be safe and near-perfect. She wanted to tell Kate she'd be there to make sure of it. At the stop sign she sat, unmoving, for several minutes.

"Get real," she mumbled. "You are not the settling down kind of woman. And Kate," she chuckled, "is not a woman interested in women."

Rolling down the other window to create a cross-draft, she tried to blast the fantasy from her muddled brain as she drove into the early morning toward home.

* * *

Kate leaned in the doorway, watching through the storm door as Tommie made her way down the driveway. It hadn't escaped her notice how dashingly handsome Tommie was in the black tux and starched white shirt she was wearing. Kate had allowed her eyes to drift from her broad shoulders, down to her muscular thighs and back to Tommie's stormy dark eyes as she pulled on her jacket.

Slowly wrapping her arms around herself, she recalled how soothing and comfortable it had felt when Tommie had held her. There was a big difference in the way someone held someone solely for the purposes of sex and the touch of someone who cared. She could tell that Tommie cared on some level. Kate was sure, though, that it could never be in a serious relationship sort of way. From the beginning Tommie had projected the image of a self-reliant loner, and, as Kate reminded herself, first impressions were lasting ones.

CHAPTER ELEVEN

Kate and Megan had a heart-to-heart on New Year's Day about the dangers of alcohol, about drugs and peer pressure and about how everything a person does and each choice she makes in her life has consequences…good or bad. Megan didn't protest much when Kate took her phone away and grounded her from her computer for two weeks. She ended up spending her two weeks of evenings reading, while Kate spent the time trying to put Tommie out of her mind. Unable to come up with a good excuse to call her, Kate poured herself into work and concentrated on helping Megan decide on a college for fall. Fall, when Megan would be leaving their nest and Kate would be freer to explore the identity she'd kept hidden away for the last decade.

* * *

Everything about Kate was burned into Tommie's memory. Her soft touch, the light and sensual scent of her perfume, the way her blond hair framed a face that held the bluest eyes she'd ever seen. Just the thought of her made Tommie's heart ache in a way she'd never felt before and other parts of her yearn for the sensation of Kate's touch.

In an attempt to get Kate off her mind, Tommie forced herself back to old habits. She'd hit one bar on Friday night, then another on Saturday, drinking and flirting, but she couldn't bring herself to go home with a woman, regardless of how inviting she was. She'd made out in more than one car, steaming its windows in the January cold, but she always found herself going home alone.

Tommie's uncharacteristic behavior raised a number of eyebrows, none, though, more than her own. She decided she might be having some kind of life crisis as she headed for that thirty-year-old milestone in just over a year.

* * *

Just before Valentine's Day, Megan and Kate were at the dining room table after dinner, poring over the brochures and information on the three colleges Megan had narrowed her list to.

Out of the blue, Megan said, "You know that was a pretty awesome present Tommie gave me for Christmas." Kate's head snapped up at the mention of the reporter's name. "I was thinking maybe I should do something nice for her for her birthday." Megan directed her eyes to meet Kate's intent gaze. "What do you think?"

Quite surprised, Kate answered, "I think that would be a very thoughtful gesture. Do you know when her birthday is?"

Megan chuckled. "Yeah, I do."

At Megan's impish grin, Kate had to ask, "Okay, I give. What's so funny?"

Megan laid down the papers in her hand and leaned away from the table. "I don't remember how the subject came up, back in the summer, you know, when I was interning at the paper, but it did." Megan furrowed her brow in thought while Kate waited anxiously for her to continue. "Anyway...she hates when her birthday is." Megan chuckled again before saying, "It's February fourteenth, Valentine's Day. Isn't that funny?"

Kate looked at her questioningly.

"Well, you have to admit, Tommie seems like the least romantic kind of person." Megan picked up another stack of papers. "I mean, it's kind of hard to picture her as a flower-and-candy-kind of girl."

She might not be the kind of girl to receive flowers and candy, but Kate would bet she'd given them a time or two in her life.

After several minutes of thought, Kate said, "Why don't we see if she'll meet us out for dinner somewhere Friday night. Her birthday isn't until Sunday so she probably wouldn't suspect anything. We could pick up a little something as a gift for her."

"Yeah, that sounds like a good idea. If we're going out somewhere, can we have the waitresses and waiters embarrass her by singing 'Happy Birthday'?"

Kate narrowed her eyes at Megan. "I don't think I would want to embarrass her like that myself, because I personally wouldn't want her to do that to me. Remember what we discussed about consequences?" The corners of her mouth curved up ever so slightly.

"But if I do it, that's a whole other matter." Megan smirked. "So what should we get her as a gift?"

"I don't know," Kate said. "I'll have to think about it." Actually, she already knew exactly what the gift should be. Megan's reason for initiating the conversation had given her the idea.

"You better call her this evening and ask before she makes plans. I have a feeling she goes out a lot on the weekends."

Kate picked up the handset in the kitchen and punched the speed dial for Tommie's number. After a half a dozen rings, the voice messaging clicked on and the familiar voice said, "Leave your scoop after the beep, thanks." How clever, Kate thought. "Tommie, hi! It's Kate. Could you give me a call when you have a minute? Thanks." The kitchen clock read just after seven thirty.

* * *

Tommie laid on the horn and yelled, "Moron!" at yet another car trying to force its way in front of her in the chaotic traffic outside the arena. The college basketball game had been one of the best she'd ever witnessed, remaining tied down to the final seconds, so everyone had stayed to watch. Hence traffic was a nightmare. It was just after eight. At the pace they were moving, she'd be lucky to get home by eleven.

Two hours and twenty minutes later she dragged her tired body into her apartment, feeling like she'd played the forty minutes of basketball herself. She only wanted to fall into bed and sleep, but the blinking red light on her machine glowed like a beacon in the dark. She huffed out a breath as she listened to the message, which came in just past seven thirty.

"Tommie, hi!" Tommie's heartbeat raced as she listened to Kate's words. She picked up the phone to return the call, then noticed on her watch it was almost ten thirty. She wondered if Kate would still be up, but before she could answer the question her fingers were automatically dialing the number. The quick response, partway through the second ring, made Tommie wonder if Kate had answered from a bedside phone. She was concerned she may have startled her or woken her up.

"Hello..." Kate's voice purred softly through the line to Tommie.

Tommie kept her own voice low. "Kate, I hope I didn't wake you. I debated whether I should or shouldn't call at this hour. From what Megan has said I know you sometimes have to start work before the chickens are up." She realized suddenly that she was rambling. "I'm sorry. I can't seem to shut up...I will now."

"It's okay, I wasn't sleeping. I was just lying here reading."

Tommie's mind pictured the attractive blond lying in bed wearing whatever she did or didn't sleep in. Kate's voice interrupted her imaginings.

"You didn't have to call back tonight. I suspected you were out at some kind of sporting event somewhere."

Tommie stammered, "Uh, yeah...I was at a college game down in Carson." *God*, she thought, *I sound like a blubbering schoolgirl. Why does she make me so damn nervous?*

"Did they win?"

"Who?"

Kate laughed lightly. "Your team, silly."

"Oh, uh..." *There I go again*, Tommie thought. "Yeah, I mean no...I was covering the game for the paper. I'm not much of a basketball fan." She couldn't believe how lame she sounded this evening. "So, um, what's up?"

"Megan and I were wondering if you were free Friday evening for dinner?"

Tommie dropped with a thud into the recliner at the thought of Kate calling with another invitation, and crap, she had no idea if she had to work Friday night or not. She blew out a silent breath before saying, "You know, Kate, I'm not certain if they have me scheduled for anything Friday evening. Can I let you know tomorrow, or is that too late?"

"Of course you can."

"Uh, yeah, okay, so…I'll call after I find out tomorrow."

"That's fine, Tommie. I'll talk to you tomorrow then."

"Right, tomorrow."

Kate's voice purred again through the phone. "Goodnight, Tommie."

"'Night," was all Tommie could manage.

* * *

Tommie rushed into her office and checked the games she was slotted to cover. "Damn it!" Then with the schedule sheet in hand, she charged over to George's office. The door was closed and she could see someone's back through the blinds that partially covered the window. She paced. Five, then ten, and finally almost fifteen minutes later, one of her coworkers emerged. She mumbled a curt greeting and pushed into her boss's office without knocking.

In an agitated tone, he looked over his reading glasses and asked, "Now what?"

She stepped briskly up to his desk. "I really need you to get someone else to cover that high school game across town Friday night."

He pulled his glasses off, dropping them on his desk. "Sorry, no can do."

"Damn it, George. I do every job you assign to me."

"Not without a lot of bitching more often than not," he mumbled under his breath, just loud enough for her to hear.

"That's beside the point. I've done it. I really need out of this Friday."

He turned his hands up. "Sorry, but I can't. You know Nick is out. His wife just had their baby. We're shorthanded." He shrugged. "I've gotta have you there."

She leaned her fists on his desk. "Hell, George, it's high school basketball. Anybody can watch the game and write a paragraph." Pushing back off his desk, she planted her fists on her hips. "Miss Goody Two-shoes who writes the society crap could cover this—"

"But she's not…you are." He narrowed his eyes. "And if you don't, I'd be happy to give you a good reference along with your resignation…or—"

She glared at him. "You wouldn't fire me. You can't."

He leaned back in his chair with a smug expression, "Wouldn't I? Just give me a reason that HR won't kick back at me and you'll find out." He cocked his head.

Tommie stomped from his office, slamming the door hard enough to rattle the windows. She cursed him silently with words she'd never speak within earshot of anyone. Tommie wouldn't call Kate back until evening, she decided. As mad as she was that she would have to decline the invitation, she wanted to hear Kate's voice, not a machine, even if only for a few minutes of conversation. She waited until she felt certain they'd be settled in for the evening. Megan answered.

"Hey, Megan. How's it going?"

She answered distractedly. "Okay."

"So school's going okay?"

"Yeah. Um, did you want to speak to Aunt Kate?"

I'd love to, Tommie thought. "Sure, if she's not busy."

"Hang on."

She heard the phone tap on something. Drumming her fingers on the end table beside her chair to the song "What A Girl Wants," which had been looping in her mind all day since she'd heard it while driving into work, Tommie waited, a minute, then two minutes. She was about to give up when Kate finally picked up the phone.

"Tommie, hi! Sorry to keep you waiting. I was just washing my hair and I had to get it rinsed out."

"I called at a bad time, sorry."

"No, no, I've done what I needed to." Tommie wondered if Kate was maybe clad in an old bathrobe walking through the house, or perhaps…just a bath towel. She quickly banished the thought.

"Well," Tommie began reluctantly. "Unfortunately I have a high school basketball game I have to attend Friday night at seven thirty so I won't be able to meet you two for dinner before nine, nine thirty and that's too late."

"Hum…that is kind of late." Kate paused a long moment. "Are you available Saturday for dinner?"

Surprised, Tommie hesitated. "Uh, yeah, sure."

"Are you sure you don't already have some plans? It is Saturday."

Tommie laughed. "And exactly what plans are you thinking I might have on a Saturday night?"

* * *

First impressions weren't always accurate ones, Kate thought, thinking back to her first encounter with Tommie. It was obvious now that besides being strong and independent, Tommie was funny and charming, compassionate and tender.

Kate guessed she appeared gruff and distant to most for a reason, and she was grateful to be someone who was privileged to see the real Tommie. She wasn't the kind of woman Kate had ever been drawn to, but she was attractive, and those eyes…Well, when she was intensely stirred by something, Kate likened them to the pitch-black of a moonless night. Kate thought now she might like to try and stir that "something."

"Kate?"

Tommie's voice startled her. "I'm sorry. What were you saying?"

"Never mind. So where are we having dinner Saturday night?"

"There's a little Italian restaurant called Burdello's across from the mall that has the best deep dish pizza. Please tell me you like pizza."

"Pizza's my number one food group. Well…that and hot dogs."

"What time would be good for you?"

Tommie chuckled. "Anytime. I really don't have any plans for Saturday."

"How about seven? Is that too late?"

"That's perfect."

"Okay, we'll see you at seven on Saturday."

"Why don't I swing by and pick you two up? I'm going to practically drive by your place on the way there."

"Are you sure?"

"Absolutely. So I'll see you about six forty-five."

"Yes, you will. Goodnight, Tommie."

"'Night, Kate."

* * *

Tommie couldn't decide what to wear to dinner. Burdello's wasn't fancy, but it wasn't casual either. As many times as she'd driven past it she'd never stopped in. She checked it out online to get an idea how to dress. It was considered "dress-casual" so she picked out her best black jeans and a button-down oxford shirt. She appraised herself in the mirror. Definitely butch, but she couldn't remember a time when she didn't look this way. Placing more gel in her hair to tame her short unruly locks, she took one last look, gave her reflection an approving nod and made her way out to her car.

Compared to Kate's car, Tommie's Nissan was an old dog, but it was clean and reliable. Her Jeep was newer, but with only a soft top it stayed garaged most of the winter months unless an unusually heavy snowfall made its four-wheel drive useful.

Twenty-four minutes later she pulled to the curb in front of the house. She was reaching out to knock when the inside door opened. By the time, Tommie stepped inside, Kate's voice was fading down the hallway.

"Make yourself comfortable. We'll be ready in a few minutes."

Tommie had learned long ago that when a femme said "a few minutes," what she really meant was "kick off your shoes and have a beer while you wait," but she'd give Kate the benefit of the doubt— she was a few minutes early.

When Kate appeared moments later, Tommie's mouth fell open. She was drop-dead gorgeous in a pair of tight, fitted black slacks and a royal blue sweater that hugged her body, leaving no doubt just how feminine and curvy she was. The blue of the sweater magnified the color of her eyes. Tommie compared them to deep pools on a sweltering summer day. Yes, she could definitely dive in and linger a long, leisurely time. Tommie forcibly pulled her gaze away, looking down at her own blue shirt, then back to Kate.

"Dress code for the evening." She nodded. "I suppose Megan's going to appear now wearing a blue top and black pants too."

Kate shook her head. "I seriously doubt she'll be going anywhere public wearing anything similar to me. She saw what I was planning to wear." Kate's eyes traveled over Tommie, head to toe. "You look nice...and comfortable, and I feel overdressed."

Tommie slowly shook her head no. "You look perfectly enticing." *God*, Tommie thought, *did I just say that out loud?* Kate blushed. "Did I just say that out loud?"

Kate's blush deepened. "You did, but I won't hold it against you. Thank you for the compliment."

Tommie thought how heavenly it would be if she could hold Kate against her. She put her hand over her mouth. She wanted to make absolutely certain that thought didn't unwittingly take the shape of spoken words too and escape her mouth.

"Are you okay?"

Tommie scrubbed her hands over her face. "Oh, yeah, I just remembered something about work. Nothing big."

Kate looked at her curiously before moving to a small table beside the door and removing a notepad and pen from the drawer. She handed them to Tommie. "Here, write it down so you don't forget again."

Tommie took the offered items as Kate turned her attention to the hall and called, "Megan, honey, come on. We should be going right this minute." Tommie stood numbly, inhaling Kate's perfume. When Kate looked back at her, she asked, "Did you forget again already?"

"Uh…no." Immediately and nervously, Tommie scribbled in almost illegible script, "This woman makes me crazy." She tore off the sheet, folded it and placed it in her shirt pocket. She patted the chest pocket. "Now if I can only remember not to wash it when I do the laundry."

Footsteps coming down the hall announced Megan's approach.

"Well, perhaps you can tell me about it at dinner. That might help you remember." Tommie knew her face was probably a shade redder than Kate's had just been.

"Are you sure you're okay?" Kate touched her fingers lightly to Tommie's cheek. "You don't feel feverish, but you look flushed." Tommie tugged the collar of her shirt as beads of perspiration popped out on the back of her neck. "Should I take your temperature before we drag you out into the cold?"

Tommie's body trembled and threatened to burst into flame as she thought of the many different and exciting ways the beautiful Kate Bellam could check her body's temperature. She ran a nervous hand through her hair.

"I'll be fine. I just need some air. Winter…furnaces, I'm always too warm." She smiled wryly as Kate held her gaze.

Megan stopped, watching the intense eye contact between her aunt and Tommie before interrupting. "Well, let's get going."

Kate turned to Megan. "Yes, let's." Tommie held Kate's coat while she shrugged into it, then grabbed up her keys. "We can take my car if that's okay with you."

Tommie slipped her keys in her pocket. "Fine by me."

When they stepped into the crisp evening air, Kate asked, "Where's your Jeep?"

Kate hit the remote to unlock the doors and Tommie moved quickly to open the driver's door for her. After closing the rear door for Megan and sliding into the front passenger seat, she answered, "I store it for a few months in the winter. It's impossible to warm it up with only the soft top. She might get lucky and see daylight in another month."

Kate headed up the street, glancing briefly at Tommie. "'She'?"

Tommie turned slightly in her seat to get a better view of the beauty beside her. "Yeah, she. It runs perfectly and has never given me any trouble, therefore it must be a 'she,' couldn't possibly be a 'he.' A 'he' would leave you broken and stranded but not a 'she.'"

"Interesting theory. I would imagine, though, that there are women out there capable of the same behavior."

Tommie pursed her lips. "Perhaps." Unfortunately she knew firsthand that to be true.

* * *

Tommie seated herself across from Kate, looking to take advantage of the view without being blatantly obvious. After they placed their drink orders, Megan immediately excused herself to the restroom. When she returned, Kate and Tommie were locked in an intense gaze, smiling like high school girls. Both turned to look at her when she took her seat.

"What?" she said, looking from Tommie to Kate.

Kate asked, "Can we leave the mushrooms off the pizza? Tommie doesn't like mushrooms and I thought we'd order the house salad to start. How's that sound?"

Megan sipped her soft drink. "Sure, fine."

* * *

During dinner they talked about Megan's college selection and, eventually, Tommie's college experience. They learned that Tommie was born and raised in a northern Chicago suburb and had attended college at Elmhurst on an academic scholarship and played volleyball. Kate couldn't quite picture Tommie as the volleyball type. With her height and build, she figured her more for a basketball player—except Tommie had recently informed her she wasn't a basketball fan. From poring over brochures with Megan, Kate also knew that Elmhurst was a religious college, though it was affiliated with a denomination that she didn't think was very fundamentalist. She wondered if Tommie had been aware of her sexuality back then.

When the waitress returned asking about dessert, Kate and Tommie declined, but Megan ordered a piece of sinful chocolate cake smothered in rich sauces. Minutes later the waitress—and half a dozen other waiters and waitresses—appeared behind Tommie carrying the dessert lit by a single candle. She placed the plate in front of Tommie as they began clapping and singing a "happy birthday" song.

Tommie's cheeks glowed red in embarrassment. When the singing stopped and they left the table, Tommie looked at Megan, then Kate. "I'll get even with you both," she said. "I promise."

"The embarrassing part was Megan's idea," Kate said, looking to her niece. "Actually, the whole thing was her idea." She retrieved the gift box from her purse and pushed it across the table to Tommie.

Tommie regarded the small, long rectangular box, then met Kate's eyes. "And what's this?"

"Just a little something from Megan and me for your birthday and for being a generally nice person."

Tommie's gaze was intent on Kate. "I'm touched, thank you."

Kate tipped her head. "You're welcome." Tommie's gaze continued to linger on her. "You might want to open it."

Tommie carefully removed the foil wrapping on a box bearing the Cross brand. Inside was a Cross Sauvage pen in the prettiest shade of blue. Tommie marveled at how closely the color was to Kate's amazing eyes and what a wonderful reminder it would always provide.

"Maybe you'll pen some great work with it," Kate said, giving Tommie a wink.

Turning the pen over in her hand, she said, "Thank you both. This is very thoughtful."

Megan ran off to the restroom, explaining that the first trip had only been a ruse to set up the birthday surprise.

Tommie returned the pen to the box. "It's a beautiful pen, Kate. An unexpected and pleasant surprise."

"Not as unexpected as the lovely pen you gave Megan for Christmas." Kate leaned in over the table. "That was an incredibly generous gesture—and very sweet." Kate's gaze lingered.

Tommie shrugged and was saved from further embarrassment when Megan returned.

"We ready to go?" She looked from Kate to Tommie.

"Absolutely." Tommie tucked her gift inside her jacket pocket and popped up.

* * *

After pulling in the drive and getting out of the car, Kate called across the roof of the car, "Would you like to come in for a bit or do you have other plans?"

Tommie shook her head. "I told you I didn't have any plans for this evening."

"Well, then, you have no excuse not to come in." Kate started for the door. "I'm not sure what I might have to offer in the way of refreshments, though."

Tommie sat on the couch while Kate disappeared into the kitchen. She was fidgeting nervously with the edge of a pillow when Kate returned with a bottle of beer and a glass of wine. She kicked off her shoes, tucking her feet under her and sat facing Tommie on the couch. Tommie shifted slightly to look at Kate, bringing her thigh into contact with Kate's knee. The innocent contact caused a rush of blood through Tommie's veins.

Kate made no attempt to move away, instead raising her glass and saying, "Even though it's a few hours away yet, happy birthday, Tommie."

Tommie tipped her beer at Kate. "Thanks." She took a long drink, trying to tamp down the heat building inside her. If Kate only knew what she did to Tommie, she wouldn't look so damned gorgeous and sit so close. Kate casually draped her arm along the back of the couch pulling the sweater taut across her breasts. Tommie couldn't keep her eyes from drifting over them.

"So do you have big plans on your birthday, also known as Valentine's Day?" Her tone was light and playful.

Tommie chuckled. "You can't imagine what it was like as a kid. I got razzed because it was my birthday and there was no way I could be a cupid. I pounded more than one kid for picking on me." She shrugged. "Then I just started ignoring them."

Kate placed her hand on Tommie's shoulder. "I'm sorry for stirring up bad memories."

Tommie shook her head. "Forget it, water under the bridge." She chuckled again. "I've actually received flowers and candy a couple of times for my birthday, if you can believe that." The warmth of Kate's hand on her shoulder was fueling a fire inside, one that Tommie felt might rage out of control at any minute. She shifted nervously and Kate moved her hand back to the couch.

Kate took a sip of wine. "I think it's sweet."

"Sweet, yeah, that's me." She gulped down the rest of her beer and stood quickly. "I should get going." She didn't trust herself not to do something stupid if she had to continue sitting so close to Kate. She needed to put some distance and cold February night air between them. She feared another touch from Kate's soft hand would fan the embers simmering inside her into a raging fire and if that happened she couldn't be sure she wouldn't cross the line that she managed her whole life to stay on the right side of.

Getting up, Kate followed Tommie to the door. When Tommie turned around to tell Kate goodnight, she stood only a breath away. So close that Tommie could smell the fresh lavender scent of her hair.

"Uh…Thanks again for the birthday surprise. Been a long time since anyone's done that, as embarrassing as it is."

"You've become a friend to us. Someone we can rely on. We wanted you to know we appreciate that." Kate rested her hand on Tommie's arm. "Thank you for being here for us when we need you."

Tommie wanted so badly to take Kate in her arms. She deserved
to be cherished and loved and Tommie wanted to be the one to
do that for her. When Kate's hand slipped down Tommie's arm to
squeeze her hand, Tommie's insides shook with raging desire.

Kate said softly, "I hope you have a wonderful day tomorrow,
Tommie."

Tommie couldn't speak; her throat was too tight.

Kate slowly released her hold. "Goodnight."

Tommie barely managed a "'Night."

Kate watched through a crack in the door until Tommie's car
drove off. Megan's voice startled her.

"Tommie leave already?"

Kate turned slowly, still feeling the flush that had warmed her
from holding Tommie's hand in her own. "Yes, she just left. What
are your plans for the remainder of the evening?"

Megan dropped onto the couch. "I don't know." She clicked on
the TV. "Maybe check out the movie channels." Kate picked up the
empty beer bottle and went to the kitchen. When she returned to
sit with Megan on the couch, Megan said, "We pulled it off, didn't
we? Tommie really was surprised, wasn't she?"

Kate remembered Tommie's rosy cheeks and her threat to get
even with them. "Yes, we did, sweetie. There's no doubt she was
surprised."

Megan stopped channel-hopping and lowered the volume on
the TV. She turned to look at Kate. "Can I ask you something?"

Kate sipped from the glass as she regarded Megan's serious
expression over the rim. She swallowed. "Sure, honey, what's on
your mind?"

"How come you never go out on dates?" She didn't give Kate
a chance to answer before adding. "And you hardly ever hang out
with your friends from the hospital."

Kate gave the question a moment's thought, then said, "Well,
I guess I just haven't met anyone yet that I want to spend time
getting to know better."

"But you don't go out anywhere to meet anyone."

"That's true. I don't like the idea of meeting someone in a bar,
though, and that's all the girls at the hospital want to do, so I've
tried to get out of going out with them whenever possible." Megan
frowned. "Besides, I believe the right someone is out there, and

it will happen without my having to be out there searching them out."

Megan lowered her eyes. "You had 'Mr. Right' until I came along."

Kate's heart ached that her niece would think she was the cause of Kate's break-up ten years earlier. She cupped Megan's chin in her hand. "Megan, look at me." When Megan's eyes met hers, she said softly, "No, sweetie. Please don't ever think you drove anyone away because you didn't." Kate stroked her hair. "It wasn't meant to be. I should thank you for saving me from a relationship that was clearly doomed to fail, and I was too blind to see it." Megan didn't appear convinced.

"So what was he like? If he wasn't 'Mr. Right', what is your type?"

Kate knew she had to tread carefully through this minefield. "Well, I can tell you what my type isn't and that's selfish and self-centered. If I'm going to invest myself in a relationship again, it would have to be someone who thoroughly appreciates *all* the things around them—like me!"

"Oh, I know, Aunt Kate, we can set you up on one of those Internet dating sites."

"Megan Bellam, don't you dare!"

Megan snickered. "I could screen them for you."

"Sweetie, you do not need to worry about my love life." *Or lack thereof.*

"I still think he left you because of me, though."

"Megan, I couldn't love you more if you were my own daughter." She pulled her niece into a hug. "My life is exactly as I wish it to be." *Well, mostly*, she thought to herself. "Please don't ever think you are a burden or are preventing me from living my life. Okay?" Megan nodded slowly. Kate stroked her cheek. "If I meet someone I think is special, you'll be the first to know, I promise."

Megan turned back to the TV. "Well, I'm glad you like to hang out with Tommie." Kate held her breath until Megan continued. "I like her…she's nice, you know, as, like, friends go."

Kate slowly exhaled. "Yes, I agree, Tommie is a nice woman and I don't doubt she's the very best kind of friend."

When Megan turned her attention back to the TV, Kate wondered about her sudden interest in her love life but dismissed it as teenage curiosity. Or…perhaps Megan had a boyfriend and inquiring about Kate dating was her way of getting around to the subject of dating herself.

"Megan, honey, is there someone special, maybe a boy, that you want to talk about?"

Megan scrunched up her face. "Guys are idiots and I don't have time for stupid. I have *big* plans for my life."

"If you ever want to talk, you know I will always listen objectively and I won't judge you."

Megan nodded.

Standing, Kate picked up her wineglass, then kissed Megan on the top of the head. "I'm going to read in bed. Don't stay up too late, okay?"

Megan shook her head. "Goodnight."

"Goodnight, sweetie."

CHAPTER TWELVE

Weeks later Kate was scanning the paper after dinner. Noticing all the airline specials to Florida and Mexico, she decided that perhaps since it was Megan's senior year they should take a spring break trip. She leaned in the doorway of Megan's room for a few minutes, watching her type like an expert on the computer keyboard.

She finally knocked lightly. "Are you in the middle of schoolwork?"

Megan quickly closed the window on the screen before turning around. Kate thought she looked guilty, then dismissed the thought.

"Nothing important. What's up?"

Kate waved the newspaper. "I was looking at all the airline deals for spring break trips to Cancun and places in Florida and wondered if you might want to go somewhere for spring break this year. Think of it as an early graduation present."

Megan shrugged her shoulders. "Yeah, that might be fun."

"Of course, I'm thinking if we want to take a trip we should be planning now before every place gets booked up."

"Can I have a day or two to think on it?"

"Sure, sweetie, just let me know." She started to move away, then turned back. "Maybe you should find out what all your friends are going to do over the break."

"Yeah, I'll do that tomorrow at school."

As Kate left, she scanned Megan's room and was reminded of how proud she was of her. She was saddened too that Megan's mother didn't live to see the amazing young woman she'd created. Kate returned to her tea and the rest of the newspaper.

The following evening when Kate arrived home Megan met her at the door. Following Kate to her bedroom, Megan plopped on the bed with her back to Kate while she undressed.

"Could we go somewhere else besides Florida or Mexico for spring break?"

Kate pulled on a comfortable old sweater and jeans. "I suppose we could. What did you have in mind?"

"Renting a cabin up at Sweetwater Lake where Ashley's folks' place is."

Kate came around the bed and sat facing her niece. "Are you sure you wouldn't rather go someplace warm and tropical where all the other kids go for spring break?" When Megan nodded a "yes," Kate regarded her with questioning eyes. "You realize the weather probably won't be that warm, even on the first of April. Why would you rather go there for the week?"

Megan sighed. "You know Ashley's parents are getting divorced?" Kate nodded. "Ashley has to spend that week with her dad because of some custody arrangement or something. Anyway, she'll be stuck there with no one around she knows, so I told her I'd ask you if we could rent a cabin up there so we can hang out."

"And what exactly do you suppose *I* might do for a week with no one around that I know?"

Megan shrugged. "Maybe we can invite Tommie to come with us. You guys don't seem to mind hanging out together, and..." She shrugged again. "She seems like she might be the outdoors type, you know."

Kate considered the proposal for a minute. She wondered if Tommie *was* the outdoors type, and if she were, if she would consider being stuck in a cabin in the woods on a lake with Megan and herself. As for herself, well, she would welcome the chance to spend more time with her. She could see lots of possibilities for deepening their friendship if they were, say, stuck in a cabin in front of a roaring fire.

"Well?" Megan snapped her out of her daydream.

"I'll tell you what, if Tommie wants to go with us, we'll go. Otherwise, I'm sorry, sweetie, but I don't think I could stand to be alone in a cabin in the woods for a week. You'll have to pick somewhere a little more exciting." Megan's eyes brightened. "And," Kate continued, "you have to do the inviting." Megan's mouth curved downward. "Agreed?"

She sighed loudly. "Agreed." She hopped off the bed and hurried out to the kitchen. Kate heard her leaving a message for Tommie as she started down the hall.

At the dinner table, Megan informed Kate, "I had to leave a message for Tommie. She's probably at a ball game somewhere, so she might not call back till tomorrow."

"I'm sure that's fine. Somehow, Megan, I'm not imagining the lake is the hot spot for Spring Breakers, although, I could be wrong."

Kate had just settled down to soak in her bubble bath when the phone rang and Megan scurried down the hall to answer it.

"Hello."

"Megan, it's Tommie. Is everything okay?"

Megan hopped on the kitchen counter. "Yeah, sure."

"So what's up?"

Megan crossed her fingers and asked, "What are you doing the first week of April?"

"Working." Tommie laughed. "Why, what are you doing?"

Megan was absently fidgeting with the dishtowel lying on the counter beside her. "Well," she hesitated, "maybe taking a little trip for spring break, depending…"

She waited long enough and Tommie asked, "Depending on what?"

Megan squeezed her already crossed fingers. "Depending on what you're doing."

Confused, Tommie said, "Megan, help me out here. What are you talking about?"

Megan blew out a breath. "Here's the thing, Aunt Kate and I are thinking about renting a cabin up at Sweetwater Lake for spring break and we want you to come along."

Tommie felt warm all over at the thought of Kate wanting to spend a week with her.

Megan asked impatiently, "Well, you get vacation time don't you? What do you think, you want to go with us?"

Tommie wanted to hop to her feet and do a little victory dance around the coffee table. "Um, I'll have to check about the time off. The first week of April? You know baseball season is starting. When do you need to know?" Tommie didn't want to sound over-anxious.

"As soon as you can find out. So you want to go with us?"

"Kate really wants me to go?"

"Uh-huh."

"I'll find out tomorrow and call you after work."

"Great!" Megan jumped off the counter. "I'll let Aunt Kate know."

"Okay. Talk to you tomorrow."

"Okay, it will be fun if you can do this with us."

"Sure, kiddo, later."

Kate was on the verge of drifting off in the tub when she heard Megan's voice on the other side of the door.

"Tommie's going to find out tomorrow if she can get off work to go with us and let us know. Okay?"

A delightful warmth enveloped her, and it wasn't her bathwater. "Okay, sweetie." Megan bounded off to her room and Kate closed her eyes again, this time to conjure up an image of Tommie, one in which she was dressed to kill in a tux and holding Kate tight, gazing into her eyes with lust and longing evident in her own smoldering dark eyes and...

Kate presses her cheek to Tommie's chest where her heart pounds a rapid rhythm. "If I don't touch you everywhere soon," Tommie whispers, "I'm going to die right here in your arms." Kate's breath catches at the sound of wanton desire in Tommie's voice. She leads Tommie down a darkened hallway to a candlelit room, which has as its centerpiece a massive bed covered in dark earth tones. Tommie sweeps Kate into her arms and lays her down gently. As Tommie begins the slow deliberate task of undressing her, Kate's hand begins a soft caress of Tommie's torso and gradually moves to stroke the pulsing need between her own legs...

The orgasm came quickly, distressingly so. Kate lay in the water until her breathing evened out, then climbed out, gathering her robe around her. She was ashamed for having fantasized about Tommie to satisfy her own physical need. She proceeded to the kitchen to pour a half glass of wine, then went to her room, hoping the wine and a few chapters in her book would clear her head.

* * *

When the phone rang the following evening Kate was at the kitchen counter loading the dishwasher. She caught the phone before Megan made it off the couch in the living room.

"Hello!"

"Kate, hi, it's Tommie."

Megan mouthed in the doorway, "Tommie?" Kate nodded a "Yes."

"I told Megan I would let her know about the spring break trip to the lake this evening."

"Would you like to speak to her?"

"No!" Tommie said abruptly, then quickly added, "Um, I can just talk to you, can't I?"

"Of course." There was a long silence. "Well?"

"Are you sure you guys want me tagging along on your getaway? I mean…I don't want to interfere with any bonding time together or anything like that."

Kate laughed lightly. "Believe me, that's not the purpose of this trip."

"Are you sure?"

"Positive. Fair warning: She's probably going to spend most of her time with Ashley."

"Great. I mean, if you're sure, why not? I can get the time off work. Just give me all the details at least a few days ahead of time."

Excitement filled Kate at the thought of a week in the woods with Tommie. Tommie was the only link Kate had to her true self, and even though she could never admit to it, she delighted in the time she could spend with her.

"I'll call as soon as the reservations are made."

Kate left Tommie a message the following evening letting her know they had a cabin reserved at Sweetwater Lake, which was located just over two hours northwest of Denton. Not that Tommie wouldn't know where the lake was located since she'd probably driven past it on her trips to and from Chicago. She assured Tommie she would call again a few days before they were to leave.

* * *

Tommie couldn't have been more excited about the trip if she herself were a teenager back in high school. Kate called Thursday evening to give Tommie their departure time. She included the extended weather forecast, which predicted normal average springtime weather, though anyone living in Indiana knew that would change at least a half a dozen times in the next forty-eight hours. But Tommie could attempt to pack accordingly. When she called Kate back to ask what she could bring, Kate said only to bring whatever alcohol she planned to consume and she would take care of the food.

Tommie fussed. "You won't let me help pay for the cabin rental and now you won't let me help pay for groceries. I have to tell you in all seriousness, Kate, I cannot be a kept woman."

Kate laughed, then said very seriously, "And what makes you think I have any intentions of keeping you after a week out in the woods?"

Tommie was silent, unsure what Kate's words meant.

Kate chuckled. "You realize I'm just kidding?"

"Uh…yeah, I know that."

"I'll tell you what. Let's plan to leave at nine instead of ten, and we can stop at the grocery on the way. We'll discuss the bill then. Does that work better for you?"

"I think I can live with that."

"Good, then we'll see you Saturday morning at nine sharp, ready for a week of…well, whatever one does at a lake in the woods in April."

Tommie's heart pounded with anticipation. "See you then."

* * *

Tommie was a few minutes early Saturday morning, but Kate's trunk was already standing open and Tommie saw her entering the house as she approached. She dropped her duffel bag on the driveway behind the car, then rapped on the storm door before pulling it open and poking her head in.

"Hello..."

Kate called from somewhere down the hall, "Come on in, we're almost ready." As Tommie stepped in, Kate added, "There's coffee in the kitchen, get you some to go."

In the kitchen Tommie found two travel mugs sitting on the counter by the coffeemaker. As she poured some, she inhaled the heavenly aroma. It didn't smell anything like the crap she got down at the paper or even the stuff that came from the Roach Coach outside her building. Yet another reason to admire Kate, she thought as she sipped the mouth-watering brew. When it came to the art of coffee making, she was obviously another Warhol or Nagel.

Kate popped into the kitchen, rousing Tommie before she could drift into a daydream about her. "Good morning!"

"Yes, it is," Tommie replied, raising her coffee mug. "Great coffee."

Kate poured the other mug full and took a sip. "It's my own special blend. I use four different kinds of beans. It's a secret recipe."

Tommie took another drink. "Well, if there's nothing else to look forward to during a week in the woods"—she raised her mug once again—"at least there's this."

Kate regarded Tommie for a moment. "Surely there'll be more to look forward to than just my coffee," she said, affecting a hurt tone.

Tommie nearly choked. She could think of dozens of things and they all started with Kate. Not that she could mention those. She shrugged. "You mean like fishing and shuffleboard?"

Kate wrinkled her nose and said in a serious tone, "No, I was thinking more like marshmallow roasts and campfire songs."

Tommie frowned until Kate finally smiled mischievously. "I hope you're kidding or I might be forced to hitch a ride to the closest drinking establishment."

Kate's hand brushed briefly across Tommie's arm as she stepped around her to a small table where several bags were sitting. "I'm sure we'll come up with something."

Tommie's eyes swept over Kate—her tight-fitting jeans, the loose sweatshirt she was wearing over some kind of collared blouse and the hikers on her feet. With her hair pulled back like that, she could pass for a gay woman...*If only*, she thought.

As for herself...She examined her own bright plaid flannel shirt, tucked into faded carpenter jeans, and her barely broken-in running shoes. The shoes were barely broken in because she hadn't been to the park or the Y to run much since before last November. Still, her stereotypical garb didn't leave much doubt about her preferences, certainly not compared to Kate's outfit.

Kate turned and caught Tommie eyeing her. "What?" She looked down at her clothes. "Am I not dressed appropriately for the whole woods thing?" Tommie's lips curved appreciatively. "Not everyone can look like you, you know. Like an authentic woods... person...woman." She tossed a hand in the air.

"You look perfect—ly fine—for the woods," Tommie said, quickly raising the mug to her mouth to hide her embarrassment.

Kate considered Tommie more closely. She didn't look like a dyke, Kate thought, just ruggedly handsome. Warmed by the memory of strong arms holding her, she swallowed, pushing away the desire to feel the tender touch of Tommie's hands everywhere. A flush crept up her neck and began to spread across her face.

At that moment, Megan came into the kitchen, breaking the tension Kate was feeling in the pit of her stomach. She needed to get hold of herself. Tommie might flirt from time to time, but Kate knew there was no way she would make a pass or come on to her. There was a tender, caring soul under the tough, coarse veneer Tommie shielded herself with, someone who had come to care about Megan and about her as well. Besides which, she reminded herself, Tommie thought she was straight.

"So are we leaving or what?"

* * *

As the clerk was scanning the groceries, Tommie whipped her wallet out of her pocket. She swiped her credit card while Kate was still trying to get hers out of her purse.

"Hey!" Kate exclaimed. "We agreed to discuss the grocery bill."

"If you insist, but I say we arm wrestle for it." She leaned a brawny elbow on the small checkout counter. "What do you say?"

The young clerk looked at Tommie like she was certifiable, then at Kate. "Go for it," she said, giving Kate a grin. "I think you can take her."

Kate closed her purse. "Very funny. Never fear. We will discuss this."

For most of the two-hour-and-fifteen-minute ride, Megan remained silent in the back with her headphones on. Kate and Tommie kept their conversation to topics such as work, music and movies. There was no disagreement over the easy listening music from the radio playing in the background. Tommie found it very "Kate" and soothing. Tommie welcomed the relaxation she experienced cruising up the highway with the Bellam women.

* * *

They arrived at the cabin outside the "one-light" town of Lakeside in Ramsey County, Indiana, just after noontime, and Megan immediately searched for a signal on her phone. "Wow! I've got more bars here than I do at home."

Tommie grabbed bags from the trunk. "It's probably that tower we passed right before we turned off the main road."

Megan's fingers began quick deliberate movements over the phone keys. "Cool."

With an armful of groceries, Kate said, "Megan, could you postpone the messaging until we've at least carried everything inside?"

"I told Ashley I'd let her know the minute I got here."

"I'm sure five minutes won't ruin your friendship." She looked at Megan. "Please."

Megan snapped the phone closed and grabbed her bag and a sack of groceries. "Fine," she grumbled her way to the door. "I hope this is all the work I have to do this week. It is my spring break, after all." Kate heard enough of her grousing to shake her head in response.

Inside the spacious living room, complete with a fireplace already stacked with logs, Tommie asked, "Where would you like your bag, Kate?"

Kate dropped the grocery sacks she carried on the island between the living area and kitchen and regarded Tommie briefly.

"Um...there's only two bedrooms and," she pointed to the couch across the room, "a sofa sleeper. I thought we'd flip for the bedroom."

Tommie tossed her bag at the end of the couch. "I'll sleep on the couch."

"It's just that the bigger rentals with more bedrooms were outrageously expensive, so I—"

Tommie cut her off. "Like I said at the hospital, I've slept in a lot worse places in college. The couch is fine."

Of course, Tommie would be gracious enough to take the couch. Kate should have expected no less. She had considered offering her half of the queen-size bed in the larger of the two bedrooms, but she suspected Tommie would not be comfortable with those arrangements. Kate knew she'd also have trouble sleeping with Tommie close enough to touch.

* * *

Megan left almost immediately to meet Ashley. As Kate began preparing lunch for Tommie and herself, Tommie got cold drinks and arranged the chairs on the back deck so the small table sat between them. She stood at the rail looking past the scattering of trees to the lake. It was so quiet, save for the distant sound of people enjoying themselves and the squirrels rustling around the perimeter of the cut grassy area off to one side of the deck, which gave way to land densely populated with every kind of tree imaginable. She breathed deep the fresh outdoors air, thinking how easy it might be to live somewhere like this instead of the city with its noise and air polluted by too many cars and industry. She was glad she had remembered to bring a notebook and pen, thinking she might find the time and inspiration to write about something other than sports during the week.

Lost in her thoughts she didn't hear Kate come out. "It's beautiful," she said, leaning against the rail next to Tommie.

Beautiful is what you are, thought Tommie, but she said, "And so peaceful. I was just thinking I could live out here."

Kate regarded her with a questioning look. "Really? You strike me as more of a city dweller."

Tommie laughed. "I think I could give up the rat race and exist in this quiet."

Tommie could probably fit comfortably into the rural environment, thought Kate, surveying Tommie's flannel shirt and jeans. "Our lunch is ready. Let's eat."

They enjoyed the peaceful quiet, talking little while they ate. When they'd finished, Kate suggested, "We can hike one of the many trails they have around here if you're up for it."

"Sure," said Tommie, standing. "I just need to put on some shorts. This sounds like a workout and I tend to overheat when I exercise in pants." After changing into cargo shorts in the bathroom, she rejoined Kate in the kitchen area.

"You know, Tommie, you can use the bedroom for dressing and a place to keep your clothes. You're just one of the girls."

Tommie simply shrugged.

"Well, I still would rather flip for the bedroom."

Tommie shook her head. "Nope, I already claimed the couch so you're stuck in the bedroom."

Noticing how powerful Tommie's calves appeared, Kate wondered if she was going to be able to keep up with her while hiking through the woods. She scooped up her keys. "Shall we?"

Tommie waved toward the door, following her out.

* * *

They drove several miles to a paved parking lot occupied by a dozen or so cars. Kate grabbed a small backpack containing two bottles of water, and they made their way to the large map of the area with the hiking trails highlighted.

As they scanned the map, Kate asked, "Should we start with the shorter, less strenuous one and work our way up?"

Tommie shoved her hands in her pockets. "Fine by me. I haven't gotten in much exercise lately. The six-or ten-mile hikes might do me in."

Kate tapped her finger on the green highlighted trail. "Okay, the three-point-five mile it is then. You ready?"

Tommie liked Kate's enthusiasm. "As I'll ever be, I'm sure."

When Kate followed up on Tommie's mention of exercise, she explained that she used to run regularly on the paved jogging path through the park close to her apartment or at the Y, but hadn't been very regular with her routine for months. What she didn't share was how meeting Kate seemed to have turned her life upside down. How she couldn't force herself to go out daily and run or cruise the bars on the weekends in search of a different form of exercise. How, lately, in fact, she felt like she was living for the rare opportunities to see Kate and just managing to get through the daily grind out of habit.

"I don't get any regular exercise," Kate offered. "Maybe a monthly visit to the gym, which results in such sore muscles for days afterward that I can't make myself go back."

"You look pretty fit to me," Tommie said casually. "Spending time in surgery must be some good kind of physical exercise."

Kate looked so fit, in fact, that Tommie let her lead on the narrow parts of the path—which let *her* enjoy the view of Kate's firm backside. The impression of fitness wasn't just cosmetic, she decided about two miles into the hike. "I really need a drink," she said in a labored breath, desperately needing to take a break. "Can we take a break?" God, she hated to think she was going soft.

Kate stopped suddenly, causing Tommie to nearly run into her. When she spun around, they were only a foot apart.

"Sure, I'm sorry. Sometimes when I'm focused on a task nothing distracts me."

Tommie swallowed hard, thinking suddenly not of her need for a drink, but of Kate making love with the unwavering focus she had just confessed to. *Oh God*, Tommie scolded herself. *Get your mind off that train of thought.*

"Thanks." She took the bottle of water Kate offered her and quickly gulped half of it down. She leaned against a tree a few feet off the path and watched as Kate drank more slowly. She couldn't help watching her breasts rise with each deep breath— and imagining having Kate in her arms and those firm full breasts pressing into her.

"Tommie," Kate whispered and placed her index finger over her lips. She pointed to her left and Tommie glanced that way. In the tranquil solitude of the woods, Tommie heard the rustling of dry leaves and snapping of small twigs. There, not more than forty feet away, was a doe and her two fawns. The fawns' white tails twitched as they foraged along in the dense woods. Tommie was awestruck by the innocent beauty of the sight. Glancing over at Kate, she was again struck by the look of pure astonishment and delight on her face.

"Wow!" Tommie spoke when they'd finally been spotted by the mom and all three sprinted away.

"Yes, wow." Kate returned her half-empty bottle to her pack. "You ready to finish this hike?"

Tommie drained her bottle and capped it. "Let's do it."

They hiked the remaining distance back to the parking lot with little more conversation. At the car, Kate took a sip of her water, then offered the remainder of the bottle to Tommie. "Looks like we need to bring extra for you on the next hike."

Tommie patted her firm abdomen. "I happen to have an extra large tank."

"Yes, I suspect you do."

* * *

Megan returned with Ashley for dinner. They resembled a family of sorts when sitting around the table, Tommie thought. It made her rethink her whole carefree single lifestyle. Getting to know and care for Kate and Megan had caused her to consider what it would be like to share a life with someone. She was beginning to dread the thought of spending so much time on her own. Perhaps if she took the time to get to know a woman, instead of hopping into bed with her, she might actually find one like Kate. *A girl can dream*, she thought.

Kate noticed the faraway look in Tommie's eyes and the pleasing curve of her mouth. "Something you'd like to share with the rest of us?" Tommie met Kate's questioning gaze with a raised brow. "You look like you just enjoyed the most delectable piece of chocolate in the world. It can't be my cooking."

"It's not…I mean…" Tommie was flustered like she'd just gotten caught doing something she shouldn't. "Uh, there's nothing at all wrong with your cooking. I was just thinking about baseball." She hoped she sounded convincing.

"Ah yes, it's that time of year, isn't it? We haven't made you miss some big important game, have we?"

Tommie shook her head. Hell, she'd miss the World Series to be here with Kate. As ridiculous as her fantasies about "straight Kate" were, she couldn't make herself not think about how wonderful she'd feel in her arms.

After dinner they played cards until Ashley's dad picked her up, then Kate and Megan went to their bedrooms. Before she turned in for the night, Tommie kicked back out on the deck, drinking a beer, enjoying the sounds of the night and wondering what she and Kate might find to get themselves into tomorrow.

CHAPTER THIRTEEN

Midmorning on Sunday, after Megan left with Ashley again, Kate and Tommie decided to hike the four-point-two-mile trail at the other end of the lake. Tommie slung the backpack, into which they put extra water bottles, over her shoulder at the trailhead, and they started out.

Although Tommie was watching more of Kate's behind than the natual beauty around them, she did manage to not run into her when she stopped abruptly again this time.

"Listen," Kate said.

Tommie tilted her head one way then the other. "I give. What are we listening for?"

Kate's eyes scanned the trees overhead. "There," she pointed. "See him up there."

Tommie tried to see what Kate was pointing out. "Who?" She squinted into the green canopy above them.

Kate stepped directly in front of Tommie. Her back pressed lightly to Tommie's chest and abdomen. She pointed again. "See him there."

Tommie sighted along Kate's forearm, her hand and to the tip of her finger. She could see the slightest trace of perspiration glistening on Kate's skin, and her familiar scent nearly buckled Tommie's knees.

"It's a Red-bellied Woodpecker."

Tommie concentrated, finally seeing the noisemaker on the side of the tree. "His belly doesn't look red to me, but the top of his head does. Does this mean this isn't Woody?"

Kate gave Tommie a light jab with her elbow. "Funny."

Tommie chuckled. "I thought so."

Two hours and two bottles of water later they were huffing and puffing along. Thinking too much about how close they might be to getting back to the car instead of where she was walking, Tommie stepped on a large tree root. When her ankle twisted under her, she went down so fast she didn't have a chance to catch herself.

"Damn!" she yelled as she thudded to the ground.

Kate, who was once again in the lead, spun around to see Tommie facedown on the trail.

Tommie slowly rolled onto her side. "Ah, crap..." She couldn't decide which was hurt worse, her pride or her ankle.

Kate hurried to kneel beside her as she attempted to push herself up. Placing a hand on Tommie's shoulder, she said, "Stay put, don't try to get up."

Tommie pushed against her hand. "Ah, it's okay, just a little sprain."

Kate gently urged Tommie back down. "You're bleeding."

Tommie's eyes widened. "Really, where?"

Kate lightly touched her finger to Tommie's forehead at her hairline. "Here..." She raised Tommie's right arm to find the source of the blood that was running down it. "And you've got a nasty gash on your arm here." She indicated the side of Tommie's forearm.

Tommie shrugged the backpack off her shoulder. "I'm tougher than a sprain and a few cuts." She pushed herself up to a sitting position while Kate dug a small first-aid kit out of the backpack. "I just need to get up and walk it off."

"You need to just sit still and let me check your injuries." Kate's tone was so insistent that Tommie complied without another word.

"Just tell me I didn't do a face plant in poision ivy or something."

Kate looked around them. "It doesn't appear you did." She pulled the bandana from Tommie's pocket, soaked it with fresh water and began dabbing at the cut on her head. Tommie sat motionless, mesmerized by Kate's tender touch.

She smoothed Tommie's hair back. "The cut's not too bad, but I'm a little concerned about this knot." Tommie flinched when Kate pressed gently on her forehead. "I'm sorry." She positioned herself to look in Tommie's eyes. "How's your vision?"

Tommie took in Kate's concerned expression. "Perfect."

Kate averted her gaze. "That's good." She lifted Tommie's arm to assess the gash. "This, however, is much worse." Kate rinsed the wound with some water, then tied the bandana around it.

Moving next to Tommie's ankle, she carefully pulled her sock down as far as she could. "I'm not going to untie or take off your shoe. I don't want it swelling to the point we can't get it back on." Tommie nodded as she very gently probed her ankle. When she touched the spot of obvious injury, Tommie's leg jerked. "I'm sorry, again." Kate quickly rubbed her hand over Tommie's calf. "It doesn't feel like anything is broken." Digging in the first-aid kit again, she removed a small bottle and shook out two pills. "Take these," she said, offering the water bottle. "They'll help with the swelling."

Kate removed a tissue from her pocket and dabbed at the small trickle of blood on Tommie's forehead. Tommie downed most of the last bottle of water, marveling at how good it felt to have Kate close enough that she could smell the fresh scent that was so uniquely her. Kate leaned in again closely to inspect the head injury, her breasts mere inches from Tommie's face. Tommie's stomach ached with a desire that quickly spread lower.

She knew she shouldn't feel this way about Kate—the woman was straight and all she'd ever been with Tommie was nice. She'd given no indications she had any desire for another woman, let alone Tommie, and yet Tommie couldn't stop wanting her. She closed her eyes, envisioning her mouth teasing Kate's nipples. When she groaned, Kate leaned back suddenly.

"What's wrong?" She lightly stroked her fingers across Tommie's cheek. "Tommie?"

Tommie slowly opened her eyes and exhaled deeply. "If I don't get up and move now, I'm not sure if I'll make it out of here under my own steam."

"You think you can walk on that ankle?"

"I've got to if the alternative is to sit here on this hard ground."

Kate stood first, offering a hand. Once Tommie was on her feet, or rather foot, Kate positioned Tommie's arm across her shoulder and her arm around Tommie's waist.

"Lean as much as you want. You need to keep as much weight as possible off that ankle."

Tommie tested it and said, "Let's do this."

The pain was excruciating and had Tommie wincing with every step. Half an hour later—probably less than a quarter of a mile down the trail—she swiped a hand across her face, streaking blood through her sweat.

"Sorry for sweating all over you."

Kate stopped. "Believe me, raising a child and being a nurse, I have been exposed to worse." She turned slightly toward Tommie, pressing her breast into Tommie's side. "Let's rest for a couple of minutes." She steered them to a fallen tree, where she helped Tommie sit. She pulled the last, nearly empty water bottle from her pack, poured a small amount on a clean tissue and then gave Tommie the bottle. "Drink it all, I'm fine." She cautiously wiped more blood from Tommie's head wound.

Tommie capped the empty bottle. "You ready to move again? I have a feeling I'm going to need something stronger than water real soon."

Kate examined Tommie's pained expression. "I think you should stay put and let me go get some help."

Tommie snorted. "No way you're leaving me here. You drug me in here...you're dragging me out." She pushed her weight up on her good leg. "Let's go, I'm dying for a cold beer."

In just under an hour they cleared the woods and stopped at the edge of the parking lot.

"Now, will you at least sit down here and let me get the car?"

Tommie nodded. "Sure thing." She called after Kate as she started away, "Hey, you don't have anything to drink in that car, do you?"

Kate shook her head, continuing across the parking lot.

Once she had Tommie comfortably situated in the backseat with her leg propped on an old blanket from the trunk they headed out. When Kate turned north on the highway instead of south toward the cabin, Tommie pulled herself up to the back of the empty front seat.

"Where you headed? Shouldn't we have turned the other way?"

"There's an urgent care facility less than a half an hour from here. I'm worried about your head injury and I'm sure your arm needs stitches."

"You're kidding, right? I feel fine—"

"I've seen people die from less-serious-looking injuries." Kate tilted her head to see Tommie's face in the rearview mirror. "So humor me, would you?"

Tommie closed her eyes and let her head drop against the seat. "I guess I'm not exactly in a position to fight you, am I?"

Tommie kept her eyes on what she could see of Kate from the backseat. She liked the feeling that having Kate worry about her evoked. Maybe, she thought, just maybe she was ready to find a good woman like Kate and settle down.

Kate was a bit surprised to discover that she was as worried about Tommie as she would be if it were Megan in the backseat with the same injuries. Oh, she knew Tommie was tough, but she wasn't taking any chances. Any of Tommie's seemingly minor injuries could be serious, especially the one to her hard head. As much as there was that was unspoken between them, Kate knew in her heart she'd be devastated if anything happened to Tommie.

* * *

Hours later they pulled into the cabin and Kate helped Tommie hobble in on her badly sprained ankle. To Kate's dismay and against her professional advice, Tommie had refused the crutches the urgent care clinic had offered, telling them to keep them for the next klutz who came in. She had some from a previous mishap that she would use when she got home if she still needed them. She promised to stay off her foot as much as possible for at least the next few days. She was armed with a mild painkiller and antibiotics.

She dropped heavily on the couch. "Can I please have a beer now?"

Kate frowned. "You have meds to take, and alcohol doesn't mix well with either one of them."

"Please, Kate. One beer couldn't possibly hurt. I promise to take my meds like a good girl." She flashed an endearing smile over teeth that were clenched. Her ankle throbbed, her head pounded and the shot given to her when she received seven stitches in her arm, two inside and five out, was wearing off. The wound was beginning to sting something fierce.

Kate shook a finger at her. "You get one beer, then you take the pills and get settled with your ankle up. Do we have a deal?"

"Deal."

Taking a long drink of beer, Tommie sighed. "That's the best beer I've ever had."

Kate sat at the opposite end of the couch and adjusted the pillow under Tommie's foot. Checking the color of Tommie's toes to be sure the ankle wrap wasn't too tight, she said, "Well, enjoy it, because that's the last one you'll be having while I'm on duty." She narrowed her eyes at Tommie.

Tommie decided she would drag herself to the fridge the first chance she got if she needed another.

"You must be hungry since we missed lunch. Do you want something to tide you over until dinner?"

Tommie raised her bottle. "This is all I need for now, but go ahead and get yourself something."

"I snuck a granola bar while they were X-raying your ankle. I'm fine till dinner."

Megan had promised to be back by five. They heard the gravel crunch in the drive around four thirty. She entered, followed by Ashley and a very tall, handsome man.

"Aunt Kate, Tommie—oh, my God! What happened?" Megan rushed to the couch.

Tommie waved her hand. "It's nothing, just some bumps and I'm sure, tomorrow, bruises."

Kate had moved to the door where Ashley and the man stood, extending her hand. "Hi, I'm Kate, and you must be Ashley's father."

"Warren, and it's very nice to meet you. Megan speaks often of you."

"Please, come in." She turned back toward Megan and Tommie.

His voice was deep and husky. "We can't stay. I just came in to meet you and to ask if you and Megan would join Ashley and myself for dinner this evening." Megan turned a hopeful gaze to her aunt. "There's a wonderful restaurant about a half an hour drive from here. We dine there frequently, and I highly recommend it."

"It's very kind of you to ask, but I'm sorry. I couldn't possibly leave our injured guest here alone." Kate's eyes wandered back to meet Tommie's.

His words lacked any emotion. "Of course, I understand."

Tommie's conscience was battling her emotions. She knew she could manage a few hours on her own, but part of her wanted to be selfish and keep Kate to herself. She finally gave voice to what her conscience dictated. "I'll be fine for a while, Kate. You and Megan go and have a nice dinner. I'm pretty tired. I'll probably just sleep anyway."

Kate moved back toward the couch. "I'm still worried about that large knot on your head." She leaned down and brushed Tommie's hair back, inspecting the bump, which was covered with a butterfly bandage to hold the small cut closed.

Tommie shrugged away from Kate's gentle touch. "I'm not a child." She nudged Kate's thigh with her arm. "Go have dinner and enjoy yourselves. I'm fine." She pushed harder. "Go on."

Kate was torn between wanting to stay and take care of Tommie's every need, and Tommie's demand that she go.

Megan helped her make the decision. "Come on, Aunt Kate. Tommie says she'll be fine. You can call to check on her if you're that worried."

Tommie's eyes were darker than Kate had ever seen them when she turned her attention back to her. "Are you sure you'll be okay?"

Tommie waved a hand dismissively. "Absolutely, you two go have a good time." Tommie nearly choked on the last words. The last thing she wanted was for Kate to go out and enjoy herself with some man.

"Well, then." Kate looked at Warren. "I need a few minutes to change and freshen up."

Warren made himself comfortable in the easy chair just inside the door as Kate disappeared to the bedroom. The silence that followed was deafening. Neither Tommie nor Warren made any attempt at conversation, as if they understood they were both vying for Kate's attention. When she emerged with her blond locks hanging loosely around her shoulders, wearing a crisp blouse and slacks, Tommie groaned inwardly. She looked amazing. Tommie hated that she was going out with the smug-looking guy seated across the room.

After a quick trip to the kitchen, Kate walked to the couch, extending one hand with two pills and the other with a bottle of water. "Anything else you need before we leave?"

"Another beer."

Kate's wry smile crinkled her eyes. "Nice try."

"Go have a nice dinner."

Kate struggled to make her feet move. "I'll call you in an hour. Where's your phone?"

Tommie patted her pockets. "It must be in my pack."

Kate rummaged through the bag sitting at the other end of the couch. Finding the phone, she placed it on the end table by Tommie. "If you need anything at all, call me," she pleaded, knowing Tommie would suffer rather than call and bug Kate while she was out.

"I'm good, just go on."

Kate's heart ached at the hard edge in Tommie's voice. She squeezed Tommie's hand quickly and said, "We won't be gone long."

Tommie didn't miss how possessively Warren cupped Kate's elbow to steer her through the door after the girls. She swung her foot to the floor, hoping to get to the window to spy on Kate as they left, but when she stood the pain that shot from her swollen ankle dropped her quickly back onto the couch.

"Damn it!" she cursed loudly. She propped her foot back on the pillow as best she could and sucked the last drip of beer from the bottle. Jealousy was the only name Tommie could give the emotion she was feeling at the moment. She had no right to be jealous of Kate being on a date with a man, and yet she wanted to tie cement blocks to the man's ankles and drop him in the lake.

* * *

Kate fiddled nervously with the strap on her purse in her lap while the girls chatted away in the backseat and Warren tried to make polite conversation with her. She'd hated leaving Tommie alone at the cabin. She was less worried about her head wound since seeing the urgent care doctor, but she felt bad leaving Tommie alone in her present injured state. Kate wanted to be there, hovering over, taking care of her. She couldn't wait another couple of hours to talk to her.

As they entered the restaurant she said, "Go on in, I'll be just a minute," and pulled the phone from her purse. Tommie answered almost immediately. "How do you feel?"

Tommie muted the TV. "Okay, and it hasn't been an hour since you left."

Kate didn't want to be standing outside the restaurant; she wanted to be sitting with Tommie and fussing over her. "I know. I just feel bad you're there alone."

Tommie pulled at a loose thread on her shorts pocket, thinking she wished she wasn't alone too. "Kate, I'm fine. You need to quit worrying and enjoy your dinner."

"Well, I can't enjoy it when I keep thinking about you there by yourself." And I'm having dinner with a stranger—a male stranger at that.

"I'll be sitting right here where you left me when you get back. Probably snoring like a bear. So you don't need to call and check on me anymore. I'll see you when you get back if I'm awake." Tommie didn't give Kate a chance to respond before she disconnected the call and dropped her phone on the table.

God, Tommie thought, she hated feeling like an invalid. And she really wanted another beer. She stood again, steadying herself on her good foot before trying to put her weight on the other. When she did, the tears sprang from her eyes and nausea washed over her.

She sat down immediately, leaning back until the feeling subsided. "I'll be damned if I'm going to let an ankle sprain handicap me this bad."

She scooted off the couch onto the floor and began dragging her butt backward across the floor toward the kitchen. The effort needed to move her large frame soon tired her, so she stopped just outside the kitchen door for a few minutes to catch her breath and rest her overworked arms.

She stared at the fridge. "Almost there."

She covered the last twelve feet without too much trouble, popped open the door and managed to reach her stash. The sound the cap made when she twisted it off the cold bottle was like music to her ears. After several huge gulps, she emitted an "ahh!" She took another drink, then raised the bottle as if to toast. "You can knock me down, but you can't take away my beer."

She finished the first in record time and reached in for another. Partway through the second, her head became fuzzy and her vision began to blur. "Whoa!" She set the bottle down and leaned her head back.

* * *

They had barely finished their meal when Kate excused herself to the ladies' room. Redialing Tommie's number, she absently tapped her nail on the sink listening as it rang and rang and went to voice mail. She hung up and dialed again and again, with the same results.

Kate whispered, "Tommie, where are you?" When the voice mail greeting finished and the phone beeped, she said anxiously, "Tommie, I'm really concerned you're not answering your phone. If you're just ignoring me…well, please call me back and let me know. Okay…"

She hung up and paced in front of the sink for several minutes. As she slipped the phone back in her purse, she muttered, "We'll just have to leave immediately." She left the ladies' room with a sick feeling in the pit of her stomach.

When she reached the table Warren said, "We were just discussing dessert. Would you like some coffee?"

Rather than sit, Kate stood behind her chair. "Actually, I really need to get back to the cabin."

Warren stood to pull out Kate's chair. "Surely, you have time for some coffee and a bite of dessert."

Kate shook her head vehemently. "No, I really need to get back now." Kate looked at Megan. "Tommie's not answering her phone and I'm worried about her."

Megan knew how her aunt was when she worried. "I'm sure she's okay, Aunt Kate." Turning to Warren she said, "But I don't want dessert so we can go"—she looked at Ashley—"unless you want some."

Ashley shook her head. "We should probably go, Daddy." It was apparent that Ashley had had enough adult company for one evening, especially that of her father.

Warren frowned but conceded. "Fine then, ladies. Shall we go?" He waved the waiter over for the check.

Kate was nearly silent on the ride home, only speaking when she was required to respond, otherwise considering the possible reasons for Tommie not answering her phone or calling her back.

As they neared the cabin, Ashley asked, "Can Megan stay over tonight?"

The question was directed to both adults in the front seat, but only Warren answered. "Sure, that's fine with me."

When Kate didn't answer, Megan asked, "Aunt Kate, would that be okay?"

"Huh?" she replied, clearly having not heard the question.

Ashley asked again, "Can Megan spend the night?"

Kate glanced at Warren. "Is that all right with you?"

"Like I just said…" He hesitated, then said, "Sure, that's fine."

"Okay, sweetie, just be home by lunchtime."

Megan readily agreed.

At the cabin, Megan and Ashley raced from the car inside to get Megan's things.

Warren started to make small talk as Kate opened the door to get out. "I'm glad you could join us for dinner."

Kate leaned in the door. "Yes, thank you, Warren, and it was nice to meet you."

Before he could continue, Kate closed the door and rushed to the cabin.

CHAPTER FOURTEEN

The first thing she noticed was the empty couch, then, the girls standing in the kitchen doorway. She dropped her purse and hurried toward them.

"Oh, God, what?" Pushing between them, she saw Tommie on the floor with her head tilted at an odd angle. "Tommie!" she called, dropping to her knees beside her.

"Aunt Kate, what's wrong with her?" Megan's voice held terror.

There were drops of blood on the floor from the soaked gauze covering Tommie's arm injury. Kate gently cradled Tommie's face in her hands and tipped her head up.

"Tommie." She slid her fingers to her neck, where she felt a strong pulse. She patted lightly on her cheek. "Tommie, open your eyes and look at me."

When Tommie's eyelids fluttered open, her eyes were pale and hazy.

"Aunt Kate?" Megan asked again.

Without removing her gaze from Tommie, Kate said, "Megan, soak a towel in cold water for me, please."

She rubbed her thumb over Tommie's cheek. "Can you talk to me?"

Tommie's lids closed slowly and she swallowed hard. Kate took the wet towel, wiping it gently over Tommie's face, and her eyes opened again.

"Tommie, I need you to answer me, do you understand?" Tommie's head nodded the tiniest bit. "What happened?"

Tommie croaked, "I…"

Recognizing the difficulty Tommie was having talking, Kate jerked open the fridge and pulled out a bottle of water. Bringing it to Tommie's lips she said, "Drink some water. Pain pills can really dry you out."

After several small swallows, Tommie managed to get her mouth working. "I feel like someone stuffed my head with cotton."

It wasn't until then that Kate noticed the empty and half-empty beer bottles on the other side of Tommie's body.

Megan asked again, "Is she okay?"

Kate made Tommie take another drink of water. "She will be. You girls run on. Ashley's dad is waiting in the car."

"Are you sure it's still okay? I mean, I can stay if you need me to."

Kate looked over her shoulder. "I can manage, Megan. You two go on." Kate returned her attention to Tommie, wiping the cold cloth gently over her face again. "I leave you for a few hours and you manage to reopen your arm wound and try to kill yourself on the kitchen floor." Kate settled close to Tommie on the floor.

Hoarsely, Tommie said, "I'm sorry, I didn't—"

Kate touched her finger to Tommie's lips. "Shh…" She wiped the cloth again over Tommie's face, then placed it around her neck.

Megan stopped in the doorway. "Okay, we're leaving, Aunt Kate, as long as you're sure."

Kate tore her eyes away from Tommie "Go on, sweetie, everything's fine. Just remember to be back by lunchtime tomorrow."

Megan bobbed her head. "Sure, okay."

When Kate looked back at Tommie, her eyes were again closed. Slipping her hand into Tommie's, she squeezed. "Hey…you want to explain what happened here?"

Slowly Tommie reopened her eyes. "I'm sorry, Kate. I didn't follow your orders."

Kate shook her head. "I would have never guessed. You obviously walked on that ankle. It's as big as a melon now." Tommie shook her head. "No?" Kate asked. "Then how did you get in here?"

Tommie gave a light chuckle. "I dragged this big butt across the floor."

Kate raised Tommie's arm. "That would explain why your arm is bleeding again." She frowned. "That and the alcohol." She eyed the beer bottles nearly hidden beside Tommie.

"I just…" Tommie stuttered. "Man, I was so thirsty and not for water."

Kate stood and grabbed another dishtowel to wrap around Tommie's arm. "Yes, well, pain meds can dry you out, but beer was a terrible choice. Number one, it doesn't mix well with pain pills, and two, alcohol thins your blood, which increases bleeding." She gingerly wrapped the towel around her arm. "We need to get you up off the floor and get that foot elevated."

Tommie pushed her body forward from the cabinet. "What I need in the worst way is to pee. Oh yeah…" She groaned. "Like a racehorse."

Kate stood, extending her hand. "Can you push yourself up with one leg?"

"I think so," Tommie said. "The question is if I can do it without wetting myself." She squeezed her eyes shut as she pushed.

"That's the least of my concerns at the moment," Kate said as she steadied Tommie with her weight on one foot. "After the bathroom, you're getting in bed for the night, no argument."

Tommie winced as they hobbled toward the kitchen door. "Yes, ma'am." When Kate had her in the bathroom, Tommie said, "I think I can manage from here."

Tommie pulled her arm from Kate's shoulder, but Kate's arm remained around her waist. "Are you sure? I don't need you falling in here and cracking your head open."

Tommie sighed. "I'm really sorry, Kate. I promise not to do anything stupid. Well, anything *more*."

Kate slowly slid her hand across Tommie's back. "Call me if you need any help."

"…*need any help*." God, did she need help. As out of it and in pain as Tommie felt, her body didn't have any trouble reacting to

Kate's nearness. The ache and the obvious fire between her thighs was becoming unbearable. When Tommie groaned quietly, Kate immediately placed a hand on Tommie's hip and stepped in front of her.

"What's wrong?"

Tommie gazed into the deepest pools of blue she'd ever seen. "Uh…I really gotta go."

Kate nodded. "Oh, of course, that's why we're in the bathroom in the first place."

Tommie wanted to slip her fingers into the silky blond hair falling across Kate's shoulders, pull her close and kiss her—more than she'd ever wanted to kiss a woman in her life. She wet her lips to speak. When Kate's eyes dropped to Tommie's mouth, she'd have sworn Kate was looking at her lips like they were a savory slice of dessert. *I'm hallucinating.* When she cleared her throat, Kate's eyes drifted back to hers. "If I'm going to bed I might as well get dressed for it now. Would you mind getting boxer shorts and a clean T-shirt out of my bag for me?"

Kate's hand still rested on Tommie's hip and her eyes were on Tommie's. She nodded slowly. "Okay." After what was a fraction of a second but seemed like long minutes, she left the room.

Tommie took a deep breath. If Kate stood that close again and looked at her again the way she had been, Tommie didn't think she could stop herself from kissing her. And maybe it was the drugs, but she wasn't so sure Kate wouldn't kiss her back. She'd had a definite look of desire in her eyes. Either that or the pills were having a serious delusional effect.

Kate returned with Tommie's clothes and placed them on the vanity. "Are you sure you don't need help?"

"I'll manage. Besides, I'm a little modest about going to the bathroom in front of someone."

Kate blushed lightly. "I just meant with your clothes…" She waved her hands around nervously. "You've never been hospitalized?"

Tommie shook her head. "Not since the tonsillectomy when I was eight, and I'm pretty sure it was my mom that helped me with the whole bathroom thing when I was drugged out then." Tommie was certain her face flushed to match Kate's. The thought of being so banged up that Kate might have to help her go to the bathroom was embarrassing.

Pulling the door closed, Kate stepped into the hall. "Well, call if you need anything."

Tommie unzipped her shorts, dropping them and her underwear to the floor as her bottom hit the seat. Her whole body sighed as her bladder finally released. She sat there for several minutes longer allowing everything some time to relax. Stepping out of her shorts and underwear, she pulled on the boxers, stood, flushed and lowered the lid to sit again, all without losing her balance or putting much weight on her throbbing ankle. Things didn't go as well with her T-shirt. She struggled once, twice, three times to pull it off but was unsuccessful. Finally admitting defeat, she called Kate's name.

Kate was instantly at the door. "What's wrong?"

"I can't get my shirt off." Kate slowly pushed the door open. Tommie had the hem of the shirt pulled under her arms. She grimaced. "I can't seem to get it up and off."

Standing in front of her, telling herself to pretend it was Megan she was helping, Kate said, "Let me. Lift your arms." She gently guided the fabric over Tommie's head and injured arm. She dropped it in the sink. "I'll soak this and see if I can get the blood out."

Tommie shrugged. "It's just a T-shirt. I have more."

Kate automatically reached behind Tommie and unclasped her bra, gingerly sliding it over her injured arm too. When she glimpsed the small firm breasts in front of her, her legs grew shaky. As Kate watched, Tommie's nipples puckered—and she could feel her own straining under her bra in response.

Oh God, she thought, her skin suddenly feeling too tight everywhere. *It's just Megan, it's just Megan*, she repeated over and over. It didn't seem to help. The throbbing between her thighs was a clear indication this wasn't Megan's bare chest she was looking at.

Tommie shivered under Kate's lingering gaze. Snapped from her lustful stare, Kate grabbed for the T-shirt on the vanity.

"You're cold. Let's get this shirt on you."

Tommie helped Kate help her as much as she could, but it wasn't easy. Kate's proximity, the smell of her perfume and the tender way she touched Tommie made her want to grab Kate around the waist and pull her down into her lap to tamp the fire down. Or…stoke it even hotter.

"You're sweating," Kate placed a cool hand on the side of Tommie's neck. "You feel a little warm."

No kidding, Tommie thought.

"Do you feel feverish?"

Tommie shook her head. "No, just like a big airhead."

"That's the pills." Kate knelt and took Tommie's injured arm in her hand. "Let's see how much damage you've done." Kate carefully removed the dressing.

"The pills make me feel warm and fuzzy." Tommie watched Kate intently. "I'm an airhead for falling in the first place and then for not listening to the advice of a medical professional."

Kate looked into Tommie's eyes. "You're hardly an airhead. Hardheaded maybe, but definitely not an airhead."

There was so little space between them now, Tommie thought, that she could kiss Kate if she just leaned slightly forward...

"I'm sorry. Am I hurting you?"

Tommie looked at Kate questioningly.

"You were biting your lip. I thought I'd hurt you."

My ego maybe, Tommie thought. *Or my reputation*. Any other woman, straight or otherwise, she would have already bedded months ago—hell, after their first meeting, probably. And even though she thought of Kate that way, Tommie couldn't let herself make a move on her.

"Tommie?"

She shook her head. "I, uh...I don't know," she shrugged. "Must be the drugs."

Kate finished inspecting her arm—"Thankfully the bleeding stopped, so it may heal without infection"—and helped steady Tommie as she stood. Slipping an arm around her waist, she said, "You're going into the bedroom to sleep in the bed." When Tommie started to protest, she said, "No argument. You need to lay somewhere that's comfortable on your back and that's not a sofa."

Tommie protested even as Kate steered her toward the bedroom. "I'm not going to take your bed."

Kate turned sideways to fit them through the door. "You're going to do exactly as I say until you're out of my care. Understood?"

Tommie sighed. "Yes, ma'am." She dropped hard on the side of the bed.

"And could you please quit making me have to treat you like a child?"

Tommie looked sheepishly up into Kate's eyes. "Yes, ma'am."

When Kate had Tommie settled comfortably in bed she got a pain pill and some water. "You might as well take this now. Once your beer wears off it's going to hurt a lot worse than it does right now." After Tommie swallowed the pill, she asked, "Is there anything else you need?"

A goodnight kiss? Tommie thought, then shook her head no. "I can't let you sleep on the couch." She patted the empty side of the bed. "There's plenty of room here. I promise not to snore too much."

"I'm not sleeping on the couch. Megan's staying over with Ashley so I'll sleep in her bed. It's just across the hall. If you need anything, just call."

Man, Tommie thought, *so far away*.

* * *

Kate readied herself for bed, then sat out on the couch until almost eleven, drinking a glass of wine and reading until she felt sleep coming on. After turning off all the lights, she stood in the doorway of the bedroom and watched Tommie's still form in the faint moonlight that filtered through the blinds. She watched a long time, marking the rise and fall of her chest and remembering with complete clarity what Tommie's half-nude body had looked like earlier. How sexy she had looked, even as banged up as she was, and how there'd never been another woman in her life that had stirred the kind of desire in her that Tommie had. Kate sighed heavily and took herself to bed.

The voice that came to her in her sleep was so soft that Kate was sure she was dreaming it. When it became louder she rolled over. Then it was clear that Tommie was calling for her.

"Kate, are you awake? Oh, God, oh, God!"

The panic in her voice made Kate jump from the bed and bolt across the hall. Flipping on the switch she saw Tommie sitting up in bed with her hand clamped on her calf just inches above the ACE wrap.

"Tommie, what's wrong?"

She turned watery eyes to Kate. "My leg's cramping and it…"— she squeezed her leg harder—"oh, God, it's curling my toes…it's killing me." She panted as Kate sat beside her on the bed.

Pushing Tommie's hand away, she said, "You've got to massage it, to get it to relax." She dug her fingers into the large muscle in the back of the calf. After a minute Kate could feel the tension ease and the muscle relaxed. "Better?"

Tommie inhaled a deep breath. "Much, thank you." Her brow was covered with sweat.

"What happened to the pillows?"

Kate had meticulously positioned two pillows under Tommie's leg and foot to keep it elevated, but they weren't anywhere to be seen now. Actually, she noticed, the bed looked like a tornado had swept across it.

"I couldn't get comfortable, and I couldn't go to sleep. I think they got kicked to the floor."

Tommie remained sitting, leaning on her good arm as Kate made her way around the bed to retrieve the pillows. Once she had Tommie settled, she started from the room.

"Hey, you gonna make me sleep with the light on?"

"I'll be right back," Kate called as she headed down the hall.

She returned several minutes later with a fresh bottle of water, another pain pill and a wet washcloth.

"You're not going to turn me into a drug addict are you?"

"You're a big girl and it's been long enough since the last one."

When Tommie had swallowed the pill, Kate sat next to her and wiped the cool cloth gently over Tommie's face. Kate thought she looked so innocent and vulnerable in that moment. Nothing at all like the woman she'd first encountered in the bar so long ago. It made her want to just take Tommie home with her and care for her for all time. With each swipe her thigh pressed into Tommie's side. *Megan*, she reminded herself when she felt again the stirrings she had experienced earlier. *Just pretend it's Megan.*

"I'm sorry." Tommie spoke so softly that Kate couldn't make out what she said.

She met Tommie's eyes. "What?"

Tommie cleared her throat, but her voice still sounded so meek. "I'm sorry for ruining your spring break vacation."

Kate brushed her fingers lightly over Tommie's cheek. "Oh, honey, you haven't ruined anything."

"But…" Her voice was hoarse. She cleared her throat and tried again. "But what are you going to do for the next five days now that you're saddled with this?" She indicated herself.

Kate watched Tommie's eyes as they flickered between shades of dark and darker. She sat back a bit, sliding her leg over the side of the bed. "Well, let's see…I brought several books I've been dying to read. So maybe I'll just relax a lot, read and enjoy the quiet out here…" She regarded Tommie for a moment. "And nurse you back to health." She patted Tommie's thigh before standing, turning off the light and rounding the bed.

When she turned the covers back on the other side, Tommie asked, "What are you doing?"

Kate slipped onto the bed, propping herself against the headboard. "I'm going to sit here with you until you fall asleep."

"You don't have to do—"

Kate cut her off. "Do you remember what I told you earlier?"

"Yes, ma'am."

Kate smiled in the moonlight. "Good, then be quiet and go to sleep. Our bodies heal faster when they are rested."

Tommie wrestled a pillow from under her head. "Here…at least be comfortable."

Kate took the offered pillow and tucked it behind her.

* * *

A faint light was filtering through the blinds when Tommie's bladder woke her. The little bedside clock read just after seven. She rolled her head slowly to see Kate cradling the pillow under her head and sleeping soundly. Tommie marveled at how beautiful she looked now without a dash of makeup and her hair falling loosely every which way. She wanted to brush the strands of hair off Kate's forehead. She wanted to touch every inch of her soft skin. She wanted so much that she couldn't have.

Knowing that Kate had planned to only sit with her until she fell asleep, Tommie had feigned sleep, thinking Kate then would move back across the hall. Instead Kate's breathing had become deep and regular, and she'd slid down into the bed with a soft murmur. Tommie had laid awake for more than an hour after that. The pain pill should have put her to sleep faster than that, she thought. It must have been the presence of Kate's sleeping body beside her that had kept her mind whirring, reeling with fantasies. Just waking next to the woman was stoking the pulse between her legs.

As quietly as Tommie could, she sat up and moved her legs over the side of the bed, fully intending to hobble herself to the bathroom if she could bear the weight on her ankle. She was about to test it when Kate bolted upright.

"What do you think you're doing?" she asked in a groggy voice.

"I was trying not to wake you."

Kate tugged her nightshirt down her thighs as she climbed out of the bed. "And?"

Tommie exhaled. "I have to pee and this is really getting old, not being able to help myself."

Kate stood in front of her, perky breasts and perkier nipples showing through the silky nightshirt. Tommie turned her gaze to the floor.

"It feels a lot better, I think I can walk on it."

Kate planted her hands on her hips and cocked her head. "What did the doctor tell you?"

"I forget…Take it easy, maybe?" She shrugged.

Kate shook her head. "Okay, then what did I tell you?"

"I have to do as you order."

"And you know what I'm about to order?"

"To get my ass back in bed?"

Kate had to fight the smile trying to escape. "Right, so I can change a wet bed? I don't think so." She extended a hand to help Tommie stand and aided her to the bathroom, Tommie grumbling all the way.

"Since I'm here, I might as well take a bath. I can manage without any help, I think."

Kate moved to the door. "Call me if you need help. I'm going to put coffee on."

"I can take this wrap off, right?"

"I'll be back to unwrap it after I start the coffee. I want to take a look."

Tommie was sitting on the side of the tub running water when Kate knocked lightly on the door.

"Can I come in?"

"Yeah."

Kate knelt beside her to unwrap her ankle. "Are you sure you can manage without getting your arm wet? You've got to keep those stitches dry."

Tommie allowed her eyes to scan Kate's womanly figure, which was covered only by the thinnest of silky material. "I'll manage."

Kate pulled the last of the wrap off. "It looks a little less swollen this morning." She rolled her eyes at Tommie. "Which surprises me after what you pulled last night."

"Enough with the scolding. I said I would follow your orders from here on out, and I will...explicitly."

Kate folded the wrap loosely and laid it on the vanity. "Let me help you with your T-shirt before I leave."

Tommie closed her eyes. "Fine." She raised her arms over her head and tried to imagine Kate as an elderly nurse's aide. That worked until Kate's fingers touched her sides, causing a sharp intake of breath.

"Sorry!" Kate said. "My hands must be colder than I thought." She finished pulling the shirt off. Tommie's nipples were erect, just as they had been the night before. "I'll get you some clothes to dress in," she said, turning toward the door. "What would you like to wear today?"

Tommie reached to turn the water off. "Surprise me."

As soon as Kate closed the door Tommie stood, dropping her boxers and returning to the edge of the tub. Cautiously putting her good foot in first, she easily swung her other leg over and lowered herself in the hot water with only minor pain from her arm. "Ahh..." She propped her injured ankle on her other thigh and slid down until her chest nearly disappeared under the water, keeping her arm high and dry on the side of the tub. Closing her eyes, she let the warmth relax her.

Kate pulled a pair of well-worn jeans and a button-up shirt from Tommie's duffel. With guilty pleasure, she raised the shirt to her face and breathed its fresh laundered smell. It reminded her of the few times her face had been pressed against Tommie's chest... against her small firm breasts and those nipples, which seemed to harden in an instant.

She wished she had the luxury of taking a hot bath right now with her favorite tub toy. Maybe then she could release some of the tension that'd been building for the last two days. Why she thought she could spend a week tucked away in a cabin in the woods with Tommie and not drive herself crazy escaped her. She dropped onto the couch, remembering when she had allowed herself to get so comfortable lying next to Tommie's warm body last night, watching the rise and fall of her chest, that she dozed off herself. That was one of the things she missed most about a relationship—sleeping close to someone and feeling the security a warm body beside her evoked. If she got through this week without making a pass at her and ruining both their lives, she was swearing off the woman. Kate had never in her life been attracted to a butch, and since shortly after meeting Tommie she'd not been able to think of another woman with any kind of desire...except for Tommie.

As a teen Kate had tried to deny her sexuality. Later, because being with one of "those" women would all but advertise whom, or rather what she was, she avoided the places that butches were known to frequent. She was too insecure to openly embrace being a lesbian. She'd not even been able to say the word for a very long time.

Then in college, when she finally did come out to her family, her parents had cast her out. She became even more aware of appearances and fiercely determined to keep her private life private. Nikki had been totally open and accepting of her sexuality, to her parents' further disgust, but Megan's unexpected addition to Kate's everyday life and her partner Hayden's departure seemed the perfect justification for staying in the closet. But there was something, or some *things*, about Tommie—Kate couldn't pinpoint exactly what—that were making her nearly irresistible.

She knocked lightly on the door. "Are you decent?" She entered before Tommie could answer.

Tommie grabbed quickly for the washcloth and covered her crotch. "So much for privacy."

Kate laid Tommie's clothes on the vanity. "I've seen more naked bodies in my job than you could ever hope to see in your lifetime," she said matter-of-factly. "Would you like me to wash your hair for you?"

Tommie sighed. "Why not?"

Remembering how it had made her feel last night, Kate tried to avoid looking at Tommie's bare chest again. It was bad enough to be sliding her fingers through her hair and wanting to tip her head back and kiss her. Still, as soon as Tommie closed her eyes, Kate stole another look. She suppressed the arousal that the sight of her erect nipples triggered, then made quick work of rinsing her hair.

"I'll give you some privacy to finish your bath." She stood, drying her hands. Hanging up the towel, she added, "Don't forget to wash the important stuff." She winked and watched as Tommie's face and neck turned a rosy hue. "Call if you need anything."

When Kate closed the door, Tommie groaned as she cupped her crotch. Under her breath she muttered, "You can come back and finish what you started." She squeezed her thighs, willing the throb to go away.

What choice did she have but to resign herself to the embarrassment? After all, to Kate she was probably just another patient. There shouldn't have been any need to feel uncomfortable. She had, however, kept the washcloth securely in her lap as she sat up and Kate settled on the side of the tub.

At the first touch of Kate's fingers massaging the shampoo into her hair, Tommie had felt her nipples tighten again and the now-familiar slow burn move lower. Thank God women didn't have penises, she thought, because otherwise her desire for Kate would no longer be a secret.

Twenty minutes later Tommie hopped down the hall and braced herself in the kitchen doorway. Her voice startled Kate from a daydream.

"You know, it's much easier to hop on one foot when I'm not under the influence of those mind-altering drugs."

Kate quickly rose and dragged a chair over to Tommie. "Sit. I'll put your wrap back on."

Puffing hard, Tommie dropped without resistance. It was getting harder and harder to resist Kate in general, she realized. She handed the ACE bandage to Kate, who propped Tommie's leg on her own tight thighs as she wrapped it. When she was done, she gently rested Tommie's foot on the floor and reached for Tommie's chest, leaning between her legs. Tommie felt her eyes grow big as saucers.

"You missed one…" Kate's fingers deftly fastened a button that had been left hanging, and she stepped back. "A couple more days off that foot and it'll be able to bear some weight, I'd guess."

She reached out a hand. "Come have coffee and I'll start some breakfast."

Tommie accepted Kate's assistance and the cup of coffee. Kate moved so naturally in the kitchen, she thought, in any kitchen, apparently. That's what she needed to start thinking about, Tommie thought as she gazed out the tiny window over the table—settling down so she could find herself a good woman. A homebody. She'd sown enough wild oats. Hadn't she?

"It's supposed to be a beautiful day."

"Huh?" Tommie looked over to where Kate was wiping her hands.

"I said, it's supposed to be a beautiful day." Tommie nodded. "Is there anything you'd like to do today?"

Tommie glanced at her bandaged ankle. "Yeah, I think I'd like to try that seven-mile hike. How long do you think it would take us?"

"Maybe by Friday you can hobble one of the short ones, but I wouldn't recommend it."

"Exactly. I suppose I'll park my big butt on the couch the rest of the week. But you have Megan. You two can go out and see the sights."

Kate came to the table carrying her coffee. "First of all, you don't have a big butt. It's in direct proportion to your stature." Kate's cheeks pinked. "Secondly, Megan's here to spend her time with her friend, not me. That's why we dragged you along, to keep me company."

Tommie shook her head. "And what wonderful company I'm proving to be."

"Don't sell yourself short. You're an interesting, intelligent woman. I enjoy hanging with you." She shrugged. "If we do nothing more than sit out on the deck and watch the grass grow, it's fine with me." She went back to the stove to start cooking breakfast. "Really, I'm looking forward to just relaxing."

* * *

Megan came back at lunchtime as promised, Ashley in tow. When they finished eating, the girls made some excuse to go off exploring. Kate and Tommie settled on the back deck, Kate with a paperback romance and Tommie with a small notebook, her phone and tiny earbuds. Normally Tommie could give a flying foul ball about the whole evolution of technology. But she was grateful now for her smartphone and its ESPN Radio app. As amazing as it was to be sequestered in the woods with Kate, she was beginning to feel out of touch with her real world.

Later, bored to tears, Tommie glanced over at Kate. Her book was folded in her lap and she was basking in the sun, her face illuminated like an angel's.

"Either that's a terribly boring book you're reading in order to put you to sleep or you really do enjoy this peace and quiet stuff."

Kate slowly rolled her head to look at Tommie. "If you knew how noisy and absolutely crazy hospitals are, you'd know why I'm drinking in every drop of this." Actually, she had just been having the most pleasant daydream, reliving the hike on Saturday and thinking how natural it felt to be sharing that with Tommie.

Tommie searched for something to keep the conversation flowing. "So just how crazy is being a surgical nurse at a hospital?"

"The routine surgeries, like tonsillectomies or appies—appendectomies—are just that, pretty routine. Unlike, say, open-heart surgeries, which are rather delicate, as you might guess. Then there are trauma surgeries. They can sometimes be like traversing a minefield. The worst are children." She sighed. "There's nothing more heartbreaking than looking at the frightened and innocent face of a child about to go into surgery. Or worse, the ones whose face you can't read because some adult didn't think a seat belt or bike helmet was that important." Tommie immediately regretted her question and the pained expression it caused on Kate's face.

She rubbed her forehead in lieu of smacking it. "I was so out of it last night I didn't even ask how your dinner was with…" She shook her head. "With Mr. Ashley. I don't even remember his name."

Kate laughed lightly. "Mr. Ashley's name is Warren, and dinner was okay."

"Just okay? By most women's standards, I'd guess he's considered a pretty hunky guy."

Kate thought for a minute. "I suppose most women would agree with that, but, just between us, he's pretty much an egotistical ass. It's no wonder Ashley's mother left him."

"Ouch!" Tommie cringed. "I guess it's a good thing, then, that you kind of like spending time with me, huh?"

"You have some redeeming qualities," Kate said.

"Do tell," Tommie said.

"Well..." Kate hesitated. "You turned me on to baseball. I'm even thinking about following the Cougars this year. Maybe you'll take me to another game this summer?"

Wow, Tommie thought, she'd provided Kate with a turn-on! She wondered if she should share with Kate how she turned her on.

"Something you want to share?"

Tommie was lost in the ache that was starting down low again. "Huh?"

"What are you smiling about?"

Tommie lied. "Another converted sports nut." She gave Kate a wide grin. "Before I'm done with you, you'll be waving one of those foam fingers and cursing the opposing teams."

Kate rolled her eyes. "I'm not seeing it, but feel free to comfort yourself with that fantasy."

Tommie wondered if the rosy color in Kate's cheeks was a result of the afternoon sun beating down on them. "Yeah, that's what I'll do." She nodded, grin still in place, considering how her world had been turned upside from how she'd envisioned it for so many years and how it all seemed insignificant in comparison to sharing this family experience with Kate. It made it much easier to picture herself being committed to just one person and perhaps finding that happily ever after.

If there was one thing that could make her change her idea of the perfect way to be with a woman or with just one person, Tommie thought, it was definitely Kate.

* * *

By the end of the week, Tommie had grown comfortable with the simple quiet at their cabin in the woods and Kate's companionship. She could do the whole relationship thing, she was now sure. She just had to find the right woman to do it with. She wished Kate could be that woman, but since that was impossible, she'd need to find a way to get Kate Bellam off her mind when they returned home. Kate stirred too many dangerous thoughts and physical responses in Tommie. If Kate ever found out, Tommie knew, she'd be appalled.

Tommie retrieved her bag from the trunk when they returned Saturday, preparing to shift it to her Jeep.

Megan grabbed her own bag and started up the drive. "Thanks for coming, Tommie. It was fun. Sorry you got hurt."

"It was still fun. Thanks for the invite." Tommie called after her.

"If you stop by the middle of this week I can take those stitches out for you," Kate said, watching to make sure Tommie didn't need help.

"I wouldn't want to bother you."

"It wouldn't be a bother at all."

"Thanks for the offer, but my doctor's office is just a few blocks from my place. I'll probably stop in there so he can lecture me about drinking beer and not eating healthy."

"At least you can tell him you ate healthy last week."

Tommie nodded her head. "That I did."

She was nervous about this parting with Kate. She'd made up her mind to avoid her in the future and concentrate her time and energy on finding the woman of her dreams. The sooner she got Kate out of her head, the sooner she could get back to living her life. A life that included real intimacy with a woman and not simply daydreams.

"Thanks again for the invite. And for taking such good care of me."

"You're welcome." Kate's eyes sparkled in the sunlight. "Anytime."

Tommie made herself look away. "Okay—I'll see you." She headed down the drive, limping only slightly.

She waved a hand over her head in acknowledgment when Kate called after her, "Remember, go easy on that ankle. No jogging for a while."

* * *

Kate watched sadly as Tommie's car drove off. The week she'd just spent with her had been so close to perfect. It didn't matter that Tommie had gotten hurt and they spent most of their time at the cabin. The only thing else Kate would have wished for was the physical closeness she knew couldn't happen between them. *Oh well*, she thought. *A girl can dream.*

Back in the house Kate breathed deeply of its familiar smells. The cabin in the woods had been relaxing, a nice diversion, but Kate was ready to get back to real life. Well, mostly real life. With any luck she could start dating again after Megan went off to college and maybe even tell Megan the truth about who she really was besides just her devoted and loving aunt. She dropped her keys on the kitchen counter as Megan entered, fresh from depositing her bag in her room, Kate assumed.

"Did you have a good break, Megan?"

"Oh yeah, it was great. Thanks, Aunt Kate."

"So what did you and Ashley spend all your time doing?"

"You know, just hanging out."

"I didn't hear any mention of any eligible guys."

Megan's cheeks colored. "Uh, well, we weren't exactly out cruising for guys."

"Good, I'm glad you both know there's a whole world out there in addition to guys."

Megan's face flushed full red. "Oh, we know."

Kate relented—assuming Megan was anticipating a "sex talk" or some such thing—and changed the topic.

"I think pizza sounds good for dinner. What do you think?"

Megan grinned. "I think I like the way you think."

CHAPTER FIFTEEN

It took two weeks before Tommie wasn't sitting around all day thinking about Kate. How great she looked dressed simply in jeans and a sweatshirt. How she smelled just after her shower and how fresh she still smelled at the end of the day. But mostly how she looked sleeping next to Tommie, the sound of her breathing and the soft murmurs she made in her sleep.

Finally, though, Tommie was ready to go out drinking and carousing again. She started after work that Friday, talking with Jamie at Lili's Pad while she waited on carryout from Pop's Diner next door. After dinner, she showered and dressed in her tightest black jeans, a simple snug white T-shirt, her black Doc Marten ankle boots and her black leather jacket, preparing for serious cruising. She was headed to The Underground.

She arrived ahead of most of the crowd and took the seat at the bar that offered the best view of the dance floor. Two beers and two hours later, a busty, attractive brunette sidled up next to her to order a "Cosmo" from the bartender. Tommie had been watching her. She was at a table with six or seven other women. She had danced plenty, but always with one or another of the women seated with her, never the same one and never to a slow number. Tommie figured she was either single or stag for the evening. She would find out soon enough.

She turned her stool to face the bar and when the bartender set the colorful drink glass before the brunette, she slapped down some money. "I've got this one."

The bartender winked as if to say, "Good luck."

"Thank you," the brunette said.

"No, thank *you*. For improving the view in this place."

"That's kind of you to say," she said, extending her hand. "I'm Jodi."

Tommie took the slender hand in hers. It was very long for someone who was perhaps only five foot five. *The better to stroke you with*, Tommie thought. She immediately scolded herself. She was supposed to be looking for Ms. Right, not Ms. Right Now.

"It's very nice to meet you, Jodi. I'm Tommie."

"It's nice to meet you too, Tommie. Thank you again for the drink."

She moved the glass to her lips and sipped. "Are you here alone or waiting for someone?"

"Both." Tommie took a quick sip of her beer. "I'm looking for the woman of my dreams." She grinned.

"Well, while you're waiting, would you like to join me and my friends?"

"Only if you promise me a dance."

Jodi took Tommie's hand, pulling her off the stool. "I'm sure that can be arranged."

At the table Jodi introduced Tommie to her friends, whose names she couldn't remember five minutes later. She watched as the pretty brunette interacted with the other women, and the more she saw, the more she liked Jodi. When the first slow number started to play, she stood, offering her hand.

"Let's dance."

Amidst raised eyebrows, Jodi stood. "Let's."

She molded perfectly against Tommie and they began to move to the music. It was hard to tell in the dim light, but Tommie guessed Jodi was a few years older than she was. Maybe Kate's age. "Stop," she told herself. Kate was history and she was prepared to possibly never see her again. They had shared some good times, but she needed to move on.

Jodi tilted her head to gaze up at Tommie.

"What?"

"You looked like you were somewhere else."

Tommie turned on the charm. "I was just thinking how good you feel in my arms." Jodi placed her head on Tommie's shoulder, drawing her arm tighter around her. When the song ended, Tommie leaned close. "This was really nice, thank you."

Jodi took her hand. "You want to get some air?" Tommie nodded and allowed Jodi to lead her through the crowd. Part of the way across the parking lot she stopped at a small pickup, lowered its tailgate and hopped up on it. Patting beside her, she said, "Join me."

Tommie did and they began talking. About jobs or, rather, careers. Jodi was an accountant, which completely blew away the image Tommie had of accountants. She worked at a firm downtown that serviced some of the bigger companies in the city. Jodi was familiar with Tommie's byline but admitted she was not a sports fan.

"I'm surprised I haven't seen you around before."

Jodi gazed up at the stars. "I had a pretty bad breakup a while back. I've been a hermit until just recently. We never did go out much. She was a doctor and worried a lot about how people perceived her."

Tommie nodded her understanding. She'd run across more than one of those kind of gals in college. "I guess I'm lucky to be doing what I do. Sports nuts don't much care if I'm a dyke, as long as I know my stuff."

Jodi turned to look at Tommie. "I wouldn't consider you a dyke. Butch maybe, but certainly not a dyke. To me dykes are rough. You know, not tender"—she touched Tommie's thigh—"like you were when we danced."

"And what kind of women does Jodi like?" Tommie asked, cocking her head.

"The kind that like women. I trust that includes you?"

Tommie slowly nodded her head. "Yeah…I do." Jodi shivered and Tommie hopped off the tailgate, shrugged out of her jacket and slipped it over Jodi's shoulders. "We should go back inside." Jodi slipped her hand into Tommie's as they walked back to the bar.

Tommie bought a round of drinks for the table but found that her old exuberant, entertaining personality was content to sit back and just take things in. She rested her arm across the back of Jodi's chair, where Jodi frequently leaned into it as she spoke. It felt comfortable, Tommie thought. Is that what a relationship is? Two people who are comfortable being close? Not the anxiousness she felt whenever Kate was close? *Comfortable*, Tommie thought again. She could do comfortable.

A little after midnight Jodi leaned over the table and told her friends, "I've got to get going. I've got to be at my folks early tomorrow. I need to rest up for it." She turned to Tommie. "Walk me out?"

Tommie pushed up out of her chair. "I should get going too. It was nice to meet all of you. I'm sure I'll see you all again."

Jodi took her hand again as they headed for the door.

When they reached the Dodge Ram again, Tommie stood an arm's reach away. "I would never figure an accountant for a truck driver."

"It's not mine. I borrowed it from a friend. I have to help my little brother move out of our parents' house tomorrow. After twenty-three years he's finally flying the coop."

"You need help?"

"Thanks, but he doesn't have much. I wouldn't mind seeing you again, though." She reached out and hooked one of her long fingers in a belt loop on Tommie's jeans. "Tomorrow...later, maybe?"

"Yeah...I wouldn't mind that either."

Jodi pulled her so close that Tommie had to straddle her legs, then threaded her fingers in the hair at the nape of Tommie's neck, pulling her in for a kiss. Not a sexually charged kiss, the kind that boiled your blood, but a tender kiss that lingered just long enough to leave Tommie wanting.

Tommie dug her phone from her pocket when Jodi released her. "What's your number?" Tommie dialed as Jodi recited it. When Jodi's began ringing in her back pocket, Tommie patted it. "And now you've got mine. Call me when you're done with your moving tomorrow and we'll make some plans."

"I will. Think about what you might want to do."

"That's all I'll be doing." Tommie leaned down and touched her lips to Jodi's again. "'Night," she said, then she spun and started across the lot to her own car.

* * *

"Hello?" Kate heard a stifled yawn.

"I woke you. I'm sorry."

"Kate, oh, it's okay. What's up?"

Tommie's voice sounded different, Kate thought, or maybe *in*different. "Well, I hadn't heard from you, so I thought I'd check if your stitches came out all right."

"Oh, uh yeah." Kate heard running water. "Doc said no problem, just a scar."

Definitely indifferent. Suddenly Kate felt very nervous about what she was about to ask. "Well, Megan's off to stay with Ashley tonight, so I thought I'd see if you wanted to come over for a movie and popcorn or something."

"I can't. Sorry, Kate. I've already got plans."

Kate felt let down and, inexplicably, jealous. "Of course, it's Saturday night, you probably have a date."

"I've just got some stuff going on."

"Well, perhaps another time then." Kate felt like she wanted to cry.

"Sure," Tommie responded without commitment or enthusiasm.

Kate hung up a minute later after some meaningless chitchat about Megan.

* * *

Tommie poured a cup of coffee and plopped into her recliner, phone in hand. She really wanted to call Kate back and accept her invitation, even though doing so would prevent her from having a date with Jodi. She liked Jodi. She was attractive. *She* was a lesbian. Tommie thought she could find herself enjoying her company on a regular basis. Wasn't that how you began a relationship? And wasn't that what she was after? Yes, she decided. Even if it didn't develop into a lasting relationship of a serious nature, dating Jodi would be a good start.

Feeling antsy, she dressed for a run in the park. On her third lap around the mile-long route she heard a persistently honking horn. When she stopped to see what was going on, Jodi's pickup pulled to the curb on the wrong side of the road, its flashers on. She jogged to the curb and leaned her hands on the roof, breathing hard.

"Hi!" Jodi swept her eyes over Tommie's sweat-soaked body. Between gasps, Tommie returned her greeting. "No wonder your body's so hard. You work out too?"

Still laboring to catch her breath, Tommie managed, "Sometimes."

"So you live close by?"

As her breathing evened out, Tommie rested her hands in the window opening on the truck door. "Yeah, in the apartments north of the park."

"My parents live just a few blocks from here. I was on my way back to have lunch with them before I headed home."

Jodi looked cute with her hair pulled through the back of the baseball cap she was wearing. Not many women could pull the look off and still appear very feminine. The way Kate had, Tommie thought. Jodi rested her hand on Tommie's wrist and stroked the back of her hand with her thumb.

"I suppose this will save me the phone call."

"What?"

Tommie leaned closer. "You're looking especially adorable today in your ball cap and your jersey," she said, taking note too of the ample breasts straining Jodi's shirt. "Even if I didn't know you I'd still have to ask you out." She grinned devilishly. "Or ask to play on my team at the very least."

Jodi rubbed her hand up and down Tommie's forearm. "Ask me out where?"

"Well, dinner for starters."

"And after we get started?"

"We can discuss that at dinner."

"Okay."

Tommie grinned. "Give me your address. I'll pick you up at seven."

Jodi rummaged in her purse, then scribbled her address on the back of a grocery receipt. When Tommie reached for the piece of paper, she tucked it into the waistband of her running shorts. "So you don't lose it." A shiver ran up Tommie's spine as Jodi pulled her hands back inside the truck. "How should I dress?"

Tommie's gaze wandered from Jodi's eyes, to her breasts and back again. "However you're most comfortable."

Jodi nodded. "I'll see you at seven." Before Tommie could step back, Jodi caught her shirt in a fist just below the neck and pulled her close. She lightly brushed her lips over Tommie's. "Seven...I'll be waiting." She released Tommie's shirt and drove away.

Trancelike, Tommie stumbled backward up onto the curb. She couldn't decide if this woman was a master seductress or if she was totally unaware of the sexuality she exuded. She was an accountant, for crying out loud, a number cruncher. Then again...She had a flash of Jodi, dressed all conservatively, tantalizing her with a striptease, then clearing her desk with the swipe of her hand for them to have sex on it. Tommie shook her head to erase the image. She walked for more than a few minutes thinking about anything but Jodi to get the throbbing between her legs to stop.

* * *

Tommie knocked on the door of the small frame house in an eastern suburb of Denton just minutes before seven. When Jodi opened the door, she froze. She stood there with her mouth open long enough for Jodi to touch Tommie's chin and then invite her in. "I'll be ready in a minute." Tommie glued her eyes to her backside as she disappeared from sight. She resumed staring when, true to her word, Jodi reappeared no more than sixty seconds later.

"Well?" She turned a slow, complete circle.

"You look..." Tommie was truly at a loss for words.

"Too much?"

Tommie silently shook her head no. "You look amazing. I hope no one steals you away."

She picked up her purse and hooked her arm through Tommie's. "I promise I won't let them."

On the way to the car Jodi commented, "You actually look quite yummy yourself."

Tommie's cheeks got warm. "Thanks."

Jodi squirmed in the Nissan seat, tugging the short skirt down her thighs. Tommie's fingers twitched, wanting to explore the pale soft skin of her thighs and whatever else lay beneath the fabric.

They shared a pleasant dinner talking about college and jobs. Tommie had trouble keeping her eyes on Jodi's as she talked. They kept wandering instead to the hint of cleavage exposed, invitingly, by her scoop neck top.

Tommie had decided when she ran into Jodi earlier in the day that she would not let this evening's date turn into every other liaison she'd ever had with a woman. So when she walked Jodi into her house, she said goodnight just inside the door.

"Stay for a drink."

"I can't."

Jodi nodded, stepping closer and twining her fingers with Tommie's. "Can I at least talk you into a goodnight kiss?"

Tommie leaned down and gently touched her lips to Jodi's. Jodi's free hand moved slowly up Tommie's back, then down her backside as she introduced her tongue to Tommie's mouth. Tommie moaned and pulled back.

Cupping Jodi's cheek, she said, "I have to go…now, but I'd like to see you again." She gazed into the luminous green eyes sparkling back at her.

Jodi squeezed her hand. "I'd like that too." She placed Tommie's hand on her hip and slid her hand around Tommie's neck. "One more for the road." Her mouth was hungry when it met Tommie's lips, and Tommie almost let herself be taken captive. She indulged a long minute before pulling back again.

She reached for the doorknob. "I had an amazing time. I'll call you."

Jodi leaned in the doorway as she stepped outside. "I pretty much work bankers' hours so call when you're free."

Tommie stopped partway down the walk and turned around. "Count on it."

One last glance before she got in the car found Jodi still in the doorway, one hand holding her shoes and the other giving another one of those finger waves. Tommie drove off thinking about those long fingers. "Am I crazy?" The ache between her legs was so fierce she had to press her hand to it while she drove hurriedly home. She dropped onto her bed, her right hand diving inside her pants even as her left unzipped them. God, she thought, if this is what just *dating* a woman was going to do to her, she might have to solicit some assistance from her friend Carly.

CHAPTER SIXTEEN

Kate had never felt so lonely in her home as she did at this moment. Megan was off enjoying her Saturday night with her best friend. And Kate's only friend, of sorts, Tommie, was most likely out enjoying a woman. The thought made Kate ache and not just because she couldn't be spending the evening with Tommie, but because she couldn't have Tommie—that way. Late in the evening she finally ran a bubble bath and slipped in to relax, a glass of wine and her favorite water toy within easy reach.

If she closed her eyes, she could feel Tommie's arms around her, could see the vulnerability in her eyes when Megan had been hurt and when she herself had gotten injured. Nothing felt more natural to Kate than caring for Tommie except caring for Megan and doing so with her heart and very soul.

Physically satisfied for the time being, Kate read herself to sleep, only to wake hours later dreaming of lying in Tommie's arms.

* * *

In the days that followed Kate kept herself busy working as many hours as she could without disrupting their lives. She rationalized that every extra dollar earned could be saved for Megan's education. What she had managed to save in the last ten years, plus the insurance money Megan's mother had left in trust, should get her through most of her college.

One evening early in May, Megan joined Kate in the backyard, where she was gardening. "Do you suppose it would be okay if I went to Senior Prom?" she asked hesitantly.

Kate pulled off her dirty gloves, tucking loose strands of hair behind her ears. "Why, of course, sweetie. Why would you think it wouldn't be okay?"

"Because a dress costs money, and I don't exactly have a date."

Kate arched a brow as she rose to sit with Megan on the steps. "Is a date a requirement these days for prom? Because even when I was in high school I recall a number of people, guys and gals, who went without dates."

Megan shrugged. "I don't think so. Ashley's dad's renting a limo and Ashley is going to meet some guy there. They're not actually going together, so she thought it would be cool if I could go with her in the limo. There's probably going to be a bunch of us going to the 'after prom.' That is, if it's okay for me to go."

"It sounds like a fun time that you shouldn't miss, date or not." Kate patted Megan's knee. "I can't believe there's not some hot guy chasing you around to go with him." Megan didn't respond. "When is it?"

"Two weekends from now."

Kate put an arm around Megan's shoulder and squeezed. "That's plenty of time, then, for all the hunky guys to line up and ask you."

* * *

That weekend they went shopping for Megan's dress. Kate had forgotten what it was like to go shopping for just the right dress to turn heads. In Kate's case, of course, she had been far more interested during prom in which girls were keeping an eye on her as she pretended to enjoy being on the arm of one of the guys that all the girls considered to be the hottest catch.

Kate was lost in a memory when Megan parted the curtains. "This is the one." The dress was a simple black tank dress that fell just inches above her knee.

"Are you sure?"

Megan nodded. Kate wondered why she hadn't gone for a trendier look, like most of the dresses displayed on the mannequins. Megan held up the price tag. "And look…it's marked half-off."

"Honey, you don't have to settle for a dress because it's on sale."

Megan turned in front of a full-length mirror next to Kate. "I'm not. I really like this one. It's me, don't you think?"

Kate stood behind Megan and looked at her in the mirror. "It certainly is. It's simply elegant." She held Megan's shoulders and kissed the top of her head. "Let's go find you some shoes and have lunch. I'm hungry, so you must be starving."

The day turned into good therapy for Kate, but as she was searching for fresh batteries for the camera so she'd be ready to capture Megan's special occasion, the memory of Tommie decked out in a tux for New Year's popped into her head. Tommie had a real soft spot for her niece. Megan's big night offered a perfect reason to call Tommie and invite her over.

Kate called Tommie Sunday afternoon. When the voice mail message clicked on, Kate assumed she was at a ball game—it was, after all, baseball season. She left a simple message asking Tommie to return her call. The phone rang a little before nine and Kate was on it before Megan could get to it.

"Hi, sorry to call late, I was at a game." Kate welcomed the sound of Tommie's voice.

"I figured as much."

"So…what's going on?"

"First of all, how's the ankle?"

Tommie slumped back in her chair. Why did Kate have to be so damned caring? She sighed. "Good as new."

"Is everything okay, Tommie?"

"Yes, no…" Tommie had a battle going on in her head. Things were going really well with Jodi. They hadn't slept together yet, but she suspected that moment was getting closer. And just now, in a fraction of a second, she had realized she didn't care the least bit about sleeping with her. The moment she heard Kate's voice, she wanted her all over again.

"Tommie?"

Tommie scrambled. "Oh…uh…sorry. I can't find my notes for a story I've been working on." That sounded like a plausible excuse, didn't it?

"I've interrupted your work. I won't keep you."

"No, no, I'm not working now, I was just looking for my notes… never mind. So, how have you been?" That sounded so lame.

"I'm just fine. Listen, I won't keep you."

Tommie wished Kate would keep her and for all times. But she sounded happy enough with status quo. Any overtures from Tommie would only complicate matters.

"Megan's Senior Prom is this Saturday. She's got her dress, if not a date, and she and Ashley are going in a limo, compliments of Ashley's dad."

"Is it that time of year already?"

"Yes, well, I was wondering if you'd like to stop over and see her all dressed up for her big night."

"I can probably stop by for a minute to two. What time?" *Damn, Kate, why do you have to tempt me like this?*

"Ashley's supposed to be here no later than eight."

"Don't tell her I'm coming by in case something comes up and I can't make it. Okay?"

"Oh, sure, I understand. The life of a sportswriter, always on the go."

At least Tommie had an out, in the event she didn't feel up to facing Kate and her feelings for her. "Well, then I'll see you Saturday, maybe."

"Have a good week, Tommie. Goodnight."

God, the way Kate just purred those words. "Yeah, you too."

* * *

Ashley had arrived in her limo just after seven thirty, and she and Megan were back in Megan's room doing their girl stuff. Kate paced the living room, hoping Tommie was going to show up. When she heard a car door slam outside, Kate rushed to the kitchen so it wouldn't appear she had been waiting anxiously.

Tommie knocked before pulling the door open and poking her head in. "Hello…?"

Kate came from the kitchen, smiling at the welcome sight of Tommie. "Come in." She moved to the door.

Tommie entered the house, followed, much to Kate's surprise, by a pretty brunette. Meeting the other woman's eyes, Kate felt her joyous mood quickly vanish.

Hoping to sound more light hearted than she felt, she said, "The girls are just putting on their finishing touches. Come in and have a seat."

"Uh...we can only stay a few minutes." Tommie not only seemed uneasy but sounded so. The woman nudged Tommie in the side. "Oh...and I'm so rude, sorry. Kate, this is Jodi. Jodi...Kate."

Kate offered her hand.

"Always nice to meet friends of Tommie's," Jodi said with a firm handshake.

"Yes, it is." Although, Kate thought, the only other friend of Tommie's she'd met was the one she'd had sex with one desperate and lonely night several years earlier.

As Kate and Tommie stood, eyes locked on one another, Jodi continued. "This is a very nice house you have. I love this neighborhood."

Kate reluctantly shifted her gaze to the other woman. "Thank you, we like it." Then, uncomfortably, "Are you sure you won't have a seat? I can offer you something to drink..."

"I think we're good." Tommie looked over at Jodi for confirmation. "We were just on our way out for a late dinner."

Kate felt light-headed. Thankfully, before the room became completely void of air for her to breathe, Megan and Ashley entered.

"Tommie!" Megan exclaimed, clearly surprised. She rushed over and threw her arms around her. Tommie gave a gentle squeeze. "What are you doing here?"

Tommie took Megan by the arms, stepping back to get a better look. "Do you think I'd miss seeing my favorite intern dressed to the nines?" When Megan blushed, she said, "You look beautiful. Every guy at the party is going to line up to dance with you."

Megan rolled her eyes. "As if."

Tommie peered over Megan's shoulder. "You're a knockout too, Ashley. Should I call ahead and warn everybody to wear their sunglasses 'cause there's two brilliant beauties on their way?"

Megan slapped Tommie's arm playfully. "Very funny."

Ashley stepped up and grabbed Megan's hand. "Come on, let's go."

Kate raised her hand. "Just a minute, girls." She moved to the coffee table and picked up the camera there. "I want to get a few pictures of you two in front of your big limo." The girls rolled their eyes. "Humor me." She followed them to the door.

Tommie caught Jodi's elbow. "Let's watch, then we can go."

Outside, Kate snapped a few shots of the girls, then Tommie suggested a few of Kate and Megan. While aunt and niece were preparing for their photo, Tommie managed to sneak a quick shot with her phone without anyone being any the wiser—including Jodi, who stood behind her.

The second after the last camera flash, Ashley grabbed Megan's arm. "Let's go." With a wave at Kate, Megan allowed herself to be pulled into the limo.

"Remember, two a.m., Megan, and not a minute later."

Jokingly, Megan responded, "Yes, mother," and slammed the door.

Standing, arms crossed over her chest, Kate jumped when Tommie's hand touched her back.

"Sorry," Tommie said quickly, holding the camera out to Kate. "Don't worry, Kate. She'll be fine. They have a very responsible driver."

Kate turned with sorrow-filled eyes. "I know…I'm just worried about all the boys, tongues wagging, that might not behave as responsibly."

"She's a smart girl, Kate. You raised her right, she'll be fine."

Kate shook her head sadly. Tommie just wanted to hold her in her arms and try to comfort her.

Jodi stepped beside Tommie. "We should probably be going if we want to make our reservation."

"Thanks for stopping and taking pictures. Megan was happy to see you."

Tommie smiled weakly. "No problem. It was good to see you both."

Jodi said, "It was nice to meet you."

"You too." Kate looked away.

Emptiness settled in the pit of Tommie's stomach.

* * *

Tommie was halfway through her beer when Jodi asked, "So what's the story?"

"What?" Tommie had been preoccupied since picking Jodi up and was now feeling terribly disjointed.

Jodi stirred her drink. "Kate and Megan. I was just wondering what the story is with them."

Tommie took a long drink. "Uh, well, Megan was my intern last summer at the paper. We just all kind of became friends." Tommie met Jodi's questioning eyes. "Not much of a story really."

"So you two never dated, or...you know...?"

Uh-oh, Tommie thought. *Was I wearing my heart on my sleeve and Jodi saw it?* "Oh, hell no. She's straight."

"I suspected as much. I just thought she looked at you like she wanted you."

Tommie drained her beer. "Let's order. I'm starved." She buried her face in the menu. Was Jodi insecure or a little jealous, maybe? Had Kate really looked at her that way? Tommie was not great at reading women—except in bed—and she knew it.

Tommie's heart fluttered. *You can't have Kate,* she reminded herself.

Besides, she and Jodi had been building a solid relationship over the last month. It was still in its infant stages, and Tommie didn't want to spoil it. They'd come close to hopping in the sack just last weekend—Jodi was definitely ready to throw caution to the wind—but Tommie had been levelheaded enough to put the brakes on. Jodi had seemed to respect her resolve.

Fortunately Jodi changed the subject, asking Tommie about the Cougars' game she was going to tomorrow. Sports she knew. All that other stuff was a bit much for Tommie to wrap her head around.

CHAPTER SEVENTEEN

Jodi gripped Tommie's shoulders and parked herself on Tommie's thigh, pinning her to the door as she had done at the end of most of their recent dates. Their kiss was hot and grew urgent. This move never failed to arouse Tommie, but tonight instead of simply feeling like she didn't want to just jump into bed with this sexy woman, Tommie found herself thinking of Kate and wondering how Kate's lips might feel against her own. After several minutes of Jodi rubbing against her thigh and her tongue playing in Tommie's mouth, Tommie gently ended the kiss.

She cradled Jodi's face in her hands. "You are so sexy…and so very hard to resist, but…I don't want to ruin anything between us." Jodi's thigh muscles tensed as she reached up to stroke Tommie's cheek. "I know there's more to a relationship than sex, and I want to know all the 'more.'"

Jodi touched a fingertip to Tommie's lips. "And I want you to know 'all the more.'" She placed her lips where her finger had just been. Lingering there only a moment, she said, "I had a wonderful evening, thank you."

Tommie slipped her fingers into the dark locks at the nape of Jodi's neck. "No, thank you." She kissed her forehead. "I'll call you."

Tommie drove down the street to the corner and sat at the stop sign there, just thinking, until a car approached from behind and honked. Without another moment's hesitation she turned left, instead of right toward her apartment.

She parked across the street from the lighted house and watched it for ten or fifteen minutes, hoping to see some movement. Spotting none, she finally got out and walked to the door. Peering through the small window there, she saw Kate stretched out on the couch sleeping. She checked her watch. It was just minutes after eleven. She knew she shouldn't wake her, but she wanted so much to talk to her again, to look into her eyes. No, what she really wanted was to stretch her body against Kate's, to hold her and feel her heart beat.

Even now, seeing that she was asleep, she wanted to just stand there and watch her. Like what? Some kind of deranged stalker? She couldn't do that. She trudged back to the car, turned it around and drove home to her lonely apartment.

By the time Tommie called Jodi after the ball game Sunday, she'd pretty much managed to put Kate out of her mind again. They made plans to go out the following Saturday for a reasonably early dinner, then dancing at The Underground. As Tommie left the apartment for a morning run that day she was thinking only of Jodi and the chance to wine and dine her that evening.

After her run she sat down to drink some coffee and sort through her mail. In it she found a fancy invitation envelope with Kate's return address on it. She stared at it a long time before opening it. A printed invitation to Megan's graduation, it also contained a small note in Megan's handwriting that invited Tommie back to the house afterward.

Tommie pushed the envelope aside. It was two weeks off so she didn't have to think too much on it just yet. Pushing the remainder of the mail to the side as well, she went to take a shower.

* * *

When Tommie and Jodi arrived at The Underground, the house was packed and heart-thumping music was bouncing off the walls. Jodi spied a few casual friends, receiving a wave-over. One of the gals yelled, "Have a seat." There was only one so Tommie told Jodi to take it.

Jodi pulled the chair out and sat while Tommie pushed her way to the bar for drinks. When she returned with them, Jodi stood again.

Tommie placed a hand on her lower back. "Go ahead. I'm fine standing."

Jodi leaned into Tommie. "No, you sit"—she cocked her head—"and I'll sit in your lap."

Tommie was on her second beer before Jodi was half-finished with her first drink. Jodi's weight on Tommie's lap, even as slight as it was, forced the inevitable. She pressed her lips to Jodi's ear. "I've got to go to the bathroom."

Jodi stood immediately, taking Tommie's hand. "I need to go too. I'll go with you."

Tommie bulldozed through the throng to take her place in a line of half a dozen women for the restroom. A beer at dinner and another one since was more than Tommie's bladder could tolerate any longer.

"Is anyone in here?" she asked, indicating the men's room. Several of the women merely shrugged, so she knocked and pushed on the door. "Anyone in here?" Receiving no response, she told Jodi, "I can't wait. I'm using the men's room." She pushed through the door. Surprisingly, Jodi followed on her heels.

"I'll watch the door for you."

The room held a urinal and a single stall with no door on it. Tommie was uneasy. "I don't usually use the bathroom in front of my dates...uh, I mean girlfriends."

Jodi turned her back. "I promise not to look."

Tommie let out a breath. If she'd had a few more beers she might not care, but she did. She'd grown up the only girl in her family and had only been seen in the bathroom by her mother. She'd made sure in school too that no other girls got a look at her privates. She could lie naked with a woman now and have sex with her, but going to the bathroom in the company of one was something else. She wondered if she'd ever get past that discomfort.

As soon as Tommie finished and raised the zipper on her pants, Jodi turned around, shimming her short, tight skirt above her hips.

"I might as well go while we're here."

Tommie got a clear look at the black thong she was wearing and nearly tripped coming out of the stall. She hurried to the sink.

"Might as well." Staring at her reflection through the film on the mirror she noticed that her cheeks looked hot. That wasn't the only part of her that was hot, she thought as she dried her hands.

She wasn't the only one, it seemed. After Jodi washed her hands, she grabbed at Tommie's waistband. "A minute, please." She hooked her hand around Tommie's neck and pulled her into a quick kiss. When she pulled back and allowed Tommie to open the door, she said, "That's better. I've been wanting to do that all evening."

In the hours that followed, they danced a number of times, Jodi talked a lot with her friends and Tommie slugged down way too many beers. She'd thought the cold brews might cool her body where Jodi sat, but it didn't have that effect. By the end of the evening, Tommie was wet with a desire that seriously needed to be unleashed—and she was pretty much loaded. As they prepared to leave, Jodi tried to slip her hand in Tommie's front pants pocket.

Tommie caught her wrist. "Not here. I can wait till we get home." She offered Jodi a lopsided grin.

Jodi smiled at Tommie's obvious less-than-in-control condition and said, "I certainly hope so, but"—she shoved her hand deeper into Tommie's pocket and pulled out her car keys—"I need these. I really don't think you should drive."

Tommie nodded her head and slipped her arm around Jodi's shoulder. "You are absolutely correct on that one."

She swayed a little as they headed for the door. Walking across the parking lot supported by Jodi vaguely reminded Tommie of something, but she couldn't quite remember what. On the other hand, from this angle she had a perfect view of Jodi's cleavage. The thought of putting her mouth on that soft flesh fanned the fire that was simmering just below the surface. It was a good sign, Tommie thought, when she got herself into the car, buckled up without any challenges and didn't pass out on the drive home. Perhaps tonight they'd finally make that physical connection.

* * *

The second Jodi closed the door and turned around, Tommie cupped Jodi's face in her hands and kissed her gently. "I want to touch you everywhere."

Tommie's vision was hazy with lust or alcohol or both, and her entire body hummed with desire—desire that she was going to satisfy, damn the circumstances. Tommie's heart hammered under the press of Jodi's hand on her chest. Their next kiss was deep and hungry, and when Tommie's hand slid down Jodi's thigh, a whimper escaped her. Tommie's hand moved up slowly, pushing the skirt up with it. Jodi rocked against Tommie's thigh.

Tommie slid her fingers past the tiny scrap of silk between Jodi's legs and was rewarded with a warm wetness. "God, you feel so good," she murmured as her lips trailed kisses along Jodi's jaw to her neck, which she bit lightly.

Jodi's fingers worked nimbly at the buttons on Tommie's shirt. She grazed her fingertips over Tommie's nipples, then gently massaged them erect. Tommie couldn't stop the deep throaty groan caused by the arousal Jodi was inciting and the slick wetness she discovered when her hand dipped inside the thong.

"Oh…" Jodi gasped, pushing against Tommie's fingers. "Oh… yes, please, please, Tommie."

Tommie's lips lightly touched Jodi's ear. "You better take me to the bedroom."

Tommie took her own shirt off in the bedroom before pulling Jodi's top over her head, unzipping and removing her skirt and leaving her in a black lacy bra that matched her thong. The body standing before Tommie was simply magnificent, and she intended to enjoy every inch of it. She gently traced her fingers down Jodi's firm abdomen before slipping her arm around her waist and, with a thigh between hers, carefully lowering her onto the bed.

"You have such a beautiful body." She lifted Jodi's legs, one at a time with a hand under her knee, and removed her shoes, then allowed her fingers to trace a path back up her calf to the inside of her thigh. Jodi's body shivered in response. Slipping her arm under Jodi, Tommie moved her to the center of the bed and settled on her side next to her. When Jodi cupped a hand over Tommie's breast, she leaned in to kiss her lips before kissing and nipping down the column of Jodi's throat to the valley between her breasts. Tommie reached under her and released her bra, then began working her lips over an already erect nipple.

"Oh…yes…" Jodi gasped as Tommie's tongue circled one, then the other nipple. Jodi arched against Tommie's mouth, cupping the back of Tommie's head to hold her against her breast.

Tommie's fingers danced lightly down Jodi's thigh and back up to the heated vortex that was pressing into her thigh. Her fingers slipped again past the thin strand of fabric there and touched Jodi's engorged flesh, prompting a throaty "Oh, God, yes!"

Tommie pulled back slightly. "You like this?" She transferred her attention to Jodi's other breast. Jodi emitted a deep moan as she continued to buck against Tommie's stroking fingers. Tommie moved them lower, teasing Jodi's hot inviting opening while continuing to stroke her throbbing clit with her thumb. "Tell me what you want."

Jodi's hand went instantly to Tommie's between her legs, pushing on it as she growled in a deep, low voice, "I need you inside me, please. I need to come…"

Her voice died away when Tommie easily slipped two fingers inside her. She dropped her head to Jodi's chest.

"God, you feel so good, Jodi…so ready…" Tommie was getting close herself, wetness soaking her jeans as the pressure from Jodi's thigh between her own pressed the seam of her jeans against her own throbbing clit.

"God!" Jodi came loudly, her entire body convulsing under Tommie. As the pulse begin to subside around Tommie's fingers, she slowly withdrew, rolling on her side and pulling Jodi tight against her.

Jodi's breath evened out and she murmured, "God, that was incredible."

Tommie kissed the top of her head. "Mmm…"

Jodi's hand traced a path up and down Tommie's bare back before moving around the waistband of her jeans to the button fly.

Tommie stilled her hand. "I can't."

Jodi gazed up at her, half-dazed, questions written all over her face.

Tommie stroked a finger over her cheek and lips and gently kissed them. "I drank too much, I can't." When Jodi's bottom lip pushed out in a pout, Tommie whispered, "I'm sorry."

Jodi moved her hand to stroke Tommie's chest, then settled it on her left breast, tweaking the nipple between her thumb and fingers. When it hardened and Tommie gave a soft grunt, Jodi asked, "Are you sure I can't…?"

Tommie stilled her hand once again. "Yeah, unfortunately, I'm sure."

She grabbed the comforter, pulling it across them as Jodi nestled into the crook of her arm, sighing her contentment. Tommie kissed her lightly again before closing her eyes. The satisfaction that she'd felt after performing her magic on the body wrapped in her arms faded quickly, though, replaced by the vision behind her eyelids of the brilliant blue eyes of a certain blond. She held her breath. Kate. Had she just somehow, subconsciously, made love to her? Was it possible her head was so screwed up that she had imagined that the whimpers and moans of pleasure were Kate's and not Jodi's?

The mere possibility of that caused her stomach to turn over. Tommie breathed deeply, slowly, to quell the nausea that threatened. After a while, the sickening feeling gave way to the uninvited, yet familiar, feeling of desire for Kate. She lay, unmoving, for another hour, waiting until she felt certain Jodi was sleeping deeply enough to allow her to slip from her embrace and her bed undetected. She buttoned her shirt on the way to the front door, where she pulled her shoes on and phoned for a cab.

Tommie gave serious thought to how disgusting her behavior with women was on the silent ride to her apartment. She treated them pretty much like prostitutes, the only difference being that she had never had to pay for a woman's company. Not with money nor with any piece of herself.

Before sunrise, she decided, when she was safe to drive, she would sneak back to Jodi's to get her car. Then she'd figure out some way to tell Jodi that she didn't—she couldn't—well, she just plain wasn't interested in anything serious. It wasn't fair. Not when she couldn't get Kate out of her head.

A few minutes before six, while the coffee was gurgling into the pot, Tommie mindlessly sifted through the mail that had accumulated on the counter. Halfway through the stack, she came across it again—the invitation to Megan's graduation the following weekend. She poured a cup of coffee, then stared at it, as if doing so would give her some indication of what she was supposed to do about all this. About all the things she was feeling, and about Kate, who had briefly been her bubbly, beautiful self the weekend of the prom but then noticeably was sad.

Well, why not? First prom, then graduation, then Megan would be off to college. Kate was saddened by the thought of Megan going away, that's all there was to it. The invitation contained no

RSVP. Kate might not even be aware Megan had sent it to her. She turned it over in her hand several times before sticking it under the magnet on the refrigerator. She didn't have to decide anything today. Hell, she didn't have to decide anything until an hour before the ceremony if she didn't want to.

The phone rang just after ten while Tommie was napping in her recliner. Seeing Jodi's number, she debated whether to answer or not. She took so long that the machine finally picked up.

"Tommie, good morning." Jodi's voice was cheery. "I was kind of surprised to wake and find you gone, then I realized you're always full of surprises, like last night." Her voice became breathy. "I get a tingle just thinking about what you did to me." Tommie closed her eyes at the ache the words started in her chest. "I can't wait to reciprocate…anyway, call me when you've got a few minutes." She made a kissing sound. "I'll be waiting."

Tommie groaned at the expectancy in Jodi's words. "What the hell have I done?" Feeling more drained than any hangover had ever left her, she forced herself to dress and leave the house. Maybe running would clear her head and give her a clue what she should do about her mess of a life.

It didn't. She came to one conclusion during her run, however. She could go to Megan's graduation. In fact, she *should* go, because she liked and respected Megan, and she felt certain the feelings were mutual.

She made herself call Jodi back on Sunday evening. Pleasantly surprised when Jodi didn't answer and she had to leave a message, Tommie said cheerfully, "Sorry I missed you. You were amazing to finally touch last night. I've got a pretty busy schedule, but I'll get hold of you later in the week."

* * *

Tommie finally called Jodi again on Thursday evening.

"Hi," Jodi answered. "You must really be having a busy week."

"Pretty much, yeah."

"I can think of some ways to help you unwind over the weekend."

"Well…" Tommie drawled, "I've got a pretty busy weekend too. The Cougars are playing a series at home and I really should be there." Her statement was truthful, Tommie told herself. She had said she should be at the games, not that she was going to be. In fact, she'd definitely decided she would attend Megan's graduation. Just the ceremony, though. She didn't want or need to go back to the house with them. She couldn't lie to herself, it was getting harder and harder to be around Kate since their spring break trip. She knew that information probably wouldn't be well received, but she liked and respected Kate so much she was even beginning to think Kate deserved to know how she really felt. And Jodi, well, she definitely deserved to know how Tommie didn't feel.

"Tommie?" Jodi's voice stirred her from her thoughts.

"Sorry, I've just got so much going on right now. It's very distracting." That also not a lie. "I might have some time free later on Sunday, but I can't be positive, so if you have other things to do, don't sit around waiting for me to call. Okay?"

"Well, don't work too hard, you know what they say about that. I'll talk to you when I talk to you. 'Night, Tommie."

Tommie heard bewilderment in Jodi's tone and got a distinct sense that she already suspected that something unpleasant was just around the corner.

CHAPTER EIGHTEEN

Kate waited impatiently with every other parent, relative and friend as the graduates began filing down the aisle. Megan's smile was brilliant when she looked at her aunt, and Kate thought her heart might burst. At the same time, it ached that Nikki couldn't be there to see the wonderful young woman Megan had blossomed into. Nikki would have been prouder than words could express.

As was Kate. It didn't matter that she wasn't Megan's biological mother. She had given her all to fill Nikki's shoes in every aspect of the word. It was more than a shame that Megan's grandparents hadn't been able to see past their prejudices to help this wonderful young woman grow to adulthood. They should be here to watch their only grandchild graduate from high school, Kate reflected, with a mix of sadness for Megan and anger toward her intolerant parents.

Megan's eyes moved past Kate and she gave a little wave. Kate shifted in her seat to look in the same direction, her breath catching in an instant when she saw, to her left and one row back, the one person who made her heart flutter.

Kate's heart stopped when Tommie's dark eyes turned from Megan and fell upon her. Megan had apparently invited Tommie—

and she'd shown up! Kate was pleased on both accounts. She gave a slight nod, receiving one from Tommie in return before she turned her attention back to the ceremony.

She chanced several glances at Tommie throughout the program—and got caught each time, almost as if Tommie knew when Kate's eyes were headed her direction. She looked away quickly, of course, then berated herself. It was childish to be embarrassed for admiring an attractive woman like Tommie, who surely was accustomed to having women "check her out." So what if she thought Kate was straight? After Megan went to college...

The possibilities came flooding into her mind—along with the memory of the possessive brunette Tommie had had with her a few weeks back. They had been headed out for the evening, dinner and who knew what else. A real date and not a one-night stand like when she'd first seen Tommie in that bar last year. Kate's heart ached at the thought.

When the ceremony ended, she looked in Tommie's direction and found her already gone. Kate made her way through the crowd searching for her, but to no avail. Weighted down with disappointment, she headed to her car. Her solemn mood changed in a heartbeat when she saw the dark-eyed woman of her dreams leaning casually on the car but looking off in the opposite direction.

Kate approached quietly. "Hi, Tommie. I'm glad to see you here today."

Tommie turned to face her. She looked like a female Adonis, Kate thought, her heart rate quickening at the memory of seeing Tommie bare-chested.

"Hi, Kate." Tommie's dark eyes burned into hers. "I'm so glad to see you too."

They stood in silence a long moment, then both started to speak at the same time. Tommie insisted Kate go first.

"I was just going to tell you that Megan is with Ashley. Ashley received a shiny new car for a graduation present, so Megan is riding with her today."

Tommie retrieved an envelope from her back pocket and held it toward Kate. "I got a little something for Megan. Could you pass it on to her?"

Kate started to reach for it, then stopped. "Why don't you come by and give it to her yourself?" When Tommie began to protest, Kate quickly added, "I know it would mean a lot to Megan if you'd stop by."

Tommie looked briefly at the envelope in her hand, then back into Kate's eyes. Seeing Kate was one of the reasons she was here today, and now Kate was offering her the opportunity to spend more time with her.

"I wasn't really planning…I mean, I thought I'd just see her here…"

Tommie shrugged.

"You have other plans, no doubt." Kate quirked an eyebrow. "A date with your pretty brunette? Of course, you do. It's Saturday night."

Tommie felt strangely nervous. "Uh…no, I don't…" She choked down her nervousness. "Have any plans, that is."

Kate placed a hand gently on Tommie's arm. "Then come by the house, at least for a few minutes. I insist."

Tommie relented. "Sure, I can stop by for a few minutes, I guess."

"Good, I'll see you there."

Kate stood for a moment, watching Tommie as she walked off. God. She wanted that woman in the most lustful ways imaginable.

* * *

Tommie waited around outside at least ten minutes after she arrived at Kate's, hoping a shiny new car would appear carrying the girls. She was apprehensive about being in the house with Kate alone, as anxious as a schoolgirl on a first date. "Relax," she told herself. It was just Kate. How much time had she spent with her in nearly a year's time? Several deep breaths later, she got out of her Jeep and walked up the drive. Knocking before pushing the door open, she called, "Kate?"

That familiar voice that generated warm waves through her called back. "In the kitchen."

Tommie entered with her hands tucked in her pockets to help conceal some of her nervous jitters. Kate was at the counter, a colorful apron covering an incredibly form-fitting dress. The light sweater she'd been wearing earlier was gone, and Tommie could see now that the back was cut low. So low, in fact, Kate couldn't possibly be wearing a bra. The thought unnerved Tommie.

Kate tossed her a quick glance. "Make yourself at home," she said, before turning on the blender. The appliance ground loudly away as Tommie whispered to herself, "Stop it, stop it, stop it." She stayed put in the doorway. Distance, that's what she needed to maintain between her and Kate. If Kate so much as breathed on her, she couldn't be sure she'd be able to keep her hands from exploring the softness of Kate's exposed flesh.

Kate was saying something when the noise stopped, but Tommie was talking so loud in her own head, she didn't hear. "I'm sorry, what?"

"I said—I've got margaritas, my own special recipe. Have one with me?"

Tommie found it hard to process her words. She was too busy watching Kate's perfectly painted lips form them. She finally managed to blurt, "Uh, sure, why not?"

Kate poured two glasses as she chatted away. "The girls should be along any minute. Ashley's joining us too. Since her parents are divorcing, and they waited until nearly the last minute to try to plan something for today, Ashley told them to forget it. That she'd rather be here today. Which of course started a world war. I can only assume they've scheduled something for her. That poor girl has had a tough time this last year. Going off to college in the fall should be a much-needed break for her."

When she turned, two slushy drinks in hand, Tommie felt herself falling into the deep blue of her eyes. She could drown in those eyes.

"It's beautiful outside. Let's sit out on the deck."

Tommie followed in silence. As they sat in the peaceful quiet, she recalled her first dinner here with Kate and how much more at ease she'd been then. That was because she'd only just met her and was only just beginning to like her. Whereas now she was crazy about her. Insane, actually. Because Kate was straight, an untouchable, and because with Megan going off to college she would undoubtedly be resuming the social life she'd put on hold so many years ago. God, how she envied the guy who would eventually win her heart.

"Tommie?" Kate's voice interrupted her thoughts.

"Hum..."

"I was asking if you think the Cougars have a chance to go all the way this year."

"Uh..." Tommie shrugged. "As good a chance as last year, I suppose, though they're getting off to a slow start."

They heard the front door close then, and a moment later Megan and Ashley appeared in the doorway.

"Tommie, you came. I'm so glad."

Tommie smiled up at Megan from her seat in the lounger. She shifted to pull the envelope out of her pocket.

"Here you go, kiddo." She winked. "Hopefully this will help you get started in college in the fall."

Megan read the congratulatory card before pulling out a very generous gift card for an office supply chain. "Wow, Tommie, thanks. This is...well, wow! Guess I don't have to worry about running out of ink cartridges or paper." She looked at her aunt. "What time are we eating?"

As Kate glanced at her watch, Tommie brought the margarita glass to her mouth and drained it. "Six o'clock. I made you girls some virgin margaritas. They're in the fridge in the juice pitcher. And don't think about sneaking any of mine. I know exactly how much is left in the blender."

Megan rolled her eyes and flashed an "as if" expression before they returned to the house.

Tommie stood, empty glass in hand. "I should get going."

Kate popped up, immediately, catching Tommie's hand. "Oh, no. Please say you'll stay and have dinner with us."

Tommie looked at Kate's perfectly manicured nails, on her perfect fingers, attached to her perfect hand—which burned where it held onto her hand, threatening to start a blaze.

Kate pulled her hand away and repeated her invitation. "Please say you'll stay."

Tommie couldn't imagine ever being able to resist any kind of pleading by Kate. "Sure, I guess. Okay."

"Let me get you a fresh drink."

Tommie shook her head. "I'll wait until you're ready for your next one." By the time they were starting on their second drinks, Kate was putting the food on the grill.

When Tommie carried the platter of shrimp kabobs into the kitchen, Kate asked, "Would you mind calling the girls out of Megan's room and away from the computer?"

Tommie handed Kate the plate and headed down the hall. "Megan..." Pushing lightly on the nearly closed bedroom door, she poked her head in—then pulled it out so fast she knocked her head on the doorframe. "Ouch," she said, rubbing the side of her head.

Megan materialized almost immediately in the doorway, her face filled with shock, embarrassment and, most evident, fear. She wrung her hands as she spoke, her voice shaking. "God, Tommie. Please don't tell Aunt Kate. Please? I beg you, not a word. She'll die, or she'll kill me. Promise?"

Tommie cut her off. "Megan, relax. I've never been a tattletale, and this is definitely not any news I want to be responsible for delivering to your aunt." Tommie put her hand over her heart. "Your secret is safe with me, I promise. I'll take it to my grave if necessary."

After a long awkward silence Megan turned to Ashley, whose face was several shades pinker even than Megan's. "See, I told you Tommie was the coolest adult ever."

"Admittedly I'm probably not the best person to give advice, but I can tell you, unless you two are just experimenting, the road ahead isn't paved with yellow bricks. Let me know if there's anything I can do to help besides keep my mouth shut until you're ready to tell Kate. Which you should and soon, because you might not realize it now, but she's a really cool adult too. Otherwise she'd have flipped out at having you intern with someone like me." *Ah damn, Kate's going to think I recruited you.* She exhaled a long breath. "You girls get yourselves together. Dinner's ready."

Conversation at the table was sparse and subdued. Megan and Ashley seemed uncomfortable to Tommie, but not nearly as uncomfortable as she was. Megan was avoiding eye contact with her like she had the plague, especially when she asked as she cleared the dishes if she could spend the night at Ashley's. They just wanted to "hang," she explained, and make some plans for the summer before they went in different directions to college.

Kate was perfectly agreeable to the request, of course, while Tommie was thinking, "Making plans. Yeah right," as she remembered what she'd witnessed earlier.

When the girls left, Kate returned from the kitchen with their drink glasses filled again to the brim. Tommie held up her hands. "I don't think I should have another. I really need to get going."

Kate frowned. "You can't leave me here all alone. Just one more, then I promise to let you go." Suspecting she was a bit depressed by Megan's departure, that evening and next fall, Tommie decided to stay to make sure she didn't get too buzzed.

* * *

They made their way to the deck, where Kate finished her drink before Tommie barely started on hers. When she popped up out of her chair to go inside for another, she stumbled back against the house. Tommie was there in a split second, steadying hands on her shoulders. Kate grabbed a fistful of Tommie's shirt.

"Are you all right?"

"Of course, I'm fine. I just stood up too fast." Kate's crooked smile immediately faded, morphing into an intense expression that froze Tommie in place. She wanted to swim in the endless depths of those incredible blue eyes. She took a slow, deep breath to clear her head—and the scent of Kate on the warm night air paralyzed her brain. She couldn't move. Or could she? The object of her desire was getting closer. Was she moving toward it? Or was Kate pulling her? Beads of perspiration forming on the back of her neck, she lowered her head slightly, never losing sight of Kate's eyes and what was smoldering in them, something that looked very much to her like desire. Then Kate's hand, fisted in her shirt, gave a light tug and brought Tommie's lips to her.

Kate's heated lips burned against her own for long, lingering seconds, their heat forcing a sensation through her body that made her tremble. Abruptly she pushed back out of Kate's grasp, gasping for air. "Oh, God, Kate…I'm sorry." She backed away further, trying to flush the desire from her brain. "So sorry…"

Kate reached for her, but Tommie had already reached the back door. "Tommie?"

"I've got to go." She was gone before Kate could stop her.

Tommie sped like a gazelle through the house, down the drive and into her Jeep. *Run, leave now.* Those were the only thoughts in her head as she drove away, fearing if she didn't escape fast enough she'd be consumed. Swallowed up by what she had allowed between her and Kate. By that kiss. A kiss, Tommie knew, that could ruin their lives.

Tommie touched her lips, still feeling the warmth Kate's lips had left behind. Kate had had too much to drink. That was obvious. That was why she had stumbled. As for herself, that was a whole other issue. Tommie had known exactly what she was doing. She'd stood there and let a fantasy, a completely unrealistic one at that, cloud her common sense.

She slammed her fist into the steering wheel. "Stupid!" She punched it again. "Stupid, stupid move." Adrenaline had her blood pumping so hard it was thundering in her ears. "I've totally fucked up everything now."

Once she got home, she couldn't get into her apartment fast enough. She almost didn't hear her machine beeping as she raced to the fridge to grab a beer. She chugged it down, reaching for another before going to the answering machine. She inhaled and exhaled a deep, slow breath before hitting the button, expecting to hear Kate's voice when the message began.

"Hey, baby..." She breathed a sigh of relief. "I was just thinking about you, so I thought I'd call and tell you that." Jodi paused. "I hope you're not working those magnificent fingers of yours to the bone. That would definitely be a tragedy. Anyway...call when you can. Goodnight."

The machine clicked off and Tommie dropped on the floor. She leaned back against the couch, guilt grabbing her like a boa constrictor and compressing her chest. She sucked in a ragged breath before downing the second beer, then leaned her head back to let it begin to numb her brain.

* * *

Kate stood, her back against the house, undone by what had just happened. She could still feel Tommie's lips upon hers, warm and sweet with the taste of margaritas. She had so wanted to feel her tongue in her mouth, her strong hands on her bare skin. And then...

She shivered, first from the loss of that intimate contact and then from the realization she was standing alone in the dark. Light-headed, she made her way to the kitchen for a cold drink of water.

"Oh, God, what have I done?" She was torn between calling Tommie right then or waiting until the morning when she would be more clear-headed. Logic won out over desire, as usual. After starting the dishwasher, she refilled her water glass and forced herself to the bathroom and a steamy, hot shower.

She awoke with a headache. Scolding herself for not taking some aspirin before she'd crawled into bed, she sipped coffee at the kitchen table and replayed the events of last night. The first chance she had to explain her behavior to Tommie, she'd blame it on those extra-strength margaritas. After all, it wasn't like she could confess she felt something for her—she wasn't completely sure of it herself—and then see if Tommie was willing to serve as a guinea pig for her emotional experimentation.

CHAPTER NINETEEN

Kate and Tommie decided, separately, to put their "moment of indiscretion" out of their minds. Days passed, and days quickly turned into weeks, and before long, it was months.

Beyond embarrassed by her behavior, Kate couldn't bring herself to face Tommie. She rationalized that Tommie would call if she weren't mad, upset or completely put off by Kate's attempt at seduction. When she didn't…Kate assumed the worst.

For her part, Tommie felt like a predator of the worst kind. She couldn't excuse her actions—taking advantage of a woman when she was most vulnerable. She figured if Kate wasn't completely appalled with her, she would have called…but she hadn't.

* * *

Tommie arrived home from work the third Friday in August to a answering machine message from Megan. She picked up the phone and dialed the number Megan had left. When Kate answered, she was at a complete loss for words.

"Uh…Kate," she stammered, then tried desperately to sound composed. "Hi."

"Hi, Tommie. How have you been?"

Tommie thought Kate sounded much more together than she did. Nervously, she answered, "Good, real good. Um…I was calling for Megan. Is she there?"

"She is, hold on a sec." Tommie heard the sound of the receiver being set down. "Megan—Tommie for you." Kate's voice started to fade. "Oh, and there's one spot left in 'Laundry one-oh-one.' I'd be thrilled if you joined the 'course' after your call."

God. Tommie kicked herself for not being able to find even the simplest words to exchange with Kate. That night several months ago had messed with her mind, though—to the point she thought she would never get past it. It had also ended her relationship with Jodi. She'd taken her out for dinner the following weekend. It was a pleasant evening, but when Tommie declined to join Jodi afterward for a nightcap in the house, she had peppered her with questions about the "straight blond" with the niece. When Tommie didn't respond Jodi had told her in no uncertain terms—until she could decide who she really wanted to be with, she should "stay the hell away." Tommie had complied with her demand, in the process becoming nearly a hermit, going out only for work or when it was absolutely necessary.

Suddenly Tommie heard Megan's voice on the other end of the line.

"Hey, Tommie, I have a favor to ask," she began.

Tommie groaned. "Please tell me this will not require any deceit."

"None at all. I need your brawn."

"For…?" Megan's message had said little more than "please call me back."

Megan explained that she had been reluctant to call, assuming that Tommie had been staying away since the day of her graduation because of the precarious position she had put her in with her aunt. But moving some of her things into the dorm was going to take more than just she and Kate could manage.

"And I miss my ol' mentor."

Tommie chuckled. "Good thing you didn't say 'old' or I'd have to decline your otherwise irresistible invitation."

"Diplomacy," Megan said with a hint of mischief.

Tommie chuckled again and against her better judgment agreed to help. She noted the move-in date on her calendar, then went to work trying once again to put the sound of Kate's voice out of her head.

Kate wandered down the hall to Megan's room with an armful of laundry ten minutes later after Megan had neglected to join her in the laundry room. "What was Tommie calling about?" she asked with what she hoped was a tone of casual curiosity.

"Tommie's going to help us move my stuff to campus."

"Really? I didn't realize you two had been talking over the summer."

"We haven't." Megan shrugged. "I figured we could use the muscle. My room's on the third floor you know and the elevator will be busy with everyone moving in over that weekend. I just asked if she'd help and she said she would. It's not a problem that I asked her, is it?"

Kate shook her head absently, recalling in great detail the very last time she'd laid eyes on Tommie. "No...it's not a problem, sweetie. The help will be welcome, I'm sure, if we have to climb the stairs more than a few times."

"Great." Megan bounded toward the kitchen, Kate following a few steps behind her. "I told her to come around ten. I thought we would get lunch on the way"—she flexed her arm—"for extra energy."

Kate made no response, already drifting back into the memory of that kiss and the woman she'd laid awake thinking about for countless nights afterward. Perhaps it was time to come out of the closet and have a talk with her niece? No, the more she thought about it, the more she worried that it would cause Megan to pull away from her.

Besides, if she came out to Megan, then what? What would she tell Tommie? That she really was a lesbian and had just let Tommie think she was straight for the last fourteen or so months? That would go over with a big thud, right? She would assume that Kate didn't trust her enough to be honest with her, and that would kill everything. Then again, Kate thought, they hadn't even talked in months. What was there left to kill?

"Aunt Kate?" When Kate stared at her blankly she asked again, "Lunch on the way to campus for some energy, okay?"

Kate nodded automatically. "Sure, honey, that sounds fine."

After Megan left the room, Kate settled at the kitchen table with her cup of tea, closing her eyes and conjuring up the image of those dark, hypnotic eyes and the feel of those tender lips. They were real enough in her mind to send a shiver up her spine and warmer sensations to places lower. While she relished the thought of seeing her again, she had to worry how Tommie felt about her now. The way she had raced from the house that night and, seemingly, from Kate's life didn't give her cause for a great deal of optimism.

* * *

It was almost time for Tommie to be there. And she was close. Just around the corner in fact, sitting in her Jeep and giving herself a pep talk. This would be fine, she told herself. Megan needed help today, she could give it and Kate, well, hadn't she and Kate sort of been friends before the whole kiss thing happened? They could just pretend it had never occurred and go back to how things had been before. Couldn't they?

Tommie pulled slowly to the curb and took her time walking up the drive. The trunk of Kate's car was open and there were numerous boxes sitting next to it. She knocked on the door but didn't enter as if she had some right to. Today she was here to work and work only. Maybe, just maybe, if Kate worked her hard enough, she could stop punishing herself for that indiscretion months ago.

Kate greeted her with a brilliant smile. "Good morning." She stepped back from the door. "Come in and get yourself some coffee." She turned toward the kitchen. "Megan's packing her last box, then we can load up and head out."

Tommie watched Kate as she rummaged in the cupboard for travel mugs with lids. God, she had missed seeing her.

"So—you said on the phone you were doing good. Anything new and exciting in your life?" Kate asked as she poured them coffee.

Yeah, Tommie thought, I dumped the pretty brunette because I couldn't get past that kiss we shared, out there on the deck. She glanced briefly at the back door. And now I'm wallowing in self-pity because I can't ever have you. That pretty much sums it up.

But what she said was, "Nope, pretty much same ol', same ol'. Nothing new. You?"

Kate turned and held a mug out to Tommie. "Black, right?" After Tommie accepted it, she added, "Not too much." Some of the light faded from her bright blue eyes. "Just trying to figure out what I'm going to do here in this house by myself. Megan has been such a big part of my life for the last ten years."

Tommie sipped her coffee. "You're probably feeling what every other mother does who's about to send her kid off to college."

Kate nodded. "I suppose you're right. You think they have a support group for us?"

"If not, you could always start one."

They heard a door close. "Ready whenever you two are," Megan said, appearing behind Tommie.

They managed to squeeze all of Megan's things into Kate's car and still leave room for the three of them. Tommie suggested driving herself down to the campus, but Kate insisted they ride together, pointing out that it could be a while before they were all together again. They traveled in companionable silence most of the way, Kate and Tommie each deep in their own thoughts while Megan listened to her music through headphones. One or another of them occasionally commented on something, like a song playing on the radio or a billboard announcing the great savings at an outlet mall.

Several hours later they arrived in Hastings. On the side of town where the campus of Indiana Arts and Sciences University was located, Kate pulled into a small café. After a pleasant lunch, during which Megan described her class load to Tommie and talked excitedly about her future plans, they drove to Megan's dorm and began the arduous task of setting up her half of the small room. The process brought back a flood of memories for Tommie, including that of the first "college girl" she'd ever made out with in her dorm room. The only girl Tommie had ever fallen in love with and the one that had broken her heart. Tommie blamed Emily for her having become the playgirl she'd become—or had been. She was Tommie's justification for how she could so readily take a woman to bed, and to that special place, all the while keeping them at an emotional distance. Until recently at least. Now she couldn't even do that. She was lost. She wondered how many memories Megan was about to make that she'd want to remember the rest of her life and how many she'd spend the rest of her life trying to forget.

Finally, after a tearful hug, Kate climbed in the car, searching her purse for tissues and leaving the last words of farewell to Tommie.

Tommie cocked her head. "Well, kiddo, welcome to the big grown-up world." She grinned. "Don't ever let it get out of control on you, but, if you do and you need anything, I hope you know you can always call me."

Her eyes sparkling with fresh tears, Megan threw her arms around Tommie's neck. Quietly she said, "Thanks for all your help. And for keeping my secret." She started to step back, then stopped. "Will you do one more thing for me?"

"If I can. What is it?"

"Will you kind of keep tabs on Aunt Kate? Check up on her, you know? Make sure she's getting out and trying to have a life."

She would have done that, Tommie knew, even if Megan hadn't asked. She would always do anything she could for Kate. "Sure thing." Tommie placed a hand on Megan's shoulder, waggling the other in the air. "Now, go…learn lots and make me proud."

"I will."

Tommie walked to the driver's side of the car, where Kate was watching Megan disappear inside the building, fresh tears cresting in her eyes. "Would you like me to drive home?"

Kate pulled her eyes from the empty sidewalk. "That's kind of you to offer. I think I could use the downtime," she answered wearily.

Ah, Kate, Tommie thought as they changed places. *I'd hold you forever and let you cry out all your sadness. If only you'd ask.*

Kate looked uncomfortable as they stood in the driveway at the house. "Thanks for all your help, Tommie. I really appreciate it."

"You're very welcome."

"Can I repay you by fixing you some dinner or ordering in some pizza?"

Tommie shoved her hands in her pockets nervously and lied. "Thanks, but I need to get going. I've got some work to do." When Kate nodded, Tommie noticed the tears brimming again in her eyes. She stepped closer, gently taking Kate's hand. "Listen, if you get lonely and need to talk, just call. I'll always have time for you."

Kate swiped at the tears that threatened to spill down her cheeks. "Thank you."

Reluctantly, Tommie released her hand. "Okay, then. I'll see you around."

"Right," Kate said. "I'm sure we'll run into each other sometime."

Tommie felt bad as she drove off, leaving Kate standing alone in the driveway. Like she'd abandoned a helpless puppy.

CHAPTER TWENTY

What was everyone so excited about? Tommie was devoting the beginning of her workweek to polishing her column for the Tuesday edition. Or trying to. But everybody in the newsroom seemed to be trampling by her door. Rising to shut it, she saw most of the staff crowded in front of the bank of televisions suspended from the ceiling at the front of the bullpen. Figuring it was as good a time as any to stretch her legs, she walked over to find out what the commotion was about.

As she crossed the room, she heard the reporter's excited voice saying, "The suspected gunman is reported to be holed up somewhere in the arts building on campus."

God, another stomach-churning school shooting. Tommie was about to turn away when one of the TVs flashed a shot of the main entrance of the campus and the name of the college she had helped deliver Megan to two weeks earlier. She froze, pain squeezing her chest. "What's going on?" she asked.

"It appears there's been a shooting," the guy next to her said, one of the business reporters, she thought.

Tommie spun and ran to her office, knocking into a desk chair on the way. Snatching up her cell phone she scrolled through her contacts to the letter M, found Megan's number and punched it. When the call finally connected, it went straight to voice mail. "Damn it!" She hit the end button, then redial, and got the same result. "Think," she said aloud, rubbing her forehead. "Just think, damn it." She tried the number once more before going back to her contacts and scrolling to the Ks. "Damn!" She didn't have anything but the number for Kate's landline at home. She reached in the bottom drawer of her desk for the phone book. Finding the number for the hospital was not difficult. Reaching Kate was. She was transferred to four different people before she finally lost her cool and unloaded on an unsuspecting woman in HR.

"Look, lady, you're the fourth and, I can assure you, the last person I'm going to speak to." She took a quick breath and forged on. "You have a surgical nurse on staff named Kate Bellam. A very serious situation has arisen concerning her niece, for whom she is the legal guardian. Now, I don't know if you have kids, but her niece is like her daughter. If you don't put me through to her or to someone who can get her on the phone with me in the next sixty seconds, I'm going to use every ounce of influence here at the paper to ensure a scathing article appears about inadequacies at your institution. And I'll make sure that you are mentioned by name, Mrs. Harris, Human Resources Advocate."

"Just, uh…please, give me a minute or two," the woman stuttered. "I promise I will locate someone who can help you."

"Please do." She was ready to explode by the time the woman came back on.

"Thank you for your patience. I'm going to connect you to the head surgical nurse. She has assured me she will do what she can to help you."

The phone began ringing. Once, twice, three times. And with each ring Tommie's anger and anxiety grew. Finally a brusque voice answered. "Marge Banks, may I help you?"

"I need to speak to Kate Bellam immediately regarding a family emergency."

"Well, I…"

Tommie cut her off. "Look, lady. This could be a matter of life or death."

"Perhaps if I had some idea what this crisis is I could be of more assistance." The woman's words were laced with suspicion.

"There has been a shooting on the campus in Hastings where Kate's niece attends college and I am unable to reach her. As you probably know, Kate is Megan's legal guardian. She needs to be aware that she could be in grave danger, but I'd rather it come from someone she knows—like me." Tommie heard the click of a computer keyboard. "Please? I'm begging you."

The woman's voice softened. "She's in a surgery that is scheduled to last another hour or so. I can try and find another nurse to scrub in and relieve her."

"Do her a favor please and don't just try. Make it happen. I'm asking for some compassion here." *And if you can't find any, I'm going to be one angry mother you-know-what, and if I were you I'd find a really good place to hide.* When the woman started to protest, she cut her off again. "I'm on my way now. I'll be there in less than twenty minutes." She pushed out of her chair and headed for the parking garage, calling in to her boss as she passed his door that she had to go out. She redialed Megan's cell, only to receive the immediate voice mail message again. The phone must be off or dead. "Oh God," Tommie whispered to herself. "Don't even *think* that word." Adrenaline pumping, she drove to the hospital, practically running a guy over in the lot before whipping her car into a parking spot and racing into the hospital main entrance.

"Where's Surgery?" she asked the woman at the information desk. On a phone call, she held up a finger in a request to wait. Tommie tapped her fingers on the desk as she finished helping the caller. "Now who was it you were looking for?"

"Surgery," said Tommie through gritted teeth.

"It's on the third floor…" The words were barely out of her mouth before Tommie was heading to the elevators. "But the waiting room is on the fourth floor."

Tommie slid past two people exiting the elevator, punched three, then slumped against the wall. On the drive over, all the radio stations had been broadcasting live reports about the campus shooting. Her stomach was in knots.

When the doors opened on the surgery floor, she burst through them and, after a brief glance, headed to her left in the direction of what appeared to be a desk.

"I'm looking for Marge…"

A young woman in a brightly printed scrub shirt and matching pants looked up. "Nurse Banks said you'd be showing up here looking for Kate. She should be back with her any minute. Is there anything I can help with while you're waiting?"

Tommie shook her head no. Her heart was in her throat. How on earth would she break this news to Kate? She was sure she didn't have a clue what was going on outside the sterile environment of the operating room at the moment. She closed her eyes, struggling to keep her emotions under control. Finally she heard a metal door close and turned to see Kate approaching.

"Tommie?" Kate's voice trembled and she pulled nervously at the mask hanging around her neck.

Tommie took a breath. "There's been a shooting on campus and I can't get hold of Megan." She watched as tears formed in Kate's eyes and threatened to spill over. "I wanted to make sure…" Tommie paused, her emotions about to rob her of her own composure. "Wanted to make sure you heard what was going on."

"Oh, no…please, not Megan." Tommie quickly slipped an arm around her waist. She'd seen Kate faint before and wanted to be prepared.

"I came to drive you down there. I don't have any details yet, but I can call the paper on the way and find out what they've been able to find out."

Kate swayed against her. "Oh God."

"Listen," Tommie said. "Let's get your things and get on the road. You can keep trying Megan's phone while I call the paper." As she steered Kate from the desk, she caught the eye of the other nurse standing there, the woman she supposed was Marge Banks. "Thank you for your help," she said. "Sorry if I was out of line."

"Completely understandable," the woman said, nodding and sending them off with a sympathetic smile.

* * *

While Tommie drove like a maniac toward the highway, Kate dialed Megan's phone repeatedly, leaving desperate messages for Megan to call her back as soon as possible. She kept her voice even and controlled, but after hanging up the last time she just flopped back in her seat, stared blankly at the scenery passing by and thought about the phone conversation she'd had with Megan yesterday.

Megan had sounded so bubbly and upbeat as she recounted her last few days on campus to Kate. They'd made it a habit to talk at least two or three times a week since Megan had left, more for Kate's sake than Megan's. She was beginning to cope with living alone but experiencing some separation anxiety, which she assumed all mothers went through. A sob wracked her as she contemplated the thought of what her life would become if Megan ceased to be a part of it.

Tommie, who had called the paper once they entered the freeway, put down her cell phone and placed her hand on Kate's thigh. "My contact at the paper said all the phone lines and cell towers down there are jammed right now. He'll call back when he has confirmation, but he thinks that the gunman has been isolated and is possibly in custody."

Kate put her fingers on top of Tommie's. Barely loud enough to hear, she said, "She has to be okay, Tommie…she has to."

Tommie grasped Kate's trembling hand. "I'm sure she's fine," she said reassuringly, "and I'm sure we'll find that out any minute."

Kate's phone rang in her lap, startling them both. "Hello?" After a pause, she said, "I know. I've been trying too. I can't get through either." There was another pause. "I will." When she closed the phone and laid her hand back in her lap, Tommie took hold of it again. "That was Ashley in Connecticut. It's all over the national news. She's been trying to call Megan for the last half hour too." A sob shook her body.

Tommie gave her hand a gentle squeeze. "She's going to be just fine, Kate. You have to believe that."

Kate nodded, unconvinced. "I have to call Ashley back if we hear anything from Megan."

"When," Tommie corrected her. "*When* we hear from her."

As Kate turned her gaze back to the window, Tommie held fast to the comfort of holding her hand. It was little solace compared to all the feelings tumbling around inside her at the moment. And poor Ashley. Tommie couldn't imagine where her head or heart had to be, hanging in limbo so far away.

Twenty minutes later and not quite half the way there, Kate's phone rang again. Tommie saw her eyes grow wide when she answered.

"Megan, honey..." Kate sucked in a deep breath as the tears rolled down her cheeks again. "Oh, God, honey..." She turned a watery smile in Tommie's direction. "We've been so worried. We've been trying to get hold of you since this thing started." She was silent for a long minute. "It's okay, sweetie, we were just so worried." She paused. "Tommie and I. Oh, and Ashley called. The news already made it to the East Coast." Another pause. "I said I'd call her but maybe you should. I'm sure she'll be glad to hear your voice." Kate exhaled a long, slow breath. "You can tell her yourself. Here..." She handed the phone to Tommie.

"Hey there, kiddo," she said in a voice that was as unruffled as she could make it. "I knew you were too smart and tough to get caught in the middle of whatever was happening there today. Is everyone okay?" A moment later she said, "It's a deal," and handed the phone back to Kate.

After a long silence, she said, "I'll be home by six if you want to call this evening." Then, "All right...be safe, sweetie. You know I love you."

She snapped her phone closed, dropped it in her purse and began crying harder than she had since Tommie had delivered the news to her. Tommie carefully steered the car onto the shoulder of the road and stopped, her flashers blinking.

"Hey, she's okay." When her words didn't seem to slow the sobs, she slid her arm around Kate's shoulder and drew her into her arms. "Shh..." she murmured against Kate's hair. "Everything's fine, Kate. Please don't cry."

After a few minutes Kate sniffed and pulled back to look in Tommie's eyes.

"Thank you," she whispered, placing a hand on Tommie's chest. "You have such a big heart. Bigger than anything imaginable."

Tommie pushed down the urge to respond with a kiss. She wasn't going to make that mistake again. Uncomfortable, she averted her eyes from Kate's and started the car again.

Kate composed herself. "We might as well head back. Megan assured me we can't get close to the campus and she promised to call later this evening." Kate looked in the visor mirror. "Her cell phone battery was dead. By the time she tried to borrow someone else's to call, the towers were jammed. She felt so bad. She said she knew how worried we would be." Tommie caught a glimpse of fresh tears, which Kate wiped away as she exited the highway and then jumped back on it to head back to Denton.

CHAPTER TWENTY-ONE

When Tommie turned the blinker on to leave the highway, Kate asked, "Can we stop at the house before we go by the hospital for my car?"

She turned the signal off. "Sure." She took the exit for Kate's house a few miles further on. She pulled in the empty drive, and Kate unbuckled her seat belt.

"Do you have to rush back to work?"

Tommie looked over at Kate. She was so beautiful even with little or no makeup and red swollen eyes. She thought she could look at that face every moment of every day and never be tired of seeing it. What the heck. Kate seemed to have all but forgotten their kiss. Why not spend as much time as she could with the most unattainable woman in her life? Chances were they wouldn't see each other much, if at all anymore, with Megan virtually out of their lives now. Well, at least out of hers.

"There's nothing pressing, no."

"Come in for a bit before you take me back to my car?"

Tommie snapped off the engine. "Sure."

Inside Kate dropped her coat onto a living room chair and started down the hall. "Make yourself at home. I'll be back in a minute."

Tommie dropped onto the couch, leaned her head back and closed her eyes. Five minutes passed, then ten. She stood, wondering where Kate had disappeared to, then made her way down the hall. The bathroom was empty, but there was a shadow across the hall in Megan's room. She moved to the open door. Kate was standing next to Megan's bed, gazing out the window above it.

Tommie waited a few moments more. "Kate?" she said softly.

She turned around, revealing the furry teddy bear she had clutched to her chest. "This was Megan's favorite when she first came to live with me. She couldn't sleep without old Mr. Bear." The tiniest smile creased her face. She looked down at the worn, stuffed bear with a missing eye and a nose hanging on by a few threads. "Well, without him and my arms around her, off and on for the first few years." Tommie smiled, easily imagining the scene. "She was so innocent and confused. First by the absence of her father, then the death of her mom and moving in with me." Kate placed the bear back on the pillow, turning back to Tommie. She looked completely together now, centered, despite the potentially life-altering terror they'd just experienced. "Thank you for today."

Tommie nodded. "No problem. I told you. I'll always do my best to help you keep Megan safe."

Kate moved to where Tommie stood in the doorway. When she looked up, there was more in her eyes than fear and anguish.

She reached her arms around Tommie's neck and hugged her. "Thank you for taking care of *me*."

Tommie gave her a gentle squeeze. "My pleasure." Having Kate's arms around her had her heart racing like a sprinter's.

What Kate did next almost exploded it. She leaned back, looked into Tommie's eyes briefly, then just—kissed her, pressing her soft warm lips firmly against hers.

Eyes wide with fear, Tommie pulled back, gasping for the breath Kate seemed to have sucked from her lungs. "Wait! Kate, I don't think this—"

Kate quickly pressed her lips to Tommie's again, for just a second, then said, "Please don't run away again. I need you."

She pulled Tommie to her for another kiss. This one was totally lacking in tenderness, though. It was fierce and fiery. Hungry. Tommie saw brilliant flashes of light behind her eyelids and felt a liquid heat begin to flow through her veins. This was unreal. She was almost convinced she'd stumbled into some kind of "other world vortex" and it would all go away when they stepped out of the room. For the time being, though…Tommie surrendered to the feel of Kate's lips on hers, her body pressed so close and the fingers she was threading through Tommie's hair to hold them together.

Eventually her haze cleared enough to allow Tommie to wonder why Kate was kissing her. She hadn't been drinking. She might not be completely in her usual, logical mind, but she was in a place where she should be able to make mostly rational decisions. And this wasn't rational.

Tommie placed gentle hands on Kate's shoulders, pushing her back far enough to gasp for air but without separating herself from Kate's hold. "This is not a good idea," she said raggedly. "You're feeling the emotional effects of what could have happened to Megan. I get that you're alone, and maybe don't want to be right now, but, Kate, you're str…"

Kate pressed her finger to Tommie's lips. "I'm not…Everything you think about that is wrong." Tommie's eyes, clouded with confusion, locked onto Kate's.

"What…?"

Kate gave her head a little shake. "I'm gay, Tommie. I've been gay as long as I can remember." Tommie's mouth fell open. "I want you so much." She stroked her finger across Tommie's cheek and down her jaw. "I've wanted you almost since we met. Don't doubt this, please." She stroked her fingers again over Tommie's cheek. "I want to take care of you. I want to feel your strong arms around me every possible moment, always." Her fingertip lightly traced Tommie's lips. "I want to show you that there's so much more than drinking in bars and hot chicks. And, I want *you* to remind me every day, what fun…" one of Kate's brows rose suggestively, "and serious things adults do."

Kate's lips curved up slightly at Tommie's continued confused expression. "Unless there's someone else? Or you don't have even the slightest attraction to me?"

Tommie lowered her forehead to meet Kate's. "No, nobody else. And God, I'm crazy about you. I can't stop thinking about you, in fact."

Kate cradled Tommie's face in her hands. "Then let's not waste another minute. Today is proof that life is too short to lose precious moments like these." She pulled Tommie's face closer, parting Tommie's lips with her tongue.

Tommie groaned. "God, Kate," she growled into Kate's mouth.

Kate responded by plunging her tongue deeper. When she ended the kiss, she pulled back again to look into Tommie's eyes, her own eyes glowing a deep violet. "I want you," she repeated. She stroked her fingers through Tommie's hair. "Please, Tommie. Make love to me."

Oh, God, Tommie thought as she moved to scoop Kate up in her arms. *I hope I don't live to regret this.* Kate held on tightly, her face pressed to Tommie's neck as she carried her across the hall on knees that threatened to buckle before she reached the bed. She set her down carefully, searching her eyes for signs of apprehension but finding only deep-burning desire.

Gently guiding Kate's scrub shirt over her head and removing her bra, Tommie laid her back and stretched out beside her. She traced her fingers down Kate's neck to the valley between her breasts, murmuring, "God, you're beautiful." Her lips replaced her fingers on the spot between Kate's breasts, freeing her hand to trail lower across her abdomen.

Kate shivered under Tommie's touch. "Please don't make me wait any longer." She pushed Tommie's hand to the top of her loosely tied scrub pants. Tommie's heart pounded so fiercely that she could feel it beating at every point where her and Kate's bodies connected.

Please, God, Tommie prayed silently. *Don't let this be a mistake.* She lowered her lips to Kate's as her fingers found their way under her scrubs and into her silk panties, sliding gently into Kate's wetness. Kate moaned into her mouth as her hips rose firmly to meet Tommie's touch and rocked in rhythm with her pressure. "God, Kate. You feel so incredible." Tommie felt her own desire surge as she continued to slide her fingers back and forth over Kate's pulsing flesh.

"I need you, Tommie. Inside me…Please?"

Tommie thought she might just come from Kate's impassioned plea. She slid one, then two fingers inside her. Kate squeezed tightly around them as they slowly filled her.

"Oh…Tommie…oh, yes." Kate gasped and reached a hand between Tommie's legs and her own thigh. "Oh, God…that's so…"

Tommie felt Kate tighten hard around her fingers, forcing her burgeoning desire to peak. Moments after Kate's spasms stilled beneath her, Tommie's body rocked with an intense orgasm of its own.

They lay unmoving for long minutes before Tommie very slowly pulled her fingers out, drawing a tiny whimper from Kate. She rolled onto her back and Kate snuggled against her, resting her head on Tommie's thumping chest. Tommie's arms crushed Kate to her. She fit perfectly there, and Tommie wanted with all her heart to always hold her this close.

When Kate's breath evened out, she said softly, "That was…"

"Mmm…yeah, it was."

Kate raised her head to look at Tommie. "Did you?"

"I did, but you know…"

"What?" Concern clouded Kate's eyes.

Tommie's expression was lustful. "I want you in my mouth." Her lips curved enticingly. "I want—I need to taste you in the worst way."

Kate felt dizzy with desire at the thought of Tommie's mouth on her. "Can I have a minute or two to catch my breath?" When Tommie nodded with a grin, Kate added, "And I'll only agree if we get completely naked."

Tommie's grin turned sly. "Not a problem." She slipped out of bed. "Not a problem at all." She pulled off Kate's remaining clothing, stripped away her own and quickly slid back in beside her.

"Mmm…" Kate pressed herself against Tommie's newly exposed flesh and snuggled back into the crook of her arm.

* * *

Tommie woke hours later, her body half covered by Kate's and a sheet. The feel of Kate's breath on her chest and her body snuggling against Tommie's own made her heart ache with what she suspected must be love. She examined the feeling more closely.

Love? Oh yeah, she thought, definitely head over heels. At least on her part. But what about Kate? Why would a woman as beautiful as Kate take up with someone like her? She recalled briefly the last time she'd felt as though she was in love, and how devastating that had turned out. Her heart had been scarred all those years ago. Maybe, just maybe, if she were lucky this time around, the scars would protect it.

A teensy tiny part of her mind told her to jump up and run. Isn't that what she'd always done with women? Sex them and leave them. She'd never had a truly serious relationship in her life. She'd not even tried since college, until Jodi, and look how that had turned out. She'd failed. Because her head was all twisted and confused over Kate. Straight Kate…who turned out to be not so straight after all.

Oh God, she'll never want to be in a relationship with me. She certainly isn't going to settle for a big ol' butch when she can have her pick of all the beautiful babes out there like herself. *Shut up, shut up,* she told her overactive mind. Live for the moment, and deal with the consequences…whenever. She tightened her arm around Kate, eliciting a tiny moan from her.

Kate gave a little moan of pleasure, savoring the feel of Tommie's arm around her and the strength of the body that was snuggling against her own. She had never felt safer or more protected in her life. She wanted that every day for the rest of her life, she realized. She'd been waiting so long. But…could she count on Tommie to provide it? She was a playgirl, a charming flirt, not at all the type of person Kate had ever pictured settling down with.

She slid her arm around Tommie's waist and pressed her leg tightly between Tommie's.

"Mmm…" Tommie moaned, lightly kissing the top of Kate's head. "If you don't stop that, you're going to start something again."

Kate slid her hand to Tommie's hip and pulled herself on top of her. She raised her eyes to meet Tommie's. "I assure you that I will finish anything I start." She moved her slickness over Tommie's thigh, the heat between them flaring again and quickly spreading like a wildfire. Kate smothered Tommie's mouth with a passionate kiss, then pulled back and looked into her eyes. "I could do this all day," she said, continuing to thrust against Tommie's thigh.

Tommie laced her fingers in Kate's hair and held her face inches away from her own. "Actually, I think we've made a pretty good start on that already. Aren't you hungry, thirsty?"

Kate squeezed Tommie's thigh between hers. "Only for you. I love the way you make me feel."

Tommie stiffened. Kate had used the word "love." She wasn't sure how to take it.

"What's wrong?"

Tommie quickly gathered herself. "Nothing." She reached down to cup Kate's ass and pull her hard against her. "You just make me crazy with want. Still, maybe we should think about getting out of this bed, at least to make sure our legs still work."

"Mmm…" Kate squeezed Tommie's thigh once more, then rolled back onto her side. She stroked her fingers up and down Tommie's chest and abdomen before letting her hand rest between her breasts. "I hope this wasn't an act of pity on your part."

"Pity?"

"Yes, pity for the poor old closeted lesbian who hasn't had any action in eons."

Tommie laughed. "No, no pity for you. I think I fell for you the first moment we met, even though I was determined not to like you. I would actually think it would be the other way around." She pressed her cheek to the top of Kate's head. "You know, pity for the big ol' dyke."

Kate rose up to look at Tommie. "It's who you are that makes you so loveable." She placed a tender kiss on Tommie's neck. "And," she kissed the spot again, "I don't think I've ever been with a more passionate and tender lover."

Lord, Tommie thought, *TWO variations of the "L" word.* "Life is too short," she chanted in her mind, not allowing Kate's words to send her running. As long as Kate wanted her in her bed, she'd be there.

Kate got a serious look on her face. "What did you mean—you were prepared not to like me when you met me?"

Tommie's eyes held nothing but tenderness when she answered, "As you know, I assumed you were a surgeon. I figured you'd be, I don't know, egotistical maybe or have that 'God-like' complex that some doctors do." She shrugged. "It was stupid for me to assume anything without actually meeting you."

Kate touched her lips briefly to Tommie's chin. "And now?"

Tommie gave Kate her most charming smile. "You're an amazing woman, Kate Bellam. A beautiful and amazing woman. Megan is a lucky girl to have you caring for her. I hope she never forgets that."

Kate blushed. She stared off for a moment, then brought her eyes back to Tommie's. "I care about you too, you know."

Tommie chuckled. "That can't be an easy thing to do."

Kate shook her head. "It requires no effort at all." She pursed her lips and Tommie could tell she was considering her last comment. "I have a confession to make."

"I'm not sure I know you well enough to be hearing your confessions."

Kate slid a hand down, cupping Tommie's crotch. "You know me on a much more personal level than anyone has in years."

"Then confess away."

Kate took a breath. "I met you, sort of, before Megan invited you to the house that first time." Tommie's mind was in overdrive trying to recall an image of Kate before the Fourth of July holiday the previous year. "Megan took a weekend trip with Ashley and I snuck out one night to Gurlz Club. You were there with a bunch of women."

Tommie raised a finger. "For the record, before you and I met I wouldn't have been at the bar 'with' anyone. If I was with any women, I would have met them there."

"Okay. In any case, I was sitting at the bar when you came up to get drinks for all your women. You spoke to me, in fact, though I didn't respond. The bartender's name was Tina or something like that."

"Tammy, her name is Tammy."

"That's right. Anyway, while you were at the bar you made some…"—she paused—"some comments, about women. I thought they sounded arrogant and crude." She grimaced. "I'm sorry, it was just the impression you gave me. I don't know. Maybe you were showing off for the bartender or for your table full of girls."

Tommie groaned as fragments of memory stirred and began to knit together. "The pretty straight blond with the nice ass."

Kate looked surprised. "You noticed my ass?"

"Oh, yeah, on your way to the door. Who wouldn't? Tammy thought I ran you off, but I told her you had just figured out you were in the wrong kind of bar."

"You assumed I was straight and just happened to wander into a gay bar?"

"It happens more than you might think. Or at least that's what they say." She remembered satisfying more than one straight woman who supposedly didn't know the bar was packed with lesbians. Tommie felt the blush coloring her cheeks.

"Now what? Or shouldn't I ask?" Tommie bit her lip. "Say no more. It surprises me, I guess, that there are gay women who want to be with straight women. I admit, I had a few crushes on straight women when I was younger, but I don't think I ever wanted to sleep with one."

"Just the pretty gay ones, I imagine."

Kate frowned. "It sounds so shallow when I think about it, but yes, I have only been with fairly feminine women before."

Tommie sighed. "And here you are with the likes of me."

Kate pushed back from Tommie to better look in her eyes. "And what is that supposed to mean?"

Tommie shrugged. "I'm big, and...oh, let's see, yeah, I'm butch. Not exactly your criteria for the perfect woman."

Kate let out an exasperated breath. "For someone so 'big,' so seemingly powerful and in control, you sure can be insecure." Kate moved her hand up to cradle her cheek. "There are so many good and wonderful hidden qualities about you. That's what attracted me to you." Kate slowly drew her hand down Tommie's neck to that spot on her chest, between her breasts, where her hand fit perfectly. "I hope you don't think this is just about sex." Tommie quirked an eyebrow. "When I said I needed you, I wasn't just asking for you to scratch an itch for me."

Seeing Tommie's eyes go wide, Kate contemplated playing with her a little. She decided against it. This was no time for games. She wanted Tommie to know how she felt. She'd spent far too much of her life hiding who she was and what she wanted. "Relax, honey, I'm not asking you to marry me today. I just want you to know I care about you, more than I probably can convey, and I would like to see where things might go." She clarified. "If there's a chance they can go somewhere besides the bedroom." Tommie exhaled a long breath and Kate braced herself, thinking Tommie was about to let her down easy.

Tommie thought her heart would burst. "Like I said, you're an amazing woman, Kate. And while I'm pretty sure I've probably never really been in love before"—Tommie touched Kate's face tenderly—"I think I might be in love with you." Kate's eyes sparkled like a million tiny diamonds. "I'd go anywhere with you that you want to take me, Kate Bellam. I love you."

Kate's response came in a choked whisper. "Oh, Tommie…you have my heart." Kate pressed her hand to Tommie's heart. "I'm so in love with you."

Tommie drew Kate near. As their lips came together, it felt as if the whole of their bodies melted into one. This is what it is all about, Tommie thought. This was truly what made life worth it all. She'd never felt more loved, more comforted or more content in the embrace of someone's arms. She'd never wanted to hang onto anything as much as she wanted to hang onto Kate. This was where she was meant to be. She was home.

* * *

She was also hungry, as her stomach announced a little while later. Kate patted it gently. "Sounds like someone needs to be fed. I'm just going to slip in the bathroom, then I'll fix us some dinner. Okay?"

"Hmm…" Tommie glanced at the clock. Where had the time gone? Oh, yeah. She reached out and laced her fingers in Kate's. "That sounds good." She watched her for a moment, then asked, "Is this for real?"

Kate leaned down and kissed Tommie briefly. When she leaned back, she said, "I certainly hope so. If it's not, it's the best, most real-life dream I've ever had."

After Kate headed to the bathroom, Tommie swung her legs over the edge of the bed. Seconds later Kate's cell phone rang. She looked at it, then to the hallway, where she could hear water running, and then back at the phone. What the heck. She picked it up. "Hello."

There was a brief pause, then, "Tommie?" Megan's voice conveyed nothing but a simple question.

"Yeah, it's me, and I bet you want to speak to your aunt. She just went to the bathroom. Hang on a minute." Tommie covered the phone with her hand, padding naked into the hall and to the bathroom door. Tapping lightly, she said, "Kate, Megan's on the phone."

Kate opened the door and ran her eyes over Tommie's big muscular frame, a tiny smile creeping across her face. After savoring Kate's curvaceous figure as well, Tommie handed her the phone and leaned in the doorway.

Kate managed to get her surging libido under control before speaking. "Megan, sweetie, hi." She listened for a moment. "I know you are." She turned to Tommie, covering the mouthpiece. "Are you available for a little road trip this weekend?"

"For you, anytime."

Kate slid her hand into Tommie's and gave it a squeeze. "We're coming down this weekend, Megs, so please set aside some time." She listened, then added, "Tommie and I." She hesitated a second. "I really need to talk with you." She squeezed Tommie's hand again. "No, sweetie, I'm fine...just fine." She was, really, though it was pure agony to have Tommie standing so close to her—and so naked. Kate closed her eyes against the torture. She finally said, "I love you too, sweetie. I'll talk to you again before the weekend."

Ending the call, she laid the phone down on the vanity and gazed into Tommie's eyes. "Are you ready for this?"

Tommie pulled Kate into her arms. "I'm ready to spend my life making you happy. Whatever it takes."

Kate laid her head against Tommie's chest. "You already have."

CHAPTER TWENTY-TWO

"Mmm…" Tommie moaned as Kate's lips brushed lightly over the corner of her mouth. Before her eyes opened Tommie could detect the mouth-watering aroma of Kate's expertly brewed coffee.

"Wake up, sleepyhead," Kate said softly. "We have a big day today."

Tommie groaned, rolling onto her back as Kate settled her hip against Tommie's side. "How can you be so cheery at"—she glanced at the bedside clock—"at seven o'clock in the morning when we were up well past midnight?"

Kate took a sip of the coffee she was carrying before handing the cup to Tommie. "Practice," she responded. "When you're responsible for getting a teenager up and off to school each day, it becomes second nature." When Tommie raised the cup to drink, Kate took the opportunity to tug the sheet down to her waist. She adored looking at Tommie's big muscular body.

Tommie felt her gaze like a gentle caress on her skin. Her nipples puckered instantly, and her body flushed with arousal.

"God, Kate, if you don't stop undressing me with those eyes, I'm going to drag you back into this bed."

Kate chuckled. "I hate to tell you this, sweetheart, but you're already undressed. And if you don't get up we're going to be late." She leaned in quickly for a kiss before swatting Tommie's thigh and popping up off the bed. "Come on, Ms. Reporter, we have big news to deliver today." She disappeared through the door.

Tommie took another sip of coffee, stood and stretched until she heard all the familiar pops, then headed to the bathroom. Her mind wandered as she stood under the shower spray. Big news to deliver indeed. She wondered how Megan would receive it.

She didn't think Megan would be too upset about Kate's revelation, given her own secret, though she might be hurt that Kate had not told her earlier and had ignored that part of her life for so long.

As for the news about Tommie...While she and Megan had had a bit of a rough start when they met at the paper, they'd not only gotten past whatever misgivings they had about each other but also developed, at the very least, a respectful relationship, a caring respectful relationship. Or so Tommie thought.

That didn't mean Megan would throw her arms around Tommie when she learned she was sleeping with her aunt, though. Nothing guaranteed that she wouldn't be as fiercely protective of Kate as Kate was of her. In which case...Tommie checked her appearance in Kate's full-length mirror as she pulled on her worn button-fly jeans that Kate liked so well and a navy rugby shirt. "Yep," she mumbled. "No doubt about it. You still look like a big ol' dyke." It would have to do. She was what she was.

She found Kate in the kitchen leaning a hip against the counter. "Bagel or muffin?"

"Whatever you're having is fine."

Kate brushed her fingers over Tommie's arm as she moved around to the bread drawer. When Tommie didn't respond to the caress, she took a closer look at her. Her expression was blank, her eyes unfocused as she sipped her coffee.

"I'm thinking of cutting my hair in a short spike and dying it pink. What do you think?"

"Hum, okay," was Tommie's absentminded response.

Kate dropped in a bagel and started the toaster, then moved in front of Tommie. "What's wrong?" she asked, her heart beating anxiously.

She and Tommie had been together every minute they could since Monday, kept apart only by their jobs. They came to Kate's every night for dinner and conversation, talking about anything and everything, learning more about each other and making short-term plans. After which, because Kate had this insatiable need for Tommie to make love to her, they would run off to bed to make further discoveries.

Was it too much too soon? Kate wondered. It wasn't for her, but Tommie was standing there looking like she was a million miles away. Like she was rethinking the whole concept of being in a relationship.

"I...uh..." *Oh, God.* "I guess I'm pretty worried about this coming out thing with Megan. Not me coming out." She gave a half laugh. "I don't have any doubt she already has my number."

"You're worried what Megan will think when she learns her aunt is a lesbian?"

"No." Tommie shook her head and pointed a thumb at herself. "What Megan will think when she learns you're involved with *this* lesbian."

Kate chuckled. "Sorry, sweetheart, I don't mean to make light of this." She grasped Tommie's hand. "Megan cares very much about you."

"That doesn't mean she wants to think about you heating the sheets with me. I don't know. I guess I'm afraid she'll think I've brainwashed you somehow...brought you over to the dark side or..."

"Stop." Kate placed her fingers on Tommie's moving lips. "The only thing you're guilty of is awakening my long-neglected woman-loving libido. Megan is a very smart girl. I don't believe for a minute she's going to blame you for anything. All she has to do is consider the fact that I've never been on a date with a man since she came to live with me. She'll figure it out. I wouldn't be surprised if she doesn't already have her suspicions. After all, she was the one who kept bringing us together." She slipped her arms around Tommie's waist, stepping between her feet until their bodies connected.

"Huh?"

"Dinner on the Fourth of July, the festival on the mall, the spring break trip, inviting you to graduation and to help her move…" She nuzzled Tommie's chest. "If she's silly enough to have any problems with you, well, I don't care how old she is. I'm still 'the mom.' I'll ground her butt until she gets her head on straight."

Tommie exhaled a long deep breath.

"What?" Kate eyed her suspiciously.

Tommie wrapped her arms possessively around her. "You are one amazing woman, Kate Bellam."

"Yes, I am." Kate nipped at her neck. "And don't you ever forget it." The toaster popped. "Breakfast awaits." She steered Tommie to the table.

Tommie insisted on driving even though they were taking Kate's car. She didn't think she could manage the two-plus hour drive without fidgeting, and she didn't want to drive Kate nuts or turn her into a nervous ball of anxiety. Hopefully with her mind on driving she'd take less notice of how heavy the bagel was sitting in the pit of her stomach and think less about feeling like she was headed to the gallows.

Kate tried to distract her by discussing her plans for landscaping the backyard and asking for her help when the time came to work on it next spring. As they reached the campus entrance, Kate called Megan to alert her they were near. She was so excited to see her that she practically jumped from the car before Tommie got them stopped in front of the dorm.

Kate and Megan raced toward one another as though they hadn't seen each other in years. Tommie turned off the car, giving them their privacy and noting, not completely amazed, the unmistakable glistening of tears in not only Kate's but in Megan's eyes as Kate's arms held her tightly. When they released each other, Kate placed a light kiss on Megan's forehead and pushed a few stray locks of hair behind her ears. "I don't know how I would have survived if anything would have happened to you."

Megan gave her aunt a squeeze. "I'm sorry you had to worry like that. I promise I'll always keep my phone charged from now on."

"Oh, honey, I don't think I'll ever be able to not worry about you." Kate stroked her hand lightly over Megan's hair. "I can't help that. I wouldn't if I could."

Tommie climbed out of the car and waited by the curb. After a bit, Megan looked past Kate to where Tommie stood and gave a wave. Accepting the wave as an invitation, she joined them.

"Hey, Megan. How's it going?"

When Kate turned to dab at her damp cheeks, Megan took the opportunity to give Tommie an unexpected hug. She whispered, "Are you making sure Aunt Kate's not getting too lonely?"

Caught off guard by the question, Tommie stepped back from Megan's embrace, practically stumbling into Kate as she did so. She wiped sweaty palms on her jeans as she stammered for a reply. "Uh, I think she's coping," she finally managed to say.

Kate hooked her arm through Megan's. "I don't know about you two, but I'm starving. Let's go have some of this pizza you've been raving about."

Tommie drove again so Kate could continue talking with Megan where she sat behind Tommie in the backseat. Tommie drummed her fingers on the wheel during the twenty-minute drive to the other side of town. Her nerves continued to twitch as they were seated around a table at Luciano's Ristorante, which was authentic Italian right down to the red-checked tablecloths.

"We have to have their ultimate supreme pizza, Aunt Kate. It's orgasmic."

Kate blushed as Tommie's eyes went wide. "Sure sweetie, sounds good."

The waitress appeared then, and not a moment too soon for Tommie. She was seriously considering the excuse of having forgotten her wallet in the car so she could escape for a while, maybe even the duration of the lunch if she could manage it.

"What can I start you gals off with to drink?" the middle-aged redhead asked.

Megan ordered a soda and Kate iced tea, and the waitress stood waiting as Tommie just stared at the menu. Kate could feel Tommie's anxiety—it was palpable. She tapped a nail on the menu. "Why don't you have one of those specialty beers?" Tommie looked blankly at her. It was a little disconcerting—and sweet. She'd never seen her be anything but strong and confident. She patted Tommie's arm. "I'll drive us home."

Megan and Kate immediately launched into easy conversation about everything they missed sharing on a daily basis. Things stalled noticeably, however, when Kate asked how Ashley was getting along in Connecticut.

Megan cast a wary glance at Tommie, who quickly averted her eyes. "Uh…she's doing good. She probably won't make it home for Thanksgiving, but she says she will for the Christmas holiday."

After witnessing Megan's careful glance at Tommie, Kate raised an eyebrow to Tommie. Tommie lifted a shoulder slightly in response. "Well, then," Kate said, "you'll have to make sure she makes it by the house when she is home for the holiday so we can visit."

"Um, sure."

She seemed inordinately uncomfortable to Kate. "Megan, are you okay, honey?"

Megan's eyes darted again to Tommie. "Uh, yeah. I'm fine, Aunt Kate." She gave Kate an uneasy smile.

Tommie was never so happy to see food in her life. Despite her nervous stomach, she dug in as soon as it arrived, happy to think about something else for a few minutes. And that's all it felt like, mere minutes, before Kate's expression grew serious and she leaned toward her niece. Tommie swallowed a final mouthful of pizza, hoping not to choke.

"Megan, there's something I need to tell you, and it's just not something I could do over the phone."

"Oh, God, Aunt Kate, you're scaring me! Are you all right? You're not sick, are you?" Megan's face paled.

"Oh, sweetie." Kate took her hand. "Nothing like that."

Megan breathed. "Okay. Then why so serious?"

Kate's eyes swept briefly to Tommie's before focusing on Megan. "There's no way to sugarcoat this, so I'll just say it. Megan," Kate swallowed nervously, "I'm gay." There, it was out. "I don't want to hide who I am from you." Kate watched as those familiar, yet now unreadable, bright eyes gazed back at her for what seemed like an eternity as Megan sat silently.

"So…this person you were with before I came along, the one I always assumed was a man…Was it a woman?" Kate nodded. "And you did break up because of me then?"

"Sweetie, no. I've told you, we split up because we just didn't fit." She cast a brief, but longing look at Tommie. "It wasn't meant to be." Megan looked crestfallen. She held her breath.

Megan's eyes dropped to the table. "You could have told me. I wouldn't have stopped loving you, Aunt Kate." When she looked up her eyes shimmered with tears.

"Oh, God, sweetie. I am so sorry I didn't tell you sooner." She rushed on, " I didn't tell you when you were little for several reasons. I was afraid you might not understand. You'd already been through so much in your young life. And I didn't know if it might somehow affect my being your guardian. I was selfish. I didn't want you with someone else—with a stranger. *I* wanted to take care of you." She all but whispered, "I needed to take care of you." She exhaled a long sigh. "And then, well, there just never seemed to be a right time. But…times are changing. You're such a mature young woman, here at college, living on your own, and, well I'm…I'm babbling." She gave Megan's hand a squeeze. "You know what I've always said about making choices. These are the choices I felt I needed to make. I hope this won't cause problems between us."

Tommie watched Kate with rapt awe. It wasn't any wonder why she'd fallen so helplessly in love with her. She was one of the most selfless people Tommie knew. She thought of her own family. She wasn't all that close to her brothers, they had been long gone from the house, scattered across the country, by the time Tommie had accepted who she was. Her dad was more of a "don't ask, don't tell" person, and he preferred such private matters remain behind closed doors, but she always knew he loved her.

Her mother, on the other hand, had seemed to struggle with it for a number of years. But now, she was always asking Tommie questions about her life whenever they talked. Wanting to know when Tommie was going to find someone special and settle down. She just wanted her only daughter to find her happiness. *Well, Mom, wait till you meet Kate!*

When Tommie had asked Kate about her own coming out, she had shared what it was like to feel leprous. To be ostracized by the ones that should love you unconditionally, namely your parents. Then again they had lots of practice, having earlier rejected Nikki because the man she married was a worthless beatnik who ran off, and because Nikki had fully accepted responsibility for and supported Megan. Their parents had disowned both Nikki and Kate—and Megan, whom they viewed as some sort of spawn of Satan.

Tommie thought the Bellam seniors were foolish people. She couldn't wait for Kate to meet her mom. Margie Tommelson would adopt Kate straightaway. Tommie knew in her heart the importance that being accepted into her family would hold for Kate—and Megan too, for that matter. She deserved loving grandparents.

Megan looked at Tommie in bewilderment. "So, what? You came along for moral support? To give her pointers on being gay?"

"I…uh…maybe?" Tommie's face got hot.

Kate released Megan's hand and reached for Tommie's. "No, Tommie is here because we've been dating."

Dating, Tommie mentally chuckled, casting a sidelong look at Kate. So that's what they were calling the hours they'd been spending in Kate's bed.

"Oh," Megan said, looking between Kate and Tommie, then back at Kate. "Are you happy?" she asked.

The light Tommie saw in Kate's eyes and the smile that claimed her perfect lips said so much more than Kate's simple answer of "yes." Tommie held her breath, watching Megan as she again sat silently—processing, Tommie thought, then finally saying, "You've sacrificed so much for me, Aunt Kate. If you're happy, then I'm happy for you. I'm glad you have someone to make you feel that way. You too, Tommie."

Kate's eyes teared. "When did you get to be so grown up?" Her voice quivered.

* * *

Everyone was quiet on the ride back to campus, Kate and Tommie in reaction to having successfully shared their news with Megan, and Megan probably giving some thought to what it might all mean for her future. Tommie hoped Megan knew that she had kept her secret. And that, when she was ready to come out to Kate, if that was who she discovered she really was, Tommie would be in her corner. Not that Kate would ever reject her, even if she were straight.

Back in front of her dorm, Megan hugged Tommie extra tight. "Please don't hurt her," she whispered.

"Never, I promise." Tommie was overwhelmed by Megan's protectiveness of Kate. "I want to make her life everything she wants it to be."

"Good," Megan responded. "And our secret is…"

"Still locked up tight."

Kate and Megan shared a long hug accompanied by lots of murmured comments. Kate's eyes were shimmering again with tears when she slid behind the wheel to drive them home.

"You okay?" Tommie placed her hand on Kate's thigh.

Kate nodded, slipping her fingers between Tommie's. "Can I ask what Megan whispered to you?"

Tommie chuckled. "She threatened to kick my butt if I did anything to hurt you." She needed Kate to know just how fiercely protective Megan was of her. Kate laughed.

"So what were you two whispering about?" Tommie asked.

"That we still have a lot to talk about. I'm sure once she gives this more thought she'll have plenty of questions for me that I am ready to answer." She laughed again. "She wants to send us rainbow stickers for our cars. Apparently the Jeep doesn't require one."

Tommie chuckled again.

"Oh, let's see…she suggested that I start paying more attention to sports." She squeezed Tommie's hand. "And she threatened to kick my butt too." Kate gave Tommie a quick glance and a heart-stopping smile. "I told her not to worry, I'm going to love and cherish you till my last breath."

Bella Books, Inc.

Women. Books. Even Better Together.

P.O. Box 10543
Tallahassee, FL 32302

Phone: 800-729-4992
www.bellabooks.com